AVEMPARTHA

By
MICHAEL J. SULLIVAN

RIDAN

A Ridan Publication

www.ridanpublishing.com
www.michaelsullivan-author.com
www.riyria.blogspot.com

Copyright © 2009 by Michael J. Sullivan
Cover Art and Map by Michael J. Sullivan

LIBRARY OF CONGRESS CONTROL NUMBER: 2009922383

ISBN: 978-0-9796211-1-6

PRINTED IN THE UNITED STATES

First Printing: April 2009

*To Robin, my partner both in life
and in the adventure of creating this series.*

To Paul Dunlap for his astute criticism.

And to the members of Dragonchow, my original fan club.

Books in the Riyria Revelations

The Crown Conspiracy

Avempartha

Nyphron Rising

The Emerald Storm

Wintertide

Percepliquis

CONTENTS

The World of Elan

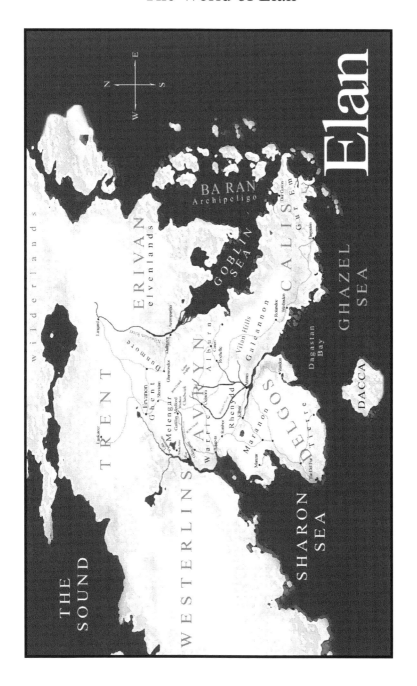

Detail of Avryn

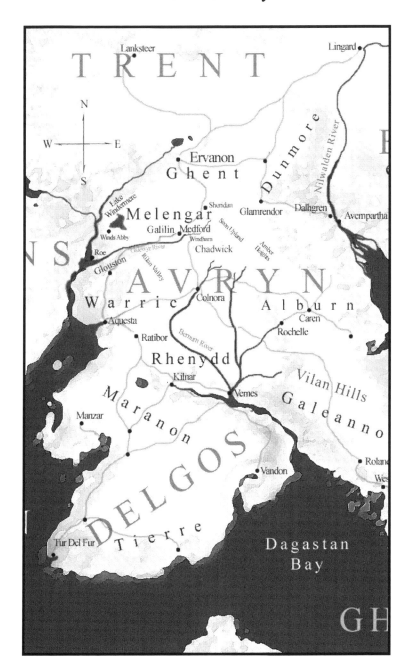

Avempartha

Chapter 1

COLNORA

A S THE MAN stepped out of the shadows, Wyatt Deminthal knew this would be the worst, and possibly the last, day of his life. Dressed in raw wool and rough leather, the man was vaguely familiar, a face seen briefly by candlelight over two years ago, a face Wyatt hoped he would never see again. The man carried three swords, each one battered and dull, the grips sweat-stained and frayed. Taller than Wyatt by nearly a foot, with broader shoulders and powerful hands, he stood with his weight distributed across the balls of his feet. His eyes locked on Wyatt the way cats stare at mice.

"Baron Dellano DeWitt of Dagastan?" It was not a question, but an accusation.

Wyatt felt his heart shudder. Even after recognizing the face, a part of him—the optimist that somehow managed to survive after all these dreadful years—still hoped he was only after his money. But with the sound of those words that hope died.

"Sorry, you must be mistaken," he replied to the man blocking his path, trying his best to sound friendly, carefree—guiltless. He even tried to mask his Calian accent to further the charade.

"No, I'm not," the man insisted as he crossed the width of the alley, moving closer, eating up the comforting space between them. His hands remained in full view, which was more worrisome than if they rested on the pommels of his swords. Even though Wyatt wore a fine cutlass, the man had no fear of him.

"Well, as it happens, my name is Wyatt Deminthal. I think therefore, that you must be mistaken."

Wyatt was pleased he managed to say all this without stammering. With great effort, he concentrated on relaxing his body, letting his shoulders droop, resting his weight on one heel. He even forced a pleasant smile and glanced around casually as an innocent man might.

They faced each other in the narrow, cluttered alley only a few yards from where Wyatt rented a loft. It was dark. A lantern hung a few feet behind him, mounted on the side of the feed store. He could see its flickering glow, the light glistening in puddles the rain had left on the cobblestone. Behind him, he could still hear the music of the Gray Mouse Tavern, muffled and tinny. Voices echoed in the distance, laughter, shouts, arguments; the clatter of a dropped pot followed the cry of an unseen cat. Somewhere a carriage rolled along, its wooden wheels clacking on wet stone. It was late. The only people on the streets were drunken men, whores, or those with business best done in the dark.

The man took another step closer. Wyatt did not like the look in his eyes. They held a hard edge, a serious sense of resolve, but it was the hint of regret he detected that jarred Wyatt the most.

"You're the one who hired me and my friend to steal a sword from Essendon Castle."

"I'm sorry. I really have no idea what you are talking about. I don't even know where this *Essendon* place is. You must have me confused with some other fellow. It's probably the hat." Wyatt took off his wide-brimmed cavalier and showed it to the man. "See, it's a common hat in that anyone can buy one, but uncommon at the same time as few people wear them these days. You most likely saw someone in a similar hat and just assumed it was me. An understandable mistake. No hard feelings I can assure you."

Wyatt placed his hat back on, tilting it slightly down in front and cocking it a bit to one side. In addition to the hat, he wore an expensive black and red silk doublet and a short flashy cape; however, the lack of any velvet trimming, combined with his worn boots, betrayed his station. The single gold ring piercing his left ear revealed even more; it was his one concession, a memento to the life he left behind.

"When we got to the chapel, the king was on the floor. Dead."

"I can see this is not a happy story," Wyatt said, tugging on the fingers of his fine red gloves—a habit he had when nervous.

"Guards were waiting. They dragged us to the dungeons. We were nearly executed."

"I am sorry you were ill-used, but as I said, I am not DeWitt. I've never heard of him. I will be certain to mention you should our paths ever cross. Who shall I say is looking?"

"Riyria."

Behind Wyatt, the feed store light winked out and a voice whispered in his ear, "It's elvish for *two*."

His heartbeat doubled and before he could turn he felt the sharp edge of a blade at his throat. He froze, barely allowing himself to breathe.

"You set us up to die," the voice behind him took over. "You brokered the deal. You put us in that chapel so we would take the blame. I'm here to repay your kindness. If you have any last words, say them now, and say them quietly."

Wyatt was a good card player. He knew bluffs and the man behind him was not bluffing. He was not there to scare, pressure, or manipulate him. He was not looking for information; he knew everything he wanted to know. It was in his voice, his tone, his words, the pace of his breath in Wyatt's ear—he was there to kill him.

"What's going on, Wyatt?" a small voice called.

Down the alley, a door opened and light spilled forth, outlining a young girl whose shadow ran across the cobblestones and up the far wall. She was thin with shoulder length hair and wore a nightgown that reached to her ankles exposing bare feet.

"Nothing Allie—get back inside!" Wyatt shouted, his accent fully exposed.

"Who are those men you're talking to?" Allie took a step toward them. Her foot disturbed a puddle that rippled. "They look angry."

"I won't allow witnesses," the voice behind Wyatt hissed.

"Leave her alone," Wyatt begged, "she wasn't involved. I swear. It was just me."

"Involved in what?" Allie asked. "What's going on?" She took another step.

"Stay where you are, Allie! Don't come any closer. Please, Allie, do as I say." The girl stopped. "I did a bad thing once, Allie. You have to understand. I did it for us, for you, Elden and me. Remember when I took that job a few winters back? When I went up north for a couple of days? I—I did the bad thing then. I pretended to be someone I wasn't and I almost got some people killed. That's how I got the money for the winter. Don't hate me, Allie. I love you, honey. Please just get back inside."

"No!" she protested. "I can see the knife. They're going to hurt you."

"If you don't, they'll kill us both!" Wyatt shouted harshly, too harshly. He did not want to do it, but he had to make her understand.

Allie was crying now. She stood in the alley, in the shaft of lamplight, shaking.

"Go inside honey," Wyatt told her, gathering himself and trying to calm his voice. "It will be alright. Don't cry. Elden will watch over you. Let him know what happened. It will be alright."

She continued to sob.

"Please honey, you have to go inside now," Wyatt pleaded. "It's all you can do. It's what I need you to do. Please."

"I—love—you, Da—ddy!"

"I know honey. I know. I love you too, and I'm *so sorry*."

Allie slowly stepped back into the doorway, the sliver of light diminishing until the door snapped shut, leaving the alley once more in darkness. Only the faint blue light from the cloud-shrouded moon filtered into the narrow corridor where the three men stood.

"How old is she?" the voice behind him asked.

"Leave her out of this. Just make it quick—can you give me that much?" Wyatt braced himself for what was to come. Seeing the child broke him. He shook violently, his gloved hands in fists, his chest so tight it was difficult to swallow and hard to breathe. He felt the metal edge against his throat and waited for it to move, waited for it to drag.

"Did you know it was a trap when you came to hire us?" The man with three swords asked.

What?—*No!*"

"Would you still have done it if you knew?"

"I don't know—I guess—yes. We needed the money."

"So, you're not a baron?"

"No."

"What then?"

"I was a ship's captain."

"Was? What happened?"

"Are you going to kill me any time soon? Why all the questions?"

"Each question you answer is another breath you take," the voice from behind him spoke. It was the voice of death, emotionless, and empty. Hearing it made Wyatt's stomach lurch as if he were looking over the edge of a high cliff. Not seeing his face, knowing that he held the blade that would kill him, made it feel like an execution. He thought of Allie, hoped she would be all right then realized—she would see him. The thought struck with surprising clarity. She would rush out after it was over and find him on the street. She would wade through his blood.

"What happened?" the executioner asked again, his voice instantly erasing all other thoughts.

"I sold my ship."

"Why?"

"It doesn't matter."

"Gambling debts?"

"No."

"Why then?"

"What difference does it make? You're going to kill me anyway. Just do it!"

He had steadied himself. He was ready. He clenched his teeth, shut his eyes. Still, the killer delayed.

"It makes a difference," the executioner whispered in his ear, "because Allie is not your daughter."

The blade came away from Wyatt's neck.

Slowly, hesitantly, Wyatt turned to face the man holding the dagger. He had never seen him before. He was smaller than his partner, dressed in a black cloak with a hood that shaded his features, revealing only hints of a face—the tip of a sharp nose, highlight of a cheek, end of a chin.

"How do you know that?"

"She saw us in the dark. She saw my knife at your throat as we stood deep in shadow across the length of twenty yards."

Wyatt said nothing. He did not dare move or speak. He did not know what to think. Somehow, something had changed. The certainty of death rolled back a step, but its shadow lingered. He had no idea what was happening and was terrified of making a misstep.

"You sold your ship to buy her, didn't you?" the hooded man guessed. "But from whom, and why?"

Wyatt stared at the face beneath the hood—a bleak landscape, a desert dry of compassion. Death was there, a mere breath away; an utterance remained all that separated eternity from salvation.

The bigger man, the one with three swords, reached out and placed a hand on his shoulder. "A lot is riding on your answer. But you already knew that, didn't you? Right now you're trying to decide what to say, and of course, you're trying to guess what we want to hear. Don't. Go with the truth. At least that way, if you're wrong, your death won't have been because of a lie."

Wyatt nodded. He closed his eyes again, took a deep breath and said, "I bought her from a man named Ambrose."

"Ambrose Moor?" the executioner asked.

"Yes."

Wyatt waited but nothing happened. He opened his eyes. The dagger was gone and the three-sword man was smiling at him. "I don't know how much that little girl cost, but it was the best money you ever spent."

"You aren't going to kill me?"

"Not today. You still owe us one hundred tenents, for the balance on that job," the man in the hood told him coldly.

"I—I don't have it."

"Get it."

Light burst into the alley as the door to Wyatt's loft flew open with a bang and Elden charged out. He held his mammoth two-headed axe high above his head as he strode toward them with a determined look.

The man with three swords rapidly drew two of them.

"Elden, NO!" Wyatt shouted. "They're not going to kill me! Just stop."

Elden paused, his axe held aloft, his eyes looking back and forth between them.

"They're letting me go," Wyatt assured him, then turned to the two men. "You are, aren't you?"

The hooded man nodded. "Pay off that debt."

As the men walked away, Elden moved to Wyatt's side and Allie ran out to hug him. The three returned to the loft and slipped inside the doorway. Elden took one last look around then closed the door behind them.

"Did you see the size of that guy?" Hadrian asked Royce, still glancing over his shoulder as if the giant might try to sneak up on them. "I've never seen anyone that big. He had to be a good seven feet tall, and that neck, those shoulders, and that axe! It would take two of me just to lift it. Maybe he isn't human, maybe he's a giant, or a troll. Some people swear they exist. I've met a few who say they have seen them personally."

Royce looked at his friend and scowled.

"Okay, so it's mostly drunks in bars who say that, but that doesn't mean it's not possible. Ask Myron, he'll back me up."

The two headed north toward the Langdon Bridge. It was quiet here. In the respectable hill district of Colnora, people were more inclined to sleep at night than to carouse in taverns. This was the home of merchant titans, affluent businessmen who owned houses grander than many of the palatial mansions of upper nobility.

Colnora had started out as a meager rest stop at the intersection of the Wesbaden and Aquesta trade routes. Originally, a farmer named Hollenbeck and his wife watered caravans here and granted room in their barn to the traders in return for news and goods. Hollenbeck had an eye for quality and always picked the best of the lot.

Soon his farm became an inn and Hollenbeck added a store and a warehouse to sell what he acquired to passing travelers. The merchants deprived of first pick bought plots next to his farm and opened their own shops, taverns, and roadhouses. The farm became a village, then a city, but still, the caravans gave preference to Hollenbeck. Legend held that the reason was their fondness for his wife, a wonderful woman who in addition to being uncommonly beautiful, sang and played the mandolin. It was said she baked the finest cobblers of peach, blueberry, and apple. Centuries later, when no one could accurately place the location of the original Hollenbeck farm, and few remembered there had ever been such a farmer, they continued to remember his wife—Colnora.

Over the years the city flourished until it became the largest urban center in Avryn. Shoppers found the latest style in clothes, the most exquisite jewelry, and the widest variety of exotic spices from hundreds of shops and marketplaces. In addition, the city was home to some of the best artisans and boasted the finest, most popular inns and taverns in the country. Entertainers had long congregated here, prompting Cosmos DeLur, the city's wealthiest resident and patron of the arts, to construct the DeLur Theatre.

Crossing the district, Royce and Hadrian halted abruptly in front of the theatre's large white painted board. It depicted the silhouette of two men scaling the outside of a castle tower and read:

THE CROWN CONSPIRACY
HOW A YOUNG PRINCE AND TWO THIEVES SAVED A KINGDOM
EVENING SHOWS DAILY

Royce raised an eyebrow while Hadrian slipped the tip of his tongue along his front teeth. They glanced at each other, but neither said a word before continuing on their way.

Leaving the hill district, they continued along Bridge Street as the land sloped downward toward the river. They passed rows of warehouses—mammoth buildings emblazoned with company brands like royal crests. Some were simply initials, usually the new businesses that had no sense of themselves. Others bore trademarks like the boar's head of the Bocant Company, an empire whose genesis was pork, or the diamond symbol of DeLur Enterprises.

"You realize he'll never be able to pay us the hundred?" Hadrian asked.

"I just didn't want him to think he was getting off easy."

"You didn't want him to think Royce Melborn went soft at the sight of a little girl's tears."

"She wasn't just *any* girl and besides, he saved her from Ambrose Moor. For that alone he earned one life."

"That's something that has always puzzled me. How is it Ambrose is still alive?"

"I've been side-tracked, I suppose," Royce said in his *let us not talk about this* tone, and Hadrian dropped it.

Of the city's three main bridges, the Langdon was the most ornate. Made from cut stone, it was lined every few feet by large lampposts fashioned in the shapes of swans that when lit, gave the bridge a festive look. Now, however, with the lights out, the stone was wet and appeared oily and dangerous.

"Well, at least we didn't spend the last month looking for DeWitt for nothing," Hadrian said sarcastically as they crossed the bridge. "I would have thought—"

Royce stopped walking and abruptly raised his hand. Both men looked around, and without a word drew their weapons as they moved back to back. Nothing seemed amiss. The only sound was the roar of the tumultuous waters that rushed and churned below them.

"Impressive, Duster," a man addressed Royce as he stepped out from behind one of the bridge lampposts. His skin was pale and his body so slender and boney that he swam in his loose britches and shirt. He looked like a corpse someone forgot to bury.

Behind them, Hadrian noted three more men crawling onto the span. They all had similar appearances, thin and muscular, each in dark colored clothes. They circled like wolves.

"What tipped you off we were here?" the thin man asked.

"I'm guessing it was your breath, but body odor really can't be ruled out," Hadrian replied with a grin while noting their positions, movements, and the direction of their eyes.

"Mind 'yer mouth bub," the tallest of the four threatened.

"To what do we owe this visit, Price?" Royce asked.

"Funny, I was about to ask you the same," the thin man replied. "This is our city after all, not yours—not anymore."

"Black Diamond?" Hadrian asked.

Royce nodded.

"And you would be Hadrian Blackwater," Price noted. "I always thought you'd be bigger."

"And you're a Black Diamond. I always thought there were more of you."

Price smiled, held his gaze long enough to suggest a threat, and returned his attention to Royce. "So what are you doing here, Duster?"

"Just passing through."

"Really? No business?"

"Nothing that would interest you."

"Well now, you see that's where you're wrong." Price stepped away from the swan lamppost and began slowly circling them as he talked. The wind blowing down the river whipped his loose shirt like a flag at mast. "The Black Diamond is interested in everything that happens in Colnora, most particularly when it involves you, Duster."

Hadrian leaned over and asked, "Why does he keep calling you, *Duster?*"

"That was my guild name," Royce replied.

AVEMPARTHA

"*He* was a Black Diamond?" asked the youngest looking of the four. He had round, chubby cheeks blown red and blotchy, a narrow mouth wreathed by a thin mustache and goatee.

"Oh yes, that's right, Etcher, you've never heard of Duster before, have you? Etcher is new to the guild, only been with us what—six months? Well, you see not only was Duster a Diamond, he was an officer, bucketman, and one of the most notorious members in the guild's history."

"Bucketman?" Hadrian asked.

"Assassin," Royce explained.

"He's a legend, this one is," Price went on, pacing around the stone bridge, carefully avoiding the puddles. "Wonder-boy of his day, he rose through the ranks so fast it unnerved people."

"Funny," Royce said, "I only remember one."

"Well, when the First Officer of the guild is nervous, so is everyone else. You see back then the Jewel had a man named Hoyte running the show. He was an ass to most of us—a good thief and administrator—but an ass just the same. Duster here had a lot of support from the lower ranks and Hoyte was concerned Duster might replace him. He began ordering Duster on the most dangerous jobs—jobs that went suspiciously bad. Still, Duster always escaped unscathed, making him even more a hero. Rumors began circulating we might have a traitor in the guild. Rather than being concerned, Hoyte saw this as an opportunity."

Price paused in his orator's trek around the bridge and stopped in front of Royce. "You see at that time there were three bucketmen in the guild and all of them good friends. Jade, the guild's only female assassin, was a beauty who—"

"Is this going somewhere, Price?" Royce snapped.

"Just giving Etcher a little background, Duster. You wouldn't begrudge me the chance to educate my boys, would you?" Price smiled and returned to his casual pacing, slipping his thumbs into the

12

loose waistline of his pants. "Where was I? Oh yes, Jade. It happened right over there." He pointed back across the bridge. "That empty warehouse with the clover symbol on its side. That's where Hoyte set them up, pitting one against the other. Then, like now, bucketmen wore masks to prevent being marked." Price paused and looked at Royce in feigned sympathy. "You had no idea who she was until it was over did you, Duster? Or did you know and kill her anyway?"

Royce said nothing but glared at Price with a dangerous look.

"The last of the three bucketmen was Cutter, who was understandably upset to learn Duster murdered Jade since Cutter and Jade were lovers. The fact that his friend was responsible made it personal, and Hoyte was happy to let Cutter settle the score.

"But Cutter didn't want Duster dead. He wanted him to suffer and insisted on something more elaborate, more painful. The man is a strategic mastermind—our best heist planner and arranged for Duster to be apprehended by the city guard. Cutter traded a few favors and with some money, bought a trial that resulted in Duster going to the Manzant Prison and Salt Mine. The hole no one ever comes back from. Escape was thought to be impossible—only somehow Duster managed it. You know we still don't know how you got out," he paused, giving Royce a chance to reply.

Again, Royce remained silent.

Price shrugged. "When Duster escaped he returned to Colnora. First, the magistrate who presided over his trial was found dead in his bed. Then the false witnesses—all three on the same night—and finally the lawyer. Soon, one by one, members of the Black Diamond started disappearing. They turned up in the strangest places: the river, the city square, even the steeple of the church.

"After losing more than a dozen members, the Jewel made a deal. He gave Hoyte to Duster who forced him to confess publicly. Then Duster killed Hoyte and left his body in the Hill Square Fountain—it was pure artistry. It stopped the war, but the wounds were too deep to forgive. Duster left only to reemerge years later working out of Crimson Hand territory up north. But you're not a member, are you?"

"I don't have much use for guilds anymore," Royce replied coldly.

"And who's that?" Etcher asked pointing at Hadrian. "Duster's servant? He's carrying enough weapons for the both of them."

Price smiled at Etcher. "That's Hadrian Blackwater, and I wouldn't point at him; you're likely to lose that arm."

Etcher looked at Hadrian skeptically. "What? He's some kind of killer swordsman? Is that it?"

Price chuckled. "Sword, spear, arrow, rock, whatever is at hand," he turned to Hadrian. "The Diamond doesn't know as much about you, but rumors abound. One says you were a gladiator; another reports you were a general in a Calian army—successful too if the stories can be trusted. There's even one story circulating that you were the enslaved courtier of an exotic eastern queen."

Some of the other Diamonds including Etcher chuckled.

"As much fun as this trip down memory lane has been, Price, do you have a reason for stopping us?"

"You mean beyond entertainment? Beyond harassment? Beyond reminding you that this is a Black Diamond controlled city? Beyond informing you that unguilded thieves like yourselves are not allowed to practice here, and that you personally are not welcome?"

"Yeah, that's what I meant."

"Actually there is one more thing. There's a girl looking for you two."

Royce and Hadrian glanced at each other curiously.

"She's been going around asking about two thieves named Hadrian and Royce. Now, as entertaining as it has been to hear your names publicly advertised, it is embarrassing for the Black Diamond to have anyone asking for thieves in Colnora that are not members of our guild. People are apt to get the wrong impression about this city."

"Who is she?" Royce asked.

"No idea."

"Where is she?"

"Sleeping under the Tradesmen's Arch on Capital Boulevard, so I think we can rule out her being a noble debutant or a rich merchant's daughter. Since she is traveling alone, I think you can also rule out the possibility that she is here to kill you or have you arrested. If I had to guess, I should think she is looking to hire you. I must say, if she is typical of the kind of patrons you two attract, I would consider a more traditional line of work. Perhaps there's a pig farm you might be able to get a job at—at least you would be keeping the same level of company."

Price's tone and expression dropped to a serious level. "Find her, and get her, and yourselves, out of our city by tomorrow night. You might want to hurry. Cleaned up she could be pretty and might fetch a fair price or at least provide several minutes of pleasure for someone. I suspect the only reason she hasn't been touched so far is that she's been dropping your names everywhere. Around here, Royce Melborn is still something of a bogeyman."

Price turned to leave and his mocking tone returned. "It's actually a shame you can't stay around; the theatre is showing a play about a couple of thieves lured into being accused of murdering the King of Medford. It's loosely based on the real murder of Amrath several years ago." Price shook his head. "Completely unrealistic. Can you imagine a seasoned thief being lured into a castle to steal a sword to save a man from a duel? Authors!"

Price continued to shake his head as he and the other thieves left Hadrian and Royce on the bridge and headed down the streets on the far bank.

"Well, that was pleasant, don't you think?" Hadrian said as they retraced their steps, heading back up the hill toward Capital Boulevard. "Nice bunch of guys. I feel a little disappointed they only sent four."

"Trust me, they were plenty dangerous. Price is the Diamond's First Officer, and the other two quiet ones were bucketmen. There were also six more, three on each side of the bridge hiding under the ambush lip, just in case. They weren't taking any chances with us. Does that make you feel better?"

"Much, thanks," Hadrian rolled his eyes. "Duster, huh?"

"Don't call me that," Royce said, his tone serious. "Don't ever call me that."

"Call you what?" Hadrian asked innocently.

Royce sighed then smiled at him. "Walk faster; apparently, we have a client waiting."

She awoke to a rough hand on her thigh.

"Whatcha got in the purse, honey?"

Disoriented and confused, the girl wiped her eyes. She was in the gutter beneath the Tradesmen's Arch. Her hair a filthy tangle of leaves and twigs, her dress a tattered rag. She clutched a tiny purse to her chest, the drawstring tied around her neck. To most passing by, she might appear as a bundle of trash discarded on the side of the road, or a pile of cloth and twigs absently left behind by the street sweepers. Still, there were those who were interested even in piles of trash.

The first thing she saw when her eyes could focus was the dark, haggard face and gaping mouth of a man crouching over her. She squealed and tried to crawl away. A hand grabbed her by the hair. Strong arms forced her down, pinning her wrists to her sides.

She felt his hot breath on her face and it smelled of liquor and smoke. He tore the tiny purse from her fingers and pulled it from around her neck.

"No!" She wrenched a hand free and reached out for it. "I need that."

"So do I." The man cackled slapping her hand aside. Feeling the weight of coins in the bag, he smiled and stuffed the small pouch in his breast pocket.

"No!" she protested.

He sat on her, pinning her to the ground, and ran his fingers down her face, along her lips, stopping at her neck. Slowly they circled her throat and he gave a little squeeze. She gasped, struggling to breathe. He pressed his lips hard against hers, so hard she could tell he was missing teeth. The rough stubble of his whiskers scratched her chin and cheeks.

"Shush," he whispered. "Were only get'n started. You need ta save your strength." He lifted off, pushing himself up to his knees, and reached for the buttons of his britches.

She struggled, clawing at him, kicking. He pinned her arms under his knees and her feet found only air. She screamed. The man replied by slapping her hard across the face. The shock left her stunned, staring blindly while he returned to work on his buttons. The pain did not hit her yet, not fully. It was there welling up, fire hot on her cheek. Through watering eyes, she saw him on top of her as if viewing the scene from a distance. Individual sounds were lost replaced by a dull hum. She saw his cracked, peeling lips moving, his throat muscles shifting, long gangly chords, but never heard the words. She freed one arm, but it was captured and stuffed back down out of sight once more.

Behind him, she could see two figures approaching. Somewhere inside her, a thread of hope came alive and she managed a weak whisper, "Help me."

The foremost man drew a massive sword and holding it by the blade, swung the pommel. Her attacker fell sprawling across the gutter.

The man with the sword knelt down beside her. He was merely an outline against the charcoal sky, a phantom in the dark.

"May I be of assistance, milady," she heard his voice—a nice voice. His hand found hers and he pulled her to her feet.

"Who are you?"

"My name is Hadrian Blackwater."

She stared at him. "Really?" She managed, refusing to let go of his hands. Before she realized it, she began to cry.

"What'd you do to her?" the other man asked coming up behind them.

"I—I don't know."

"Are you squeezing her hand too hard? Let her go."

"I'm not holding her. She's holding me."

"I'm sorry. I'm sorry." Her voice quivered. "I just never thought I would ever find you."

"Oh, okay. Well, you did." He smiled at her. "And this fellow here is Royce Melborn."

She gasped and threw her arms around the smaller man's neck, hugging him tight and crying even harder. Royce stood awkward and stiff while Hadrian peeled her off.

"So I get the impression you're glad to see us, that's good," Hadrian told her. "Now, who are you?"

"I'm Thrace Wood of Dahlgren Village." She was smiling. She could not help herself. "I have been looking for you for a very long time."

She staggered.

"Are you alright?"

"I'm a little dizzy."

"When was the last time you had anything to eat?"

Thrace stood thinking, her eyes shifting back and forth trying to remember.

"Never mind," Hadrian turned to Royce, "This was once your city. Any ideas where we can get help for a young woman in the middle of the night?"

"It's a shame we aren't in Medford. Gwen would be great for this sort of thing."

"Well, isn't there a brothel here? After all we're in the trade capital of the world. Don't tell me they don't sell *that*."

"Yeah, there's a nice one on South Street."

"Okay, Thrace, is it? Come with us, we'll see if we can get you cleaned up and perhaps a bit of food in you."

"Wait." She knelt down beside the unconscious man and pulled her purse from his pocket.

"Is he dead?" She asked.

"Doubt it. Didn't hit him that hard."

Rising, she felt light-headed and darkness crept in from the edges of her vision. She hovered a moment like a drunk, began to sway and finally collapsed. She woke only briefly and felt arms gently lifting her. Through a dull buzzing she heard the sound of a chuckle.

"What's so funny?" she heard one of them say.

"This is the first time I suspect anyone has ever visited a whore house and brought his own woman."

Chapter 2

THRACE

"SHINES UP PURTY as a new copper piece, that one does," Clarisse noted as the three looked through the doorway at Thrace waiting in the parlor. Clarisse was a large rotund woman with rosy cheeks and short pudgy fingers that had a habit of playing with the pleats of her skirt. She and the other women of the Bawdy Bottom Brothel had done wonders with the girl. Thrace was clothed in a new dress. It was cheap and simple, a brown linen kirtle over a white smock with a starched brown bodice, but still decidedly more fetching than the rag she had worn. She hardly resembled the ragamuffin they met the night before. In addition to giving her a bed to sleep in, the women scrubbed, combed, and fed her. Even her lips and eyes were painted and the results were stunning. She was a young beauty with startling blue eyes and golden hair.

"Poor girl was in awful shape when you dropped her off. Where'd you find her?" Clarisse asked.

"Under the Tradesmen's Arch," Hadrian replied.

"Poor thing," the large woman shook her head sadly. "You know if she needs a place, I'm sure we could put her on the roster.

She'd get a bed to sleep in, three meals a day, and with her looks she could do well for herself."

"Something tells me she's not a prostitute," Hadrian told her.

"None of us are, honey. Not until you find yourself sleeping under the Tradesmen's Arch that is. You shoulda seen her at breakfast. She ate like a starved dog. 'Course she wouldn't touch a thing 'till we convinced her that the food was free, given by the Chamber 'a Commerce to visitors of the city as a welcome. Maggie came up with that one. She's a hoot, she is. That reminds me, the bill for the room, dress, food, and general clean up comes to sixty-five silver. We threw in the make-up for free 'cause Delia just wanted to see how she'd look on account she says she's never worn it 'afore."

Royce handed her a gold tenent.

"Well, well, you two really need to drop by more often, and next time without the girl, eh?" she winked. "Seriously though, what's the story with this one?"

"That's just it, we don't know," Hadrian replied.

"But I think it's time we found out," Royce added.

Not nearly as nice as Medford House back home, the Bawdy Bottom Brothel was decorated with gaudy red drapes, rickety furniture, pink lampshades, and dozens of pillows. Everything had tassels and fringe, from the threadbare carpets to the cloth edging adorning the top of the walls. It was old, weathered, and worn but at least it was clean.

The parlor was a small oval room just off the main hall with four bay windows that looked out on the street. It contained two loveseats, a few tables crowded with ceramic figures, and a small fireplace. Seated on one of the loveseats, Thrace waited, her eyes darting about like a rabbit in an open field. The moment they entered, she leapt from her seat, knelt, and bowed her head.

"Hey! Watch it, that's a new dress," Hadrian said with a smile.

"Oh!" she scrambled to her feet blushing, then curtseyed and bowed her head once more.

"What's she doing?" Royce whispered to Hadrian.

"Not sure," he whispered back.

"I am trying to show the proper reverence, your lordships," she whispered to both of them while keeping her head down, "I'm sorry if I'm not very good at it."

Royce rolled his eyes and Hadrian began to laugh.

"Why are you whispering?" Hadrian asked her.

"Because you two were."

Hadrian chuckled again. "Sorry, Thrace—ah your name is, Thrace, right?"

"Yes, my lord, Thrace Annabell Wood of Dahlgren Village," she awkwardly curtseyed again.

"Okay, well—Thrace," Hadrian struggled to continue with a straight face. "Royce and I are not lords, so there is no need to bow or curtsy."

The girl looked up.

"You saved my life," she told them in such a solemn tone Hadrian stopped laughing. "I don't remember a lot of last night, but I remember that much. And for that you deserve my gratitude."

"I would settle for an explanation," Royce said, moving to the windows. He began closing the drapes. "Straighten up for Maribor's sake, before a sweeper sees you, thinks we're noble, and marks us. We're already on thin ice here as it is. Let's not add to it."

She stood up straight, and Hadrian could not help but stare. Her long yellow hair, now free of twigs and leaves, shimmered in waves over her shoulders. She was a vision of youthful beauty and Hadrian guessed she could not be more than seventeen.

"Now, why have you been looking for us?" Royce asked, closing the last curtain.

"To hire you to save my father," she said, untying the purse from around her neck and holding it up with a smile. "Here. I have twenty-five silver tenents. Solid silver stamped with the Dunmore crown."

Royce and Hadrian exchanged looks.

"Isn't it enough?" She asked, her lips starting to tremble.

"How long did it take you to save up this money?" Hadrian asked.

"All my life. I saved every copper I was ever given, or earned. It was my dowry."

"Your dowry?"

She lowered her head looking at her feet. "My father is a poor farmer. He would never—I decided to save for myself. It's not enough, is it? I didn't realize. I'm from a very small village. I thought it was a lot of money; everyone said so, but…" She looked around at the battered loveseat and faded curtains. "We don't have palaces like this."

"Well, we really don't—" Royce began in his usual insensitive tone.

"What Royce is about to say," Hadrian interrupted, "is we really don't know yet. It depends on what you want us to do."

Thrace looked up, her eyes hopeful.

Royce just glared at him.

"Well it does, doesn't it?" Hadrian shrugged. "Now, Thrace you say you want us to save your father. Has he been kidnapped or something?"

"Oh no, nothing like that. As far as I know he's fine. Although I have been away a long time looking for you. So, I'm not sure."

"I don't understand. What do you need us for?"

"I need you to open a lock for me."

"A lock? To what?"

"A tower."

"You want us to break into a tower?"

"No. I mean—well yes, but it isn't like—it's not illegal. The tower isn't occupied; it has been deserted for years. At least I think so."

"So you just want us to open a door to an empty tower?"

"Yes!" She said nodding vigorously so that her hair bounced.

"Doesn't sound too hard," Hadrian looked at Royce.

"Where is this tower?" Royce asked.

"Near my village on the west bank of the Nidwalden River. Dahlgren is very small and has only been there a short time. It's in the new province of Westbank, in Dunmore."

"I've heard about that place. It's supposedly being attacked by elven raiders."

"Oh, it's not the elves. The elves have never caused us any trouble."

"I knew it," Royce said to no one in particular.

"Leastways I don't think so," Thrace went on. "We think it's a beast of some kind. No one has ever seen it. Deacon Tomas says it's a demon, a minion of Uberlin."

"And your father?" Hadrian asked. "How does he fit into this?"

"He's going to try and kill the beast, only…" she faltered and looked at her feet once more.

"Only you think it will kill him instead?"

"It has killed fifteen people and over eighty head of livestock."

A freckle-faced woman with wild red hair entered the parlor dragging a short, pot-bellied man who looked like he had shaved for the occasion, his face nicked raw. The woman was laughing, walking backward as she hauled him along with both hands. The man stopped short when he saw them. His hands slipped through hers and she fell to the wooden floor with a hollow thud. The man looked from the woman to them and back, frozen in place. The woman glanced over her shoulder and laughed.

"Oops," was all she could manage. "Didn't know it was taken. Give us a hand up, Rubis."

The man helped her to her feet. She paused to give Thrace a long appraising look then winked at them. "We do good work, don't we?"

"That was Maggie," Thrace told them after the woman hauled her man back out again.

Hadrian moved to the sofa and gestured for Thrace to sit, while taking a seat across from her. She sat gingerly and straight, not allowing her back to touch the rear of the sofa, and carefully smoothed out her skirt.

Royce remained on his feet. "Does Westbank have a lord? Why isn't he doing something about this?"

"We had a fine margrave," she said, "a brave man with three good knights."

"Had?"

"He and his knights rode out to fight the beast one evening. Later, all that was found was bits and pieces of armor."

"Why don't you just leave?" Royce asked.

Thrace's head drooped and her shoulders slouched a bit. "Two nights before I left to come here, the beast killed everyone in my family except for me and my father. We weren't home. My father had worked late in the fields and I went to look for him. I—I accidentally left the door open. Light attracts it. It went right for our house. My brother, Thad, his wife, and their son were all killed.

"Thad—he was the joy of my father's life. The reason we moved to Dahlgren in the first place—so he could become the town's first cooper." Tears welled in her eyes. "Now they're all gone and my father has nothing left but his grief and the beast that brought it.

He'll see it dead, or die himself before the month is out. If I had only closed the door. If I had just checked the latch…"

Her hands covered her face and her slender body quivered. Royce gave Hadrian a stern look, shaking his head very slightly and mouthing the word "No."

Hadrian scowled back and moved to sit beside her. He placed his hand on her shoulder and brushed the hair away from her eyes. "You're going to ruin all your pretty make-up," he said.

"I'm sorry. I really don't want to be such a bother. These aren't your problems. It is just that my father is all I have left and I can't bear the thought of losing him too. I can't reason with him. I asked him to leave, but he won't listen."

"I can see your problem, but why us?" Royce asked coldly. "And how does a farmer's daughter from the frontier know our names and how to find us in Colnora?"

"A crippled man told me. He sent me here. He said you could open the tower."

"A cripple?"

"Yes. Mister Haddon told me the beast can't—"

"Mister Haddon?" Royce interrupted.

"Uh-huh."

"This Mister Haddon…he wouldn't be missing his hands, would he?"

"Yes, that's him."

Royce and Hadrian exchanged glances.

"What exactly did he say?"

"He said the beast can't be harmed by weapons made by man, but inside the tower of Avempartha there is a sword that can kill it."

"So, a man with no hands told you to find us in Colnora, and hire us to get a sword for your father from a tower called *Avempartha?*" Royce asked.

The girl nodded.

Hadrian looked at his partner. "Don't tell me…it's a dwarven tower?"

"No…" Royce replied, "it's elvish." He turned away with a thoughtful expression.

Hadrian returned his attention to the girl. He felt awful. It was bad enough that her village was so far, but now they faced an elven tower. Even if she offered them a hundred gold tenents, he would not be able to convince Royce to take the job. She was so desperate, so in need of help. His stomach knotted as he considered the words he would say next.

"Well," Hadrian began reluctantly, "the Nidwalden River is several days travel over rough ground. We'd need supplies, for what, a six—seven day trip? That's two weeks there and back. We'd need food and grain for the horses. Then you'd have to add in time at the tower. That's time we could be doing other jobs, so that right there is money lost. Then there is the danger involved. Risk of any kind can bump our price and a mass-murdering phantom-demon-beast that can't be harmed by weapons, has got to be classified as a risk."

Hadrian looked into her eyes and shook his head. "I hate to say it, and I am very sorry, but we can't take—"

"Your money," Royce abruptly interjected as he spun around. "It's too much. To take the full twenty-five silver for this job, ten really seems like more than enough."

Hadrian raised an eyebrow and stared at his partner but said nothing.

"Ten silver each?" she asked.

"Ah—no," Hadrian replied, keeping his eyes on Royce. "That would be together. Right? Five each?"

Royce shrugged. "Since I will be doing the actual picking I think I should get six, but we can work that out between us. It's not something she needs to be concerned about."

"Really?" Thrace asked looking as if she might explode with happiness.

"Sure," Royce replied, "After all…we're not thieves."

"Want to explain why we are taking this job?" Hadrian asked, shielding his eyes as they stepped outside. The sky was a perfect blue, the morning sun already working to dry the lingering puddles from the night before. All around them people rushed to market. Carts loaded with spring vegetables and tarp covered barrels sat trapped behind three wagons mounded high with hay. Out of the crowd in front of them, a fat man charged forward with a flapping chicken gripped tightly under each arm. He danced around the puddles dodging people and carts and offering a muttered "excuse me," as he pressed by.

"She's paying us ten silver for a job that has already cost us a gold tenent," Hadrian continued after successfully skirting the chicken man. "It will cost us several more before we're done."

"We're not doing it for the money," Royce informed him as he cut a path through the crowd.

"Obviously, but why are we doing it? I mean sure, she's cute as a button and all, but unless you're planning on selling her, I don't see the angle here."

Royce looked over his shoulder, displaying an evil grin, "I never even considered selling her. That could defray the costs considerably."

"Forget I brought it up. Just tell me why we're doing this."

Royce led them out of the crowd toward Ognoton's Curio Shop, whose window exhibited hookahs, porcelain animal figurines, and jewelry boxes with brass latches. They ducked around the side into the narrow bricked space between it and a confectioner shop that was offering free samples of hard candy.

"Don't tell me you haven't wondered what Esrahaddon has been doing," Royce whispered. "That wizard was imprisoned for nine hundred years then disappears the day we break him out and we don't hear a word about him until now? The church must know, and yet the Imperialists haven't launched search parties or posted notices. I would think that if the most dangerous man alive was on the loose there might be a bit more of a commotion.

"Two years later he turns up in a tiny village and invites us to come visit. On top of that, he picks the elven frontier and Avempartha as the meeting place. Don't you want to find out what he wants?"

"What is this Avempartha?"

"All I know is that it's old. Real old. Some kind of ancient elven citadel. Which also begs the question, wouldn't you like to get a peek inside? If Esrahaddon thinks there's value in opening it, I'm guessing he's right."

"So we're going after ancient elven treasure?"

"I have no idea, but I'm sure there is something valuable in there. But for that we need supplies and we need to get out of town before Price lets loose the hounds."

"Well, as long as you promise not to sell the girl."

"I won't—if she behaves herself."

Hadrian felt Thrace leaning again, this time gazing at a two-story country home of stucco and stone with a yellow thatch roof and orange clay chimney. It was surrounded by a waist-high wall overgrown with lilacs and ivy.

"It's so beautiful," she whispered.

It was early afternoon and they were only a few miles out of Colnora, traveling east along the Alburn road. The country lane twisted through the tangle of tiny villages that comprised the hill region surrounding the city. Little hamlets where poor farmers worked their fields alongside the summer cottages of the idle rich, who for three months a year, pretended to be country squires. Royce rode beside them or trotted forward as congestion demanded. His hood was up despite the pleasant weather. Thrace rode behind Hadrian on his bay mare, her legs dangled off one side, bobbing to the rhythm of the horse's stride.

"It's a different world here," she said, "a paradise. Everyone is wealthy, everyone a king."

"Colnora does alright, but I wouldn't go that far."

"Then how do you explain all the grand houses and palaces? The horse carts have metal rims on their wheels—metal! The vegetable stands overflow with bushels and bushels of onions and green peas and it is only spring. Look how smooth the road is, even after the rain, and do you see all the cows on that hillside? They even put street names on posts and back there a farmer was wearing gloves— gloves on his hands while working. My father won't believe it when I tell him. In Dahlgren, even the church deacon doesn't own fancy gloves, and he certainly wouldn't work in them if he did. You all are so rich."

"Some of them are."

"Like you two."

Hadrian laughed.

"But you have nice clothes and beautiful horses."

"She's not much of a horse really."

"No one in Dahlgren but the lord and his knights own horses, and yours are so pretty. I especially like her eyes—such long lashes. What's her name?"

"I call her Millie after a woman I once knew who had the same habit of not listening to me."

"Millie is a pretty name. I like it. What about Royce's horse?"

Hadrian frowned and looked over at him. "I don't know. Royce, did you ever name her?"

"What for?"

Hadrian glanced back at Thrace who returned an appalled look.

"How about…" she paused, shifting and twisting as she scanned the roadside. "Lilac, or Daisy? Oh wait, no, how about Chrysanthemum."

"*Chrysanthemum?*" Hadrian repeated. As funny as it might be to have Royce riding a Chrysanthemum, or even a Lilac or Daisy, he had to point out that flower names just did not fit Royce's short, dirty, gray mare. "How about Shorty or Sooty?"

"No!" Thrace scolded him. "It will make the poor animal feel awful."

Hadrian chuckled. Royce ignored the conversation. He clicked his tongue, kicked the sides of his horse and trotted forward to avoid an approaching wagon, but remained there even after the road was clear.

"How about Lady?" Thrace asked.

"It seems a bit haughty, don't you think? She's not exactly a prancing show horse."

"Then it will make her feel better. Give her confidence."

They were coming upon a stream where honeysuckle and raspberry bushes crowned the heads of smooth granite banks with brilliant springtime green. A gristmill stood at the edge, its great wheel creaking and dripping. A pair of small square windows, like dark eyes, created a face in the stone exterior beneath the steeply peaked wooden roof. A low wall separated the mill from the road and on it rested a white and gray cat. Its green eyes opened lazily and blinked at them. When they drew closer, the cat decided they had come close enough and leapt from the wall, darting across the road into the thickets.

Royce's horse reared and whinnied, dancing across the dirt. He cursed and tightened the reins as the horse shuffled backward, pulling her head down and forcing her to turn completely around.

"Ridiculous!" Royce complained once the horse was under control. "A thousand pound animal terrified by a five pound cat, you'd think she was a mouse."

"Mouse! That's perfect." Thrace shouted causing Millie's ears to twist back.

"I like it," Hadrian agreed.

"Oh, good lord," Royce muttered, shaking his head as he trotted forward again.

As they rode farther northeast, the country estates became farms, rosebushes became hedges, and fences that divided fields gave way to mere tree lines. Still Thrace pointed out curiosities, like the unimagined luxury of covered bridges and the ornately decorated carriages that still occasionally thundered by.

They climbed higher, losing the shade as the land opened up into vast fallow fields of goldenrod, milkweed, and wild salifan. Flies dogged them in the heat and the drone of cicadas whined. In her discomfort, Thrace at last grew quiet and laid her head against Hadrian's back. He became concerned she might fall asleep and topple off, but occasionally she would stir to look about or swat at a fly.

The broad road narrowed to a single carriage width and rose steadily upwards. To their left lay Chadwick. They steered clear and this drove them east toward Amber Heights. The prominent highland stood out as a bald spot of short grass and bare rock. Part of a long ridge that ran along the eastern edge of Warric, it served as the border between Colnora and the kingdom of Alburn. Reaching the crest, Colnora could be seen spread out below them along with the southern villages of Chadwick to the north. Ahead to the northeast lay endless miles of dense forest.

Amber Heights was a curiosity even to the local residents due to the standing stones, massive blue-gray rocks carved into uniquely fluid shapes. They appeared almost organic in their rounded curves, like a series of writhing serpents burrowing in and out of the hilltop. Hadrian did not have the slightest idea what purpose the stones might have originally served. He doubted anyone did. Remnants of campfires were scattered around the stones etched with messages of true love or the occasional slogan: "Maribor is God!", "Nationalists are Barmy", "The Heir is Dead", and even "Gray Mouse Tavern—it's all downhill from here". Because the wind on the hilltop was cool and strong enough to drive off the flies, it made a perfect place to break for a midday meal.

They ate salted pork, hard dark bread, onions, and pickles. It was the kind of meal Hadrian would loathe to eat in a town, but seemed somehow wonderful on the road where his appetite was greater and options fewer. He watched Thrace sitting on the grass, nibbling on a pickle, being careful not to stain her new dress. She gazed off with a faraway look, inhaling the air in deep appreciative breaths.

"What are you thinking?" he asked.

She smiled at him a bit self-consciously and he thought he noticed a sadness about her. "I was just thinking how wonderful it is here. How nice it would be to live on one of those farms we passed. We wouldn't need anything grand, not even a house—my father can build a house all by himself and he can turn any soil. There's nothing he can't do once he sets his mind to it, and once he sets his mind, there's no changing it."

"Sounds like a great guy."

"Oh, he is. He's very strong, very determined."

"I'm surprised he would allow you to set off alone across the country like you did."

Thrace smiled.

"You didn't walk all the way, did you?"

"Oh no, I got a ride with a peddler and his wife who stopped in Dahlgren. They refused to spend a second night and let me ride in the back of their wagon."

"Have you done much traveling before?"

"No. I was born in Glamrendor, the capital of Dunmore. My family worked a tenant farm for his lordship there. We moved to Dahlgren when I was about nine, so I've never been out of Dunmore until now. I can't even say I remember all that much of Glamrendor. I do recall it was dirty though. All the buildings were made of wood and the roads very muddy—at least that's how I remember it."

"Still that way," Royce mentioned.

"I can't believe you had the courage to just go off like that," Hadrian said shaking his head. "It must have been a shock leaving Dahlgren and a few days later finding yourself in the largest city in the world."

"Oh it was," she replied, using her pinky finger to draw away a number of hairs that had blown into her mouth. "I felt foolish when I realized just how hard it was going to be to find you. I expected it would be like back home where I would be able to walk up to anyone and they would know who you were. There are a lot more people in Colnora than I expected. To be honest, there's a lot more of everything. I looked and looked and I thought I would never find you."

"I expect your father will be worried."

"No he won't," she said.

"But if—"

"What are these things?" she asked pointing at the standing stones with her pickle. "These blue stones. They're so odd."

"No one knows," Royce replied.

"Were they made by elves?" she asked.

Royce cocked his head and stared at her. "How did you know that?"

"They look a bit like the tower near my village—the one I need you to open. Same kind of stone—at least I think so—the tower looks bluish too, but it might be because of the distance—ever notice how things get blue in the distance? I suppose if we could actually get near it we might find it was just a common gray, you know?"

"Why can't you get near it?" Hadrian asked.

"Because it's in the middle of the river."

"Can't you swim?"

"You would have to be a real strong swimmer. The tower is built on a rock that hangs over a waterfall. Beautiful falls—really high, you know? Lots of water going over. On sunny days, you can see rainbows in the mist. Of course, it's very dangerous. At least five people have died, only two are for sure, the other three are just guesses because—" She paused when she saw the looks on their faces. "Is something wrong?"

"You might have said something earlier," Royce replied.

"About the waterfall? Oh, I thought you knew. I mean you acted like you knew the tower when I mentioned it before. I'm sorry."

They ate in silence for a few moments. Thrace finished her lunch and walked around looking at the stones, her dress billowing behind her. "I don't understand," she finally said raising her voice over the wind. "If the Nidwalden is the border, why are there elven stones here?"

"This used to be elven land," Royce explained. "All of it. Before there was a Colnora, or a Warric, it was part of the Erivan Empire. Most don't like to acknowledge that; they prefer to think that men always ruled here. It bothers them. Funny thing is many of the names we use are elvish. Ervanon, Rhenydd, Glamrendor, Galewyr, and Nidwalden are all elven. The very name of this country Avryn means *green fields*."

"Try and tell that to someone in a bar sometime and see how fast you get cracked in the head," Hadrian mentioned, drawing looks from both of them.

While they finished eating, Thrace stood among the great stones staring west, her hair and dress whipping about her. Her sight rose to the horizon, out beyond Colnora, beyond the blue hills to the thin line of the sea. She looked so small and delicate he half expected the wind to carry her away like some golden leaf and then he noticed the look in her eyes. She was little more than a child and yet they were not the eyes of a child. The glow of innocence, the sparkle of wonder was absent. There was a weight to her face, a determination in her gaze. Whatever childhood she had known had long since abandoned her.

They finished their food, packed up, and set off again. Descending the far side of the heights, they continued to follow the road for the remainder of the day but as sunset neared, the road narrowed to little more than a simple trail. Farmhouses still appeared from time to time, but they were less frequent. The forest grew thicker and the road darker.

As sunlight faded, Thrace grew very quiet. There was nothing to see or point out anymore but Hadrian guessed it was more than that. Mouse skipped a stone into a windblown pile of last year's leaves and Thrace jumped, grabbing his waist. She dug her nails in deep enough to make him wince.

"Shouldn't we find shelter?" she asked.

"Not much chance of that out here," Hadrian told her. "There might be a few more inns on the road ahead as we pass near Alburn, but nothing that will help us tonight. Besides, it's a lovely evening. The ground is dry and it looks like it will be warm."

"We're sleeping outside?"

Hadrian turned around to see her face. Her mouth was open slightly, her forehead creased, her eyes wide and looking up at the sky. "We're still a long way from Dahlgren," he assured her. She nodded, but held on to him tighter.

They stopped at a clearing near a little creek that flowed over a series of rocks, making a friendly rushing sound. Hadrian helped Thrace down and pulled the saddles and gear off the horses.

"Where's Royce?" Thrace asked in a whispered panic. She stood with her arms folded across her chest, looking around anxiously.

"It's okay," Hadrian told her as he pulled the bridle off Millie's head. "He always does a bit of scouting whenever we stop for the night. He'll circle the area making sure we're alone. Royce hates surprises."

Thrace nodded but remained huddled, as if standing on a stone amidst a raging river.

"We'll be sleeping right over there. You might want to clear it some. A single stone can ruin a night's sleep. I ought to know; it seems whenever I sleep outside I always end up with a stone under the small of my back."

She walked into the clearing and gingerly bent over, tossing aside branches and rocks, nervously glancing skyward and jumping at the slightest sound. By the time Hadrian had the horses settled Royce had returned. He carried an armload of small branches and a few shattered logs which he used to build a fire.

Thrace stared at him, horrified. "It's so bright," she whispered.

Hadrian squeezed her hand and smiled. "You know, I bet you're a wonderful cook, aren't you? I could make us dinner, but it would be miserable. All I know how to do is boil potatoes. How about you give it a try? What do you say? There are pots and pans in that sack over there and you'll find food in the one next to it."

Thrace nodded silently, and with one last glance upwards, shuffled over to the packs. "What kind of meal would you like?"

"Something edible would be a pleasant surprise," Royce said, adding more wood.

Hadrian threw a stick at him. The thief caught it and placed it on the fire.

She dug into the packs, going so far as to stick her head inside, and emerged moments later with an armload of items. She borrowed Hadrian's knife and began cutting vegetables on the bottom of a turned-up pan.

It grew dark quickly, the fire becoming the only source of light in the clearing. The flickering yellow radiance illuminated the canopy of leaves around them, creating the feel of a woodland cave. Hadrian picked out a grassy area upwind from the smoke and laid out sheets of canvas coated in pitch. It blocked the wetness that would otherwise soak in. The treated fabric was something they had come up with after years on the road. But they did not have time to make one for Thrace. He sighed, threw Thrace's blankets on his canvas and went in search of pine boughs for his own bed.

When dinner was ready, Royce called for Hadrian. He returned to the fire where Thrace was dishing out a thick broth of carrots, potatoes, onions and salted pork. Royce was sitting with a bowl on his lap and a smile on his face.

"You don't have to be that happy," he told him.

"Look, Hadrian—food," Royce taunted.

They ate mostly in silence. Royce made a few comments about things they should pick up when they passed through Alburn such as another length of rope and a new spoon to replace the cracked one. Hadrian mostly watched Thrace who refused to sit near the fire; she ate alone on a rock in the shadows near the horses. When they finished, she stole away to the river to wash the pot and wooden bowls.

"Are you alright?" Hadrian asked, finding her along the stony bank.

Thrace was crouched on a large moss capped rock, her gown tucked tight around her ankles as she washed the pots by scooping up what sand she could find and scrubbing them with her fingers.

"I'm fine, thank you. I'm just not used to being out at night."

Hadrian settled down beside her and began cleaning his bowl.

"I can do that," she said.

"So can I. Besides, you're the customer so you should get your money's worth."

She smirked at him. "I'm not a fool, you know. Ten silver won't even cover the feed for the horses, will it?"

"Well, what you have to understand is Mouse and Millie are very spoiled. They only eat the best grain." He winked. She could not help but smile back.

Thrace finished the pot and the other bowls and they walked back to camp.

"How much farther is it?" she asked replacing the pots in the sack.

"I'm not sure. I've never been to Dahlgren, but we made good time today so maybe only another four days."

"I hope my father is alright. Mister Haddon said he would try to convince him to wait until I returned before hunting the beast. I hope he did. As I said my father is a very stubborn man and I can't imagine anyone changing his mind."

"Well, if anyone can, I suspect that Mister Haddon could," Royce remarked prodding the coals of the fire with a long stick. "How did you meet him?"

Thrace found the bed Hadrian had laid out for her near the fire and sat down on her blanket. "It was right after my family's funeral. It was very beautiful. The whole village turned out. Maria and Jessie Caswell hung wreaths of wild salifan on the markers. Mae Drundel and Rose and Verna McDern sang the *Fields of Lilies*, and

Deacon Tomas said a few prayers. Lena and Russell Bothwick held a reception at their house. Lena and my mother were very close."

"I don't remember you mentioning your mother, was she—"

"My mother died two years ago."

"I'm sorry. Sickness?"

Thrace shook her head.

No one spoke for awhile then Hadrian said, "You were telling us how you met Mister Haddon—"

"Oh yeah, well I don't know how many funerals you've been to, but it starts to feel…smothering. All the weeping and old stories. I snuck out. I was just wandering really. I ended up at the village well and there he was—a stranger. We don't get many of those, but that wasn't all. He had on this robe that shimmered and kinda seemed to change colors from time to time, but the big thing was he had no hands. The poor man was trying to get himself a drink of water struggling with the bucket and rope.

"I asked his name and then, oh I don't know, I did something stupid like starting to cry and he asked me what was wrong. The thing was, at that moment, I wasn't crying because my brother and his wife just died. I was crying because I was terrified my father would be next. I don't know why I told him. Maybe because he was a stranger. It was easy to talk to him. It all just spilled out. I felt stupid afterwards, but he was very patient. That's when he told me about the weapon in the tower and about you two."

"How did he know where we were?"

Thrace shrugged. "Don't you live there?"

"No…we were visiting an old friend. Did he talk oddly? Did he use *thee* and *thou* a lot?"

"No, but he spoke a bit more educated than most. He said his name was Mister Esra Haddon. Is he a friend of yours?"

"We only met him briefly," Hadrian explained. "Like you, we helped him with a little problem he was having."

"The question is why is he keeping tabs on us?" Royce asked. "And how since I don't recall dropping our names and he couldn't have known we would be going to Colnora."

"All he told me is that you were needed to open the tower and if I left right away I could find you there. Then he arranged for me to ride with the peddler. He's been very helpful."

"Rather amazing isn't it, for a man who can't even get himself a cup of water," Royce muttered.

Chapter 3

THE AMBASSADOR

ARISTA STOOD AT the tower window looking down at the world below. She could see the roofs of shops and houses. They appeared as squares and triangles of gray, brown, and red pierced by chimneys left dormant on the warm spring day. The rain had washed through, leaving the world below fresh and vibrant. She watched the people walking along the streets, gathering in squares, moving in and out of doorways. Occasionally a shout reached her ears, soft and faint. Most of the noise came from directly below in the courtyard where a train of seven coaches had just arrived and servants were loading trunks.

"No. No. No. Not the red dress!" Bernice shouted at Melissa. "Novron protect us. Look at that neckline. Her highness has a reputation to protect. Put that in storage, or better yet—burn it. Why, you might as well salt her, put a garnish behind her ear, and hand her over to a pack of starving wolves. No, not the dark one either; it's nearly black—it's spring for Maribor's sake. Where's your head?—the sky blue gown—yes, that one can stay. Honestly, it's a good thing I'm here."

Bernice was an old plump woman with a dough-like face that sagged at the cheeks and doubled at the chin. The color of her hair was unknown as she always wrapped it in a barbette veil that looped her head from crown to neck. To this she added a tall cloth filet that made it seem like the top of her head was flat. She stood in the center of Arista's bedroom, flailing her arms and shouting amidst the chaotic maelstrom that she had created.

Piles of clothes lay everywhere except in Arista's wardrobes. Those stood empty, waiting with doors wide, as Bernice sorted each gown, boxing the winter dresses for storage. In addition to Melissa, Bernice had drafted two other girls from downstairs to assist in the packing. Bernice had filled one chest but still her bedroom remained carpeted in gowns and Arista already had a headache from all the shouting.

Bernice had been one of her mother's handmaids. Queen Ann had kept several. Drundiline, a beautiful woman, had been her secretary and close friend. Harriet ran the residence, organizing the cleaning staff, seamstresses, and laundry. Nora, whose lazy eye always made it impossible to tell who she was actually looking at, handled the children. Arista remembered how she would tell her fairy tales at bedtime about greedy dwarves who kidnapped spoiled princesses, but how a dashing prince always saved them in the end. In all, Arista could remember no fewer than eight maids, but she could not remember Bernice.

She came to Essendon Castle nearly two years ago, only a month after Arista's father, King Amrath, was murdered. Bishop Saldur explained that she had served the queen and was the only maid to survive the fire that had killed her mother so many years ago. He mentioned Bernice had been away for years suffering from melancholy and sickness, but after Amrath's death, she insisted on returning to care for her beloved queen's daughter.

"Oh, Your Highness," Bernice said holding two separate pairs of Arista's shoes, "I do wish you would come away from that window. The weather may look pleasant, but drafts are not something to toy with. Trust me, I know all about it—intimately. Pray you never have to go through what I did—the aches, the pains, the coughing. Not that I am complaining, of course, I am still here, aren't I? I am blessed with the vision of seeing you grow into a lady and, Maribor willing, I will see you as a bride. What a fine bride you will make! I hope King Alric picks a husband for you soon. Who knows how long I have left and we don't want people gossiping about you any more than they already are."

"People are gossiping?" Arista turned and sat on the open windowsill.

Watching her on the edge, Bernice panicked and froze in place, her mouth opening and closing with silent protests, both hands waving the shoes at her. "Your Highness," she managed to gasp, "you'll fall!"

"I'm fine."

"No. No, you're not." Bernice shook her head frantically. "Please. I beg of you."

She dropped the shoes, planted her feet, and reached out her hand as if standing on the edge of a precipice, "Please."

Arista rolled her eyes and standing up, walked away from the window. She crossed the room to her bed that lay beneath several layers of clothes.

"No, wait!" Bernice shouted again. She shook her hands at the wrists as if trying to dry them. "Melissa, clear her highness a place to sit."

Arista sighed and ran a hand through her hair while she waited for Melissa to gather the dresses.

"Careful now, don't wrinkle them," Bernice cautioned.

"I'm sorry, Your Highness," Melissa told her as she gathered an armful. She was a small redhead with dark green eyes, who served Arista for the past five years. The princess got the distinct impression the maid's apology did not refer to the mess on the bed.

Arista fought to keep from laughing and a smile emerged. It only made matters worse when she saw Melissa grinning as well.

"The good news is the bishop delivered a list of potential suitors to his majesty this morning," Bernice said and Arista no longer had any trouble quelling laughter, the smile disappeared as well. "I'm hoping it will be that nice Prince Rudolf, King Armand's son." Bernice was raising her eyebrows and grinning mischievously like some deranged pixie. "He's very handsome, many say dashing, and Alburn is a very nice kingdom—at least so I have heard."

"I've been there and I've met him. He's an arrogant ass."

"Oh, that tongue of yours!" Bernice clasped her hands to the sides of her face and gazed upward mouthing a silent prayer. "You must learn to control yourself. If anyone else had heard you—thankfully we're the only ones here."

Arista glanced at Melissa and the other two girls busy sorting through her things. Melissa caught her look and shrugged.

"Alright, so you aren't certain about Prince Rudolf, that's fine. How about King Ethelred of Warric? You can't do better than him. The poor widower is the most powerful monarch in Avryn. You would live in Aquesta and be queen of the Wintertide festivals."

"The man has to be in his fifties. Not to mention he's a staunch Imperialist. I'd slit my throat first."

Bernice staggered backward threw one hand to her own neck while the other reached for the wall.

Melissa snickered and tried to cover it with a pretend cough.

"I think you're done here, Melissa," Bernice said. "Take the chamber pot when you go."

"But the sorting isn't—" Melissa protested.

Bernice gave her a reproachful look.

Melissa sighed. "Your Highness," she said and curtseyed to Arista, then picked up the chamber pot and left.

"She didn't mean anything by it," Arista told Bernice.

"It doesn't matter. Respect must be maintained at all times. I know I am only an old crazy woman who doesn't matter to anyone, but I can tell you this: If I were here—if I had been well enough to help raise you after your mother died, people wouldn't be calling you a witch today."

Arista's eyes widened.

"Forgive me, Your Highness, but that's the truth of it. With your mother gone, and me away, I fear you were brought up poorly. Thank Maribor I came back when I did or who knows what would become of you. But no worries my dear, we have you on the right track now. You'll see, everything will work out once we find you a suitable husband. All that nonsense from your past will soon be forgotten."

Her dignity, as well as the length of her gown, prevented Arista from running down the stairs. Her bodyguard Hilfred trotted behind her, struggling to keep up with the sudden burst of speed. She had caught him by surprise. She had surprised herself. Arista had every intention of walking calmly up to her brother and politely asking if he had gone mad. The plan had worked fine up until she passed the chapel, then she started moving faster and faster.

The good news is that the bishop delivered a list of potential suitors to his majesty this morning.

She could still see the grin on Bernice's face, and hear the perverse glee in her words, as if she were a spectator at the foot of a gallows waiting for the hangman to kick the bucket.

I'm hoping it will be that nice Prince Rudolf, King Armand's son.

It was hard to breathe. Her hair broke loose from the ribbon and flew behind her. Rounding the turn near the ballroom, Arista's left foot slipped out from under her and she nearly fell. Her shoe came off and spun across the polished floor. She left it, pressing on, hobbling forward like a wagon with a broken wheel. She reached the west gallery. It was a long, straight hallway lined with suits of armor, and here she picked up speed. Jacobs, the royal clerk, spotted her from his perch outside the reception hall and jumped to his feet.

"Your Highness," he exclaimed with a bow.

"Is he in there?" she barked.

The little clerk with the round face and red nose nodded. "But his majesty is in a state meeting. He's requested that he not be disturbed."

"The man is already disturbed. I'm just here to beat some sense into his feeble little brain."

The clerk cringed. He looked like a squirrel in a rainstorm. If he had a tail, it would be over his head. Behind her she heard Hilfred's familiar footsteps approach.

She turned toward the door and took a step.

"You can't go in," Jacobs told her, panicking. "They are having a state meeting," he repeated.

The soldiers that stood to either side of the door stepped forward to block her.

"Out of my way!" she yelled.

"Forgive us, Your Highness, but we have orders from the king not to allow anyone entrance."

"I'm his sister," she protested.

"I am sorry, Your Highness, his majesty—he specifically mentioned you."

"He—what?" She stood stunned for a moment then spun on the clerk, caught wiping his nose with a handkerchief. "Who's in there with him? Who's in this *state meeting?*"

"What's going on?" Julian Tempest, the Lord Chamberlain asked, as he rushed out of his office. His long black robe with gold hash marks on the sleeve trailed behind him like the train of a bride. Julian was an ancient man who had been Lord Chamberlain of Essendon Castle since before she was born, perhaps even before her father was born. Normally he wore a powdered wig that hung down past his shoulders like the floppy ears of an old dog, but she had caught him by surprise and all he had on was his skullcap—a few tuffs of white hair sticking out like seed silk from a milkweed pod.

"I want to see my brother," Arista demanded.

"But—but, Your Highness, he's in a state meeting, surely it can wait."

"Who is he meeting with?"

"I believe Bishop Saldur, Chancellor Pickering, Lord Valin, and oh I'm not sure who else." Julian glanced at Jacobs for support.

"And what is this meeting about?"

"Why, actually I think it has to do with," he hesitated, "your future."

"My future? They are determining my life in there and I can't go in?" She was livid now." Is Prince Rudolf in there? Lanis Ethelred, perhaps?"

"Ah…I don't know—I don't think so," again he glanced at the clerk who wanted no part of this. "Your Highness, please calm down. I suspect they can hear you."

"Good!" she shouted. "They should hear me. I want them to hear me. If they think I am going to just stand here and wait for the verdict, to see what they will decide my fate to be, I—"

"Arista!"

She turned to see the doors to the throne room open. Her brother Alric stood trapped behind the guards who quickly stood aside. He was wearing the white fur mantle Julian insisted he drape over his shoulders at all state functions and the heavy gold crown that he pushed to the back of his head. "What is your problem? You sound like a raving lunatic."

"I'll tell you what my problem is. I'm not going to let you do this to me. You are not going to send me off to Alburn or Warric like some—some—state commodity."

"I'm not sending you to Warric or Alburn. We've already decided you are going to Dunmore."

"Dunmore?" The word hit her like a blow. "You're joking. Tell me you're joking."

"I was going to tell you tonight. Although, I thought you'd take it better. I figured you'd like it."

"Like it? Like it! Oh yeah, I love the idea of being used as a political pawn. What are they giving you in return? Is that what you were doing in there, auctioning me off?" She rose on her toes trying to get a look over her brother's shoulders to see who he was hiding in the throne room. "Did you have them bidding on me like a prized cow?"

"Prized cow? What are you talking about?" Alric glanced behind him self-consciously and closed the doors. He waved at Julian and Jacobs shooing them away. In a softer voice he said, "It will give you some respect. You'll have genuine authority. You won't be just *the princess* anymore and you'll have something to do. Weren't you the one that said you wanted to get out of your tower and contribute to the well-being of the kingdom?"

"And—and this is what you thought of?" She was ready to scream. "Don't do this to me Alric, I beg of you. I know I've been an embarrassment. I know what they say about me. You think I don't hear them whispering *witch* under their breath? You think I don't know what was said at the trial?"

"Arista, those people were coerced. You know that." He glanced briefly at Hilfred who stood beside her holding the lost shoe.

"I'm just saying I know about it. I'm sure they complain to you all the time," she gestured toward the closed door behind him. She did not know whom she meant by *they* and hoped he did not ask.

"But I can't help what people think. If you want, I will come to more events. I will attend the state dinners. I will take up needlepoint. I will make a damn tapestry. Something cute and inoffensive. How about a stag hunt? I don't know how to make a tapestry, but I bet Bernice does—she knows all that crap."

"*You're* going to make a tapestry?"

"If that's what it takes. I'll be better—I will. I haven't even put the lock on my door in the new tower. I haven't done a thing since you were crowned, I swear. Please don't sentence me to a life of servitude. I don't mind being just a princess—I don't."

He looked at her confused.

"I mean it. I really do, Alric. Please, don't do this."

He sighed, looking at her sadly. "Arista, what else can I do with you? I don't want you living like a hermit in that tower for the rest of your life. I honestly think this is for the best. It will be good for you. You might not see it now but—don't look at me like that! I am king and you'll do as I tell you. I need you to do this for me. The kingdom needs you to do this."

She could not believe what she was hearing. Arista felt tears working their way forward. She locked her jaw, squeezing her teeth together breathing faster to stave them off. She felt feverish and a little light-headed. "And I suppose I am to be shipped off immediately. Is that why the carriages are outside?"

"Yes," he said firmly. "I was hoping you would be on your way in the morning."

"Tomorrow?" Arista felt her legs weaken, the air empty from her lungs.

"Oh for Maribor's sake, Arista—it's not like I'm ordering you to marry some old coot."

"Oh—well! I am so pleased you are looking out for me," she said. "Who is it then? One of King Roswort's nephews? Dearest Maribor, Alric! Why Dunmore? Rudolf would have been misery enough, but at least I could understand an alliance with Alburn, but Dunmore? That's just cruel. Do you hate me that much? Am I that horrible that you must marry me to some no account duke in a backwater kingdom? Even father wouldn't have done that to me—why—why are you laughing? Stop laughing, you insensitive little hobgoblin!"

"I'm not marrying you off, Arista," Alric managed to get out.

She narrowed her eyes at him. "You're not?"

"God no! Is that what you thought? I wouldn't do that. I'm familiar with the kind of people you know. I'd find myself floating down the Galewyr again."

"What then? Julian said you were deciding my fate in there."

"I have—I've officially appointed you Ambassador of Melengar."

She stood silent, staring at him for a long moment. Without turning her head, she shifted her eyes and grabbed her shoe from Hilfred. Leaning on his shoulder, she slipped it back on.

"But Bernice said Sauly brought a list of eligible suitors," she said tentatively, cautiously.

"Oh yes, he did," Alric said chuckling. "We all had a good laugh at that."

"We?"

"Mauvin and Fanen are here," he hooked his thumb at the door. "They're going with you. Fanen plans to enter the contest the church is organizing up in Ervanon. You see it was supposed to be this big surprise, but you ruined everything as usual."

"I'm sorry," she said, her voice quivering unexpectedly.

"Oh now, don't start crying."

"I can't help it." She threw her arms around her brother and hugged him tight. "Thank you."

The front wheels of the carriage bounced in a hole, followed abruptly by the rear ones. Arista nearly struck her head on the roof and lost her concentration, which was frustrating because she was certain she was on the verge of recalling the name of Dunmore's Secretary of the Treasury. It started with a Bon, a Bonny or a Bobo—no, it could not be Bobo, could it? It was something like that. All these names, all these titles, the third Baron of Brodinia, the Earl of Nith—or was it the third Baron of Nith and the Earl of Brodinia? Arista looked at the palm of her hand wondering if she could write them there. If caught it would be an embarrassment not just for herself, but Alric, and all of Melengar as well. From now on everything she did, every mistake, every stumble would not just hurt her it would reflect poorly on her kingdom. She had to be perfect. The problem was she did not know how to be perfect. She wished her brother had given her more time to prepare.

Dunmore was a new kingdom, only seventy years old. An overgrown fief reclaimed from the wilderness by ambitious nobles with only passing pedigrees. It had none of the traditions or refinement found in the rest of Avryn, but it did have a plethora of mind-numbing titled offices. She was convinced King Roswort created them the way a self-conscious man might over-decorate a modest house. He certainly had more ministers than Alric, with titles twice as long and uniquely vague, such as The Assistant Secretary of the Second Royal Avenue Inspection Quorum. *What does that even mean?* And then there was the simply unfathomable, since Dunmore was landlocked, Grandmaster of the Fleet! Nevertheless, Julian had provided her with a list and she was doing her best to memorize it, along with a tally sheet of their imports, exports, trade agreements, military treaties, and even the name of the king's dog. She laid her head back on the velvet upholstery and sighed.

"Something wrong, my dear?" Bishop Saldur inquired from his seat directly across from her where he sat pressing his fingers together. He stared at her with unwavering eyes that took in more than her face. She would have considered his looks rude if it had been anyone else. Saldur, or Sauly as she always called him, had taught her the art of blowing dandelions that had gone to seed when she was five. He had shown her how to play checkers and pretended not to notice when she climbed trees or rode her pony at a gallop. For commencement on her sixteenth birthday, Sauly had personally instructed her on the Tenements of the Faith of Nyphron. He was like a grandfather. He always stared at her. She had given up wondering why.

"There's too much to learn. I can't keep it all straight. The bouncing doesn't help either. It's just that…" she flipped through the parchments on her lap, shaking her head, "I want to do a good job, but I don't think I will."

The old man smiled at her, his eyebrows rising in sympathy. "You will do fine. Besides, it's only Dunmore," he gave her a wink. "I think you will find his majesty, King Roswort, an unpleasant sort of man to deal with. Dunmore has been slow to gain the virtues that the rest of civilization has learned to enjoy. Just be patient and respectful. Remember that you will be standing in *his* court, not Melengar and there you are subject to his authority. Your best ally in any discussion is silence. Learn to develop that skill. Learn to listen instead of speaking and you will weather many storms. Also, avoid promising anything. Give the impression you are promising, but never actually say the words. That way Alric always has room to maneuver. It is a bad practice to tie the hands of your monarch."

"Would you like something to drink, milady?" Bernice asked, sitting beside Arista on the cushioned bench guarding a basket of travel treats. She sat straight, her knees together, hands clutching the basket, thumbs rubbing it gently. Bernice beamed at her, fanning deep lines from the corners of her eyes. Her round pudgy cheeks were forced too high by a smile too broad—a condescending smile, the sort displayed to a child who had scraped her knee. At times Arista wondered if the old woman was trying to *be* her mother.

"What have you got in there, dear?" Saldur asked. "Anything with a bite to it?"

"I brought a pint of brandy," she said, hastily adding, "in case it got cold."

"Come to think of it, I feel a bit chilled," Saldur said rubbing his hands up and down his arms pretending to shiver.

Arista raised an eyebrow. "This carriage is like an oven," she said while pulling on the high dress collar that ran to her chin. Alric emphasized that she needed to wear properly modest attire, as if she had made a habit of strolling about the castle in bosom-baring, scarlet tavern dresses. Bernice took this edict as carte blanche to imprison Arista in antiquated costumes of heavy material. The sole exception was the dress for her meeting with the King of Dunmore. Arista wanted all the help she could get to make a good impression and decided to wear the formal reception gown that once belonged to her mother. It was simply the most stunning dress Arista had ever seen. When her mother wore it, every head had turned. She had looked so impressive, so magnificent—every bit the queen.

"Old bones, my dear," Saldur told her. "Come Bernice, why don't you and I share a little cup?" This brought a self-conscious smile to the old lady's face.

Arista pulled the velvet curtain aside and looked out the window. Her carriage was in the middle of a caravan consisting of wagons and soldiers on horseback. Mauvin and Fanen were somewhere out there, but all she could see was what the window framed. They were in the Kingdom of Ghent, although Ghent had no king. The Nyphron

Church administered the region directly and had for several hundred years. There were few trees in this rocky land and the hills remained a dull brown as if spring was tardy—off playing in other realms and neglecting its chores here. High above the plain a hawk circled in wide loops.

"Oh dear!" Bernice exclaimed as the carriage bounced again. *Oh dear!* was as close as Bernice ever came to cursing. Arista glanced over to see that the jostling was making the process of pouring the brandy a challenge. Sauly with the bottle, Bernice with the cup, their arms shifting up and down struggling to meet in the middle like some test-of-skill at a May Fair—a game designed to look simple but ultimately embarrassed the players. At last, Sauly managed to tip the bottle and they both cheered.

"Not a drop lost," he said pleased with himself. "Here's to our new ambassador. May she do us proud." He raised the cup, took a large mouthful and sat back with a sigh. "Have you been to Ervanon before, my dear?"

She shook her head.

"I think you will find it spiritually uplifting. Honestly, I am surprised your father never brought you here. It is a pilgrimage every member of the Church of Nyphron needs to make once in their life."

Arista nodded, failing to mention her late father was not terribly devout. He had been required to play his part in the religious services of the kingdom, but often skipped them if the fish were biting, or if the huntsmen reported spotting a stag in the river valley. Of course, there were times when even he sought solace. She had long wondered about his death. Why was he in the chapel the night that miserable dwarf stabbed him? More importantly, how did her Uncle Percy know he would be there and use this knowledge to plot his death? It puzzled her until she realized he was not there praying to Novron or Maribor—he was talking to *her*. It was the anniversary of the fire. The date Arista's mother died. He probably visited the chapel every year and it bothered Arista that her uncle knew more about her father's habits than she did. It also disturbed her that she had never thought to join him.

"You will have the privilege of meeting with his holiness the Archbishop of Ghent."

She sat up surprised. "Alric never mentioned anything about a meeting. I thought we were merely passing through Ervanon on our way to Dunmore."

"It is not a formal meeting. He is eager to see the new Ambassador of Melengar."

"Will I be meeting with the patriarch as well?" she asked concerned. Not being prepared for Dunmore was one thing, but meeting the patriarch with no preparation would be devastating.

"No," Saldur smiled like a man amused by a child's struggle to take her first steps. "Until the Heir of Novron is found, the patriarch is the closest thing we have to the voice of god. He lives his life in seclusion, speaking only on rare occasions. He is a very great man, a very holy man. Besides, we can't keep you too long. You don't want to be late for your appointment with King Roswort in Glamrendor."

"I suppose I will miss the contest then."

"I don't see how," the bishop said after taking another sip that left his lips glistening.

"If I push on to Dunmore I won't be in Ervanon to see—"

"Oh, the contest won't be held in Ervanon," Saldur explained. "Those broadsides you've no doubt seen only indicated that contestants are to *gather* there."

"Then where will it be?"

"Ah, well now, that is something of a secret. Given the gravity of this event, it is important to keep things under control, but I can tell you this, Dunmore will be on the way. You will stop there long enough to have your audience with the king and then you will be able to continue on to the contest with the rest of them. Alric will most assuredly want to have his ambassador on hand for this momentous occasion."

"Oh wonderful, I would like that—Fanen Pickering is competing. But does that mean you won't be coming?"

"That will be up to the archbishop to decide."

"I hope you can. I'm sure Fanen would appreciate as many people as possible cheering him on."

"Oh, it's not a competition. I know all those heralds are promoting it that way, which is unfortunate because the patriarch did not intend it so."

Arista stared at him confused. "I thought it was a tournament. I saw an announcement declaring the church was hosting a grand event, a test of courage and skill, the winner to receive some magnificent reward."

"Yes, and all of that is true, but misleading. Skill will not be needed so much as courage and…well, you'll find out."

He tipped the cup and frowned, then looked hopefully at Bernice.

Arista stared at the cleric a moment longer, wondering what all that meant, but it was clear Sauly would not be adding anything further on the topic. She turned back to the window peering out once more. Hilfred trotted beside the carriage on his white stallion. Unlike Bernice, her bodyguard was unobtrusive and silent. He was always there, distant, watchful, respectful of her privacy, or as much as a man could be who was required to follow her everywhere. He was always in sight of her but never looking—the perfect shadow. It had always been that way, but since the trial, he was different. It was a subtle change but she sensed he had withdrawn from her. Perhaps he felt guilty for his testimony, or maybe, like so many others, he believed some of the accusations brought against her. It was possible

Hilfred thought he was serving a witch. Maybe he even regretted saving her life from the fire that night. She threw the curtain shut and sighed.

It was dark by the time the caravan arrived in Ervanon. Bernice had fallen asleep, her head hanging limp over the basket that threatened to fall. Saldur had nodded off as well, his head drooping lower and lower, popping up abruptly only to droop again. Through her window, Arista felt the cool, dewy night air splash across her face as she craned her neck to look ahead. The sky was awash in stars giving it a light dusty appearance and Arista could see the dark outline of the city rising on the great hill. The lower buildings were nothing more than shadows, but from within them rose a singular finger. The Crown Tower was unmistakable. The alabaster battlements that ringed the top appeared like a white crown floating high in the air. The ancient remnant of the Steward's Empire was distinctive as the tallest structure ever made by man. Even at a distance it was awe-inspiring.

Surrounding the city Arista saw campfires, flickering lights scattered across the flats like a swarm of resting fireflies. As they approached, she heard voices, shouts, laughter, arguments rising up from the many camps along the roadside. They were the contestants, and there must be hundreds of them. Arista saw only glimpses as they rolled past. Faces illuminated by the glow of firelight. Silhouetted figures carried plates; men and boys sat on the ground laughing, tipping cups to their mouths. Tents filled the spaces in between and lines of tethered horses and wagons lay in the shadows.

The wheels and hooves of her carriage began a loud click-clack as they rolled onto cobblestone. They entered through a gate and all she could see were torches illuminating the occasional wall, or a light in a nearby window. Arista was disappointed. She had learned about the city's history at Sheridan University and looked forward to seeing the ancient seat that once ruled the world. Since the fall of the Novronian Empire, only one ruler ever managed to make a serious attempt at unifying the four nations of Apeladorn. Glenmorgan of Ghent ended the era of civil wars, and through brilliant and brutal conquests unified Trent, Avryn, Calis and Delgos under one banner once more. Still holding out for Novron's heir, the church nevertheless threw its support behind him and appointed Glenmorgan Defender of the Faith and Steward to the Heir. They solidified the union by moving to Ervanon and built their great cathedral alongside Glenmorgan Castle.

It did not last. According to Arista's professor, Glenmorgan's son was ill suited to the task he inherited, and the Steward's Empire ended only seventy years after it began, collapsing with the betrayal of Glenmorgan III by his nobles. It was not long before Calis and Trent broke away and Delgos declared itself a republic.

Ervanon was mostly ruined in the warfare that followed, but in the aftermath the patriarch moved into the last remaining piece of Glenmorgan's great palace—the Crown Tower. From then on, the tower and the city became synonymous with the church and recognized as the holiest place in the world behind the ancient—but lost—Novronian capital of Percepliquis itself.

The carriage stopped with a jerk that rocked the inhabitants, waking Saldur and causing the old maid to gasp when her basket spilled to the floor.

"We've arrived," Saldur said with a groggy voice as he wiped his eyes, yawned, and stretched.

The coachman locked the brake, climbed down, and opened the door. A rush of cool damp air flooded inside and chilled her. She stepped out, stiff and weak, her head hazy. It felt strange to be standing still. They were at the very base of the massive Crown Tower. She looked up and doing so made her dizzy. Even at that dark hour, the top stood out brightly against the night sky. The tower rested on a domed crest known as Glenmorgan's Rise, which was the highest point for miles. Even without climbing a step, it appeared as if she stood at the top of the world as she looked beyond the ancient wall and down to the sprawling valley below.

She yawned and shivered and instantly Bernice was there, throwing a cloak over her shoulders and buttoning it. Sauly took longer getting out of the carriage. He slowly extended each thin leg, stretching them out and testing his weight.

"Your grace," a boy appeared. "I hope you had a pleasant journey. The archbishop asked me to tell you he is waiting in his private chambers for the princess."

Arista looked stunned, "Now?" she turned to the bishop, "You don't expect me to meet him with a day's coating of road dust and sweat on me. I look a fright, smell like a pig, and I'm exhausted."

"You look lovely as always, milady," Bernice cooed while stroking the princess' hair. It was a habit that Arista particularly disliked. "I'm sure the archbishop, being a spiritual man, will be looking at your soul not your physical person."

Arista gave Bernice a quizzical look then rolled her eyes.

Servants dressed in clerical frocks appeared around them, hauling luggage, breaking down the harnesses, and watering the horses.

"This way, your grace," the boy said and led them into the tower.

They entered a large rotunda with a polished marble floor and columns that divided the center from a walkway that encircled the wall. Soft, as if from a great distance, she could hear singing. Dozens of voices, perhaps a choir, was rehearsing. Flickering light from unseen lamps bounced off polished surfaces. Their footsteps echoed loudly.

"Couldn't I see him in the morning?"

"No," Saldur said, "this is a very important matter."

Arista furrowed her brow and pondered this. She took for granted that visiting the archbishop was just a formality, but now she was not so sure. As part of his plot to usurp the Kingdom of Melengar, Percy Braga had placed her on trial for her father's death. Barred from attending the proceedings, she later heard rumors of testimony others had given, including her beloved Sauly. If the stories were true, Sauly denounced her not only for killing her father, but also for witchery. She never spoke to the bishop about the allegations nor had she demanded an explanation from Hilfred. Percy Braga was to blame for all of it. He had tricked everyone. Hilfred and Sauly had only done what they thought best for the sake of the kingdom. Still, she could not help wondering if perhaps she had been the one fooled.

According to the church, witchery and magic of any kind was an abomination to the faith. *If Sauly thought I was guilty, might he take steps against me?* She considered it incredible that the bishop, who had been like a family member to her, who always seemed so kind and benevolent, could do such a thing. On the other hand, Braga had been her actual uncle, and after nearly twenty years of loyal service, he had murdered her father and tried to kill her and Alric as well. His desire for power knew no loyalties.

She was increasingly aware of Hilfred's presence coming up the stairs behind her. Normally a comfortable feeling of security, it now felt threatening. *Why was it he never looked at me?* Perhaps she was wrong. Perhaps it was not guilt or dislike; perhaps it was a matter of distancing himself. She heard farmers who raised cows for milking often named them Bessie or Gertrude, but those same farmers never named the beef cows, those destined for slaughter.

Arista's mind began to race. Were they leading her to a locked cell in yet another tower? Would they execute her the way the church had executed Glenmorgan III? Would they burn her at a stake and later justify it as a purifying act for the crime of heresy? What would Alric do when he found out? Would he declare war on the church? If he did, all the other kingdoms would turn against him. He would have no choice but to accept the edict of the church.

They reached a door and the bishop asked Bernice to go and prepare the princess' room for her arrival. He asked Hilfred to wait outside while he led Arista in and closed the door behind her.

It was a surprisingly small room, a tiny study with a cluttered desk and only a few chairs. Wall sconces revealed old thick books, parchments, seals, maps, and clerical vestments for various occasions.

Two men waited inside. Seated behind the desk was the archbishop, an old man with white hair and wrinkled skin. He sat wrapped in a dark purple cassock with an embroidered shoulder cape and a golden tower stole. He had a long and pallid face made longer by his unkempt beard which, when seated as he was, reached to the floor. Similarly, his eyebrows were whimsically bushy. He sat on a high wooden seat bent in a hunched posture giving the impression he was leaning forward with interest.

Searching through the clutter was another, much younger, thin little man with long fingers and darting eyes. He, too, was pale, as if he had not seen the sun in years. His long black hair pulled back in a tight tail gave him the stark and intense look of a man consumed by his work.

"Your holiness Archbishop Galien," Saldur said after they had entered, "may I introduce the Princess Arista Essendon of Melengar."

"So pleased you could come," the old cleric told her. His mouth, which had lost many of its teeth, frequently sucked in his thin lips. His voice was windy with a distinctive rasp. "Please, take a seat. I assume you had a rough day bouncing around in the back of a carriage. Dreadful things really. They tear up the roads and shake you to a frazzle. I hate getting in one. It feels like a coffin and at my age you are wary of getting into boxes of any kind. But I suppose I must endure it for the sake of the future, a future I won't even see." He unexpectedly winked at her. "Can I offer you a drink? Wine perhaps? Carlton, make yourself useful you little vagabond and get her highness a glass of Montemorcey."

The little man said nothing but moved rapidly to a chest in the corner. He pulled a dark bottle from the contents and drew out the cork.

"Sit down Arista," Saldur whispered in her ear.

The princess selected a red velvet chair in front of the desk and, brushing out her dress, sat down stiffly. She was not at ease, but made an effort to control her growing fear.

Carlton presented her with a glass of red wine on an engraved silver platter. She considered how it might be drugged or even poisoned, but dismissed this notion as ridiculous. *Why poison or drug me? I already made the fatal error of blindly blundering into your web.* If Hilfred had defected to their side, she had only Bernice to protect her against the entire armed forces of Ghent. She was already at their mercy.

Arista took the glass, nodded at Carlton, and sipped.

"The wine is imported through the Vandom Spice Company in Delgos," the archbishop told her. "I have no idea where Montemorcey is, but they do make incredible wine. Don't you think?"

"I must apologize," Arista blurted out nervously. "I was unaware I was coming directly here. I assumed I would have a chance to freshen up after the long trip. I am generally more presentable. Perhaps I should retire and meet you tomorrow?"

"You look fine. You can't help it. Lovely young princesses are blessed that way. Bishop Saldur did the right thing bringing you here immediately, even more than he knows."

"Has something happened?" Saldur asked.

"Word has come down," he looked up and pointed at the ceiling, "literally, that Luis Guy will be traveling with us."

"The sentinel?"

Galien nodded.

"That might be good, don't you think? He'll bring a contingent of seret, won't he? And that will help maintain order."

"I am certain that is the patriarch's mind as well. I, however, know how the sentinel works. He won't listen to me and his methods are heavy handed. But that is not what we are here to discuss."

He paused a moment, took a breath, and returned his attention to Arista. "Tell me my child, what do you know of Esrahaddon?"

Arista's heart skipped a beat but she said nothing.

Bishop Saldur placed his hand on hers and smiled. "My dear, we already know that you visited him in Gutaria Prison for months and that he taught you what he could of his vile black magic. We also know that Alric freed him. Yet none of that matters now. What we need to know is where he is and if he has contacted you since his release. You are the only person he knows who might trust him and therefore the only one he might reach out to. So tell us child, have you had any communication with him?"

"Is this why you brought me here? To help you locate an alleged criminal?"

"He *is* a criminal, Arista," Galien said. "Despite what he told you he is—"

"How do you know what he told me? Did you eavesdrop on every word the man said?"

"We did," he replied passively.

The blunt answer surprised her.

"My dear girl, that old wizard told you a story. Much of it is actually true; only he left out a great deal."

She glanced at Sauly, whose fatherly expression looked grim as he nodded his agreement.

"Your Uncle Braga wasn't responsible for the murder of your father," the archbishop told her. "It was Esrahaddon."

"That's absurd," Arista scoffed. "He was in prison at the time and couldn't even send messages."

"Ah—but he could, and he did—through you. Why do you think he taught you to make the healing potion for your father?"

"Besides curing him of sickness, you mean?"

"Esrahaddon didn't care about Amrath. He didn't even care about you. The reality is he needed your father dead. Your mistake was going to him. Trusting him. Did you think he would be your friend? Your sage old tutor like Arcadius? Esrahaddon is no tame beast, no honorable gentleman. He is a demon and he is dangerous. He used you to escape. From the moment you visited him, he calculated your use as a tool. To escape he needed the ruling monarch to come and release him. Your father knew who and what he was, so he would never do it. But Alric, because of his ignorance, would. So he needed your father dead. All Esrahaddon had to do was make the church believe your father was the heir. He knew it would cause us to act against him."

"But why would the church want the heir dead? I don't understand."

"We'll get to that in due time. But suffice it to say his interest in you and your father got our attention. It was the healing potion Esrahaddon had you create that sealed your father's fate. It tainted his blood to appear as if he was a descendent of the imperial bloodline. When Braga learned this he followed what he thought was the church's wishes and put plans in motion to remove Amrath and his children."

"Are you saying that Braga was working for the church when he had my father murdered?"

"Not directly—or officially. But Braga was devout in his beliefs. He acted rashly not waiting for the church *bureaucracy*, as he used to call it. Both the bishop and I speak for the whole church when we tell you we are truly sorry for the tragedy that occurred. Still, you must understand we did not orchestrate it. It was the design of Esrahaddon that set the wheels of your father's fate in motion. He used the church just as he used you."

Arista glared at the archbishop and then at Sauly. "You knew about this?"

The bishop nodded.

"How could you allow Braga to kill my father? He was your friend."

"I tried to stop it," Sauly told her. "You must believe me when I tell you this. The moment the test was done and your father implicated, I called for an emergency council of the church, but Braga couldn't be stopped. He refused to listen to me and said I was wasting valuable time."

Fears of her own murder fled and anger filled the vacuum. She stood up, fists clenched, her eyes filled with hate.

"Arista, I know you are upset, and have every right to be but let me explain further," the archbishop waited for her to sit down again. "What I am about to tell you is the most highly guarded secret of the Church of Nyphron. This information is strictly reserved for top ranking members of the clergy. I am trusting you with this information because we need your help and I know you will not extend it unless you understand why." He took the glass of wine, sipped it, then leaned forward and spoke to Arista in a quiet tone. "In the last few years of the Empire, the church uncovered a dark and twisted scheme whose goal was no less than to enslave all of humanity. The conspiracy led directly to the Emperor. Only the church could save mankind. We killed the Emperor and tried to eliminate his bloodline, but the Emperor's son was aided by

Esrahaddon. His heritage contains the power to raise the demons of the past and once more bring humanity to the brink. For this reason, the church has sought to find the heir and destroy the lineage whose existence is a knife at the throat of all of us. After so long, the heir might not even be aware of his power, or even who he is. But Esrahaddon knows. If that wizard finds the heir, he can use him as a weapon against us. No one will be safe."

The archbishop looked at her carefully, "Esrahaddon was once part of the high council. He was one of the key members in the effort to save the Empire from the conspirators but at the last moment, he betrayed the church. Instead of a peaceful transition, he callously caused a civil war that destroyed the Empire. The church cut off his hands and locked him away for nearly a millennium. What do you think he'll do if he has the chance to exact revenge? Whatever humanity he might have possessed died in Gutaria Prison. What remains is a powerful demon bent on our destruction—revenge for revenge's sake; he is mad with it. He is like a wildfire that will consume all if not stopped. As a princess of a kingdom, you must understand—sacrifices must be made to ensure the security of the realm. We deeply regret the error that occurred in respect to your father, but hope you will come to understand why it happened, accept our apologies, and help us prevent the end of all that we know.

"Esrahaddon is an incredibly intelligent mad man bent on destroying everyone. The heir is his weapon. If he finds him before we do, if we cannot prevent him from reawakening the horror we managed to put to sleep centuries ago, then all this—this city, your kingdom of Melengar, all of Apeladorn will be lost. We need your help Arista. We need you to help us find Esrahaddon."

The door opened abruptly and a priest entered.

"Your grace," he said out of breath. "The sentinel is calling the curia to order."

Galien nodded and looked back at Arista. "What say you, my dear? Can you help us?"

The princess looked at her hands. Too much was whirling in her head: Esrahaddon, Braga, Sauly, mysterious conspiracies, healing potions. The one image that remained steadfast was the memory of her father lying on his bed, his face pale, blood soaking the covers. It took so long to put the pain behind her and now…had Esrahaddon killed him? Had they? "I don't know," she muttered.

"Can you at least tell us if he has contacted you since his escape?"

"I haven't seen or heard from Esrahaddon since before my father's death."

"You understand, of course," the archbishop, told her, "that be this as it may, you are the most likely person he would trust and we would like you to consider working with us to find him. As Ambassador of Melengar you could travel between kingdoms and nations and never be suspected. I also understand that right now you may not be ready to make such a commitment, so I won't ask; but please consider it. The church has let you down grievously; I only request that you give us a chance to redeem ourselves in your eyes."

Arista drained the rest of her wine and slowly nodded.

"Do you think she is telling the truth?" The archbishop asked him. There was a faint look of hope on his face, clouded by an overall expression of misery. "There was a great deal of resistance in her."

Saldur was still looking at the door Arista exited. "Anger would be a more accurate word, but yes, I think she was telling the truth."

He did not know what Galien expected. Did he think Arista would embrace him with open arms after they admitted to killing her father? The whole idea was absurd, desperate measures from a man sinking in quicksand.

"It was worth it," the archbishop said without any conviction.

Saldur played with a loose thread on his sleeve, wishing he had taken the remainder of Bernice's bottle with him. He never cared much for wine. More than anything the tragedy of Braga's death was the loss of a great source of excellent brandy. The archduke really knew his liquor.

Galien stared at him. "You're quiet," the archbishop said. "You think I was wrong, of course. You said so, didn't you? You were very vocal about it at our last meeting. You were watching her every move. You have that—that—" the old man waved his hand toward the door as if this would make his fumbling clearer, "—that old handmaid monitoring her every breath. Isn't that right? And if Esrahaddon had contacted her we would have known and they would be none the wiser, but now…" the archbishop threw up his hands, feigning disgust in a sarcastic imitation of Saldur.

Saldur continued to fiddle with the thread, wrapping it around the end of his forefinger, winding it tighter and tighter.

"You're too arrogant for your own good," Galien accused defensively. "The man is an imperial wizard. What he is capable of is beyond your comprehension. For all we know he may have been visiting her in the form of a butterfly in the garden or a moth that entered her bedroom window each night. We had to be sure."

"A butterfly?" Saldur said, genuinely amazed.

"He's a wizard. Damn you. That's what they do."

"I highly doubt—"

"The point is we didn't know for sure."

"And we still don't. All I can say is I don't think she was lying, but Arista is a clever girl. Maribor knows she has proven that already."

Galien lifted his empty wine glass. "Carlton!"

The servant looked up. "I'm sorry, your grace, but I can't say I know her well enough to offer much of an opinion."

"Good god man. I'm not asking you about her; I want more wine, you fool."

"Ah," Carlton said and headed for the bottle, pulling the cork out with a dull, hollow pop.

"The problem is that the patriarch blames me for Esrahaddon's disappearance," Galien continued.

For the first time since Arista's departure Saldur leaned forward with interest. "He's told you this?"

"That's just it; he's told me nothing. He only speaks to the sentinels now. Luis Guy and that other one—Thranic. Guy is unpleasant, but Thranic…" He trailed off shaking his head and frowning.

"I've never met a sentinel."

"Consider yourself lucky. Although your luck, I think, is running out on that score. Guy spent all morning upstairs in a long meeting with the patriarch." He played with the empty glass, running his finger around the rim. "He's in the council hall right now giving his address to the curia."

"Shouldn't we be there?"

"Yes," he said miserably, but he made no effort to move.

"Your grace?" Saldur asked.

"Yes, yes." He waved at him. "Carlton, Get me my cane."

Saldur and the archbishop entered to the sound of a man's booming voice. The grand council chamber was a three-story circular room encompassing the entire width of the tower. Lined in thin ornate columns set in groups of two that represented the relationship between Novron, the Defender of Faith, and Maribor, the god of man. Between each set was a tall thin window, which provided the room with a complete panoramic view of the surrounding countryside. Seated in circular rows, radiating out from the center, gathered the curia, the college of chief clerics of the Nyphron Church. The other eighteen bishops were present to hear the words of the patriarch as spoken by Luis Guy.

Sentinel Luis Guy, a tall thin man with long black hair and disquieting eyes stood in the center of the room. He was sharp; that was Saldur's first impression of the man, clean, ordered, focused, both in manner and looks. His hair was very black yet his skin was light, providing a striking contrast. His moustache was narrow, his beard short and severe, trimmed to a fine point. He dressed in the traditional red cassock, black cape and black hood with the symbol of the broken crown neatly embroidered on his chest. Not a hair or a pleat was out of place. He stood straight, his eyes not scanning the crowd but glaring at them.

"...the patriarch feels that Rufus has the strength to persuade the Trent nobles and the church will deliver the rest. Remember, this isn't about picking the best horse. The patriarch must choose the one that can win the race and Rufus is the most likely candidate. He's a hero to the south and a native of the north. He has no visible ties to the church. Crowning him emperor will immediately stifle a large segment of the population that might otherwise oppose us."

"What about the Royalists?" Bishop Tildale of Kilnar asked. "They aren't likely to accept this without a struggle. They have lands and titles. They aren't about to simply hand over their wealth and power."

"The Royalists will be given assurances of their own sovereignties. That is all they really want. It is where their greatest fear lies. They might not like the idea of bending a knee to an emperor, but they will not risk their lands and titles over it."

"And the Nationalists?" the Prelate of Ratibor asked. "They have been growing in number. You can't simply ignore them."

"The Nationalists will be an issue," Guy admitted. "For years now the seret have been watching Gaunt and his followers and it's been discovered they are being covertly funded by the DeLur family and several other powerful merchant cartels in the Republic of Delgos. Delgos has enjoyed its freedom from monarchies for too long. They already fear the very idea of a unified empire. So yes, we know they will fight. They will need to be defeated on the battlefield, which is another reason why the patriarch has selected Rufus. He's a ruthless warlord. He'll crush the Nationalists as his first act as emperor. Delgos will fall soon after."

"Do we have the troops to take Delgos?" Prelate Krindel, the resident historian, asked. "Tur Del Fur is defended by a dwarven fortress. It held out against a two year siege by the Dacca."

"I have been working on that very problem and I think I will have a—unique—solution."

"And what might that be?" Galien asked suspiciously.

Luis Guy looked up. "Ah, archbishop so good of you to join us. I sent word we were beginning nearly an hour ago."

"Do you plan to spank me for being tardy, Guy? Or are you simply trying to avoid my question?"

"You are not ready to hear the answer to that question," the sentinel replied which brought a reproachful look from the archbishop. "You would not believe me if I told you and certainly would not approve, but when the time comes...rest assured that if necessary, Drumindor will fall."

"What about the people? Will they embrace a new emperor?" Saldur asked.

"I have traveled the length and breadth of the four nations promoting the contest. Heralds have announced it to the very edges of Apeladorn. There is no one who is not aware of the event. In the marketplaces, taverns and castle courts—anticipation is high. Once we announce the true intent of the contest, the people will be beside themselves. Gentlemen, these are exciting times. It is no longer a question of if, but when will the Empire rise. The ground work is laid. All we need to do is bestow the crown."

"And Ethelred?" Galien asked. "Is he on board?"

Guy shrugged. "He isn't pleased with giving up his throne to become a viceroy, but few of the monarchs are. I assured him that being the first to take off his crown will give him special privileges in the new order. I told him he would be a regent for a time, until Lord Rufus squelched any uprisings. I also suggested that he might remain as chief council. He appeared satisfied with that."

"I still don't like handing over power to Rufus and Ethelred," Galien grumbled.

"We won't be," Guy assured him. "The church will be in control. They are the faces, but we are the mind. The patriarch informed me he will personally select a member of this body to serve as co-regent alongside Ethelred so we will have a representative in the palace."

"And who will that be?" the archbishop asked, and Saldur could tell from his tone, perhaps everyone could, that he knew it would not be him.

"His holiness has not yet decided." There was a pause as they waited for Guy to speak again. "This is a historic moment. All that we have worked for, all that has been carefully nurtured for centuries is about to bear fruit. We now stand at the threshold of a new dawn for mankind. What began nearly a millennium ago will conclude with this generation. May Novron bless our hands."

"He's impressive," Saldur told Galien.

"You think so?" The archbishop replied. "Good, because you're coming with us."

"To the contest?"

He nodded. "I need someone to counter-balance Guy. Perhaps you can be just as big a pain to him as you've been to me."

Arista hesitated outside the door, holding a single candle. The boy who escorted her had since left. She stared at the door. Inside she could hear Bernice shuffling about, turning down the bed, pouring water into the basin, laying out Arista's bed clothes in that ghastly nursemaid way of hers. As tired as she was, Arista had no desire to open that door. She had too much to think about and could not bear Bernice just now.

How many days?

She tried counting them in her head, ticking them off, trying to track her memories of those muddled times between the death of her father and the death of her uncle; so much had happened so quickly. She still remembered the pale white look of her father's face as he lay on the bed, that single tear of blood on his cheek, and the dark stain spreading across the mattress beneath him.

Arista glanced awkwardly at Hilfred who stood behind her. "I'm not ready to go to bed yet."

"As you wish, milady." He said quietly as if understanding her need not to alert the nurse-beast within.

Arista began walking aimlessly. She traveled down the hallway. This simple act gave her a sense of control, of heading toward something instead of being swept along. Hilfred followed three paces behind, his sword clapping against his thigh, a sound she had heard for years like the swing of a pendulum ticking off the seconds of her life.

How many days?

Sauly had known Uncle Percy would kill her father. He knew before it happened! How long in advance did he know? Was it hours? Days? Weeks? He said he tried to stop him. That was a lie—it had to be. Why not expose him? Why not just tell her father? But maybe Sauly had. Maybe her father refused to listen. Was it possible Esrahaddon really had used her?

The dimly lit hall curved as it circled around the tower. The lack of decoration surprised Arista. Of course, the Crown Tower was only a small part of the old palace, a mere corner staircase. The stones were old hewn blocks set in place centuries ago. They all looked the same—dingy, soot covered, and yellow like old teeth. She passed several doors then came to a staircase and began climbing. It felt good to exert her legs after being idle so long.

How many days?

She remembered her uncle searching for Alric, watching her, having her followed. If Saldur knew about Percy, why did he not intervene? Why did he allow her to be locked in the tower and put through that dreadful trial? Would Sauly have allowed them to execute her? If he had just spoken up. If he had backed her. She could have called for Braga's imprisonment. The Battle of Medford could have been avoided and all those people would still be alive.

How many days before Braga's death had Saldur known...and done nothing?

It was a question without an answer. A question that echoed in her head, a question she was not certain she wanted answered.

And what was all this about the destruction of humanity? She knew they thought she was naïve. *Do they think I am ignorant as well?* No one person had the power to enslave an entire race. Not to mention the very idea that this threat emanated from the Emperor was absurd. The man was already the ruler of the world!

The stairs ended in a dark circular room. No sconces, torches, nor lanterns burned. Her little candle was the only source of illumination. Arista exited the stairs followed by Hilfred. They had entered the alabaster crown near the tower's pinnacle. An immediate sense of unease washed over her. She felt like a trespasser on forbidden grounds. There was nothing to give her that impression except perhaps the darkness. Still, it felt like exploring an attic as a child, the silence, the shadowy suggestion of hidden treasures lost to time.

Like everyone, she grew up hearing the tales of Glenmorgan's treasures and how they lay hidden at the top of the Crown Tower. She even knew the story about how they were stolen yet returned the following night. There were many stories about the tower, tales of famous people imprisoned at its top. Heretics like Edmund Hall, who supposedly discovered the entrance to the holy city Percepliquis and paid by spending the remainder of his life sealed away—isolated where he could tell no one of its secrets.

It was here. It was all here.

She walked the circle of the room. The sounds of her footsteps echoed sharply off the stone, perhaps because of the low ceiling, or maybe it was just her imagination. She held up her candle and found a door at the far side. It was an odd door. Tall and broad, not made of wood as the others in the tower, nor was it made of steel or iron. This door was made of stone, one single solid block that looked like granite and appeared out of place beside the walls of polished alabaster.

She looked at it perplexed. There was no latch, knob, or hinges. Nothing to open it with. She considered knocking. *What good will it do to knock on granite except to bloody my knuckles?* Placing her hand on the door, she pushed but nothing happened. Arista glanced at Hilfred who stood silently watching her.

"I just wanted to see the view from the top," she told him, imagining what he might be thinking.

She heard something just then, a shuffle, a step from above. Tilting her head, she lifted the candle. Cobwebs lined the underside of the ceiling, which was made of wood. Clearly someone or something was up there.

Edmund Hall's ghost!

The idea flashed through her mind and she shook her head at her foolishness. Perhaps she should go and cower in bed and have Auntie Bernice read her a nice bedtime story. Still, she had to wonder. What lay behind that very solid looking door?

"Hello?" a voice echoed and she jumped. From below Arista saw the glow of another light rising, the sound of steps climbing. "Is someone up here?"

She had an instant desire to hide and she might have tried if there were anything to hide behind and Hilfred was not with her.

"Who's there?" A head appeared, coming around the curve of the steps from below. It was a man—a priest of some sort by the look of him. He wore a black robe with a purple ribbon that hung down from either side of his neck. His hair was thin and from that angle, Arista could see the beginning of a bald spot on the back of his head, a tanned island in a sea of graying hair. He held a lantern above his head and squinted at her, looking puzzled.

"Who are you?" he asked in a neutral tone. It was neither threatening nor welcoming, merely curious.

She smiled self-consciously. "My name is Arista, Arista from Melengar."

"Arista from Melengar?" he said thoughtfully. "Might I ask what you are doing here, Arista from Melengar?"

"Honestly? I was—ah—hoping to get to the top of the tower to see the view. It's my first time here."

The priest smiled and began to chuckle. "You are sight-seeing then?"

"Yes, I suppose so."

"And the gentleman with you—is he also sight-seeing?"

"He is my bodyguard."

"Bodyguard?" The man paused in his approach. "Do all young women from Melengar have such protection when they travel abroad?"

"I am the Princess of Melengar, daughter of the late King Amrath and sister of King Alric."

"Ah-hah!" the priest said, entering the room and walking the curve toward them. "I thought so. You were part of the caravan that arrived this evening, the lady who came in with the Bishop of Medford. I saw the royal carriage, but didn't know what royalty it contained."

"And you are?" she asked.

"Oh yes, I'm very sorry, I am Monsignor Merton of Ghent, born and raised right down below us in a small village called Iberton, a stone's throw from Ervanon. Wonderful fishing in Iberton. My father was a fisherman, by the way. We fished year round, nets in the summer and hooks in the winter. Teach a man to fish and he'll never go hungry, I always say. I suppose in a way that's how I came to be here, if you get my meaning."

Arista smiled politely and glanced back at the stone door.

"I'm sorry but that door doesn't go to the outside, and I'm afraid you can't get to the top." He tilted his head toward the ceiling and lowered his voice. "That's where *he* lives."

"He?"

"His holiness, Patriarch Nilnev. The top floor of this tower is his sanctuary. I come up here sometimes to just sit and listen. When it is quiet, when the wind is still, you can sometimes hear him moving about. I once thought I heard him speak, but that might have just been hopeful ears. It is as if Novron himself is up there right now, looking down, watching out for us. Still if you like, I do know where you can get a good view. Come with me."

The Monsignor turned and descended back down the stairs. Arista looked one last time at the door then followed.

"When does he come out?" Arista asked. "The patriarch, I mean."

"He doesn't. At least not that I have ever seen. He lives his life in isolation—better to be one with the Lord."

"If he never comes out, how do you know he's really up there?"

"Hmm?" Merton glanced back at her and chuckled. "Oh well he does speak with people. He holds private meetings with certain individuals who bring his words to the rest of us."

"And who are these people? The archbishop?"

"Sometimes, though lately his decrees have come down to us by way of the sentinels." He paused in their downward trek and turned to look at her. "You know about them, I assume?"

"Yes," she told him.

"Being a princess, I thought you might."

"We actually haven't had one visit Melengar for several years."

"That's understandable. There are only a few left and they have a very wide area to cover."

"Why so few?"

"His holiness hasn't appointed any new ones, not since he ordained Luis Guy. I believe he was the last."

This was the first good news Arista heard all day. The sentinels were notorious watchdogs of the church. Originally charged with the task of finding the lost heir, they commanded the famous Order of Seret Knights. These knights enforced the church's will—policing layman and clergy alike for any signs of heresy. When the seret investigated, it was certain someone would be found guilty and usually anyone who protested would find themselves charged as well.

Monsignor Merton led her to a door two floors down and knocked.

"What is it?" an irritated voice asked.

"We've come to see your view," Merton replied.

"I don't have time for you today, Merton, go bother someone else and leave me be."

"It's not for me. The Princess Arista of Medford is here, and she wants to see a view from the tower."

"Oh no, really," Arista told him shaking her head. "It's not that important. I just—"

The door popped open and behind it stood a fat man without a single hair on his head. He was dressed all in red, with a gold braided chord around his large waist. He was wiping his greasy hands on a towel and peering at Arista intently.

"By Mar! It is a princess."

"Janison!" Merton snapped. "Please, that is no way for a prelate of the church to speak."

The fat man scowled at Merton. "Do you see how he treats me? He thinks I am Uberlin himself because I like to eat and enjoy an occasional drink."

"It is not I that judges you, but our Lord Novron. May we enter?"

"Yes, yes, of course, come in."

The room was a mess of clothes, parchments, and paintings that lay on the floor or leaned on baskets and chests. A desk stood at one end and a large flat, tilted table was at the other. On it were stacks of maps, ink bottles, and dozens of quills. Nothing appeared to be in its place or even to have one.

"Oh—" Arista nearly said *dear*, but stopped short, realizing she had almost imitated Bernice.

"Yes, it is quite the sight, isn't it? Prelate Janison is less than tidy."

"I am neat in my maps and that is all that matters."

"Not to Novron."

"You see? And, of course, I can't retaliate. How can anyone hope to compete with his holiness Monsignor Merton who heals the sick and speaks to god."

Arista, who was following Merton across the wretched room toward a curtain-lined wall, paused as a memory from her childhood surfaced. Looking at Merton, she recalled it. "You're the savior of Fallon Mire?"

"Ah-ha! Of course, he didn't tell you. It would be too prideful to admit he is the chosen one of our lord."

"Oh stop that." It was Merton's turn to scowl.

"Was it you?" she asked.

Merton nodded, sending Janison a harsh stare.

"I heard all about it. It was some years ago. I was probably only five or six when the plague came to Fallon Mire. Everyone was afraid because it was working its way up from the south and Fallon Mire was not very far from Medford. I remember my father spoke of moving the court to Drondil Fields, only we never did. We didn't have to because the plague never moved north of there."

"Because *he* stopped it," Janison said.

"I did not!" Merton snapped. "Novron did."

"But he sent you there, didn't he? Didn't he?"

Merton sighed. "I only did what the lord asked of me."

Janison looked at Arista. "You see, how can I hope to compete with a man whom God himself has chosen to hold daily conversations with?"

"You actually heard the voice of Novron telling you to go save the people of Fallen Mire?"

"He directed my footsteps."

"But you talk to him too." Janison pressed looking at Arista. "He won't admit that, of course. Saying so would be heresy and Luis Guy is just downstairs. He doesn't care about your miracle." Janison sat down on a stool and chuckled. "No, the good Monsignor here won't admit that he holds little conversations with the lord, but he does. I've heard him. Late at night, in the halls when he thinks everyone else is asleep." Janison raised his voice an octave as if imitating a young girl. "*Oh lord, why is it you keep me awake with this headache when I have work in the morning? What's that? Oh I see, how wise of you.*"

"That's enough, Janison," Merton said, his voice serious.

"Yes, I'm certain it is Monsignor. Now take your view and leave me to my meal."

Janison picked up a chicken leg and resumed eating while Merton threw open the drapes to reveal a magnificent window. It was huge. Nearly the width of the room divided only by three stone pillars. The view was breathtaking. The large moon revealed the night as if it were a lamp one could reach out and touch, hanging amongst a scattering of brilliant stars.

Arista placed a hand on the windowsill and peered down. She could see the twisting silver line of a river far below, shimmering in the moonlight. At the base of the tower, campfires circled the city, tiny flickering pinpricks like stars themselves. Looking straight down, she felt dizzy and her heartbeat quickened. Wondering how close she was to the top of the tower, she looked up and counted three more levels of windows above her, to the alabaster crown of white.

"Thank you," she told Merton, and nodded toward Janison.

"Rest assured, Your Highness. He is up there."

She nodded, but was not certain if he was referring to god or the patriarch.

Chapter 4

DHALGREN

FOR FIVE DAYS, Royce, Hadrian, and Thrace made their way north through the nameless sea of trees that made up the eastern edge of Avryn, a region disputed by both Alburn and Dunmore. Each laid claim to the vast, dense forest between them, but until the establishment of Dahlgren, neither appeared in any hurry to settle the land. The great forest, referred to merely as either The East or The Wastes, remained uncut, untouched, unblemished. The road they traveled, once a broad lane as it plowed north out of Alburn, quickly became two tracks divided by a line of grass and finally squeezed down to a single dirt trail that threatened to vanish entirely. No fences, farms, nor wayside inns broke the woodland walls, nor did travelers cross their path. Here in the northeast, maps were vague with few markings and went entirely blank past the Nidwalden River.

At times, the beauty of the forest was breathtaking, even spiritual. Monolithic elms towered overhead, weaving a lofty tunnel of green. It reminded Hadrian of the few times he had poked his head into Mares Cathedral in Medford. The long trunked trees arched over the trail like the buttresses of the great church, forming a natural nave. Delicate shafts of muted light pierced the canopy at angles as if entering through a gallery of windows far above. Along the ground, fans of finely fingered ferns grew up from last year's brown leaves, creating a soft swaying carpet. A choir of birds sang in the unseen heights, and from the bed of brittle leaves came the rustle of squirrels and chipmunks like the coughs, whispers, and shifts of a congregation. It was beautiful yet disturbing, like swimming out too far, delving into unknown, unseen, and untamed places.

Over the last days, travel became increasingly difficult. The recent spring storms dropped several trees across the trail that blocked the route as formidably as any castle gate. They dismounted and struggled through the thick brush as Royce searched for a way around. Hours passed yet they failed to rejoin the road. Scratched and sweaty, they led their horses across several small rivers, and on one occasion faced a sharp drop. Looking down from the rocky cliff, Hadrian offered Royce a skeptical look. Usually, Hadrian never questioned Royce's sense of direction or his choice of path. Royce had an unerring ability to find his way in the wilderness, a talent proven on many occasions. Hadrian tilted his head up. He could not see the sun or sky, there was no point of reference—everything was limbs and leaves. Royce had never let him down, but they had never been in a place like this.

"We're alright," Royce told them, a touch of irritation in his voice.

They worked their way down, Royce and Thrace leading the horses on foot while Hadrian cleared a path. When they reached the bottom, they found a small stream, but no trail. Again, Hadrian glanced at Royce, but this time the thief made no comment as they pressed on along the least dense route.

"There," Thrace said, pointing ahead to a clearing revealed by a patch of sun that managed to sneak through the canopy. A few more steps revealed a small road. Royce looked at it for a moment then merely shrugged, climbed back on his horse, and kicked Mouse forward.

They emerged from the forest as if escaping from a deep cave, into the first open patch of direct sun they had seen in days. Standing in the glade, beside a rough wooden wellhead, stood a child among a pack of eight grazing pigs. The child, no more than five years old, held a long, thin stick, and an expression of wonder on a little round face covered in sweat-trapped dirt. Hadrian had no idea if it was a boy or girl as the child displayed no definite indication of either, wearing only a simple smock of flax linen, dirty and frayed with holes and rips so plentiful they appeared by design.

"Pearl!" Thrace called out as she scrambled off Millie so quickly the horse sidestepped. "I'm back." She walked over and tousled the child's matted hair.

The little girl—Hadrian now guessed—gave Thrace little notice and continued to stare at them, eyes wide.

Thrace threw out her arms and spun around, "This is Dahlgren. This is home."

Hadrian dismounted and looked around, puzzled. They stood on a small patch of close-grazed grass beside a well constructed of ill-fitted planks with a wooden bucket resting on a rail wet and dripping. Two other rutted trails intersected with the one they followed forming a triangle with the well at its center. On all sides, the forest surrounded them. Massive trees of dramatic size still blocked the sky, except for the hole above the clearing through which Hadrian could see the pale blue of the late afternoon sky.

Hadrian scooped a handful of water from the bucket to wash the sweat from his face and Millie nearly shoved him aside as she pushed her nose into the bucket, drinking deeply.

"What's with the bell," Royce mentioned, climbing down off Mouse and gesturing toward the shadows.

Hadrian looked over, surprised to see a massive bronze bell hanging from a rocker arm that in turn hung from the lower branch of a nearby oak. Hadrian guessed that if it were on the ground Royce could stand inside it. A rope dangled with knots tied at several points along its length.

"That's different," he said, walking toward it. "How does it sound?"

"Don't ring it!" Thrace exclaimed. Hadrian pivoted his eyebrows up. "We only ring it for emergencies."

He looked back at the bell noting the relief images of Maribor and Novron, along with lines of religious script circling its waist. "Seems sort of extravagant for…well…" he looked around at the empty clearing.

"It was Deacon Tomas' idea. He kept saying: A village isn't a village without a church, and a church isn't a church without a bell. Everyone pitched in a little. The old margrave matched what we had and ordered it for us. The bell was finished long before we had time to build the church. Mr. McDern took his oxen and fetched it all the way from Ervanon. When he got back, we had no place to put it and he needed his wagon. It was my father's idea to hang it here and use it as an alarm until the church went up. That was a week before the attacks started. At the time no one had any idea how much use we'd get out of it." She stared at the huge bell for a moment and then added. "I hate the sound of that bell."

A gusty breeze rustled the leaves and threw a lock of hair in her face. She brushed it back and turned away from the oak and the bell. "Over there," she pointed across the rutted path, "is where most of us live." Hadrian spotted structures hidden in shadow within a shallow dip, behind a blind of goldenrod and milkweed. Small wooden frame buildings plastered with wattle and daub—a mixture of mud, straw, and manure. The roofs were thatch, the windows no more than holes in the walls. Most lacked doors, making due with curtains across the entrances that fluttered with the wind, revealing dirt floors. Beside one, he spotted a vegetable garden that managed to catch a sliver of sun.

"That's Mae and Went Drundel's place there in front," Thrace said. "Well, I guess it's just Mae's now. Went and the boys—they—were taken not long ago. To the left, the one with the garden is the Bothwick's. I used to babysit Tad and the twins, but Tad's old enough now to watch the twins himself. They are like family really. Lena and my mother were very close. Behind them—you can just see the McDern's roof. Mr. McDern is the village smith and the owner of the only pair of oxen. He shares them with everyone, which makes him popular come spring. To the right, the place with the swing is the Caswell's. Maria and Jessie are my best friends. My father hung that swing for us not long after we moved here. I spent some of the best days of my life on that swing."

"Where's your place?" Hadrian asked.

"My father built our house a ways down the hill." She gestured toward a small trail that ran to the east. "It was the best house—best farm really—in the village. Everyone said so. There's almost nothing left now."

Pearl was still staring at them, watching every move.

"Hello," Hadrian said to her with a smile, bending down on his hunches, "my name is Hadrian, and this is my friend Royce." Pearl glared and took a step back, brandishing the stick before her. "You don't talk much, do you?"

"Her parents were both killed two months ago while planting," Thrace told them looking at the girl with sympathetic eyes. "It was daylight and like everyone else they thought they were safe, but it was a stormy day. The clouds had darkened the sky." Thrace paused then added, "A lot of people have died here."

"Where is everyone else?" Royce asked.

"They'll all be in the fields now, bringing in the first cutting of hay, but they'll be coming back soon, it's getting late. Pearl minds the pigs for the entire village, don't you, Pearl?" The girl nodded fiercely, holding her stick with both hands and keeping a wary eye on Hadrian.

"What's up there?" Royce asked. He had moved down off the green and was looking up the trail as it ran north.

Hadrian followed, leaving Millie with the bucket, her tail swishing vigilantly against a handful of determined flies. Moving past a stand of spruce, Hadrian could see a hill cleared of trees rising just a few hundred yards away. On its crest rested a stockade style wall of hewn logs and in the center a large wooden house.

"That's the margrave's castle. The Deacon Tomas has taken on the responsibility of steward until the king appoints a new lord. He's very nice and I don't think he'd mind you using the stables, considering there aren't any other horses in the village. For now just tie them to the well I guess, and we can go see my father.

"Pearl, watch their stuff, and keep the pigs away. If Tad, Hal, or Arvid come back before I do, have them take the horses up to the castle and ask the deacon if they can stable them there, okay?"

The little girl nodded.

"Does she talk?" Hadrian asked.

"Yes, just not very often anymore. Com'on, I'll take you to—to what used to be my home. Dad's probably there. It's not far and a pretty pleasant walk." She began leading them east along a footpath that ran downhill behind the houses. As they circled around, Hadrian got a better look at the village. He could see more houses, all of them tiny things, most likely single rooms with lofts. There were other smaller structures, a few crated feed bins built on stilts to keep clear of rodents and what looked to be a community outhouse; it too lacked a solid door.

"I'll ask the Bothwicks to take you in while you're here. I'm staying with them myself, they—" Thrace stopped. Her hands flew to her face as she sucked in a sudden breath and her lips started to quiver.

Beside the path, not far from the house with the swing, two wooden markers stood freshly driven into the earth. Carved into them were the names Maria and Jessie Caswell.

The Wood farm appeared down the footpath. Several acres lay cleared of trees, most at the bottom of a hill where lush wheat grew in perfectly straight rows. A low stone wall built from carefully stacked rocks ran the perimeter. It was a beautiful field of rich dark earth, well turned, well planted, and well drained.

The homestead itself stood on the rise overlooking the field. The house was a ruined shell, its roof gone, thatch scattered across the yard, blown by the wind. Only a few timbers remained—splintered poles jutting up like broken bones punching through skin. The lower half of the building along with the chimney were both made of irregularly shaped fieldstone and remained mostly intact. Some stones lay in piles where they slipped from their stacks, but the majority appeared eerily untouched.

Little things caught Hadrian's attention. Mounted beneath one window hung a flowerbox with a scallop-edge and the image of a deer carved into it. The front door, made of solid oak, had a latch formed of hand-beaten iron, revealing not a single peg or visible joint. The stones that created the walls, alternated colors of gray, rose, and tan, each chipped to a fine flat profile. The curved walkway was bordered with bushes trimmed to resemble a hedge.

Theron Wood sat amidst the ruins of his home. The big farmer, with dark leathery skin, had a short mangle of forgotten gray hair that crowned a face cut by wind and sun. He looked like a part of the earth itself, a gnarled trunk of a great tree with a face like a weathered cliff. He rested on the remaining wall of his home, a grass cutter held between his legs, slowly dragging a sharpening stone along the length of the huge curved scythe blade. Back and forth the stone scrapped while the man stared down at the green field below, an expression on his face Hadrian could only describe as contempt.

"Daddy! I'm back." Thrace ran to the old farmer hugging him around his neck. "I missed you."

Theron endured the squeeze and glared at them. "Are these the ones then?"

"Yes. This is Hadrian and Royce. They've come all the way from Colnora to help. They can get the weapon Esra told us about."

"I have a weapon," the farmer growled and resumed sharpening his blade. The sound was cold and grating.

"This?" Thrace asked. "Your grass cutter? The margrave had a sword, a shield, and armor and he—"

"Not this, I have another weapon, much bigger, much sharper."

Puzzled, she looked around. The old man offered no insight.

"I don't need what lies in that tower to kill the beast."

"But you promised me."

"And I am a man of my word," he replied and drew the stone along the edge of the blade once more. "The waiting only made my weapon sharper." He dipped the stone into a bucket of water that sat beside him. He raised it back to the blade but paused and said, "Every day I wake up, I see Thad's broken bed and Hickory's cradle. I see the shattered barrel that Thad made, the fields I planted for him—growing despite me. Best season in a decade. I woulda reaped more than enough to pay for the contract and tools. I woulda had extra. I coulda built him a shop. I might even have afforded a sign and real glass windows. He coulda had a planed wooden door with hinges and studs. His shop woulda been better than any house in the village. Better then the manor. People would walk by and stare, wondering what great man owned such a business. How great an artisan was this town's cooper that he could manage such a fine store?

"Those bastards back in Glamrendor who wouldn't let Thad hang a shingle. They would never have seen the like. It woulda had a shake roof and scalloped eaves, a hard oak counter and iron hooks to hold lanterns for when he needed to work late at night to complete all his orders. His barrels would be stacked in a storage shed beside the shop. A beautiful barn-size one, and I would paint it bright red so no one could miss it. I'd 'a got him a wagon too even if I had to build it myself, that way he could send orders all over Avryn—back to Glamrendor too. I'd 'a driven them there myself just to see the shock and anger on their faces.

"Morning! I'd say grinning like a lipless crocodile. Here's another fine delivery of barrels from Thaddeus Wood, the best cooper in Avryn. They'd cringe and curse. Yep, that boy 'o mine, he's no farmer, no sir. Starting with him, the Woods were gonna be artisans and shopkeepers.

"This village, it'd have grown. People woulda moved in and started businesses of their own, only Thad's woulda always been the first, the biggest, and the best. I'd seen to that. Soon this here woulda been a city, a fine city and the Woods the most successful family—a merchant family giv'n money to the arts and riding around in fine carriages. This here house woulda been a true mansion 'cause Thad woulda insisted, but I wouldn't care 'bout that, no sir. I'd been content just watching Hickory grow up, seeing him learn to read and write—appointed magistrate maybe. My grandson in the black robes! Yes sir, Magistrate Wood is going to court in a fine carriage and me standing there watching him.

"I see it. Every morning I get up; I sit; I look down Stony Hill and I see all of it. It's right there, right in that field growing in front of me. I haven't hoed. I haven't tilled, but look at it. The best crop I ever grew getting taller every day."

"Daddy, please come back with us to the Bothwicks. It's getting late."

"This is my home!" the old man shouted, but not at her. His eyes were still on the field. He scraped the blade again. Thrace sighed.

There was a long silence.

"You and your friends go. I swore not to seek it, but there is always a chance it might come to me."

"But, Daddy—"

"I said take them and go. I don't need you here."

Thrace glanced at Hadrian. There were tears in her eyes. Her lips trembled. She stood for a moment, wavering, then abruptly broke and ran back up the path toward town. Theron ignored her. The old farmer tilted the blade of his grass cutter to the other side and resumed sharpening. Hadrian watched him for a moment, the sounds of the stone on metal drowning out Thrace's fading sobs. He never looked up, not at Hadrian, not to glance down the trail. The man was indeed a rock.

Hadrian found Thrace only a few dozen yards up the trail. She was on her knees crying. Her small body jerked, her hair rocking with the movement. He placed his hand gently on her shoulder. "Your father is right. That weapon of his is very sharp."

Royce caught up with them carrying a fractured piece of wood. He looked down at Thrace with an uncomfortable expression.

"What's up?" Hadrian asked before Royce said anything callous.

"What do you think of this?" Royce replied, holding out the scrap that might have been part of the house framing. The beam was wide and thick, good strong oak taken from the trunk of a well aged tree. The piece bore four deeply cut gouges.

"Claw marks?" Hadrian took the wood and placed his hand against the board with his fingers splayed out. "Giant claw marks."

Royce nodded. "Whatever it is, it's huge. So how come no one has seen it?"

"It gets very dark here," Thrace told them, wiping her cheeks as she stood. A curious expression crossed her face and she walked to where a yellow-flowered forsythia grew at the base of a maple tree. Taking a hesitant step, Thrace bent down and drew back what Hadrian thought was a wad of cloth and old grass. As she carefully cleaned away the leaves and sticks he saw it was a crude doll with thread for hair and X's sewn for eyes.

"Yours?" Hadrian ventured.

She shook her head but did not speak. After a moment Thrace replied, "I made this for Hickory, Thad's son. It was his Wintertide gift, his favorite. He carried it everywhere." Plucking the last bits of grass from the doll, she rubbed it. "There's blood on it." her voice quivered. Clutching the doll to her chest she said softly, "He forgets—they were my family too."

Royce guessed it was still early evening when they returned to the village common, but already the light was fading, the invisible sun quickly consumed by the great trees. The little girl and her herd of pigs were gone and so were their horses and gear. In their place, they found a host of people rushing about with an urgency that left him uneasy.

Men crossed the clearing carrying hoes, axes, and piles of split wood over their shoulders. Most were barefoot, dressed in sweat-stained tunics. Women came behind, carrying bundles of twigs, reeds, thick marsh grasses, and stalks of flax. They too traveled barefoot with their hair pulled up, hidden under simple cloth wraps. Royce could see why Thrace made such a big deal out of the dress they bought her as all the village women wore simple homemade smocks of the same natural off-white color, lacking any adornment.

They looked hot and tired, focused on reaching the shelter of their homes and dumping their burdens. As the three approached the village, one boy looked up and stopped. He had a long handled hoe across his shoulders, his arm threaded around it.

"Who's that?" he said.

This got the attention of those nearby. An older woman glared, still clutching her bag of twigs. A bare-chested man with thick, powerful arms lowered his pack of wood, holding tight to his axe. The topless man glanced at Thrace who was still wiping her red eyes, and advanced on them, shifting the axe to his right hand.

"Vince, we got visitors!" he shouted.

A shorter, older man with a poorly kept beard turned his head and dropped his bundle as well. He looked at the boy who first spotted them. "Tad, go fetch your pa." The boy hesitated. "Go now son!"

The boy ran off toward the houses.

"Thrace honey," the old woman said, "are you alright?"

The bearded man glared at them, "What they do to you girl?"

As the men advanced, Royce and Hadrian moved together, each one looking expectantly at Thrace. Royce's hand slipped into the folds of his cloak.

"Oh no!" Thrace burst out. "They didn't do anything."

"Doesn't look like nothing. Disappear for weeks and you pop up crying dressed like—"

Thrace shook her head. "I'm fine. It's just my father—"

The men stopped. They kept a wary eye on the strangers, but shot looks of sympathy at Thrace.

"Theron's a fine man," Vince told her, "a strong man. He'll come around, you'll see. He just needs some time."

She nodded, but it was forced.

"Now, who might you two be?"

"This is Hadrian and Royce," Thrace finally got around to saying, "from Colnora in Warric. I asked them here to help. This is Mr. Griffin, the village founder."

"Came out here with an axe, a knife, and not much else—the rest of these poor souls were foolish enough to follow, on account I told them life was better and they was stupid enough to believe me." He extended his hand. "Just call me Vince."

"I'm Dillon McDern," the big, bare-chested man said, "I'm the smith round here. Figure you fellas might want to know that. You got horses, right? My boys say they took two up to the manor a bit ago."

"This is Mae," Vince said, presenting the old woman. She nodded solemnly. Now that it was clear that Thrace was all right, the old woman slouched, the look in her eyes became dull and distant as she turned away with her bundle of twigs.

"Don't mind her. She's—well, Mae's had it hard lately." He glanced at Dillon who nodded.

The boy sent running returned with another man. Older than McDern, younger than Griffin, thinner than both, he dragged his feet as he walked, his eyes squinting despite the dim light. In his hands he held a small pig that struggled to escape.

"Why'd you bring your pig, Russell?" Griffin asked.

"Boy said, you needed me—said it was an emergency."

Griffin glanced at Dillon who looked back and shrugged. "You find emergencies often call for pigs, do you?"

Russell scowled. "I just got hold of her. She gets riled up with Pearl all day, hard as can be to catch her. No way I'm letting her go with night coming on. What is it? What's the emergency?"

"Turns out there ain't one. False alarm," Griffin said.

Russell shook his head. "By Mar, Vince, scare a body to death. Next you'll be swinging from the bell rope just to see folks faint."

"Twarn't on purpose," he dipped his head at Royce and Hadrian. "We thought these fellas were up to something."

Russell looked at them. "Visitors, eh? Where'd you two come from?"

"Colnora," Thrace answered, "I invited them. Esra said they could help my father. I was hoping you'd let them stay with us."

Russell looked at her and sighed heavily, a frown pulling hard at the corners of his mouth.

"Oh, well—ah, that's okay, I guess," Thrace stumbled looking embarrassed. "I can ask Deacon Tomas if he'll—"

"Of course, they can stay with us, Thrace. You know better than to even ask." Tucking the pig under one arm, he placed his hand to the side of her face and rubbed her cheek. "It's just that, well Lena and me—we was sure you were gone for good. Figured you'd found a new home, maybe."

"I'd never leave my father."

"No. No, I 'spose you wouldn't. You and your pa—you're alike that way. Rocks, the both of you, and Maribor help the plow that finds either of you in its path."

The pig made an attempt to escape, twisting, kicking its legs and squealing. Russell caught it just in time. "Need to get back. The wife will be after me. Com'on, Thrace, and bring your friends." He led them toward the clump of tiny houses. "By Mar girl, where'd you get that dress?"

Royce remained where he was as the rest started to go. Hadrian gave him a curious look but continued ahead with the others. Royce remained on the trail, unmoving, watching the villagers racing the light: fetching water, hanging out clothes, gathering animals. Pearl wandered past the well, her herd of pigs reduced to only two. Mae Drundel came out of her house, her kerchief pulled free, her gray hair hanging. Unlike the rest, she walked slowly. She crossed to the side of her home, where Royce noticed three markers like those of the Caswell's. She stood for a moment, knelt down for a time, then walked slowly back inside. She was the last villager to disappear indoors.

That left only Royce and the man at the well.

He was no farmer.

Royce spotted him the moment they returned, his long slender frame leaning silently against the side of the wellhead, resting in shadow where he nearly faded into the background. The man's hair hung loose to his shoulders, dark with a few threads of gray. He had high cheekbones and deep brooding eyes. His long enveloping robe shimmered with the last rays of sunlight. He sat motionless. This was a man comfortable with waiting and well versed in patience.

He did not look old, but Royce knew better. He had not changed much in the two years since Royce, Hadrian, a young prince Alric, and a monk named Myron, aided his escape from Gutaria Prison. The color of his robe was different, yet still not quite discernible. This time Royce guessed it shimmered somewhere between a turquoise and a dark green, as always the sleeves hung down, hiding the absence of his hands. He also bore a beard, but that of course, was new.

They watched each other, staring across the green. Royce walked forward, crossing the distance between them in silence. Two ghosts meeting at a crossroad.

"It's been a while—Esra is it? Or should I call you Mister Haddon?"

The man tilted his head, lifting his eyes. "I am delighted to see you as well, Royce."

"How do you know my name?"

"I'm a wizard, or did you miss that from our last meeting?"

Royce paused and smiled. "You know you're right, I might have, perhaps you should write it down for me lest I forget again."

Esrahaddon raised an eyebrow. "That's a bit harsh."

"How do you know who I am?"

"Well, I did see *The Crown Conspiracy* while in Colnora. I found the sets pathetic and the orchestration horrible, but the story was good. I particularly loved the daring escape from the tower, and the little monk was hilarious—by far my favorite character. I was also pleased there was no wizard in the tale. I wonder who I should thank for that oversight, certainly not you."

"They also didn't use our real names. So again, how do you know it?"

"How would you find out your name, if you were me?"

"I'd ask people that would know. So who did you ask?"

"Would *you* tell me?"

Royce frowned. "Do you ever answer a question with an answer?"

"Sorry, it's a habit, I was a teacher most of my free life."

"Your speech has changed," Royce observed.

"Thank you for noticing. I worked very hard. I sat in many taverns over the last six months and listened. I have a talent for languages; I speak several. I don't know all the colloquial terms yet, but the general grammar wasn't hard to adjust to. It is the same language after all, the dialect you speak is merely—less sophisticated than what I was used to. It's like talking with a crude accent."

"So you found out who we were by asking around and watching bad plays and you picked up the language by listening to drunks. Now tell me, why are you here, and why do you want us here?"

Esrahaddon stood up and slowly walked around the well. He looked at the ground where the last light of the sun spilled through the leaves of a poplar tree.

"I could tell you that I am hiding here and that would sound plausible. I could also say that I heard about the plight of this village and came here to help, because that's what wizards do. Of course, we both know you won't believe those answers. So let's save time. Why don't *you* tell me why I am here? Then you can try and judge by my reaction if you are correct or not, since that's what you're planning to do anyway."

"Were all wizards as irritating as you are?"

"Much worse, I'm afraid. I was one of the youngest and nicest."

A young man, Royce thought his name was Tad, trotted over with a bucket. "It's getting late," he said with a harried look filling his bucket with water. A few yards away Royce spotted a woman struggling to pull a stubborn goat into a house as a small boy pushed the animal from behind.

"Tad!" a man shouted, and the boy at the well turned abruptly.

"Coming!"

He smiled and nodded at each of them, grabbed his bucket of water and ran back the way he came, spilling half the contents in the process.

They were alone again.

"I think you're here because you need something from Avempartha," Royce told the wizard. "And I don't think it is a sword of demon-slaying either. You're using this poor girl and her tormented father to lure me and Hadrian here to turn a knob you obviously can't manage."

Esrahaddon sighed. "That's disappointing. I thought you were smarter than that, and these constant references to my disability are dull. I am not *using* anyone."

"So you are saying there really is a weapon in that tower?"

"That is exactly what I am saying."

Royce studied him for a moment and scowled.

"Can't tell if I am lying or not, can you?" Esrahaddon smiled smugly.

"I don't think you're lying, but I don't think you're telling the truth either."

The wizard's eyebrows rose. "Now that's better. There might be hope for you yet."

"Maybe there is a weapon in that tower. Maybe it can help kill this—whatever it is they have here, but maybe you also conjured the beast in the first place as an excuse to drag us here."

"Logical," Esrahaddon said, nodding. "Morbidly manipulative, but I can see the reasoning. Only if you recall, the attacks on this village started while I was still imprisoned."

Royce scowled again. "So, why are you here?"

Esrahaddon smiled. "Something you need to understand my boy is that wizards are not fonts of information. You should at least know this much—the farmer Theron and his daughter would be dead today if I hadn't arrived and sent her to fetch you."

"Alright. Your purpose here is none of my business, I can accept that. But why am *I* here? You can tell me that much, can't you? Why go to the bother of finding out our names and locating us in Colnora—which was really impressive by the way—when you could have gotten any thief to pick your lock and open the tower for you?"

"Because not just anyone will do. You are the only one I know who can open Avempartha."

"Are you saying I am the only thief you know?"

"It helps if you actually listen to what I say. You are the only one I know who can open Avempartha."

Royce glared at him.

"There is a monster here that kills indiscriminately," Esrahaddon told him with great and unexpected seriousness. "No weapon made by man can harm it. It comes at night and people die. Nothing will stop it except the sword that lies in that tower. You need to find a way inside and get that sword."

Royce continued to stare.

"You are right. That is not the whole truth, but it is the truth nonetheless and all that I am willing to explain…for now. To learn more you need to get inside."

"Stealing swords," Royce muttered mostly to himself. "Okay, let's take a look at this tower. The sooner I see it the sooner I can start cursing."

"No," the wizard replied. He looked back at the ground where the sun had already faded. He glanced up at the darkening sky. "Night is coming and we need to get indoors. In the morning we will go, but tonight we hide with the rest."

Royce considered the wizard for a moment. "You know when I first met you there was all this talk about you being this scary wizard that could call lightning and raise mountains and now you can't even fight a little monster, or open an old tower. I thought you were more powerful than this."

"I was," Esrahaddon said and for the first time the wizard held up his arms letting his sleeves fall back revealing the stumps where his hands should have been. "Magic is a little like playing the fiddle. It's damn hard to do without hands."

Dinner that evening was a vegetable pottage, a weak stew consisting of leeks, celery, onions, and potatoes in a thin broth. Hadrian took only a small portion that was far from filling, but he found it surprisingly tasty, filled with a mixture of unusual flavors that left a burning sensation in his mouth.

Lena and Russell Bothwick made good on their promise to put them up for the night, a kindness made all the more generous when they discovered how cramped the little house was. The Bothwicks had three children, four pigs, two sheep, and a goat they called Mammy, all of whom clustered in the single open room. Mosquitoes joined them as well, taking over the night shift from the flies. It was hard to breathe in the house filled with smoke, the scent of animals, and the steam from the stew pot. Royce and Hadrian staked out a bit of earth as near the open doorway as possible and sat on the floor.

"I didn't know the first thing about farming," Russell Bothwick was saying. Like most men in the village, he was dressed in a frayed and flimsy shirt that hung to his knees, belted around the waist with a length of twine. There were large, dark circles under his eyes, another trait consistent with the other inhabitants of Dahlgren. "I was a candle maker back in Drismoor. I worked as a journeyman in a trade shop on Hithil Street. It was Theron who kept us alive our first year here. We woulda starved or froze to death if not for Theron and Addie Wood. They took us under their wing and helped build this house. It was Theron that taught me how to plow a field."

"Addie was my midwife when I had the twins," Lena said while ladling out bowls, which Thrace handed to the children. The twin girls and Tad, exiled to the loft, looked down from their beds of straw, chins on hands, eyes watchful. "And Thrace here was our babysitter."

"There was never a question about taking her in," Russell said. "I only wish Theron would come too, but that man is stubborn."

"I just can't get over how beautiful that dress is," Lena Bothwick said again, looking at Thrace and shaking her head. Russell grumbled something, but with a mouthful of stew, no one understood him.

Lena scowled. "Well it is."

She stopped talking about it, but continued to stare. Lena was a gaunt woman with light brown hair, cut straight and short, giving her a boyish look. Her nose came to a point so sharp it looked like it could cut parchment. She had a rash of freckles and no eyebrows to speak of. The children all took after her, each sporting the same cropped hairstyle, son and daughters alike, while Russell had no hair at all.

Thrace entertained them with stories of her adventure to the big city, of the sights and number of people she found there. She explained that Hadrian and Royce took her to a lavish hotel. This brought worried looks from Lena but she relaxed as more details were revealed. Thrace raved about her bath in a hot water tub with perfumed soap and how she spent the night in a huge feather bed under a solid beamed roof. She never mentioned the Tradesmen's Arch, or what happened underneath it.

Lena was mesmerized to the point of nearly letting the remainder of the stew boil over. Russell continued to grunt and grumble his way through the meal. Esrahaddon sat with his back to the side wall between Lena's spinning wheel and the butter churn. His robe was now a dark gray. He was so quiet he could have been just a shadow. During dinner, Thrace spoon-fed the wizard.

How must that feel? Hadrian thought while watching them. *What is it like to have held so much power and now unable to even hold a spoon?*

After dinner, while helping Lena clean up Thrace was placing the washed bowls on a shelf and called out, "I remember this plate." A smile appeared on her face as she spotted the only ceramic dish in the house. The pale white oval with delicate blue traceries lay carefully tucked in a back corner of the cupboard with all the other treasured family heirlooms. "I remember when I was little, Jessie Caswell and I—" she stopped and the house quieted. Even the children stopped fussing.

Lena stopped cleaning the dishes and put her arms around Thrace, pulling her close. Hadrian noticed lines on the woman's face he had not seen previously. The two stood before the bucket of dirty water and silently cried together. "You shouldn't have come back," Lena whispered. "You should have stayed in that hotel with those people."

"I can't leave him," Hadrian heard Thrace's small voice muffled by Lena's shoulder. "He's all I have left."

Thrace pulled back and Lena struggled to offer her a smile.

It was dark outside now. From his vantage point at the doorway, Hadrian could not see much of anything—a tiny patch of moonlight scattered here and there. Fireflies blinked leaving trails of light. The rest was lost in the vast black of the forest.

Russell pulled over a stool to sit across from Royce and Hadrian. Lighting a long clay pipe with a thin sliver of wood, he commented, "So, you two are here to help Theron kill the monster?"

"We'll do what we can," Hadrian replied.

Russell puffed hard on his pipe to ensure it lit and then crushed the burning tip of the wooden sliver into the dirt floor. "Theron is over fifty years old. He knows the sharp end of a pitchfork from the handle, but I don't 'spect he's ever held a sword. Now you two look to me like the kind of fellas that have seen a fight up close and Hadrian here not only has a sword—he's got three. A man carries three swords he, like as not, knows how to use 'em. Seems to me, a couple fellas like you could do more than just help an old man get himself killed."

"Russell!" Lena reprimanded. "They're our guests. Why don't you scald them with hot water while you're at it?"

"I just don't want to see that damn fool kill himself. If the margrave and his knights didn't stand a chance, how well will Theron do out there? An old man with that scythe of his. What's he trying to prove? How brave he is?"

"He's not trying to prove anything," Esrahaddon said suddenly and his voice silenced the room like a plate dropping. "He's trying to kill himself."

"What?" Russell asked.

"He's right," Hadrian said, "I've seen it before. Soldiers—career soldiers—brave men just reach a point where it's all too much. It can be anything that sets them off—one too many deaths, a friend dying, or even something as trivial as a change in the weather. I knew a man once who led charges in dozens of battles. It wasn't until a dog he befriended was butchered for food that he gave up. Of course, a fighter like that can't surrender, can't just quit. He needs to go out swinging. So they rush in unguarded, picking a battle they can't win."

"Then I needn't have wasted your time," Thrace said. "If my father doesn't want to live—whatever is in the tower can't save him."

Hadrian regretted speaking and added, "Every day your father is alive there is the chance he can find hope again."

"Your father will be fine, Thrace," Lena told her. "That man is tough as granite. You'll see."

"Mom," one of the kids from the loft called.

Lena ignored the child. "You shouldn't listen to these people talking about your father that way. They don't know him."

"Mom."

"Honestly, telling a poor girl something like that right after she's lost her family."

"Mom!"

"What on earth is it, Tad?" Lena nearly screamed at the child.

"The sheep. Look at the sheep."

Everyone noticed it then. Crowded into the corner of the room, the sheep were quiet through the meal. A content wooly pile that Hadrian forgot was there. Now they pushed each other struggling against the wooden board Russell had put up. The little bell around Mammy's neck rang as the goat shifted uneasily. One of the pigs bolted for the door and Thrace and Lena tackled it just in time.

"Kids. Get down here!" Lena shouted in a whisper.

The three children descended the ladder with precision movements, veterans of many drills. Their mother gathered them near her in the center of the house. Russell got off his stool and doused the fire with the wash water.

Darkness enveloped them. No one spoke. Outside the crickets stopped chirping. The frogs fell silent an instant later. The animals continued to shift and stomp. Another pig bolted. Hadrian heard its little feet skitter across the dirt floor in the direction of the door. Beside him he felt Royce move, then silence.

"Here, someone take this," Royce whispered. Tad crawled toward the sound and took the pig from him.

They waited.

The sound began faint and hollow. A puffing, thought Hadrian, like bellows stoking a furnace. It grew nearer, louder, less airy—deep and powerful. The sound rose overhead and Hadrian instinctively looked up, but found only the darkness of the ceiling. His hands moved to the pommels of his swords.

Thrump. Thrump. Thrump.

They sat huddled in the darkness, listening, as the sound withdrew then grew louder once more. A pause—total silence. Inside the house, even the sound of breathing vanished.

Crack!

Hadrian jumped at the loud burst as if a tree across the common exploded. Snapping, tearing, splintering, a war of violent noise erupted. A scream. A woman's voice. The shriek cut across the common, hysterical and frantic.

"Oh dear Maribor! That's Mae," Lena cried.

Hadrian leapt to his feet. Royce was already up.

"Don't bother," Esrahaddon told them. "She's dead, and there's nothing you can do. The monster cannot be harmed by your weapons. It—"

The two were out the door.

Royce was quicker and raced across the common toward the little house of Mae Drundel. Hadrian could not see a thing and found himself blindly chasing Royce's footfalls.

The cries stopped—a harsh, abrupt end.

Royce halted and Hadrian nearly plowed through him.

"What is it?"

"Roof is ripped away. There's blood all over the walls. She's gone. It's gone."

"It? Did you see something?"

"Through a patch in the canopy—just for a second, but it was enough."

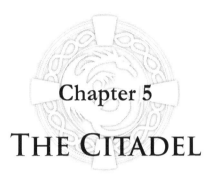

Chapter 5

THE CITADEL

ROYCE AND ESRAHADDON left at first light, following a small trail out of the village. Ever since they arrived in Dahlgren, Royce had noticed a distant sound, a dull, constant noise. As they approached the river, the sound grew into a roar. The Nidwalden was massive—an expanse of tumultuous green water flowing swiftly, racing by and bursting against rocks. Royce stood for a moment just staring. He spotted a branch out in the middle, a black and gray fist of leaves bobbing helplessly against the current. It sped along, riding through gaps in the boulders, ripping over rocks until it vanished into a cloud of white. In the center, he saw something tall rising up, most of it lost in the mist and tree branches that extended over the water.

"We need to go farther down river," Esrahaddon explained as he led Royce to a narrower trail that hugged the bank. River grass grew along the edge, glistening with dew and songbirds sang shrill melodies in the soft morning breeze. Even with the thundering river, and the vivid memory of a roofless home and bloodstained walls, the place felt tranquil.

"There she is," Esrahaddon said reverently as they reached a rocky clearing that afforded them an unobstructed view of the river.

It was wide and the water rushed by with a furious strength then disappeared over the edge of a sudden fall.

They stood very near the ridge of the cataract and could see the white mist rising from the abrupt drop like a fog. Out in the middle of the river, at the edge of the falls, a massive shelf of bedrock jutted out like the prow of a mighty ship that ran aground just before toppling over the precipice. On this fearsome pedestal rose the citadel of Avempartha. Formed entirely of stone, the tower burst skyward from the rock shelf. A bouquet of tall, slender shards stretched upward like splinters of crystal or slivers of ice, its base lost in the billowing white clouds of mist and foam. At first sight it looked to be a natural stone formation, but a more careful study revealed windows, walkways and stairs carefully integrated into the architecture.

"How am I suppose to get out there?" Royce asked yelling over the roar, his cloak whipping and snapping like a snake.

"That would be problem number one," Esrahaddon shouted back, offering nothing more.

Was this some kind of test, or does he really not know?

Royce followed the river over the bare rocks to the drop. Here the land plummeted more than two thousand feet to the valley below. What stood before him was a vision of unsurpassed beauty. The falls were magnificent. The sheer power of the titanic surge was hypnotizing. The massive torrent of blue-green water spilled and sparkled into the billowing white bejeweled mist, the voice of the river thundering in his ears, rattling his chest. Beyond it, to the south, was an equally breathtaking vision. Royce could see for miles and marked the remaining passage of the river as it wound like a long shiny snake through the lush green landscape to the Goblin Sea.

Esrahaddon moved to a more sheltered escarpment farther inland and behind a brace of upward thrust granite that blocked him from the gusting wind and spray. Royce climbed toward him when he noticed a depressed line in the trees running away from the river. A course of trees stood shorter than those around them, creating a trench in the otherwise uniform canopy. He made his way down to the forest floor and found that what he thought might be a gully was instead a section of younger growth. More importantly, the line was perfectly straight. Old vines and thorn bushes masked unnatural mounds. He dug away some of the undergrowth and swept layers of dirt and dead leaves back until he touched on flat stone.

"Looks like there might have been a road here," he shouted up to the wizard.

"There was. A great bridge once reached out across the river to Avempartha."

"What happened to it?"

"The river," the wizard told him. "The Nidwalden does not abide the efforts of man for long. Most of it likely washed away, leaving the remains to fall."

Royce followed the buried road to the river's edge where he stood looking at the tower across the violent expanse. A vast gray volume rushed by him, its speed concealed by its size. The dark gray became a swirling translucent green as it reached the edge. The moment it fell, the water burst into white foam, billions of flying droplets, and all he could hear was the thundering roar.

"Impossible," he muttered.

He returned to where the wizard stood and sat down on the sun-warmed rock, looking at the distant tower that rose up in the haze where rainbows played.

"Do you want me to open that thing?" the thief asked with all seriousness. "Or is this some kind of game?"

"It's no game," Esrahaddon replied as he sat leaning against a rock, folding his arms and closed his eyes.

It irritated Royce how comfortable he looked. "Then you'd better start saying more than you have so far."

"What do you want to know?"

"Everything—everything you know about it."

"Well, let's see, I was here once a very long time ago. It looked different then, of course. For one thing Novron's bridge was still up and you could walk right out to the tower."

"So the bridge was the only way to reach it?"

"Oh no, I don't think so. At least it wouldn't make any sense if that were the case. You see the elves built Avempartha before mankind walked on the face of Elan. No one—well, no human—knows why or what for. Its location here on the falls facing south toward what we call the Goblin Sea suggests perhaps the elves might have employed it as a defense against the Children of Uberlin—I believe you call them by the dwarven name, the Ba Ran Ghazel—*goblins of the sea*. But that seems unlikely, as the tower predates them as well. There might have even been a city here at one time. So little is left of their achievements in Apeladorn, but the elves had a fabulous culture rich in beauty, music, and The Art."

"When you say *The Art*, you mean magic?"

The wizard opened a single eye and frowned at him. "Yes, and don't give me that look, as if magic is dirty or vile. I have seen that too many times since I escaped."

"Well, magic isn't something people consider a good thing."

Esrahaddon sighed and shook his head with a stern look. "It is demoralizing to see what has happened to the world during my years of incarceration. I stayed alive and sane because I knew that one day I would be able to do my part to protect humanity, but now I discover it's almost no longer worth the effort. When I was young, the world was an incredible place. Cities were magnificent. Your Colnora wouldn't even rank as a slum in the smallest city of my time. We had indoor plumbing—spigots would pump water right into people's homes. There were extensive, well-maintained sewer systems that kept the streets from smelling like cesspools. Buildings were eight and nine stories tall, and some reached as high as twelve. We had hospitals where the sick were treated and actually got better. We had libraries, museums, temples, and schools of every kind.

"Mankind has squandered its inheritance from Novron. It's like having gone to sleep a rich man and waking up a pauper." He paused. "Then there's what you so feebly call magic. The Art separated us from the animals. It was the greatest achievement of our civilization. Not only has it been forgotten, it is now reviled. In my day, those who could weave The Art, and summon the natural powers of the world to their bidding, were considered agents of the gods—sacrosanct. Today they burn you if you accidentally guess tomorrow's weather.

"It was very different then. People were happy. There were no poor families living on the streets. No destitute hopeless peasants struggling to find a meal, or forced to live in hovels with three children, four pigs, two sheep, and a goat, where the flies in the afternoon are thicker than the family's evening stew."

Esrahaddon looked around sadly. "As a wizard, my life was devoted to the study of truth and the application of it in the service of the Emperor. Never had I managed to find more truth or serve him more profoundly than when I came here. And yet, in many ways I regret it. Oh, if only I had stayed home. I would be long dead, having lived a happy, wonderful life."

Royce smiled at him. "Wizards aren't a font, I thought."

Esrahaddon scowled.

"Now, what about the tower?"

The wizard looked back at the elegant spires rising above the mist. "Avempartha was the site of the last battle of the Great Elven Wars. Novron drove the elves back to the Nidwalden, but they held on by fortifying their position in the tower. Novron was not about to be stopped by a little water and ordered the building of the bridge. It took eight years and cost the lives of hundreds, most of whom went over the falls, but in the end, the bridge was completed. It took Novron another five years after that to take the citadel. The act was as much symbolic as it was strategic and it forced the elves to accept that nothing would stop Novron from wiping them off the face of Elan. A very curious thing happened then, something that is still unclear. Novron is said to have obtained the Horn of Gylindora and with it forced the unconditional surrender of the elves. He ordered them to destroy their war agents and machines and to retreat across the river—never to cross it again."

"So there was no bridge until Novron built one? Not on either side?"

"No, that was the problem. There was no way to reach the tower."

"How did the elves get there?"

"Exactly." The wizard nodded.

"So you don't know?"

"I'm old, but not that old. Novron is farther in the past for me, than my day is to you."

"So there is an answer to this puzzle. It's just not obvious."

"Do you think Novron would have spent eight years building a bridge if it was?"

"And what makes you think I can find the answer?"

"Call it a bunch."

Royce looked at him curiously. "You mean *hunch?*"

The wizard look irritated. "Still a few holes in my vocabulary, I suppose."

Royce stared out at the tower in the middle of the river and considered why jobs involving stealing swords were never simple.

THE CITADEL

❧

The service they held for Mae Drundel was somber and respectful, although to Hadrian it felt rehearsed. There were no awkward moments, no stumbling over words or miscues. Everyone was well versed in his or her role. Indeed, the remaining residents of Dahlgren were about as professional about funerals as mourners could be without being paid.

Deacon Tomas said the only customized portion of the service where he mentioned her devotion to her late family and her church. Mae was the last of them to pass. Her sons died of sickness before their sixth year and her husband was killed by the beast less than five months ago. In his eulogy, Tomas publicly shared what nearly everyone was thinking, that as awful a thing as her death was, perhaps for Mae it was not so terrible. Some even reported that she had left an inviting candle in her window for the last two nights.

As usual, there was nobody to bury so they merely drove a whitewashed stake into the ground with her name burned into it. It stood next to the stakes marked Davie, Firth, and Went Drundel.

Everyone turned out for the service except Royce and Esrahaddon. Even Theron Wood made a showing to pay his respects. The old farmer looked even more haggard and miserable than he had the day before and Hadrian suspected he had been awake all night.

After the service ended, the village shared their midday dinner. The men placed a row of tables, end to end across the village common, and each family brought a dish. Smoked fish, black pudding (a sausage made from pig's blood, milk, animal fat, onions, and oatmeal), and mutton were the most popular.

Hadrian stood back, leaning against a cedar tree, watching the others form lines.

"Help yourself," Lena told him.

"There doesn't look like there is a lot here. I have provisions in my bag," he assured her.

"Nonsense—we'll have none of that—everyone eats at a wake. Mae would want it that way, and what else is a funeral for if not to pay respects to the dead."

She glared at him until he nodded and began looking about the tables for a plate.

"So those are your horses I have up in the castle stables?" a voice said and he turned to see a plump man in a cleric frock. He was the first person who did not look in desperate need of a meal. His cheeks were rosy and large and when he smiled his eyes squinted nearly shut. He did not look terribly old, but his hair was pure white, including his short beard.

"If you are Deacon Tomas, then yes," Hadrian replied.

"I am indeed, and think nothing of it. I get rather lonely up on the hill at night all by myself with all those empty rooms. You hear every sound at night, you know. The wind slapping a shutter, the creak of rafters—it can be quite unnerving. Now at least I can blame the noises I hear on your horses. Being way down in the stables, I doubt I could hear them, but I can pretend, can't I?" The deacon chuckled to himself. "But honestly, it can be miserable up there. I'm used to being with people, and the isolation of the manor house is such a burden," he said while heaping his plate full of mutton.

"It must be awful for you. But I'll bet there is good food. Those nobles really know how to fill a store house, don't they?"

"Well, yes, of course," the deacon replied. "As a matter of fact, the margrave had put by a remarkable amount of smoked meats, not to mention ale and wine, but I only take what I need of course."

"Of course," Hadrian agreed. "Just looking at you I can tell that you're not the kind of man to take advantage of a situation. Did you supply the ale for the funeral?"

"Oh no," the deacon replied, aghast. "I wouldn't dare pillage the manor house like that. Like you just said, I am not the kind of man to take advantage of a situation and it's not my stores to give, now is it?"

"I see."

"Oh my, look at the cheese," said the deacon, scooping up a wedge and shoving it in his mouth. "Have to admit one thing," he spoke with his mouth full, "Dahlgren can really throw a funeral."

When they reached the end of the tables, Hadrian looked for a place to sit. The few benches were filled with folks eating off their laps.

"Up you kids!" the deacon shouted at Tad and Pearl, "you don't need to be taking up a bench. Go sit on the grass." They frowned but got up. "You there, Hadrian is it? Come sit here and tell me what brings a man who owns a horse and three swords to Dahlgren. I trust you aren't noble or you'd have knocked on my door last night."

"No, I'm not a noble, but that brings up a question. How did you inherit the manor house?"

"Hmm? Inherit? Oh, I didn't inherit anything. It is merely my station as a public servant to help in a crisis like this. When the margrave and his men died, I knew I had to administer to this troubled flock and watch after the king's interests. So I endure the hardships and do what I can."

"Like what?"

"What's that?" the deacon asked, tearing into a piece of mutton that left his lips and cheeks shiny with grease.

"What have you done to help?"

"Oh—well, let's see…I keep the house clean, the yard maintained, and the garden watered. You really have to keep after those weeds you know, or the whole garden would be swallowed up and not a single vegetable would survive. And oh—the toll it takes on my back. I've never had what you would call a good back as it is."

"I meant about the attacks. What steps have you taken to safeguard the village?"

"Well now," the deacon chuckled, "I'm a cleric, not a knight. I don't even know how to hold a sword properly and I don't have an army of knights at my disposal, do I? So aside from diligent prayer, I'm not in a position where I can really *do* anything about that."

"Have you considered letting the villagers stay in the manor at night? Whatever this creature is, it doesn't have much trouble with thatched roofs, but the manor has what looks to be a sturdy roof and some thick walls."

The deacon shook his head, still smiling at Hadrian as an adult might look at a child who just asked why there must be poor people in the world. "No, no that wouldn't do at all. I am quite certain the next lord of the house would not appreciate having a whole village taking over his home."

"But you are aware that the responsibility of a lord is to protect his subjects? That is why his subjects pay him a tax. If the lord isn't willing to protect them, why should they honor him with money, crops, or even respect?"

"You might not have noticed," the deacon replied, "but we are between lords at the moment."

"So then, you don't intend to continue taxing these people for the time they are without protection?"

"Well, I didn't mean that—"

"So, you do intend to uphold the responsibility of a steward?"

"Well, I—"

"Now I can understand your hesitation to overstep your authority and open the manor house to the village, so I am certain you will want to take the other option."

"Other option?" The cleric was holding another slice of mutton to his mouth, but sat too distracted to bite.

"Yes, as steward and acting lord it falls on you to protect this village in his stead, and since inviting them into the house at night is out of the question then I presume you will be taking to the field to fight the beast."

"Fight it?" He dropped the mutton on his lap. "I don't think—"

Before he could say any more, Hadrian went on. "The good news is that I can help you there. I have an extra sword if you are missing one, and since you have been so kind as to let me board my horse at the stable I think the least I can do is lend her to you for the fight. Now I have heard that some people have determined where the lair of the beast is so it really seems a simple matter of—"

"I—I don't recall saying that lodging the people in the manor at night was out of the question," the deacon said loudly enough to interrupt Hadrian, so loud that several heads turned. He lowered his voice and added. "I was merely stating that it was something I had to consider carefully. You see, the mantle of leadership is a heavy one indeed, and I need to weigh the consequences of every act I make as they can break as well as mend. No, no, you can't rush into these things."

"That is very understandable and very wise, I might add," Hadrian agreed, keeping his voice loud enough for others to hear him. "But the margrave was killed well over two weeks ago, so I am certain you have come to a decision by now?"

The deacon caught the interested looks of several of the villagers. Those who had finished their meals wandered over. One was Dillon McDern, who was taller than the rest and stood watching them.

"I—ah."

"Everyone!" Hadrian shouted. "Gather round, the deacon wants to talk with us about the defense of the village."

The crowd of mourners, plates in hand, turned and gathered in a circle around the well. All eyes turned to Deacon Tomas who suddenly looked like a defenseless rabbit caught in a trap.

"I—um," the deacon started to say then slumped his shoulders and said in a loud voice, "in light of the recent attacks on houses, everyone is invited to spend nights in the protection of the castle."

The crowd murmured to each other and then Russell Bothwick called out, "Will there be enough room for everyone?"

The deacon looked as if he was about to reconsider when Hadrian stood up. "I'm sure there's plenty of room in the house for all the women and children and most of the married men. Those single men, thirteen or older, can spend the night in the stables, smokehouse, and other outbuildings. Each of them has stronger walls and roofs than any of the village homes."

The inhabitants of the village began to cluster now in earnest.

"And our livestock? Do we abandon them to the beast?" another farmer asked. Hadrian did not recognize him. "Without the livestock we'll have no meat, no wool, or field animals for work."

"I've got Amble and Ramble to think of," McDern said. "Dahlgren would be in a sorry state if 'n I let sumpin' happen to those oxen."

Hadrian jumped to the rim of the well where he stood above them with one arm on the windlass. "There's plenty of room inside the stockade walls for all the animals where they will be safer than they have been in your homes. Remember there is safety in numbers. If you sit alone in the dark it is easy for anything to kill you, but the creature will not be so bold as to enter a fenced castle with the entire village watching. We can also build bonfires outside the walls for light."

This brought gasps. "But light draws the creature!"

"Well, from what I can see. It doesn't have difficulty finding you in the dark."

The villagers looked from Hadrian to Deacon Tomas and back again.

"How do you know?" Someone asked from the crowd. "How do you know any of this? You're not from here. How do you know anything?"

"It's a demon from Uberlin!" Someone Hadrian did not recognize shouted.

"You can't stop it!" A woman on the right yelled. "Grouping together could just make killing us that much easier."

"It doesn't want to kill you all at once and it isn't a demon," Hadrian assured the villagers.

"How do you know?"

"It kills only one or two, why? If it can tear apart Theron Wood's house, or rip the roof off Mae Drundel's home in seconds, it could easily destroy this whole village in one night, but it doesn't. It doesn't because it isn't trying to kill you all. It's killing for food. The beast isn't a demon; it's a predator." The villagers considered this and while they paused, Hadrian continued, "What I have heard about this creature is that no one has ever seen it and no victim has survived. Well, that doesn't surprise me at all. How do you expect to survive when you sit alone in the dark just waiting to be eaten? No one has ever seen it because it doesn't want to be seen. Like any predator, it conceals itself until it springs and like a predator, it hunts the weakest prey; it looks for the stray, the young, the old, or the sick. All of you have been dividing yourselves up into tidy little meals. You've made yourselves too convenient to resist. If we group together it might prefer to hunt a deer or a wolf that night instead of us."

"What if you're wrong? What if no one has seen it because it is a demon and can't be seen? It could be an invisible spirit that feeds on terror. Isn't that right, deacon?"

"Ah—well—" the deacon began.

"It could be, but it isn't," Hadrian assured them.

"How do you know?"

"Because my partner saw it last night."

This caught the group by surprise and several conversations broke out at once. Hadrian spotted Pearl sitting on the grass staring at him. Several asked questions at once and Hadrian waved at them to quiet down.

"What did it look like?" a woman with a sunburned face and a white kerchief over her head asked.

"Since I didn't see it, I would prefer Royce tell you himself. He'll be back before dark."

"How could he have seen anything in the dark?" one of the older farmers asked skeptically. "I looked outside when I heard the scream and it was as black as the bottom of that well 'yer standing on. There's no way he could have seen anything."

"He saw the pig!" Tad Bothwick shouted.

"What's that, boy?" Dillon McDern asked.

"The pig, in our house last night," Tad said excitedly. "It was all dark and the pig ran, but he saw it and caught him."

"That's right," Russell Bothwick recalled. "We had just put the fire out and I couldn't see my hand in front of my face, but this fellow caught a running pig. Maybe he did see something."

"The point is," Hadrian went on, "we'll all stand a better chance of survival if we stick together. Now the deacon has graciously invited all of us to join him behind the protection of walls and a solid roof. I think we should listen to his wisdom and start making plans to resettle and gather wood before the evening arrives. We still have plenty of time to build up strong bonfires."

They were looking at Hadrian now and nodding. There were still those that looked unconvinced, but even the skeptics appeared hopeful. Small groups were forming, talking, planning.

Hadrian sat back down and ate. He was not a fan of blood pudding and stayed with the smoked fish, which was wonderful.

"I'll bring the oxen over," he heard McDern say. "Brent, you go bring 'yer wagon and fetch 'yer axe too."

"We'll need shovels and Went's saw," Vince Griffin said. "He always kept it sharp."

"I'll send Tad to fetch it," Russell announced.

"Is it true?" Hadrian looked up from his plate to see Pearl standing before him. Her face was just as dirty as the day before. "Did 'yer friend—did he really catch a pig in the dark?"

"If you don't believe me, you can ask him tonight."

Looking over the little girl's head, he spotted Thrace. She was sitting alone on the ground down the trail past the Caswell's graves. He noticed her hands wiping her cheeks. He set his empty plate on the table, smiled at Pearl and walked over. Thrace did not look up so he crouched down beside her. "What is it?"

"Nothing," she shook her head, hiding her face with her hair.

Hadrian glanced around the trail and then back up at the villagers. The women were putting away the uneaten food as the men gathered tools, all of them chattering quickly.

"Where's your father. I saw him earlier."

"He went back home," she said sniffling.

"What did he say to you?"

"I told you it's alright." She stood up, brushed off her dress, and wiped her eyes. "I should help with the cleaning, excuse me."

Hadrian entered the clearing and once more faced the remains of the Wood's farmhouse. The roofing poles listed to one side, framing splintered, thatch scattered—*this is what shattered dreams look like.* The farm felt cursed, haunted by ghosts, only one of the ghosts was not at home. There was no sign of the old farmer and the scythe rested, abandoned, up against the ruined wall. Hadrian took the opportunity to peer inside at the shattered furniture, broken cupboards, torn clothes, and blood stains. A single chair stood in the center of the debris beside a wooden cradle.

Theron Wood came up from the river a few moments later carrying a shoulder yoke with two buckets full of water hanging from the ends. He did not hesitate when he spotted Hadrian standing before the ruins of his house. He walked right by. He set the buckets down and began pouring them into three large jugs.

"You back again?" he asked without looking up. "She told me she paid you silver to come here. Is that what you do? Take advantage of simple girls? Steal their hard-earned money, then eat their village's food? If you came here to see if you can squeeze more coins out of me you're gonna be disappointed."

"I didn't come here for money."

"No? Then why did you?" he asked, tipping the second bucket. "If you really are here to get that club or sword or whatever that crazy cripple thinks is in the tower, shouldn't you be trying to swim the river right now?"

"My partner is working on that as we speak."

"Uh-huh, he's the swimmer, is he? And what are you, the guy that squeezes the money out of poor miserable farmers? I've seen your kind before, highwaymen and cheats—you scare people into paying you just to live. Well, that's not gonna work this time, my friend."

"I told you I didn't come here for money."

Theron dropped the bucket at his feet and turned. "So why did you come here?"

"You left the wake early and I was concerned you might not have heard the news that everyone in the village is going to spend the night inside the castle walls."

"Thanks for the notice," he said and turning back corked the jugs. When he finished he looked up, annoyed. "Why are you still here?"

"What exactly do you know about combat?" Hadrian asked.

The farmer glared at him. "What business is it of yours?"

"As you pointed out, your daughter paid my partner and me good money to help you kill this monster. He's working on providing you with a proper weapon. I am here to ensure you know how to use it when it gets here."

Theron Wood ran his tongue along his teeth. "You're fixin' to educate me, are you?"

"Something like that."

"I don't need any training." He picked up his buckets and yoke and began walking away.

"You don't know the first thing about combat. Have you ever even held a sword?"

Theron whirled on him. "No, but I plowed five acres in one day. I bucked half a cord of wood before noon. I survived being caught eight miles from shelter in a blizzard and I lost my whole damn family in a single night! Have *you* done any of that?"

"Not your *whole* family," Hadrian reminded him.

"The ones that mattered."

Hadrian drew his sword and advanced on Theron. The old farmer watched his approach with indifference.

"This is a bastard sword," Hadrian told him and dropped it at the farmer's feet and walked half a dozen steps away. "I think it suits you rather well. Pick it up and swing at me."

"I have more important things to do than play games with you," Theron said.

"Just like you had more important things to do than take care of your family that night?"

"Watch 'yer mouth boy."

"Like you were watching that poor defenseless grandson of yours? What was it really, Theron? Why were you really working so late that night, and don't give me this bull about benefitting your son. You were trying to get some extra money this year for something *you* wanted. Something you felt you needed so badly you let your family die."

The farmer picked up the sword. His breath hissing through his teeth, puffing his cheeks and rocking his shoulders back. "I didn't let them die. It wasn't me!"

"What did you trade them for, Theron? Some fool's dream? You didn't give a damn about your son; it was all about you. You wanted to be the grandfather of a magistrate. You wanted to be the big man, didn't you? And you'd do anything to make that dream come true. You worked late. You weren't there. You were out in the field when it came, because of your dream, your desires. Is that why you let your son die? You never cared about them at all. Did you? All you care about is yourself."

The farmer charged Hadrian with the sword in both hands and swung at him. Hadrian stepped aside and the wild swing missed, but the momentum carried the farmer around and he fell to the dirt.

"You let them die Theron. You weren't there like a man is supposed to be. A man is supposed to protect his family, but what were you doing? You were out in the fields working on what *you* wanted. What *you* had to have."

Theron got up and charged again. Once more Hadrian stepped aside. This time Theron managed to remain standing and delivered more wild swings. Hadrian drew his short sword and deflected the blows. The old farmer was in a rage now and struck out maniacally, swinging the sword like an axe with single, hacking strokes that stole his balance. Soon Hadrian did not need to parry anymore and merely sidestepped out of the way. Theron's face grew redder with each miss. Tears filled his eyes. At last, the old man collapsed to the dirt, frustrated and exhausted.

"It wasn't me that killed them," he yelled. "It was *her!* She left the light on. She left the door open."

"No, Theron," Hadrian took the sword from the farmer's limp hands, "Thrace didn't kill your family and neither did you—the beast did." He slipped his sword back in its sheath. "You can't blame her for leaving a door open. She didn't know what was coming. None of you did. Had you known, you would have been there. Had your family known, they would have put out the light. The sooner you stop blaming innocent people and start trying to fix the problem the better off everyone will be.

"Theron, that weapon of yours may be mighty sharp, but what good is a sharp weapon when you can't hit anything, or worse, hit the wrong target. You don't win battles with hate. Anger and hate can make you brave, make you strong, but they also make you stupid. You end up tripping over your own two feet." The fighter stared down at the old man. "I think that's enough for today's lesson."

Royce and Esrahaddon returned less than an hour before sunset and found a parade of animals driving up the road. It looked like every animal in the village was on the move and most of the people were out along the edges with sticks and bells, pots and spoons banging away, herding the animals up the hill toward the manor house. Sheep and cows followed each other fine enough, but the pigs were a problem and Royce spotted Pearl with her stick, masterfully bringing up the rear.

Rose McDern, the smithy's wife, was the first to spot them and suddenly Royce heard the words, "He's back!" excitedly repeated amongst the villagers.

"What's going on?" Royce asked Pearl, purposely avoiding the adults.

"Mov'n the critters to the castle. We all stay'n there tonight they says."

"Do you know where Hadrian is?" You remember, the man I arrived with? Thrace was riding with him?"

"The castle," Pearl told him and narrowed her eyes at the thief. "You really catch a pig in the dark?"

Royce looked at her, puzzled. Just then, a pig darted up the road and the girl was off after it, waving her long switch in the air.

The castle of the lord of Westbank was a typical motte and bailey fortress with the great manor house built on a steep man-made hill, surrounded by a wall of sharp tipped wooden logs that enclosed the outbuildings. A heavy gate barred the entrance. A half-hearted attempt at a moat ringed it, but amounted to nothing more than a shallow ditch. Cut trees left about forty yards of sharpened stumps in all directions.

A group of men worked at the tree line cutting pines. Royce was still a bit vague on names but he recognized Vince Griffin and Russell Bothwick working a dual handled saw. Tad Bothwick along with a few other boys raced around, trimming branches with axes and hatches. Three girls tied the branches into bundles and stacked them on a wagon. Dillon McDern and his sons used his oxen to haul the logs up the hill to the castle where more men labored to cut and split the wood.

He found Hadrian splitting logs near the stockade gate. He was naked to the waist except for the small silver medallion that dangled from his neck as he bent forward to place another wedge. He had a solid sweat worked up along with a sizeable pile of wood.

"Been meddling, have you?" Royce asked, looking around at the hive of activity.

"You must admit they didn't have much in the way of a defense plan," the fighter said, pausing to wipe the sweat from his forehead.

Royce smiled at him, "You just can't help yourself, can you?"

"And you? Did you find the doorknob?"

Hadrian picked up a jug and quickly downed several swallows, drinking so quickly some of the water dripped down his chin. He poured some in his palm and rinsed his face, running his fingers through his hair.

"I didn't even get close enough to see a door."

"Well, look on the bright side," Hadrian smiled, "at least you weren't captured and condemned to death this time."

"That's the bright side?"

"What can I say? I'm a glass half-full kinda guy."

"There he is," Russell Bothwick shouted, pointing, "that's Royce over there."

"What's going on?" Royce asked as throngs of people suddenly moved toward him from the field and the castle interior.

"I mentioned that you saw the thing and now they want to know what it looks like," Hadrian explained. "What did you think? They were coming to lynch you?"

He shrugged. "What can I say? I'm a glass half-empty kinda guy."

"Half empty?" Hadrian chuckled, "was there ever any drink in that glass?"

Royce was still scowling at Hadrian when the villagers crowded around them. The women wore kerchiefs over their hair, dark and damp where they crossed their foreheads, their sleeves rolled up, faces smudged with dirt. Most of the men, like Hadrian, were topless, wood shavings and pine needles sticking to their skin.

"Did you see it?" Dillon asked. "Did you really get a look at it?"

"Yes," Royce replied and several people murmured.

"What did it look like?" Deacon Tomas asked. The priest stood out from the crowd looking fresh, clean, and rested.

"Did it have wings?" Russell asked.

"Did it have claws?" Tad asked.

"How big was it?" Vince Griffin asked.

"Let the man answer!" Dillon thundered and the rest quieted.

"It does have wings and claws. I saw it only briefly because it was flying above the trees. I caught sight of it through a small opening in the leaves, but what I saw was long, like a snake, or lizard, with wings and two legs that—that were still clutching Mae Drundel."

"A lizard with wings?" Dillon repeated.

"A dragon." A woman declared. "That's what it is. It's a dragon!"

"That's right," Russell said. "That's what a winged lizard is."

"There's suppose to be a weak spot in their armor near the armpit, or whatever a dragon has for an armpit," a woman with a particularly dirty nose explained. "I heard an archer once killed a dragon in mid-flight by hitting him there."

"I heard you weaken a dragon by stealing its treasure horde," a bald-headed man told them all. "There was a tale where this prince was trapped in the lair of a dragon and he threw all the treasure into the sea and it weakened the beast so much the prince was able to kill him by stabbing him in the eye."

"I heard that dragons were immortal and couldn't be killed," Rose McDern said.

"It's not a dragon," Esrahaddon said with a tone of disgust. He stepped out from the crowd and they turned to face him.

"Why do you say that?" Vince Griffin asked.

"Because it isn't," he replied confidently. "If it was a dragon whose wrath you had incurred, this village would have been wiped from the face of Elan months ago. Dragons are very intelligent beings, far more than you or even I and more powerful than we can begin to comprehend. No, Mrs. Brockton, no archer ever killed a dragon by shooting him in a soft spot with an arrow. And no, Mr. Goodman stealing a dragon's treasure doesn't weaken it. In fact, dragons don't have treasures. What exactly would a dragon do with gold or gems? Do you think there is a dragon store somewhere? Dragons don't believe in possessions, unless you count memories, strength, and honor as possessions."

"But that's what he said he saw," Vince countered.

The wizard sighed. "He said he saw a snake or lizard with long dark wings and two legs. That should have been your first clue." The wizard turned to Pearl who had finished driving the last of the pigs into the courtyard of the castle and had run back out to join the crowd. "Tell me, Pearl, how many legs does a dragon have?"

"Four," the child said without thinking.

"Exactly, this is not a dragon."

"Then what is it?" Russell asked.

"A Gilarabrywn," Esrahaddon replied casually.

"A—a what?"

"Gil...lar...ah...brin," the wizard pronounced slowly, mouthing the syllables carefully. "Gilarabrywn, a magical creature."

"What does that mean? Does it cast spells like a witch?"

"No, it means it's unnatural. It wasn't born—it was created, conjured if you will."

"That's just crazy," Russell said. "How gullible do you think we are? This thingamabob—whatever you called it—killed dozens of people. It ain't no made up thing."

"No, wait," Deacon Tomas intervened, waving to them from deep in the sea of villagers. They backed away to reveal the cleric standing with his hand still up in the air, his eyes thoughtful. "There *was* a beast known as the Gilarabrywn. I learned about it in seminary. In the Great Elven Wars they were tools of the Erivan Empire, beasts of war, terrible things that devastated the landscape and slaughtered thousands. There are accounts of them laying waste to cities and whole armies. No weapon could harm them."

"You know your history well, deacon," Esrahaddon complimented. "The Gilarabrywn were devastating instruments of war—intelligent, powerful, silent killers from the sky."

"How could such a thing still be alive after so long?" Russell asked.

"They aren't natural. They can't die a normal death because they really aren't alive as we understand living to be."

"I think we're going to need more wood," Hadrian muttered.

As the sun set, the farmers provisioned the castle for the night. The children and women gathered beneath the great beams of the manor house while the men worked to the last light of day building the woodpiles. Hadrian had organized effective teams for cutting, dragging, and tying the stacks such that by nightfall they had six great piles surrounding the walls and one in the center of the yard itself. They doused the piles in oil and animal fat to make the lighting faster. It was going to be a long night and they did not want the fires to burn out, nor would it do to have them lit too late.

"Hadrian!" Thrace yelled as she ran frantically through the courtyard.

"Thrace," Hadrian said, working to the last minute on the courtyard woodpile. "It's dark. You should be in the house."

"My father's not here," she cried. "I've looked everywhere around the castle. No one saw him come in. He must still be at home. He's out there alone, and if he's the only one alone tonight—"

"Royce!" Hadrian shouted, but it was unnecessary as Royce was already leading their saddled horses out of the stable.

"She found me first," the thief said, handing him Millie's reins.

"That damn fool," Hadrian said grabbing his shirt and weapons and pulling himself up on the horse. "I told him about coming to the castle."

"So did I," she said, her face a mask of fear.

"Don't worry Thrace. We'll bring him back safe."

They spurred the animals and rode out the gate at a gallop.

Theron sat in the ruins of his house on a wooden chair. A small fire burned in a shallow pit just outside the doorway. The sky was finally dark and he could see stars. He listened to the night music of the crickets and frogs. A distant owl began its hunt. The fire snapped and popped and beneath it all, the distant roaring of the falls. Mosquitoes entered the undefended house. They swarmed, landed, and bit. The old man let them. He sat as he had every night, staring silently at memories.

His eyes settled on the cradle. Theron remembered building the little rocker for his first son. He and Addie decided to name their firstborn Hickory—a good, strong, durable wood. Theron had hunted the forest for the perfect hickory tree and found it one day on a hill, bathed in sunlight as if the gods had marked it. Each night Theron had carefully crafted the cradle and finished the wood so it would last. All five of his children had slept in it. Hickory died there before his first birthday from a sickness for which there was no name. All of his sons died young, except for Thad, who had grown to be a fine man. He had married a sweet girl named Emma and when she had given birth to his grandson, they had named him Hickory. Theron remembered thinking how it seemed as if the world was finally trying to make up for the hardships in his life, that somehow the unwarranted punishment of his firstborn's premature death was healed through the life of his first grandson. But it was all gone now. All he had left was the blood-sprayed bed of five dead children.

Behind the cradle lay one of Addie's two dresses. It was a terrible, ugly thing, stained and torn, but to his watering eyes it looked beautiful. She had been a good wife. For more than thirty years she had followed him from one dismal town to the next as he had tried to find a place he could call his own. They had never had much, and many times, they had gone hungry, and on more than one occasion nearly froze to death. In all that time, he had never heard her complain. She had mended his clothes and his broken bones, made his meals and looked after him when he was sick. She had always been too thin, giving the biggest portions of each meal to him and their children. Her clothes had been the worst in the family. She never found time to mend them. She had been a good wife and Theron could not remember ever having said he loved her. It had never seemed important before. The beast had taken her too, plucked her from the path between the village and the farm. Thad's Emma had filled the void, making it easy to move on. He had avoided thinking about her by staying focused on the goal, but now the goal was dead, and his house had caved in.

What must it have been like for them when the beast came? Were they alive when it took them? Did they suffer? The thoughts tormented the farmer as the sounds of the crickets died.

He stood up his scythe in his hands, preparing to meet the darkness, when he heard the reason for the interruption of the night noises. Horses thundered up the trail and the two men Thrace hired entered the light of the campfire in a rush.

❧

"Theron!" Hadrian shouted as he and Royce arrived in the yard of the Wood's farm. The sun was down. The light gone, and the old man had a welcome fire burning—only not for them. "Let's go. We've got to get back to the castle."

"You go back," the old man growled. "I didn't ask you to come here. This is my home and I'm staying."

"Your daughter needs you. Now get up on this horse. We don't have much time."

"I'm not going anywhere. She's fine. She's with the Bothwicks. They'll take good care of her. Now get off my land!"

Hadrian dismounted and marched up to the farmer who stood his ground like a rooted tree.

"My god, you're a stubborn ass. Now either you're going to get on that horse or I'll put you on it."

"Then you'll have to put me on it," he said putting his scythe down and folding his arms across his chest.

Hadrian looked over his shoulder at Royce who sat silently on Mouse. "Why aren't you helping?"

"It's really not my area of expertise. Now if you want him dead—that I can do."

Hadrian sighed. "Please get on the horse. You're going to get us all killed staying out here."

"Like I said, I never asked you to come."

"Damn," Hadrian cursed as he removed his weapons and hooked them on the saddle of his horse.

"Careful," Royce leaned over and told him. "He's old, but he looks tough."

Hadrian ran full tilt at the old farmer and tackled him to the ground. Theron was larger than Hadrian with powerful arms and hands made strong by years of unending work, but Hadrian was fast and agile. The two grappled in a wrestling match that had them rolling in the dirt grunting as each tried to get the advantage.

"This is so stupid," Hadrian muttered, getting to his feet. "If you would just get on the horse."

"You get on the horse. Get out of here and leave me alone!" Theron yelled at them as he struggled to catch his breath, standing bent over, hands resting on his knees.

"Maybe you can help me this time?" Hadrian said to Royce.

Royce rolled his eyes and dismounted. "I didn't expect you'd have so much trouble."

"It's not easy to subdue a person bigger than you and not hurt him in the process."

"Well, I think I found your problem then. Why don't we try hurting him?"

When they turned back to face Theron, the farmer had a good size stick in his hand and a determined look in his eyes.

Hadrian sighed, "I don't think we have a choice."

"Daddy!" Thrace shouted, running into the ring of firelight, her face streaked with tears. "Daddy," she cried again and reaching the old man, threw her arms around him.

"Thrace, what are you doing here?" Theron yelled. "It's not safe."

"I came to get you."

"I'm staying here," he pulled his daughter off and pushed her away. "Now you take your hired thugs and get back to the Bothwicks right now. You hear me?"

"No." Thrace cried at him, her arms raised, still reaching. "I won't leave you."

"Thrace," he bellowed, his huge frame towering over her, "I am your father and you will do as I say!"

"No!" she shouted back at him, the firelight shining on her wet cheeks. "I won't leave you to die. You can whip me if you want, but you'll have to come back to the castle to do it."

"You stupid little fool," he cursed. "You're gonna get yourself killed. Don't you know that?"

"I DON'T CARE!" her voice ran shrill, her hands crushed into fists, arms punched down at her sides. "What reason do I have to live if my own father—the only person I have left in the world—hates me so much he would rather die than look at me."

Theron stood stunned.

"At first," she began in a quivering voice, "I thought you wanted to make sure no one else was killed, and then I thought maybe it was—I don't know—to put their souls to rest. Then I thought you wanted revenge. Maybe the hate was eating you up. Maybe you had to see it killed—but none of that is true. You just want to die. You hate yourself—you hate me. There's nothing in this world for you anymore, nothing you care about."

"I don't hate you," Theron said.

"You do. You do because it was my fault. I know what they meant to you—and I wake up every morning with that." She wiped the tears enough to see. "If it was me, it would have been just like it was with Mom—you would have driven a stick into Stony Hill with my name on it, and the next day gone back to work. You would have driven the plow and thanked Maribor for his kindness in sparing your son. I should have been the one to die, but I can't change what happened and your death won't bring him back. Nothing will. Still, if all I can do now—if all that's left for me—is to die here with you, then that's what I'll do. I won't leave you, Daddy. I can't. I just can't." She fell to her knees exhausted and in a fragile voice said, "We'll all be together again at least."

Then as if in response to her words, the wood around them went silent once more. This time the crickets and frogs stopped so abruptly the silence seemed suddenly loud.

"No," Theron said shaking his head. He looked up at the night sky. "NO!"

The farmer grabbed his daughter and lifted her up. "We're going." He turned. "Help us."

Hadrian pulled Millie around. "Up both of you." Millie stomped her hooves and started to pull and twist, nostrils flaring, ears twitching. Hadrian gripped her by the bit and held tight.

Theron mounted the horse and pulled Thrace up in front of him then with a swift kick, he sent Millie racing up the trail back toward the village. Royce leapt on the back of Mouse and throwing out a hand, swung Hadrian up behind him even as he sent the horse galloping into the night.

The horses needed no urging as they ran full out with the sweat of fear dampening their coats. Their hooves thundered, pounding the earth like violent drum beats. The path ahead was only slightly lighter than the rest of the wood and for Hadrian it was often a blur as the wind drew tears from his eyes.

"Above us!" Royce shouted. Overhead they heard a rush of movement in the leaves.

The horses made a jarring turn into the thick of the wood. Invisible branches, leaves, and pine boughs slapped them, whipped them, beat them. The animals raced in blind panic. They drove through the underbrush glancing off tree trunks, bouncing by branches. Hadrian felt Royce duck and mimicked him.

Thrump. Thrump. Thrump.

He could hear a slow beating overhead, a dull, deep pumping. A blast of wind came from above, a massive downdraft of air. Along with it came the frightening sound of cracking, snapping, splintering. The treetops shattered and exploded.

"Log!" Royce shouted as the horses jumped.

Hadrian kept his seat only by virtue of Royce's agile grab. In the darkness, he heard Thrace scream, a grunt, and a sound like an axe handle hitting wood. The thief reined Mouse hard, wrestling with her, pulling the animal's head around as she reared and snorted. Ahead, Hadrian could hear Millie galloping.

"What's going on?" Hadrian asked.

"They fell," Royce growled.

"I can't see them." Hadrian leapt down.

"In the thickets, there to your right," Royce said, climbing off Mouse who was in a panic, thrashing her head back and forth.

"Here," Theron said, his voice labored, "over here."

The farmer stood over his daughter. She lay unconscious, sprawled and twisted. Blood dripped from her nose and mouth.

"She hit a branch," Theron said, his voice was shaking, frightened. "I—I didn't see the log."

"Get her on my horse," Royce commanded. "Move, Theron, take Mouse, both of you ride for the manor. We're close. You can see the light of the bonfires burning."

The farmer made no protest. He climbed on Mouse who was still stomping and snorting. Hadrian picked up Thrace. A patch of moonlight showed a dark blemish on her face, a long wide mark. He lifted. Her head fell back limp, her arms and legs dangled free. She felt dead. He handed her to Theron who cradled his daughter to his chest and held her tight. Royce let loose the bit and the horse thundered off racing for the open field, leaving Royce and Hadrian behind.

"Think Millie's around?" Hadrian whispered.

"I think Millie is already an appetizer."

"I suppose the good news is that she bought Thrace and Theron safe passage."

They slowly moved to the edge of the wood. They were very close to where Dillon and his boys were hauling logs earlier that day. They could see three of the six bonfires blazing away, illuminating the field.

"What about us?" Royce asked.

"Do you think the Gilarabrywn knows we're still in here?"

"Esrahaddon said it was intelligent, so I presume it can count."

"Then it will come back and find us. We have to reach the castle. The distance across the open is about—what? Two hundred feet?"

"About that," Royce confirmed.

"I guess we can hope it's still munching on Millie. Ready?"

"Run spread out so it can't get both of us. Go." The grass was slick with dew and filled with stumps and pits. Hadrian only got a dozen yards before falling on his face.

"Stay behind me," Royce told him.

"I thought we were spreading out?"

"That's before I remembered you're blind."

They ran again, dodging in and out, as Royce picked the path up the hillside. They were nearly halfway across when they heard the bellows again.

Thrump. Thrump. Thrump.

The sound rushed toward them. Looking up, Hadrian saw something dark pass across the face of the rising moon, a serpent with bat-like wings gliding, arcing, circling like a hawk hunting mice in a field.

The bellows stopped.

"It's diving!" Royce shouted.

A massive burst of wind blew them to the ground. The bonfires instantly snuffed out. A second later, a loud rumble shook the earth and a monolithic wall of green fire exploded in a great ring, surrounding the entire hill. Astounding flames, thirty feet high, flashed up like trees of light spewing intense heat.

No longer having any trouble seeing his way, Hadrian jumped to his feet and sped to the gate, Royce on his heels. Behind them the flames roared. Above them they heard a chilling scream.

Dillon, Vince, and Russell slammed the gate shut the instant they were inside. The bonfire in the courtyard, which had been unlit so far, startled everyone as it exploded into a brilliant blue-green flame, reaching like a pillar into the sky. Once more from the darkness above, the Gilarabrywn screamed at them.

The emerald inferno slowly burned down. The flames lost their green color and diminished until only natural flames remained. The fires crackled and hissed, sending storms of sparks skyward. The men in the courtyard stared upward, but there were no further signs of the beast, only darkness and the distant sound of crickets.

Chapter 6

THE CONTEST

I CAN ASSURE YOU, your Royal Majesty," Arista said in her most congenial voice, "there will be no change in foreign or domestic policy under King Alric's reign. He will continue to pursue the same agenda as our father—upholding the dignity and honor of the House of Essendon. Melengar will continue to remain your friendly neighbor to the west."

Arista stood before the King of Dunmore in her mother's best dress—the stunning silver silk gown. Forty buttons lined the sleeves. Dozens of feet of crushed velvet trimmed the embroidered bodice and full skirt. The rounded neckline clung to her shoulders. She stood erect, chin high, eyes forward, hands folded.

King Roswort, who sat on his throne wearing furs that looked to have come from wolves, drained his cup and belched. He was short and immensely fat. His round pudgy face sagged under its own weight, gathering at the bottom and forming three full chins. His eyes were half closed, his lips wet, and she was certain she could see a bit of spittle dribbling down through the folds of his neck. His wife Freda sat beside him. She, too, was a large woman, but thin by comparison. Whereas the King seeped liquid, she was dry as a desert—in both looks and manner.

The throne room was small with a wooden floor and beams that supported a lofty cathedral ceiling. Heads of stags and moose protruded from the walls, each covered in enough dust to make their fur look gray. Near the door stood the famous nine-foot stuffed bear named Oswald, its claws up, mouth open, snarling. Dunmore legend held that Oswald killed five knights and an unknown number of peasants before King Ogden—King Roswort's grandfather—slew him with nothing more than a dagger. That was seventy years ago when Glamrendor was just a frontier fort and Dunmore little more than a forest with trails. Roswort himself could not claim such glory. He had abandoned the hunting traditions of his sires in favor of courtly life, and it showed.

The king held up his cup and shook it.

Arista waited and the king yawned. Somewhere behind her, loud heels crossed the throne room. There was a muttering, then the heels again, followed by the snapping of fingers. Finally, a figure approached the dais, thin and delicate—an elf. He was dressed in a rough woolen uniform of dull brown. Around his neck was a heavy iron collar that was riveted in place. He approached with a pitcher and filled the king's cup then backed away. The king drank, tipping the cup too high, wine dribbling down, leaving a faint pink line and a droplet dangling from his stubbly whiskers. He belched again, this time more loudly, and sighed with contentment. The king looked back at Arista.

"But what about this matter of Braga's death?" Roswort asked. "Do you have evidence to show that he was involved in this so-called conspiracy?"

"He tried to kill me."

"Yes, so you say, but even if he did, he had good reason it seems. Braga was a good and devout Nyphron and you are—after all—a witch."

Arista squeezed her hands together. It was not for the first time and her fingers were starting to ache. "Forgive me, your Royal Majesty, but I fear you may be misinformed on that subject."

"Misinformed? I have—" he coughed, coughed again, then spat on the floor beside the throne. Freda glared rigidly at the elf until he stepped over and wiped it up with the bottom of his tunic.

"I have very good information gatherers," the king went on, "who tell me both Braga and Bishop Saldur brought you to trial to answer charges of witchcraft and the murder of your father. Immediately afterwards Braga was dead, decapitated, and accused of the very charges he leveled against you. Now you come before us as Ambassador of Melengar—a woman. I fear this is all too convenient for my tastes."

"Braga also accused me of killing his Royal Majesty King Alric, who appointed me to this office, or do you also deny his existence?"

The royal eyebrows rose. "You are young," he said coldly. "This is your first audience as ambassador. I will ignore your affront—this time. Insult me again, and I will have you expelled from my kingdom."

Arista bowed her head silently.

"It does not bode well with us that the throne of Melengar was taken by blood. Nor that House Essendon pays only lip-service to the church. Also, your kingdom's tolerance for elves is disgusting. You let the vile beasts run free. Novron never meant for this to be. The church teaches us that the elf is a disease. They must be broken into service or vanquished altogether. They are like rats and Melengar is the woodpile next door. Yes, I have no doubt that Alric will continue his father's policies. Both were born with blinders.

Changes are coming and I can already see that Melengar is too foolish to bend with the wind. All the better for Dunmore I think."

Arista opened her mouth, but the king held up a finger.

"This interview is over. Go back to your brother and tell him we fulfilled the favor of seeing you and were not impressed."

The king and queen stood together and walked out through the rear archway, leaving Arista facing two empty wooden chairs. The elf, which stood nearby, watched her intently but said nothing. She half considered going on with the rest of her prepared speech. The level of futility would remain; empty thrones could not be any less responsive and most certainly would be more polite.

She sighed. Her shoulders drooped. *Could it have gone any worse?* She turned and walked out, listening to her beautiful dress rustling.

She stepped outside the castle gate and looked down at the city. Deep baked ruts scarred the uneven dirt roads, so rough and littered with rocks they appeared as dry riverbeds. Sun bleached the tight rows of similarly framed wooden buildings to a pale gray. Most of the residents wore drab colors, clothes made of undyed wool or linen. Dozens of people with weary faces sat on corners or wandered about aimlessly with hands out. They appeared invisible to those walking by. It was Arista's first visit to Glamrendor, the capital of Dunmore. She shook her head and muttered softly, "We have seen you too."

Despite the meager offerings, the city was bustling, but she suspected few of those rushing by were locals. It was easy to tell the difference. Those from out of town wore shoes. Wagons, carriages, coaches, and horses flowed through the center of the capital that morning, all heading east. The church opened the contest to all comers, common and noble alike. It was their shot at glory, wealth, and fame.

Her own coach waited, flying the Melengar falcon, and Hilfred stood holding the door. Bernice sat inside with a tray of sweets on her lap and a smile on her lips. "How did it go, my dear? Were you impressive?"

"No, I wasn't impressive, but we are also not at war, so I should thank Maribor for that kindness." She sat opposite Bernice making certain to pull the full length of her gown inside the door before Hilfred closed it.

"Have a gingerbread man?" Bernice asked holding up the tray with a look of pity that included pushing out her lower lip. "He is bound to steal the pain away."

"Where is Sauly?" She asked eyeing the man-shaped cookies.

"He said he had some things to speak to the archbishop about and would ride in his grace's coach. He hoped you did not mind."

Arista did not mind and only wished Bernice had joined him. She was tired of the constant company and missed the solitude of her tower. She took a cookie and felt the carriage rock as Hilfred climbed up with the driver. The coach lurched and they were off, bouncing over the rutted road.

"These are stale," Arista said with a mouthful of gingerbread that was hard and sandy.

Bernice looked horrified. "I'm so sorry."

"Where did you get them?"

"A little bakery up—" she started to point out the window, but the movement of the carriage confused her. She looked around then gave up and put her hand down again. "Oh, I don't know now, but it was a very nice shop and I thought you might need—you know— something to help you feel better after the meeting."

"*Need* them?"

Bernice nodded her head with a forced smile and reaching out she patted the princess' hand and said, "It's not your fault dear. It really isn't fair of his majesty to put you in this position."

"I should stay in Medford and receive suitors," Arista guessed.

"Exactly. This just isn't right."

"Neither is this cookie." She placed the gingerbread man back on the tray minus the leg she had bitten off. She then sat raking her tongue across her upper teeth like a cat with hair in its mouth.

"At least his Royal Majesty must have been impressed by how you looked," Bernice said, eyeing her with pride. "You're beautiful."

Arista gave her a side-long glance. "The dress is beautiful."

"Of course, it is but—"

"Oh dear Maribor!" Arista cut her off as she glanced out the window. "How many are there now? It will be like traveling with an army."

As the carriage reached the end of town, she saw the masses. There could be as many as three-hundred men standing behind the banners of the Nyphron Church. They all waited in a single line, but they could not have been more different—the muscular, scrawny, tall, and short. All ranks were represented: knights, soldiers, nobles, and peasants. Some wore armor, some silk, others linen or wool. They sat on chargers, draft horses, ponies, mules, or inside coaches, open-air carriages, wagons, or buckboards. They appeared a strange and unlikely assortment, but each bore the same smile of expectation and excitement, all eyes looking east.

Arista's first official session as ambassador was finished. As bad as it was, it was over. With Sauly gone, she could shelve thoughts of church and state, guilt and blame. Stress that had smothered her for days evaporated and at last she was able to feel the growing excitement that bubbled all around her.

From everywhere people rushed to join the growing train. Some arrived with nothing but a small linen bag tucked under one arm, while others led their own personal train of packhorses.

There were those who commanded multiple wagons loaded with tents, food, and clothes. One well-dressed merchant carried velvet upholstered chairs and a canopy bed on top of a wagon.

A loud banging hammered the roof of the coach, shocking both of them. Gingerbread men flew. "Oh dear!" Bernice gasped. A moment later Mauvin Pickering's head appeared in the window, looking down and inside from the back of his horse so that his dark hair hung wildly.

"So how did it go?" he grinned mischievously. "Do I need to prepare for war?"

Arista scowled.

"That good, huh?" Mauvin went on heedless of the commotion he had caused. "We'll talk later. I have to find Fanen before he starts dueling someone. Hiya Hilfred. This is going to be great. When was the last time we were all camping together? See ya."

Bernice was fanning herself with both hands, her eyes staring up at the roof of the coach, her mouth slack. Seeing her and the little army of gingerbread men scattered on the benches, in the curtains, on the floor, and in her lap, Arista could not help but smile.

"You were right, Bernice. The cookies did cheer me up."

"See him?" Fanen pointed to the man in the brown suede doublet. "That's Sir Enden, possibly the greatest living knight after Sir Breckton."

After another day's travel that left her drowsy, Arista was at the Pickering's camp, hiding from Bernice. The two boys shared an elegant, single-peak tent of alternating gold and green stripes, which they pitched at the eastern edge of the main camp. The three sat out front under the scallop-edged canopy held up by two tall wooden poles. On the left flew the gold falcon on the red field of the House of Essendon, on the right the gold sword on the green field, of the House of Pickering. It was a modest camp compared to most of the nobles. Some looked like small castles and took hours for a team of servants to erect. The Pickerings traveled lightly, carrying everything they needed on their stallions and two packhorses. They did not have tables or chairs and Arista sprawled in a modest gown on a sheet of canvas. If Bernice saw, the old woman would have a heart attack.

Arista did not mind. She thought it was wonderful to lie back and stretch out under the sky. It reminded her of Summersrule when they were kids. At night the adults would dance and the children would lie on the south hill at Drondil Fields counting the falling stars and fireflies. It was all of them then—Mauvin, Fanen, Alric, even Lenare—back before the Pickering's sister became too much of a lady. She remembered feeling the cool night breeze rush over her, the sensation of grass on her bare feet, the vast spray of stars above, and the faint melody of the band as it played *Calide Portmore*, the Galilin folk song.

"And there, see the large man in the green tunic? That's Sir Gravin; he's a quester. He does most of his work for the Church of Nyphron. You know recovering artifacts, slaying monsters, those kinds of things. He's known to be one of the greatest adventurers alive. He's from Vernes, that's all the way down near Delgos."

"I know where Vernes is, Fanen," Arista replied.

"That's right, you have to know all that stuff now, don't you?" Mauvin said. "Your high exulted ambassadorship." The elder Pickering offered an elaborate seated bow.

"Laugh now—just you wait," she told him. "You'll get yours—one day you'll be marquis. Then it won't be all fun and games. You'll have responsibilities, mister."

"I won't," Fanen said sadly.

If not for him being three years younger, Fanen could be Mauvin's twin. Both had the dashing Pickering features, sharp angled faces, dark thick hair, bright white teeth, and sweeping shoulders that tapered to narrow, athletic waists. Fanen was just leaner and a bit shorter and unlike Mauvin, whose hair was always a frightful mess, Fanen kept his neatly combed.

"That's why you need to win this thing," Mauvin told his brother. "And, of course, you will, because you're a Pickering, and Pickerings never fail. Look at that guy over there. He doesn't stand a chance."

Arista did not bother sitting up. He had been doing this all night—pointing out people and explaining how he could tell by the way they walked or wore their sword that Fanen could best them. She had no doubt he was right; she was just tired of hearing it.

"What is the prize for this contest?" she asked.

"They haven't said yet," Fanen muttered.

"Gold most likely," Mauvin replied, "in the form of some award, but that's not what makes it valuable. It's the prestige. Once Fanen takes this trophy he will have a name; well, he already has the Pickering name, but he hasn't any titles yet. Once he does, opportunities will open up for him. Of course, it could be land. Then he'd be set."

"I hope so; I certainly don't want to end up at a monastery."

"Do you still write poetry, Fanen?" Arista asked.

"I haven't—in a while."

"It was good, what I remember at least. You used to write all the time. What happened?"

"He learned the poetry of the sword. It will serve him far better than the pen," Mauvin answered for him.

"Who's that?" Fanen asked, pointing to the west.

"That's Rentinual," Mauvin replied, "the self-proclaimed genius. Get this. He's brought this thing, a huge contraption with him."

"Why?"

"He says it's for the contest."

"What is it?"

Mauvin shrugged. "Don't know, but it's big. He keeps it covered under a tarp and wails like a girl whenever the wagon team bounces it through a rut."

"Say, isn't that Prince Rudolf?"

"Where?" Arista popped her head up, moving to her elbows.

Mauvin chuckled. "Just kidding. Alric told us about—your misunderstanding."

"Have you met Rudolf?" she asked.

"Actually I have," Mauvin said. "The man has donkeys wondering why they got stuck with him as a namesake." It took a second then Fanen and Arista broke into laughter, dragging Mauvin with them. "He's a royal git that's certain, and I'd have been plenty upset if I thought I was facing a life kissing that ass. Honestly Arista, I'm surprised you didn't turn Alric into a toad or something."

Arista stopped laughing. "What?"

"You know, put a hex on him. A week as a frog would—what's wrong?"

"Nothing," she said, lying back down and turning onto her stomach.

"Hey—look—I didn't mean anything."

"It's okay," she lied.

"It was just a joke."

"Your first joke was better."

"Arista, I know you're not a witch."

A long uncomfortable silence followed.

"I'm sorry," Mauvin offered.

"Took you long enough," she said.

"It could have been worse," Fanen spoke up, "Alric could have forced you to marry Mauvin."

"That's really sick," Arista said, rolling over and sitting up. Mauvin looked at her with hurt, surprised eyes. She shook her head.

"I just meant it would be like marrying a brother. I've always thought of you all as family."

"Don't tell Denek," Mauvin replied, "he's had a crush on you for years."

"Seriously?"

"Oh, and don't tell him I told you either. Uh—better yet just forget I said that."

"What about those two?" Fanen asked abruptly, pointing toward a massive red and black striped tent from which two men just exited. One was huge with a wild red moustache and beard. He wore a sleeveless scarlet tunic with a green draped sash and a metal cap with several dents in it. The other man was tall and thin with long black hair and a short trimmed beard. He was dressed in a red cassock and black cape with the symbol of a broken crown on his chest.

"I don't think you want to mess with either of them," Mauvin finally said. "That's Lord Rufus of Trent, Warlord of Lingard, a clan leader and veteran of dozens of battles against the wild men of Estrendor, not to mention being the hero of the battle of Vilan Hills."

"That's Rufus?" Fanen muttered.

"I've heard he's got the temperament of a shrew and the arm of a bear."

"Who's the other guy, the one with the broken crown standard?" Fanen asked pointing at the other man.

"That, my dear brother, is a sentinel and let's just hope this is the closest either of us ever get to one."

While Arista was watching the two men, she saw a silhouette appear against the light of the distant campfire—very short, with a long beard and puffy sleeves.

"By the way, I want to start early tomorrow, Fanen," his brother said. "I want to get out ahead of the train. I'm tired of eating dust."

"Anyone know exactly where we are going?" Fanen asked. "It feels like we are traveling to the end of the world."

Arista nodded. "I heard Sauly talking about it with the archbishop. I think it is a little village called Dahlgren."

She looked back trying to find the figure once more, but it was gone.

Chapter 7

OF ELVES AND MEN

THRACE LAY ON the margrave's bed in the manor house, her head carefully wrapped in strips of cloth. Her hair was bunched and snarled, blond strands slipping out between the bandages. Purple and yellow bruises swelled around her eyes and nose. Her upper lip puffed up to twice its size and a line of dark dried blood ran its length. Thrace coughed and mumbled but never spoke, never opened her eyes.

And Theron never left her side.

Esrahaddon ordered Lena to boil feverfew leaves in a big pot of apple cider vinegar. She did as he instructed. Everyone did now. After last night, the residents of Dahlgren treated the cripple with newfound respect and looked at him with awe and a bit of fear. It was Tad Bothwick and Rose McDern who saw him raise the green fire that chased away the beast. No one said the word witch or wizard. No one had to. Soon the steam from the pot filled the room with a pungent flowery odor.

"I'm so sorry," Theron whispered to his daughter.

The coughing and mumbling had stopped and she lay still as death. He held her limp hand to his cheek, unsure if she could hear him. He had been saying that for hours, begging her to wake up. "I didn't mean it. I was just so angry. I'm sorry. Don't leave. Please come back to me."

He could still hear the sound in the dark of his daughter's cry cut horribly short by a muffled crack! If it had been a tree trunk or a thicker branch, Theron guessed she would have died instantly. As it was, she still might die.

No one but Lena and Esrahaddon dared enter the room that Theron filled with his grief. They all expected the worst. Blood had covered the girl's face and her father's shirt by the time they arrived at the manor. Skin white, lips an odd bluish hue, Thrace had not moved nor opened her eyes. Esrahaddon had whispered to her and instructed them to take the girl to the manor and keep her warm. It was the kind of thing one did for the dying, making them as comfortable as possible. Deacon Tomas had prayed for her and remained on hand to bless her departing soul.

In the last year, the village of Dahlgren had seen so many deaths. Not all were by the beast. There were the normal accidents, sicknesses, and in the winter, wolves hunted the area. There were also some unexplained disappearances. Often attributed to the beast, they could just as likely have been the result of getting lost in the forest or an accidental fall in the Nidwalden. In no more than a year, over half the village's population had perished or gone missing. Everyone knew someone who had died, and nearly every family had lost at least one member. The people of Dahlgren had grown accustomed to death. He was a nightly visitor, a guest at every breakfast table. They knew his face, the sound of his voice, the way he walked, his peculiar habits. He was always there. If it were not for the mess he left, they might neglect to notice him altogether. No one expected Thrace to survive.

The sun came up, casting a dull light into the room where Theron wept for his daughter. The last of his family was leaving him. Only now he realized how much she meant to him. Thoughts came, uninvited, to his mind. Time and time again it was she who always came for him. He remembered the night the beast attacked his farm, when he was coming home late. Only she had braved the darkness to search for him. It was Thrace, a young girl, little more than a child, who traveled alone halfway across Avryn, and spent her life savings to bring him help. Then last night, when his stubbornness kept him at the farm, she came to him in the darkness, running alone through the forest, ignoring the dangers. There was only one thought in her mind—to save him. She succeeded. She had deprived the beast of his flesh, but more than that. She had pulled him back into the world of the living. She had ripped the black veil away from his eyes and freed his heart from the weight of guilt, but the price had been her life.

Tears ran down his cheeks. They hung on his upper lip. He kissed his daughter's hand leaving a wet spot, an offering, an apology.

How could I have been so blind?

The even constant breaths his daughter took slowed with each inhale, less frequent, shorter than the one before. He listened to their descent, like the sound of footsteps receding, walking away, growing fainter, quieter.

He clutched her hand, kissing it repeatedly and rubbing it to his wet cheek. It felt like his heart was being ripped out through his chest.

At last, the regular pace of her breathing stopped.

Theron sobbed. "Oh, god."

"Daddy?" He jerked his head up. His daughter's eyes were open. She was looking at him. "Are you alright?" she whispered.

His mouth opened but he could not speak. His tears continued to flow, and like a barren bit of land seeing water for the first time in years, a smile of joy grew on his face.

OF ELVES AND MEN

ↄ

Swift clouds moved across a capricious sky as growing winds and the portents of a coming storm marked the new day. Royce sat on the rock ledge where the cliff met the river and the spray of the falls dampened the stone. His feet and legs were soaked from a morning spent trekking through the damp forest underbrush. His eyes stared out across the ridgeline of the falls at the promontory rock and the towering citadel that sat tantalizingly upon it. He thought that perhaps there might be a tunnel running under the river. He looked for an access in the trees, but found nothing. He was getting nowhere.

After almost two days, he was no closer to his goal. The tower still lay out of reach. Unless he could learn to swim the current, walk on water, or fly, he had no chance of traversing the gulf that lay between.

"They're over there right now, you know," Esrahaddon said.

Royce had forgotten about the wizard. He had arrived some time ago, mentioning only that Thrace survived, that she was awake and looked to make a full recovery. After that, he took a seat on a rock and spent the next hour or so staring across the river much as Royce had done all day.

"Who?"

"The elves. They're on their side of the river looking back at us. They can see us I suspect, even at this range. They are surprising like that. Most humans consider them inferior—lazy, filthy, uneducated creatures—but the fact is they are superior to humans in nearly every way. I suppose that's why humans are so quick to denounce them; they are unwilling to concede that they may be second best.

"Elves are truly remarkable. Just look at that tower. It's fluid and seamless as if growing right out of the rock. How elegant. How perfect. It fits into the landscape like a thing of nature, a natural wonder, only it isn't. They created it using skills and techniques that our best masons couldn't begin to understand. Just imagine how glorious their cities must be! What wonders those forests across the river must hold."

"So you have never crossed the river?" Royce asked.

"No man ever has, and no man is ever likely to. The moment a man touches that far shore, he will likely fall dead. The thread by which the fate of man hangs is a thin one indeed."

"How's that?"

Esrahaddon only smiled. "Did you know that no human army ever won a battle against the elves before the arrival of Novron? At that time, elves were our demons. The Great Library of Percepliquis had reams on it. Once we even thought they were gods. Their life span is so long that no one noticed them aging. Their death rites are so secret no human has ever seen an elven corpse.

"They were the firstborn, the Children of Ferrol, great and powerful. In combat, they were feared above all things. Sickness could be treated. Bears and wolves could be hunted and trapped. Storms and droughts prepared for—but nothing, nothing could stand before the elves. Their blades broke ours, their arrows pierced our armor, their shields were impenetrable, and, of course, they knew The Art. Imagine a sky darkened with a host of Gilarabrywn. And they are only one of their weapons. Even without all that, without The Art, their speed, eyesight, hearing, balance, and ancient skills are all beyond the abilities of man."

"If that's true how come they're over there and we're sitting here?"

"It is all because of Novron. He showed us their weaknesses. He taught mankind how to fight, how to defend, and he taught us the art of magic. Without it we were naked and helpless against them."

"I still don't see how we won," Royce challenged. "Even with that knowledge, they still seem to have the advantage."

"True, and in an even fight we would have lost, but it wasn't even. You see, elves live for a very long time. I don't think any human actually knows how long, but they live for many centuries at least. There may be elves right now watching us that remember what Novron looked like. But no people can live that long and reproduce quickly. Elves have few children and a birth for them is quite significant. Birth and death in the elven world are rare and holy things.

"You can imagine the devastation and misery it must have been during the wars. No matter how many battles they won against us, each time their numbers were fewer afterwards than before. While we humans recovered our losses in a generation, it would take a millennium for the elves. They were consumed, drowned if you will, in a flooding sea of humanity." Esrahaddon paused then added, "Only now Novron is gone. There will be no savior this time."

"This time?"

"What do you think keeps them over there? These are their lands. To us it seems eons ago, but to them it is just yesterday when they walked this side of the river. By now, their numbers have likely recovered."

"What keeps them on that side of the river then?"

"What keeps anyone from what they want? Fear. Fear of annihilation, fear that we would destroy them utterly, but Novron is dead."

"You mentioned that," Royce pointed out.

"I told you before that mankind has squandered the legacy of Novron, and it has done so at its own peril. Novron brought magic to man, but Novron is gone and the magic forgotten. We sit here like children, naked and unarmed. Mankind is inviting the wrath of a race so far beyond us they won't even hear our cries. The elves' ignorance of our weakness and this fragile agreement between the Erivan Empire and a dead emperor is all that remains of humanity's defense."

"It's a good thing they don't know then."

"That's just it," the wizard told him, "they are learning."

"The Gilarabrywn?"

Esrahaddon nodded. "According to Novron's decree, the banks of the river Nidwalden are ryin contita."

"Off limits to everyone," Royce roughly translated, garnering a faint smile from the wizard. "I can read and write too."

"Ah, a truly educated man. So as I was saying, the banks of the river Nidwalden are ryin contita."

A look of realization washed the thief's face. "Dahlgren is in violation of the treaty."

"Exactly. The decree also stipulates that elves are forbidden to take human lives, except should they cross the river. It says nothing about humans killed through benign actions. If I release a boulder it could roll anywhere, but odds are it will roll down hill. If houses and people are downhill it may destroy them, but it isn't me that is killing them, it is the boulder and the unfortunate fact they live downhill from it."

"And they are watching what we do, how we deal with it. They are sizing up our strengths and weaknesses. Much like you are doing with me."

Esrahaddon smiled. "Perhaps," he said. "There is no way to be certain if they are responsible for the beast's presence, but one thing is certain, they are watching. When they see we are helpless against one Gilarabrywn, if they feel the treaty is broken, or when it runs out, fear will no longer be a deterrent."

"Is that why you are really here?"

"No," the wizard shook his head. "It plays a part, but the war between the elves and man will come despite any action I can take.

I am merely trying to lessen the blow and give humanity a fighting chance."

"You might begin by teaching some others to do what you did last night."

The wizard looked at the thief. "What do you mean?"

"Coy doesn't suit you," Royce told him.

"No, I suppose not."

"I thought you couldn't do your art without your hands?"

"It is very hard and takes a great deal of time and it isn't very accurate. Imagine trying to write your name with your toes. I began working on that spell before you arrived here, thinking it would come in handy at some point. As it was, the flame wall nearly consumed you two. It was suppose to be several yards farther away, and last for hours instead of minutes. With hands I could have…" he trailed off. "No sense going there I suppose."

"Were you really that powerful before?"

Esrahaddon showed him a wicked smile. "Oh my dear boy, you couldn't begin to imagine."

Word of Thrace's recovery quickly spread through the village. She was still a little groggy, but remarkably sound. She could see clearly, all her teeth were in her head, and she had an appetite. By midmorning, she was sitting up eating soup. That day there was a decidedly different look in the villagers' eyes. The unspoken thought in every mind was the same—the beast had attacked and no one had died.

Most saw the winged beast outlined in the brilliant green flames that night. Alongside each of them that morning walked a strange

companion, a long lost friend who had returned so unexpectedly—
hope.

They got busy at dawn preparing more wood fires. They had a
system down now and were able to build up the piles with just a few
hours work. Suspecting that the beast—obviously able to see well
in the dark—might not be able to see through thick smoke, Vince
Griffin suggested they use smudge pots. For centuries, farmers had
used smudge pots to drive off insects that threatened to devour
their crops and Dahlgren was no different. Old pots were promptly
gathered and filled as if a cloud of locusts was on its way. At the same
time, Hadrian, Tad Bothwick, and Kline Goodman began surveying
the outbuildings of the lower bailey for the best shelters.

Hadrian busied himself organizing small groups of men. One
group started to expand the cellar they found in the smokehouse,
and another went to work digging a tunnel with the idea of trying to
capture the beast. A huge serpent chasing a man might follow him
into a tunnel, but if the tunnel gradually narrowed, they might be
able to seal the exits before it realized its mistake. No weapon made
by man may be able to slay it, but Hadrian guessed there were no
restrictions on imprisoning the beast.

Deacon Tomas was far from delighted with all the digging,
cutting and burning inside the castle grounds, but already it was
clear that the villagers had found a new leader in Hadrian. Tomas
remained quietly indoors caring for Thrace.

"Hadrian?"

He was washing at the well in the village where he could find
some privacy when he looked up to see Theron.

"Been doing some digging I see," the farmer said. "Dillon
mentioned you had them making a tunnel. Pretty smart thinking."

"The odds of it working are slim," Hadrian explained, dousing
his face with handfuls of water. "But at least it's a shot."

"Listen," the farmer began with a pained look on his face and then said nothing.

"Thrace is doing well?" Hadrian asked after a minute or so.

"She's great, as solid as her old man," he said proudly thumping his own chest. "It'll take more than a tree to break her. That's the thing about us Woods. We might not look like it, but we're a strong lot. It might take us a while, but we come back and when we do, we're stronger than ever. Thing is, we need something—you know—a reason. I didn't have one—at least I didn't think I did. Thrace showed me different."

They stood facing each other in an awkward silence.

"Listen," Theron said again, and once more paused. "I'm not used to being beholden to anyone, you see. I've always paid my own way. I got what I have by work and lots of it. I don't ask anyone's help and I don't apologize for the way I am, see?"

Hadrian nodded.

"But—well, a lot of what you said yesterday was true. Only today, some things are different—you follow? Thrace and me, we're gonna be leaving this place just as soon as she's able. I'm figuring a couple of days rest and she'll be okay to travel. We'll head south maybe to Alburn or even Calis; I hear it stays warm longer there, better growing season. Anyway, that still leaves a few nights we'll be here. A few more nights we'll have to live under this shadow. I'm not gonna lose my little girl the way I lost the others. Now I know an old farmer like me ain't much good to her swinging a scythe or a pitchfork against that thing, but if it comes to that, it would be good if I knew how to fight proper. That way if it comes calling before we leave, at least there will be a chance. Now, I haven't got much, but I do have some silver set aside and I was wondering if your offer to teach me how to fight was still good?"

"First, we need to get something straight," Hadrian told him sternly. "Your daughter already paid us in full to do whatever we could to help you, so you keep your silver for the trip south or I won't teach you a thing. Agreed?"

Theron hesitated then nodded.

"Good. Well, I suppose we can begin right now if you're ready?"

"Should we get your swords?" Theron asked.

"That would be a problem considering I put my swords on Millie last night and no one has seen her since, but that shouldn't matter for now."

"Should I cut sticks then?" the farmer asked.

"No."

"What then?"

"How about sitting down and just listening. There's a lot to learn before you're ready to swing at anything."

Theron looked at Hadrian skeptically.

"You want me to teach you, right? If I said I wanted you to teach me to be a great farmer in a few hours what would you say?"

Theron nodded in submission and sat down on the dirt not far from where Hadrian first met Pearl. Hadrian slipped his shirt on and, taking a bucket, turned it over and sat down in front of him.

"As with everything, fighting takes practice. Anything can look easy if you're watching someone who's mastered whatever it is they are doing, but what you don't see is the hours and years of effort that go into perfecting their craft. I am sure you can plow a field in a fraction of the time it would take me for this very reason. Sword fighting is no different. Practice will allow you to react without thought to events, and even to anticipate those events. It becomes a form of foresight, the ability to look into the future and know exactly what your opponent will do even before he does. Without practice, you'll need to think too much. When fighting a more skilled opponent even a split second of hesitation can get you killed."

"My opponent is a giant snake with wings," Theron said.

"And it has killed more than a score of men. Most certainly a more skilled opponent, wouldn't you say? So practice is paramount. The question is what do you need to practice?"

"Swinging a sword, I should think."

"True, but that is only a small part of it. If it were merely swinging a sword everyone with two legs and at least one arm would be experts. No, there is much more to it. First, there is concentration, and that means more than just paying attention to the fight. It means not worrying about Thrace or thinking about your family, the past or the future. It means focusing on what you are doing beyond all else. It might sound easy, but it isn't. Next comes breathing."

"Breathing?" Theron asked dubiously.

"Yeah, I know we breathe all the time, but sometimes we stop breathing or stop breathing correctly. Ever get startled and discover you were holding your breath? Ever find yourself panting when you're really nervous or frightened? Some people can actually pass out that way. Trust me, in a real fight, you'll be scared and unless you train, you'll end up breathing shallow or not at all. Less air saps your body of strength and makes it hard to think clearly. You'll become tired and slow, something you can't afford in a battle."

"So, how do you breathe correctly?" Theron asked, still with a hint of sarcasm.

"You have to breathe deep and slow even before you need to, before your exertion demands it. At first, it will be a conscious thought and it will feel counterproductive, even distracting. But over time, it will become second nature. It is also good to keep in mind that you have the most strength for a blow on an exhale. It adds power and focus to a stroke. Sometimes actually yelling or shouting helps. I will want you to do that during your training. I want to hear it when you swing. Later on, it won't be necessary although sometimes it can help to startle your opponent." Hadrian paused briefly and Theron noted the faint hint of a smile tug at his lips.

"Next comes balance, and that means more than not falling down. Sadly, humans only have two feet. That's only two points to support us. Pick up one and you are vulnerable. This is why you want to keep your feet on the ground. That doesn't mean you don't move, but when you move, you slide your feet rather than pick them up. You need to keep your weight forward, your knees slightly bent, and your balance on the balls of your feet rather than in your heels. Drawing your feet together reduces your two points of balance to one, so keep your feet apart, about shoulder width.

"Timing is, of course, very important. I warn you now, you'll be terrible at it to begin with, as timing improves with experience. You saw from swinging at me yesterday how frustrating it can be to swing and miss. Timing is what allows you to hit, and not only to hit, but also to do damage. You will learn to see patterns in movement. You'll know when to expect an opening, or a weakness. Frequently you can anticipate an attack by watching how your opponent moves—the placement of his feet, the look in his eyes, a telltale drop of his shoulder, the tightening of a muscle."

"But I'm not fighting a person," Theron interrupted. "And I don't even think it has a shoulder."

"Even animals give signs about what they will do. They hunch up, twist and shift their weight just like people. Such signals do not have to be obvious. Most skilled fighters will try to mask their intentions, or worse, purposely try to mislead you. They want to confuse your timing, throw you off balance, and make an opening for themselves. Of course, this is exactly what you want to do to them. If done well, your opponent sees the false move, but not the attack. The result—in your case—is a headless flying serpent.

"The last thing to learn is the hardest. It can't be taught. It can barely be explained. It is the idea that the fight—the battle—doesn't really exist so much in your hands or your feet, but in your head. The real struggle is in your own mind. You must know you are going to win before you start the fight. You have to see it, smell it, and believe it utterly. It is a form of confidence, but you must guard against over confidence. You have to be flexible—able to adapt in an instant and never allow yourself to give up. Without this, nothing else is possible. Unless you believe you will win, fear and hesitation will hold you down while your opponent kills you. Now, let's get a couple of stout sticks and we will see how well you listened."

That night they lit the bonfires once more and everyone stayed sheltered in either the manor house or the cellar of the smokehouse. Royce and Hadrian were the only two moving outside and even they remained in the shelter of the smokehouse doorway watching the night by bonfire light.

"How's Thrace doing?" Royce asked, his eyes on the sky.

"Great considering the fact that she broke a tree branch with her head," Hadrian replied as he sat on a barrel cleaning a mutton bone of the last of its meat. "I even heard she was walking around asking to help with dinner." He shook his head and smiled. "That girl, she's something that's for sure. Hard to imagine it seeing her under that arch in Colnora, but she's tough. The real change is in the old man. Theron says they plan on leaving in a day or two, as soon as Thrace can travel."

"So we're out of a job?" Royce feigned disappointment.

"Why, were you getting close?" Hadrian asked, throwing the bone away and wiping his hands on his vest.

"Nope. I can't figure out how to reach it."

"Tunnel?"

"I thought of that, but I've been over every inch of the forest and the rocks and there's nothing; no cave, no sunken dell, nothing that could be confused with a tunnel. I'm completely stumped on this."

"What about Esra? Doesn't the wizard have any ideas?"

"Maybe, but he's being elusive. He's hiding something. He wants access to that tower, but won't say why and avoids direct questions about it. Something happened to him here years ago. Something he doesn't want to talk about. But maybe I can get him to open up more tomorrow if I let him know the Woods no longer require our services and that there is no reason for me to try anymore."

"Don't you think he'll see through that?"

"See through what?" Royce asked. "Honestly, I'm giving it one more try tomorrow and if I can't find something, I say we head out with Theron and Thrace."

Hadrian was silent.

"What?" Royce asked.

"I just hate to run out on them like that. I mean they're starting to turn it around now."

"You do this all the time. You get these lost causes under your skin—"

"I'd like to remind you, coming here was your idea. I was in the process of declining the job, remember?"

"Well, a lot can happen in a day; maybe I'll find a way in tomorrow."

Hadrian stepped to the doorway and peered out. "The forest is loud. Looks like our friend isn't coming to visit us tonight. Maybe Esrahaddon's flames singed its wings and it's dining on venison this evening."

"The fires won't keep it away forever," Royce said. "According to the wizard, the fires didn't hurt it; they just confused it—bright lights do that, apparently. Only the sword in the tower can actually harm it. It will be back."

"Then we'd best take advantage of its absence and get a good night's sleep."

Hadrian went down into the cellar, leaving Royce staring out at the night sky and the gathering clouds that crossed the stars. The wind was still up, whipping the trees and battering the fires. He could almost smell it; change was in the air and it was blowing their way.

Chapter 8
MYTHS AND LEGENDS

ROYCE STOOD ON the bank of the river in the early morning light trying to skip stones out toward the tower. None of them made more than a single jump before the turbulent water consumed them. His most recent idea for reaching the tower centered on building a small boat and launching himself upriver in the hopes of landing on the rocky parapet before the massive current washed him over the falls. Although there was no clear landing ground for such an attempt, it might be possible, if he caught the current just right and landed against the rock. The force of the water would likely smash the boat or drive it under when it met the wall, but he might be able to scramble onto the precipice before going over. The problem was, even if he managed to perform this harrowing feat, there was no way back.

He turned to see the wizard walking up the river trail. Perhaps to keep an eye on him but more likely to be on hand should he discover the entrance.

"Morning," the wizard said. "Any epiphanies today?"

"Just one. There is no way to reach that tower."

Esrahaddon looked disappointed.

"I have exhausted all the possibilities I can think of. Besides, Theron and Thrace are going to be leaving Dahlgren. I no longer have a reason to bang my head against this tower."

"I see," Esrahaddon said, staring down at him, "what about the welfare of the village?"

"Hardly my problem. This village shouldn't even be here, remember? It's a violation of the treaty. It would be best if all these people left."

"If we allow it to be wiped out, it could be seen as a sign of weakness and invite the elves to invade."

"And allowing the village to survive is breaking the treaty, resulting in the same possibility. Fortunate for me, I am not wearing a crown. I am not the Emperor, or a king, so it's not something I need to deal with."

"You're just going to leave?"

"Is there a reason for me to stay?"

The wizard raised an eyebrow and looked long at the thief. "What do you want?" he asked at length.

"Are you proposing to pay me now?"

"We both know I have no money, but still you want something from me. What is it?"

"The truth. What are you after? What happened here nine hundred years ago?"

The wizard studied Royce for a moment and looked down at his feet. After a few minutes, he nodded. He walked over to a beech log that lay across the granite rock and sat down. He looked out toward the water and the spray as if searching for something in the mist, something that was not there.

"I was the youngest member of the Cenzar. We were the council of wizards that worked directly for the Emperor. The greatest wizards the world had ever seen. There was also the Teshlor, comprised of the greatest of the Emperor's knights. Tradition dictated that a mentor from each council was to serve as teacher and full-time protector to the Emperor's son and heir. Because I was the youngest it fell to me to be Nevrik's Cenzar instructor, while Jerish Grelad was picked from the Teshlor. Jerish and I didn't get along. Like most of the Teshlor, he held a distrust of wizards, and I thought little of him and his brutish, violent ways.

"Nevrik, however, brought us together. Like his father, the Emperor Nareion, Nevrik, was a breed apart, and it was an honor to teach him. Jerish and I spent nearly all our time with Nevrik. I taught him lore, books, and The Art, while Jerish instructed him in the schools of combat and warfare. Though I still felt the practice of physical combat was beneath the Emperor and his son, it was very clear that Jerish was as devoted to Nevrik as I was. In that middle ground, we found a foothold where we could stand together. When the Emperor decided to break tradition and travel here to Avempartha with his son, we went along."

"Break tradition?"

"It had been centuries since an emperor had spoken directly to the elves."

"After the war, there wasn't tribute paid or anything like that?"

"No, all contact was severed at the Nidwalden, so it was a very exciting time. No one really knew what to expect. I personally knew very little about Avempartha beyond the historical account of how it was the sight of the last battle of the Great Elven Wars. The Emperor met with several top officials of the Erivan Empire in the tower while Jerish and I attempted, without much luck, to continue Nevrik's studies. The sight of the waterfall and the elven architecture was too much to compete with for the attention of a twelve-year-old boy.

"It was around dusk, nearly night. Nevrik had been pointing things out to us all day, reveling in the fact that neither Jerish nor I could identify any of the elven things he found. This was, of course, the first time in centuries that humans had met with elves; we were at a distinct disadvantage. We found several sets of elven clothes drying in the sun, made of a shimmering material we couldn't identify. Nevrik delighted in stumping his teachers, so when he asked about the *thing* he saw flying toward the tower, I thought he saw a bird, or a bat, but he said it was too large and that it looked like a serpent. He mentioned it had flown into one of the high windows of the tower. Nevrik was so adamant about it that we all went back inside. We had just started up the main staircase when we heard the screams.

"It sounded like a war was being fought above us. The personal bodyguards of the Emperor—a detachment of Teshlors—were fighting off the Gilarabrywn, protecting the Emperor as they fled down the stairs. I saw groups of elves throwing themselves at the creature, dying to protect our emperor."

"The elves were?"

Esrahaddon nodded. "I was amazed by the sight. The whole scene is still so vivid to me even after nearly a thousand years. Still nothing the knights or the elves could do stopped the attacking beast, which seemed determined to kill the Emperor. It was a terrible battle with knights falling on the stairs and dying upon the wet steps, elves joining them. The Emperor ordered us to get Nevrik to safety.

"Jerish grabbed the boy and dragged him out of the tower kicking and screaming, but I hesitated. I realized that once outside, the flying beast would be able to swoop down and kill at will. The Art could not defeat it. The creature was magic and without the key to unlock the spell, nothing I could do would alter that enchantment. A thought came to me and as the Emperor exited the door, I cast an enchantment of binding—not on the beast, but on the tower trapping the Gilarabrywn inside. Those knights and elves still inside died, but the beast was trapped."

"Where did it come from? What caused the thing to attack?"

Esrahaddon shrugged. "The elves insisted they knew nothing of the attack, and that they had no idea where the Gilarabrywn came from except that one Gilarabrywn had been left unaccounted for after the wars. They assumed it destroyed. They mentioned a militant society, a growing movement of elves within the Erivan Empire that sought to incite a war. It was speculated they were responsible. The elven lords apologized and assured us they would investigate the matter fully. The Emperor, convinced that to retaliate or even make the incident public was unwise, chose to ignore the attack and returned home."

"So what's this about a weapon?"

"The Gilarabrywn is a conjured creature, a powerful magic endowed with a life of its own beyond the existence of its creator. The creature is not truly alive; it cannot reproduce, grow old, or appreciate existence, but it also cannot die. It can, however, be dispelled. No enchantment is perfect; every magic has a seam where the weave can be unraveled. In the case of the Gilarabrywn, the seam is its name. Whenever a Gilarabrywn is created, so is an object—a sword, etched with its name—it is used to control the beast and if necessary, destroy it. According to the elves, at the end of the war they placed all the Gilarabrywn swords in the tower per Novron's orders. At that time all the swords were accounted for and all but one was notched to show their associated beast was destroyed."

Royce got up to stretch his legs. "Okay, so the elven lords held one of their monsters back just in case, or this militant group hid one to cause trouble. The elven leaders tell you all the swords are in there. Maybe they are, or maybe they aren't, and they just want—"

"It's in there," Esrahaddon interrupted.

"You saw it?"

"We were given a tour when we first arrived. Near the top is a sort of memorial to the war. All the swords are on display."

"Alright so there is a sword," Royce granted, "but that's not why you want in. You didn't come here to save Dahlgren. Why are you really here?"

"You didn't allow me to finish," Esrahaddon replied, sounding every bit like the wise teacher letting his student know to be patient. "The Emperor believed he had prevented a war with the elves and returned home, but what waited for him was an execution. While we were away, the church, under the leadership of Patriarch Venlin, planned the Emperor's assassination. The attack came on the steps of the palace during a celebration commemorating the anniversary of the Empire's founding. Jerish and I escaped with Nevrik. I knew that many of the Cenzar and the Teshlor were involved in the church's plot and that they would find us, so Jerish and I came up with a plan—we hid Nevrik and I created two talismans. One I gave to Nevrik and the other to Jerish. These amulets would hide them from the clairvoyant search the Cenzar were certain to make, but allow me to find them. Then I sent them away."

"And you?" Royce asked.

"I stayed behind. I tried to save the Emperor." He paused, looking far away. "I failed."

"So what happened to the heir?" Royce asked.

"How should I know, I was locked up in a prison for nine hundred years. Do you think he wrote me? Jerish was supposed to take him into hiding." The wizard allowed himself a grim smile. "We both thought it would only be for a month or so."

"So, you don't even know if an heir exists anymore?"

"I'm pretty confident the church didn't kill him or they would have killed me shortly thereafter, but what became of Jerish and Nevrik I don't know. If anyone could have kept Nevrik alive, it would have been Jerish. Despite his age, he was one of the best knights the Emperor had. The fact that he trusted his son to his care was testament to that. Like all Teshlor knights, Jerish was a master of all the schools of combat; there wouldn't have been a man alive who could beat him in battle and he would have died before surrendering Nevrik. They would both be dead now, of course, time would have seen to that, so would their great, great grandchildren if they had any. I suspect Jerish would have known the need to perpetuate the line and would have settled down somewhere quiet and encouraged Nevrik to marry and have children."

"And wait for you?"

"What's that?"

"That was the plan, wasn't it? They run and hide and you stay behind and find them when it was safe?"

"Something like that."

"So, you had a way to contact them. A way to locate the heir? Something to do with the amulets."

"Nine hundred years ago I would have said yes, but the odds of finding their decedents now is probably a fool's dream. Time can destroy so many things."

"But you are trying nevertheless."

"What else is there for an old crippled outlaw to do?"

"Care to tell me how you plan to find them?"

"I can't do that. I've already told you more than I should have. The heir has enemies and, as fond as I have grown of you, that kind of secret stays with me. I owe that much to Jerish and Nevrik."

"But something in that tower is part of it. That's why you want to get inside." Royce thought a moment. "You sealed that tower just before you went to prison, and since the Gilarabrywn was only recently released you can be almost certain that the interior of that tower hasn't been touched in all that time. It's the only place that is still the same as the day you left it. There's something in there you saw that day, or something you left there; something you need to find the heir."

"It is a shame you aren't as good at deciphering a way to get into the tower."

"About that," Royce said, "you mentioned that the Emperor met with the elves in the tower. They aren't allowed on this bank, right?"

"Correct."

"And there was no bridge on their side of the river, right?"

"Again correct."

"But you never saw how they entered the tower?"

"No." Royce thought a moment then asked, "Why were the stairs wet?"

Esrahaddon looked at him puzzled. "What's that?"

"You said earlier that when the knights were fighting off the Gilarabrywn, they died on the wet steps. Was it blood?"

"No, water I think, I remember how the stairs were wet when we were climbing up because it made the stone so slippery I nearly fell. Some of the knights did fall, that's why I remember it."

"And you said the elves had clothes drying in the sun?"

Esrahaddon shook his head. "I see where you are going with this, but not even an elf can swim to the tower."

"That may be true, but then why were they wet? Was it a hot day? Could they have been swimming?"

Esrahaddon raised his eyebrows incredulously. "In that river? No, it was early spring and still cold."

"Then how'd they get wet?"

Royce heard a faint sound behind him. He started to turn but stopped himself.

"We're not alone," he whispered.

"When you lunge, step in with the leg on your weapon side, it will give you more reach and better balance," Hadrian told Theron.

The two were at the well again. They had gotten up early and Hadrian was putting Theron through some basic moves using two makeshift swords they had created out of rake handles. To his surprise, Theron was spryer than he looked and despite his size, the old man moved well. He had gone over the basics of parries, ripostes, fleches, presses, and the lunge, and they were now working on a compound attack comprised of a feint, parry, and riposte.

"Cuts and thrusts must follow one upon the other without pause. The emphasis is always on speed, aggression, and deception. And everything is kept as simple as possible," Hadrian explained.

"I'd listen to him. If anyone knows stick fighting, it's Hadrian."

Hadrian and Theron turned to see two equestrians riding into the village clearing, each leading a pack pony laden with poles and bundles. They were young men not much older than Thrace, but dressed like young princes in handsome doublets and hose complete with box-pleated frill and lace edging.

"Mauvin! Fanen?" Hadrian said astonished.

"Don't look so surprised." Mauvin gave his horse reign to graze on the common's grass.

"Well, that's a little hard at this point. What in Maribor's name are you two doing here?"

Just then a procession of musicians, heralds, knights, wagons and carriages emerged from the dense forest. Long banners of red and gold streamed in the morning light as standard-bearers preceded the march, followed by the plumed Imperial Guards of the Nyphron Church.

Hadrian and Theron moved aside against the trees for safety as the grand parade of elegantly draped stallions and gold etched white carriages rolled in. There were well-dressed clergy and chain-mailed soldiers, knights with their squires leading packhorses laden with fine sets of shining metal armor. There was nobility with standards from as far away as Calis and Trent, but also commoners, rough men with broad swords and scarred faces, monks in tattered robes, and woodsmen with long bows and green hoods. Such an assortment of diverse characters made Hadrian think of a circus he had once seen, although this column of men and horses was far too grim and serious to be a carnival. Bringing up the rear echelon was a group of six riders in black and red with the symbol of a broken crown on their chests. At their head rode a tall thin man with long black hair and a short trimmed beard.

"So they've finally decided to do something about this," Hadrian said. "I'm impressed the church would go to such an effort to save a little village so far out that even its own king doesn't care. But that still doesn't explain why you two are here."

"I'm hurt," Mauvin feigned a chest pain. "Granted, I'm only here to help Fanen, but I might try my hand as well. Although, if you're going to be competing it looks as if we shouldn't have bothered with the trip."

Theron whispered to Hadrian, "Who are these people? And what is he talking about?"

"Ah—sorry, this is Mauvin and Fanen Pickering, sons of Count Pickering of Galilin in Melengar, who are apparently very lost. Mauvin, Fanen, this is Theron Wood, he's a farmer."

"And he's paying you for lessons? Smart idea, but how did you two get here ahead of the rest of us? I didn't see you at any of the camps. Oh, what am I thinking? You and Royce probably had no trouble discovering the location of the contest."

"Contest?"

"Royce was probably hiding under the archbishop's desk as he set up the rules. So will it be swords? If it's swords Fanen has a real chance to win, but if it's a joust, well…" he glanced at his brother who scowled. "He's really not that good. Do you know how the eliminations will work? I can't imagine they will pit noble against commoner, which means Fanen won't be competing with you, so—"

"You're not here to slay the Gilarabrywn? Are you saying these people are here for that stupid contest?"

"Gilarabrywn? What's a Gilarabrywn? Is that like Oswald the bear? Heard about him coming through Dunmore. Terrorized villages for years until the king killed him with just a dagger."

The entourage traveled past them without pause up toward the manor house. One of the coaches separated from the group just after it cleared the well. It stopped and a young well-dressed woman exited and ran to them, holding the edge of her skirt up to avoid the dirt.

"Hadrian!" she cried with a bright smile.

Hadrian bowed, and Theron joined him.

"Is this your father, Hadrian?" she asked.

"No, Your Highness. May I present Theron Wood of Dahlgren Village. Theron, this is her Royal Highness, Princess Arista of Melengar."

Theron stared at Hadrian, shocked, "You really get around, don't you?"

Hadrian smiled awkwardly and shrugged.

"Hey Arista, guess what. Hadrian says the contest is to kill a beast."

"I didn't say that."

"Which is just fine by me because if Hadrian was going to be competing I think, I would have to withdraw. But now, a hunt is a much different story. You know luck is often a deciding factor in these things."

"These things?" Arista laughed at him. "Attended several beast slaying contests have you, Fanen?"

"Bah!" Fanen scoffed. "You know what I mean. Sometimes you are just in the right place at the right time."

Mauvin shrugged. "Doesn't sound like much of a contest for noblemen really. If it turns out to be true, I'll be disappointed. Slaughtering a poor animal is no good use for a Pickering's sword."

"Say, did you also hear what the prize will be?" Fanen asked. "The way they've been selling this contest in every square, church and tavern across Avryn, it has to be big. Will it just be a gold trophy, or is it land? I'm hoping to get an estate out of this. Mauvin will inherit our father's title, but I have to fend for myself. What does this animal look like? Is it a bear? Is it big? Have you seen it?"

Hadrian and Theron exchanged stunned looks.

"What is it?" Fanen asked. "It's not dead already?"

"No," Hadrian said. "It's not dead already."

"Oh good."

"Your Highness!" A woman's voice came from the carriage still lingering up the trail. "We need to be going—the archbishop will be waiting."

"I'm sorry," she told them, "I have to go. It was good seeing you again. She waved and ran back to her waiting carriage.

"We should probably be going too," Mauvin said. "We want to get Fanen's name as near to the top of the list as we can."

"Wait," Hadrian told them. "Don't enter the contest."

"What?" they both said.

"We rode days to get here for this," Fanen complained.

"Take my advice. Turn around right now and head back home. Take Arista with you too and anyone else you can convince to go. If it is a competition to kill the Gilarabrywn, don't sign up. You don't want to fight this thing. I'm serious. You don't know what you're dealing with. If you try and fight this creature it will kill you."

"But, you think you can kill it?"

"I'm not fighting it. Royce and I were just here doing a job for Theron's daughter and we were about to leave."

"Royce is here too?" Fanen asked, looking around.

"Do your father a favor and leave now."

Mauvin frowned. "If you were anyone else I would take your tone as insolent, I might even call you a coward and a liar, but I know you're neither." Mauvin sighed and rubbed his chin thoughtfully. "Still, we did ride an awfully long way to just turn around. You say you were preparing to leave? When will that be?"

Hadrian looked at Theron.

"Another two days I think," the old farmer told Hadrian. "I don't want to go until I know Thrace will be okay."

"Then we will stay here for that long and see for ourselves what's what. If it turns out to be as you say, we will leave with you. Is that fair, Fanen?"

"I don't see why you can't go and I stay. After all, I'm the one going to enter the contest."

"No one is going to kill that thing, Fanen," Hadrian told him. "Listen, I have been here for three nights. I have seen it and I know what it can do. It's not a matter of skill or courage. Your sword won't harm it, no one's will. Fighting that creature is nothing more than suicide."

"I'm not deciding yet," Fanen declared. "We aren't even certain what the contest is. I won't sign up right away, but I'm not leaving either."

"Do me a favor then," Hadrian told them, "at least stay indoors tonight."

Something, or someone, was in the thickets.

Royce left Esrahaddon and moved away to the river's edge, careful not to look in the direction of the sound. He descended from the rocks to the depression near the river and slipped into the trees, circling back. Something was there and it was working hard to be quiet.

At first, Royce caught a glimpse of orange and blue through the leaves and almost thought it was nothing more than a bluebird, but then it shifted. Far too large to be a bird, Royce drew closer and saw a light brown braided beard, a broad flat nose, a blue leather vest, large black boots, and a bright orange shirt with puffed sleeves.

"Magnus!" Royce greeted the dwarf loudly, causing him to stumble and fall out of the bramble. He slipped backward off the little grassy ledge and fell on his back on the bare rock not far from where Esrahaddon sat. With the wind knocked out of him, the dwarf lay gasping for breath.

Royce leapt down and placed his dagger to the dwarf's throat.

"A lot of people have been looking for you," Royce told him menacingly. "I have to admit, I rather wanted to see you again myself to thank you for all the help you gave me in Essendon Castle."

"Don't tell me this is the dwarf that killed King Amrath of Melengar?" Esrahaddon asked.

"His name is Magnus, or at least that is what Percy Braga called him. He's a master trap builder and stone carver, isn't that right?"

"It's my business!" the dwarf protested, still struggling for air. "I'm a craftsman. I take jobs the same as you. You can't fault a guy for working."

"I almost died due to your work," Royce told him. "And you killed the king. Alric will be very pleased when I tell him I finally eliminated you. And as I recall there's a price on your head."

"Wait—hang on!" Magnus shouted. "It was nothing personal. Can you tell me you never killed anyone for money, Royce?"

Royce hesitated.

"Yes, I know who you are," the dwarf told him. "I wanted to find out who beat my trap. You used to work for the Black Diamond and not as a delivery boy either. It was my job, I tell you. I don't care about politics, or Braga, or Essendon."

"I suspect he's telling the truth," Esrahaddon said. "I've never known a dwarf to care at all for the affairs of humans beyond the coin they can obtain."

"See, he knows what I am saying. You can let me go."

"I said you were telling the truth, not that he should let you live. In fact, now that I can see you have been eavesdropping on our conversations, I have to encourage the notion of ending your life. I can't be sure how much you heard."

"What?" the dwarf cried.

"After slitting his throat you can just roll his little body off the ledge here." The wizard stepped up and looked over the cliff.

"No," Royce replied, "it will be better to toss him off the falls. He's not that heavy; his body will likely carry all the way to the Goblin Sea."

"Do you need his head?" Esrahaddon asked. "To take back to Alric?"

"It would be nice, but I'm not carrying a severed head for a week while traveling through those woods. It would draw every fly for miles and it would stink after a few hours. Trust me, I speak from experience."

The dwarf looked at both of them in horror.

"No! No!" he shouted in panic as Royce pressed his blade to his neck. "I can help you. I can show you how to get to the tower!"

Royce looked at the wizard who appeared skeptical.

"For the love of Drome. I'm a dwarf. I know stone. I know rock. I know where the tunnel to the tower is."

Royce relaxed his dagger.

"Let me live and I'll show it to you," he turned his head toward Esrahaddon. "And as for what I heard, I care nothing about the affairs of wizards and men. I'll never say a word. If you know dwarves, well then you know we're a lot like stone when we choose to be."

"So there *is* a tunnel," Royce said.

"Of course there is."

"Before I decide," Royce asked, "what are you doing here?"

"I was finishing another job, that's all."

"And what was this job?"

"Nothing sinister, I just made a sword for a guy."

"All the way out here? Who is this person?"

"Lord Rufus somebody, I was hired to make it and deliver it to him here, honest, no traps, no killings."

Royce heard the sound of footfalls. Someone was running up the trail. Thinking it might be the dwarf's associates, he slipped behind Magnus. He gripped his hair, pulled his head back, and prepared to slit his throat.

"Royce!" Tad Bothwick shouted up to them from down near the water.

"What is it, Tad?" he asked cautiously.

"Hadrian sent me. He says you should come back to the village right away, but that Esra should steer clear."

"Why?" the wizard asked.

"Hadrian said to tell you that the Church of Nyphron just arrived."

"The church?" Esrahaddon muttered. "Here?"

"Is there a Lord Rufus with them?" Royce asked.

"Could be. There's a whole lot of fancy folk around. Must be at least one lord in the bunch."

"Any idea why they're here, Tad?"

"Nope."

"You might want to make yourself scarce," Royce told the wizard. "Someone might have mentioned your name. I'll go see what's happening. In the meantime," he looked down at the dwarf, "your death sentence has been suspended. This kindly old man is going to watch you this afternoon, and you're going to stay right here. Then later you're going to show us where this tunnel is and if you're telling the truth about knowing, then you live. Anything short of that and you're going over the falls in two pieces. Agreed? Good." He looked back at the wizard, "Want me to tie him up or just hit him over the head with a rock?" Royce asked, panicking the dwarf again.

"Won't be necessary, Magnus here looks like the honorable type. Besides, I can still manage a few surprisingly unpleasant things. Do you know what it is like to have live ants trapped inside your head?"

The dwarf did not move or speak. Royce searched him. He found a belt under his clothes with little hammers and some rock shaping tools and a dagger. Royce looked at the dagger, surprised.

"I tried copying it," the dwarf told him nervously. "It's not very good, I was working from memory."

Royce compared it to his own dagger. The two were very similar in design, though the blades were clearly different. Royce's weapon was made of an almost translucent metal that shimmered in the light while Magnus' dagger seemed dull and heavy by comparison. The thief threw the dagger over the cliff.

"That's a magnificent weapon you have," the dwarf told him, his eyes mesmerized by the blade that a moment before had been at his throat. "It's a Tur blade, isn't it?"

Royce ignored him and spoke to Esrahaddon. "Keep an eye on him. I'll be back later."

Arista took her seat on the balcony above the entrance to the great hall of the manor house, along with the entourage of the archbishop, which included Sauly and Sentinel Luis Guy. It was a very small balcony created of rough logs and thick ropes, where only a few could fit, but Bernice managed to squeeze her way in and remained standing just behind her. Having Bernice hovering out of sight was as irritating as a mosquito in the dark.

Arista had no idea what was going on—few people appeared to.

When they arrived, everything was in chaos. The lord of the manor was apparently dead and the place was filled with peasants. They were promptly chased out. Luis Guy and his seret established order, properly assigning quarters based on rank. She was given a cramped but private room on the second level. It was a ghastly place lacking even a single window. A bear rug lay on the floor, the head of a moose looked down at her from above the bed, and a coat rack made from deer antlers hung from the wall. Bernice was busy unpacking her clothes from the trunk when Sauly stopped by, insisting Arista join him on the balcony. At first, she thought the contest might be starting, but it was common knowledge it would begin at nightfall.

A trumpeter stepped up to the rail and blared a fanfare on his horn. Below in the courtyard a crowd formed. Men rushed over, some holding drinks or half-eaten meals. One man trotted up still buttoning his pants. The growing audience created a mass of heads and shoulders bunched together, all staring up at them.

The archbishop slowly stood up. Dressed in full regalia of long embroidered robes, he spread his arms in a grand gesture and spoke, his raspy voice barely adequate to the task.

"It is time to announce the details of this event and reveal the profound happening that you, the devoted of Novron, are about to take part in, an event so monumental that its conclusion will see the world altered forever."

Several people in the back complained they could not hear, but the archbishop ignored them and went on. "I know some of you came believing this contest was to be a battle of swords or lances like some Wintertide tournament. Instead, what you will see is nothing less than a miracle. Some of you will die, one will succeed, and the rest will bear witness to the world.

"A terrible evil haunts this place. Here on the Nidwalden River, at the edge of the world, there is a beast. Not a great bear like Oswald that terrorized Glamrendor. This creature is none other than the legendary Gilarabrywn, a horror not seen since the days of Novron himself. A monster so terrible that even in those days of heroes and gods, only Novron, or one of his blood, could slay it. It will be your task, your challenge, to slay the creature and save this poor village from the ancient curse."

A murmur broke out among those gathered and the archbishop raised his hands to quiet them. "Silence. For I have not yet told you of the reward!"

He waited as the mob grew quiet, many pushing closer to hear.

"As I said, the Gilarabrywn is a beast that only Novron, or one of his bloodline, can slay and as such, he that succeeds in vanquishing this terror can be none other than the heir to the imperial crown, the long lost Heir of Novron!"

The reaction was surprisingly quiet. There were no cheers, no shouts of jubilation. The crowd as a whole appeared stunned. They remained staring as if expecting more. The archbishop in turn looked around equally bewildered by the hesitancy of the congregation.

"Did he just say the winner would be the heir?" Arista asked, looking at Sauly who appeared as if he'd just smelled something unpleasant. He smiled at her and, standing up, whispered in the archbishop's ear. The older man took his seat and Bishop Saldur addressed the crowd.

"For centuries the church has struggled to find the true heir, to restore the bloodline of our holy lord Novron the Great," Sauly's voice was loud and warm and carried well on the pine scented afternoon air. "We have searched, but all we had to guide us were old books and rumors. Speculation really, hopes and dreams. There has never been a means of finding him, no absolute method to determine where the heir was, or who he may be. Many have falsely claimed to be his descendent, many unworthy men have striven to take that lofty crown, and the church has sat helpless.

"Still, we have faith he is out there. Novron would not allow his own blood to die. We know he lives. He may be oblivious to who he is. A thousand years have passed since his disappearance and who of us can accurately trace our lineage back to the days of the Empire? Who knows if one of us might have an ancestor who went to his grave with a terrible secret? A terrible, wonderful secret.

"The Gilarabrywn is a miracle Novron has sent. It is a tool to show us his son. He has confided this to the patriarch and told his holiness that he should hold a contest and if he did, the heir would be among the contestants, the truth of his lineage, oblivious even to himself.

"So you see, you—any one of you—may be the Heir of Novron, possessor of divine blood—a god. Have any of you sensed a power within? A belief in your own worth beyond that of others? This is your chance to prove to all of Elan that you are no fool, no mere man. Place your name upon the roster, ride out at nightfall, slay the beast, and you will become our divine ruler. You will not be a mere king, but *emperor*, and all kings will bow to you. You will take the imperial throne in Aquesta. All loyal Imperialists and the full force of the church will support you as we usher in a new age of order that will bring peace and harmony to the land. All you need do is destroy one lonely beast.

"What say you?"

This time the crowd cheered. Saldur glanced briefly at the archbishop and stepped away from the balcony to take a seat.

When Royce reached Dahlgren, the village was in turmoil. People were everywhere. Most of the villagers were heading toward the common well. There were plenty of new faces, all of them men, most carrying some sort of weapon. Royce found Hadrian at the well mobbed by villagers. None of them looked happy.

"Where do we go now?" Selen Brockton asked in tears.

Hadrian once more stood on the well, standing over the crowd and looking like he wanted to break something. "I don't know, Mrs. Brockton, home I guess, for now at least."

"But our home has a thatched roof."

"Try digging cellars and getting as low as possible."

"What's going on?" Royce asked.

"The Archbishop of Ghent has arrived and moved into the manor house. He and his clergy, as well as a few dozen nobles, have taken over the castle and driven everyone else out. Well, except for Russell, Dillon, and Kline, whom he ordered to fill in the shelter and the tunnel we were digging, saying they could repair the damages or hang for destruction of property. Good old Deacon Tomas, he stands there nodding and saying, 'I told them not to do it, but they wouldn't listen.' They kept most of the livestock too, saying it was in the castle so it belonged to the manor. Now everyone blames me for losing their animals."

"What about the bonfires?" Royce asked, "We could still build one here in the commons."

"No good," Hadrian told him. "His lordship declared it unlawful to cut trees in the area and confiscated the oxen with the rest of the animals."

"Did you tell him what will happen when the sun goes down?"

"I can't tell him anything." Hadrian threw up his hands, running his fingers through his hair as if he might start pulling it out. "I can't get past the twenty or so odd soldiers he has at the castle gate. Which is a good thing too or I might kill the guy."

"Why is the church here at all?"

"That's the kicker," Hadrian told him. "You know that competition the church has been announcing? Turns out that contest is to slay the Gilarabrywn."

"What?"

"They intend to send contestants out to fight the thing at nightfall and if they die, they'll send the next one. They've got a damn list nailed to the castle gate."

"It's alright, it's alright," Deacon Tomas shouted.

Everyone turned to see the cleric coming down the trail from the castle approaching the crowd at the well. He walked with his hands raised as if in blessing. He had a great smile on his face, which turned his eyes into half-moons. "Everything is going to be fine," he told them in a loud confident voice. "The archbishop has come to help us. They are going to kill the beast and save us from this nightmare."

"What about our livestock?" Vince Griffin asked.

"They will need most of them to feed the troops, but what isn't used will be returned after the beast has been slain."

The crowd grumbled.

"Now, now, what price do you put on safety? What price do you put on the lives of your children? Are a pig and a cow worth the lives of your children? Your wife? Consider it a tithe and be thankful the church has come to Dahlgren to save us. No one else has. The King of Dunmore ignored us, but your church has responded by sending not just some knight or margrave, but the Archbishop of Ghent himself. Soon the beast will be dead and Dahlgren will be a place of happiness once more. If that means one year of no meat, and plowing without an ox, surely that is not too high a price to pay. Now everyone please, back to your homes. Stay out of their way and let them do their work."

"What about my daughter?" Theron growled and pushed forward looking like he might kill the deacon.

"It's alright, I've spoken with the archbishop and Bishop Saldur; they have agreed to let her stay. They have moved her to a smaller room but—"

"They won't let me in to see her!" the old farmer snapped.

"I know, I know," Tomas said in a soothing voice, "but I can. I just came down to explain things. I am heading right back and I promise you, I will stay by her side and watch over her until she is well."

Hadrian slipped out of the crowd that now shifted around the deacon. He turned to Royce with a bitter look. "Tell me you found a way into the tower."

Royce shrugged, "Maybe. We'll need to check it out tonight."

"Tonight?" he asked. "Shouldn't such things be done in the daylight? When we can both see and things with complicated names aren't flying around?"

"Not if I'm right."

"And if you're wrong?"

"If I'm wrong we'll both certainly die—most likely by being eaten."

"The thing is, I know you're not kidding. Did I mention I lost my weapons?"

"With any luck we won't need them. What we will need, however, is a good length of rope, sixty feet at least," Royce told him. "Lanterns, wax, a tinderbox—"

"I'm not going to like this, am I?" Hadrian asked miserably.

"Not at all," Royce replied.

Chapter 9

TRIALS BY MOONLIGHT

"BACK IN BED," the man shouted. "Back in bed this instant!" Arista was wandering the hallway of the manor house in as much an attempt to get to know her surroundings as to evade Bernice who was insisting she take a nap. Initially she thought the yelling was directed at her, and while she put up with Bernice and her pampering, she was certainly not about to allow anyone to address her in such a manner as this brassy fellow seemed to be doing. She was no longer in her native kingdom of Melengar where she was princess of the realm, but she was still a princess and an ambassador and no one had the right to speak to her like that.

With a fury in her countenance, she marched forward and turning a corner, spotted a middle-aged man and a young girl. The girl was dressed only in her nightgown, her face battered and bruised. He held her wrist, attempting to drag her into a bedroom.

"Unhand her!" Arista ordered. "Hilfred! Guards!"

The man and girl both looked at her, bewildered.

Hilfred raced around the corner and in an instant stood with sword drawn between his princess and the source of her anger.

"I said get your filthy hands off her this instant, or I will have them removed at the wrists."

"But I—" the man began.

From the other direction, two Imperial guards arrived. "Milady?" the guards greeted her.

Hilfred said nothing, but merely pointed his sword at the man's throat.

"Take this wretch into custody," Arista ordered. "He's forcing himself on this girl."

"No, no please," the girl protested. "It was my fault I—"

"It is not your fault." Arista looked at her with pity. "And you needn't be afraid. I can see to it that he never bothers you, *or anyone*, again."

"Oh dear Maribor, protect me," the man prayed.

"Oh no, you don't understand," the girl said. "He wasn't hurting me. He was trying to help me."

"How's that?"

"I had an accident," she pointed to the bruises on her face. "Deacon Tomas was taking care of me, but I was feeling better today and wanted to get up and walk, but he thought it best if I stay in bed another day. He is really only trying to look out for me. Please don't hurt him. He's been so kind."

"You know this man?" Arista asked the guards.

"He was cleared for entrance by the archbishop as the deacon of this village milady, and he was indeed attending to this girl who is known as Thrace." Tomas, with eyes wide with fear and Hilfred's sword steady at his throat, nodded as best he could and attempted a friendly though strained smile.

"Well," Arista said pursing her lips, "my mistake then." She looked at the guards. "Go back about your business."

"Princess." The guards bowed briskly, turned and walked back the way they had come.

Hilfred slowly sheathed his sword.

She looked back at the two. "My apologies, it's just that—that—well, never mind." She turned away embarrassed.

"Oh no, Your Highness." Thrace said attempting as best she could to curtsy. "Thank you so much for coming to my aid, even if I didn't actually need it. It is good to know that someone as great as you would bother to help a poor farmer's daughter." Thrace looked at her in awe. "I've never met a princess before. I've never even seen one."

"I hope I'm not too much of a disappointment then." Thrace was about to speak again but Arista beat her to it. "What happened to you?" She gestured at her face.

Thrace reached up, running her fingers over her forehead. "Is it that bad?"

"It was the Gilarabrywn, Your Highness," Tomas explained. "Thrace and her father Theron were the only two to ever survive a Gilarabrywn attack. Now please my dear girl, please get back in bed."

"But really, I am feeling much better."

"Let her walk with me a bit, deacon," Arista said, softening her tone. "If she feels worse I'll get her back to bed."

Tomas nodded and bowed.

Arista took Thrace by the arm and led her up the hallway, Hilfred walking a few steps behind. They could not travel far, only thirty yards or so; the manor house was not a real castle. Built from great rough-cut beams—some with the bark still on—she guessed there were only about eight bedrooms. In addition, there was a parlor, an office, and the great hall with a high ceiling and mounted heads of deer and bear. It reminded Arista of a cruder, smaller version of King Roswort's residence. The floor was made of wide pine planks and the outer walls were thick logs. Nailed along them were iron lanterns holding flickering candles that cast semi-circles of quivering light, for even though it was midafternoon, the interior of the manor was dark as a cave.

"You're so kind," the girl told her. "The others treat me—as if I don't belong here."

"Well, I'm glad you are here," Arista replied. "Other than my handmaiden Bernice, I think you are the only other woman here."

"It is just that everyone else was sent back home and I feel so out of place, like I'm doing something wrong. Deacon Tomas says I'm not. He says I'm hurt and I need time to recover and that he'll see to it no one bothers me. He's been very nice. I think he feels as helpless as everyone else around here. Maybe taking care of me is a battle he feels he can win."

"I misjudged the deacon," Arista told her, "and you. Are all farmers' daughters in Dahlgren so wise?"

"Wise?" Thrace looked embarrassed.

Arista smiled at her. "Where is your family?"

"My father is in the village. They won't let him in to see me, but the deacon is working on that. I don't think it matters as we will be leaving Dahlgren as soon as I can travel, which is another reason I want to get my strength back. I want to get away from here. I want us to find a new place and start fresh. I'll find a man, get married, have a son and call him Hickory."

"Quite the plan, but how are you feeling—really?"

"I still have headaches and to be honest I'm getting a little dizzy right now."

"Maybe we should head back to your bedroom then," Arista said and they turned around.

"But, I am feeling so much better than I was. That's another reason why I got up. I haven't been able to thank Esra. I thought he might be in the halls here somewhere."

"Esra?" Arista asked. "Is he the village doctor?"

"Oh no, Dahlgren's never had a doctor. Esra is—well, he's a very smart man. If it hadn't been for him both me, and my father, would be dead by now. He was the one who made the medicine that saved me."

"He sounds like a great person."

"Oh he is. I try to pay him back by helping him eat. He's very proud you understand and he would never ask, so I offer and I can see he appreciates it."

"Is he too poor to afford food?"

"Oh no, he just doesn't have any hands."

"Tur is a myth," Esrahaddon was saying to the dwarf as Royce and Hadrian arrived at the falls.

"Says you," Magnus replied.

The wizard and the dwarf sat on the rocky escarpment facing each other, arguing over the roar. The sun, having dropped behind the trees, left the two in shadow, but the crystalline spires atop Avempartha caught the last rays of dying red light.

Esrahaddon sighed, "I'll never understand what it is about religion that causes otherwise sensible people to believe in fairy tales. Even in the world of religion, Tur is a parable, not a reality. You're dealing with myths based on legends based on superstitions and taking it literally. That is very undwarf-like. Are you certain you don't have some human blood in your ancestry?"

"That's just insulting," Magnus glared at the wizard. "You deny it, but the proof is right before you. If you had dwarven eyes you could see the truth in that blade." Magnus gestured at Royce.

"What's this all about?" Hadrian asked. "Hello Magnus, murder anyone lately?"

The dwarf scowled.

"This dwarf insists that Royce's dagger was made by Kile," Esrahaddon explained.

"I didn't say that," the dwarf snapped. "I said it was a Tur Blade. It could have been made by anyone from Tur."

"What's Tur?" Hadrian asked.

"A misguided cult of lunatics that worship a fictitious god. They named him Kile of all things. You'd think they could have at least come up with a better name."

"I've never heard of Kile," Hadrian said. "Now I'm not a religious scholar, but if I remember what a little monk once told me, the dwarven god is Drome, the elvish god is Ferrol, and the human god is Maribor. Their sister, the goddess of flora and fauna, is… Muriel, right? And her son Uberlin is the god of darkness. So, how does this Kile fit in?"

"He's their father," Esrahaddon explained.

"Oh right, I forgot about him, but his name isn't Kile its… Erebus, or something isn't it? And he's dead, so how—"

Esrahaddon chuckled, "It doesn't make any sense. Religion never does. Anyway, have you heard the tale of how Erebus raped his daughter Muriel?"

"More or less."

"How his sons banded together and killed him for it?"

Hadrian nodded.

"Well, the Cult of Tur, or Kile as it is also known, insists that a god is immortal and cannot die. This strange group of people appeared during the imperial reign of Estermon II and began circulating this story that Erebus had been drunk, or whatever equivalent there is to a god, when he raped his daughter, and was ashamed. Erebus, the story goes, allowed his children—the gods—to believe they had killed him. Then Erebus came to Muriel and begged her forgiveness. She told her father that she would only forgive him if he were to do penance for his crime. The penance she set for him was to do good deeds throughout Elan, but to do them as a commoner, not as a god or even a king. For each act of sacrifice and kindness that she approved of, she would grant him a feather from her marvelous robe, and when her robe was gone then she would forgive him and welcome him home.

"The Kile legend says that ages ago a stranger came to a poor village called Tur. No one knows where it was, of course, and over the centuries its location has changed in response to various claims, but the most common legend places it in Delgos because it was being regularly attacked by the Dacca and, of course, because of the similarity in names to the port city of Tur Del Fur. The story goes that this stranger called himself Kile, and entering into Tur and seeing the terrible plight of the desperate villagers, taught them the art of weapon making to help in their defense. The weapons he taught them to make were reputed to be the greatest in the world, capable of cleaving through solid iron as if it were soft wood. Their shields and armor were light and yet stronger than stone. After he taught them the craft, they used it to defend their homes. After driving off the Dacca, legend says there was a thunderclap on a cloudless day and from the heavens, a single white feather fell into Kile's hands. He wept at the gift and bid them all farewell, never to be seen again. At least not by the residents of Tur. Throughout the various reigns of different emperors there always seemed to be at least one or two stories of Kile appearing here and there doing good deeds and obtaining his feather. The legend of the village of Tur stood out beyond all others because the poor village of Tur was now famous for its great weaponry."

"I'll have to agree with the wizard then. I've never heard of a town making anything that fits that description," Hadrian said.

"There's more. Supposedly, the village was inundated with requests for arms. The Turists didn't feel it was right to make weapons for just anyone, so they only made a few, and only for those who had a just and good need. Powerful kings, however, decided to take the god given craft secrets for themselves and prepared to battle for control of the village. On the day of the battle, however, the armies marched in to discover the village of Tur—all its inhabitants and buildings—were gone. Not a trace was left of their existence except for a single white feather that came from no known bird."

"Any dwarf in Elan would give his beard for the secrets of Tur, or even the chance to study a Tur blade."

"And you think Alverstone is a Tur blade?" Hadrian asked.

"What did you call it?" Magnus asked his beady eyes abruptly focusing on the fighter.

"Alverstone, that's what Royce calls his dagger," Hadrian explained.

"Don't encourage him," Royce said, his eyes fixed on the tower.

"Where did he get this, Alverstone?" the dwarf asked, lowering his voice.

"It was a gift from a friend," Hadrian said, "right?"

"Who? And where did the friend get it from?" the dwarf persisted.

"You are aware I can hear you?" Royce told them, then seeing something, he pointed toward Avempartha. "There, look."

They all scrambled up to peer at the outline of the fading tower. The sun was down now and night was upon them. Like great mirrors, the river and the tower captured the starlight and the luminous moon. The mist from the falls appeared as an eerie white fog skirting the base. Near the top of the spires, a dark shape spread its wings and flew down along the course of the river. It wheeled and circled back over the falls, catching air currents and rising higher until, with a flap of its massive wings, the beast headed out over the trees above the forest, flying toward Dahlgren.

"That's its lair?" Hadrian asked incredulously. "It lives in the tower?"

"Convenient isn't it," Royce remarked, "that the beast resides at the same place as the one weapon that can kill it."

"Convenient for whom?"

"I guess that remains to be seen," Esrahaddon said.

Royce turned to the dwarf. "Alright my little mason, shall we head to the tunnel? It's in the river, isn't it? Somewhere underwater?"

Magnus looked at him surprised.

"I am only guessing, but from the look on your face I must be right. It's the only place I haven't looked. Now in return for your life, you will show us exactly where."

Arista stood with the Pickerings on the south stockade wall watching the sunset over the gate. The wall provided the best view of both the courtyard and the hillside beyond, while keeping them above the turmoil. Below, knights busied themselves dressing in armor; archers strung their bows, horses decorated in caparisons shifted uneasily, and priests prayed to Novron for wisdom. The contest was about to commence. Beyond the wall the village of Dahlgren remained silent. Not a candle was visible. Nothing moved.

Another scuffle broke out near the gate where the list of combatants hung on the hitching post. Arista could see several men pushing and swinging, rising dust.

"Who is it this time?" Mauvin asked. The elder Pickering leaned back against the log wall. He was in a simple loose tunic and a pair of soft shoes today. This was the Mauvin she most remembered, the carefree boy who challenged her to stick duels back when she stood a foot taller and could overpower him, in the days when she had a mother and father and her greatest challenge was making Lenare jealous.

"I can't tell," Fanen replied, peering down, "I think one is Sir Erlic."

"Why are they fighting?" Arista asked.

"Everyone wants a higher place on the list," Mauvin replied.

"That doesn't make sense. It doesn't matter who goes first."

"It does if the person in front of you kills the beastie before you get a chance."

"But they can't. Only the heir can kill the beast."

"You really think that?" Mauvin asked, turning around, grasping the sharpened points of the logs and peering down the outside of the wall. "No one else does."

"Who's first on the list?"

"Well, Tobis Rentinual was."

"Which one is he?" she asked.

"He's the one we told you about with the big mysterious wagon."

"There," Fanen pointed down in the courtyard, "the foppish looking one leaning against the smokehouse. He has a shrill voice and a superior attitude that makes you want to throttle him."

Mauvin nodded. "That's him. I peeked under his tarp, there's this huge contraption made of wood, ropes, and pulleys. He managed to find the list first and sign his name. No one had a problem with it when they thought the contest was a tournament. Everyone was just itching to have a go at him, but now, well, the thought of Tobis as emperor has become a communal fear."

"What do you mean *was?*"

"He got bumped," Fanen said.

"Bumped?"

"Luis Guy's idea," Mauvin explained. "The sentinel decreed that those farther down on the list could move up via combat. Those unsatisfied with their place could challenge anyone for their position to a fight. Once issued, the challenged party could trade positions on the list or enter into combat with the challenger. Sir Enden of Chadwick challenged Tobis who gave up his position. Who could blame him? Only Sir Gravin had the courage to challenge Enden, but several others drew swords against one another for lesser spots. Most expected the duels would be by points, but Guy declared battles over only when the opponent yielded so they have gone on for hours. Many have been injured. Sir Gravin yielded only after Enden pierced his shoulder. He's announced he's withdrawing and will be leaving tomorrow, and he's not the only one. Several have already left wrapped in bandages."

Arista looked at Fanen. "You aren't challenging?"

Mauvin chuckled. "It was kinda funny. The moment Guy made the announcement, everyone looked at us."

"But you didn't challenge?"

Fanen scowled and glared at Mauvin. "He won't let me. And my name is near the bottom."

"Hadrian Blackwater told us not to sign up," Mauvin explained.

"So?" Fanen stared at his brother.

"So, the one man here who could take that top spot without breaking a sweat doesn't even have his name on the list. Either he knows something we don't, or he thinks he does. That's worth waiting out the first night at least. Besides, you heard Arista, it doesn't matter who goes first."

"You know who else isn't on the list?" Fanen asked. "Lord Rufus."

"Yeah, I saw that. Thought he'd be the one to challenge Enden—it would have been worth the trip just to see that duel. He's not even out in the yard with the rest."

"He's been with the archbishop a lot."

Trials by Moonlight

From their elevated position, Arista scanned the courtyard below. The light was gone from the yard, the walls and trees casting the interior in shade. Men went around lighting torches and mounting them. There were hundreds assembled within the grounds and more outside all gathered into small groups. They talked, some shouted. She could hear laughter and even a bit of singing—she could not tell the song, but by its rhythm she guessed it was a bawdy tavern tune. There was a lot of toasting going on. Dark figures in the failing light, broad, powerful men slamming cups together with enough force to spill foam. Above it all, on a wooden platform raised in the center of the yard, stood Sentinel Luis Guy. He was high enough to catch the last rays of the sun and the last breaths of the evening wind. The light made his red cassock look like fire and the wind blowing his cape lent him an ominous quality.

She looked back at the brothers. Mauvin had his mouth open, struggling to clear something from a back tooth with his forefinger. Fanen had his head up looking at the sky. She was glad they were with her. It was a little bit of home in the wilderness and she imagined the smell of apples.

Arista and Alric had spent summer months at Drondil Fields to escape the heat of the city. She remembered how they used to climb the trees in the orchard outside the country castle and have apple fights in early autumn. The rotten apples would burst on the branches and spray pulp, soaking them until they all smelled like cider. Each tree a sovereign castle, they would make alliances. Mauvin always teamed with Alric shouting "My king! My king!" Lenare paired with Fanen wanting to protect her younger brother from the 'brutes' as she called them. Arista always remained on her own fighting both groups. Even when Lenare stopped climbing trees, it became the boys against the girl. She did not mind. She did not notice. She did not even think about it until now.

There was so much in her head. So much she needed to sort out. It had been hard to think bouncing around in the coach with Bernice staring at her. She desperately wanted to talk to someone, if only to hear her own words aloud. The idea that Sauly was a conspirator was growing in her mind despite her reluctance to accept it. If Sauly could betray her father, who could be trusted? Could Esrahaddon? Had he used her to escape? Was he responsible for her father's death? Now it seemed the old wizard was nearby, somewhere just outside the walls perhaps, spending the night in one of the village houses. She did not know what to do, or who to trust.

Mauvin found what he was looking for and flicked it from his finger over the wall.

She opened her mouth to speak, hesitating on the proper words to say. The whole trip there she planned to discuss the issues raised at Ervanon with the Pickerings; well, Mauvin at least. She closed her mouth and bit her lip, once more thinking back to the long ago orchard and the smell of apples.

"There you are, Your Highness," Bernice said, rushing to her with a shawl for her shoulders. "You shouldn't be out so late; it's not proper."

"Honestly Bernice, you should have had children when you had the chance. This preoccupation with pampering me has got to stop."

The older woman only smiled warmly. "I'm just looking after you, dear. You need looking after. This foul place is full of rough men. There is little but thin walls and the grace of the archbishop separating them from your virtue. A lady such as yourself is a strong temptation, and given the untamed surroundings of this wilderness it could easily drive many a good man to acts of rashness." She glanced suspiciously at the brothers who looked back sheepishly. "And there are more than a few here who I couldn't even describe as good men. In a great castle with a proper retinue men can be kept at bay by holding them in awe of royalty, but here my lady, in this barbaric, feral landscape, they will surely lose their heads."

"Oh, Bernice, please."

"Here we go," Fanen said excitedly.

As the last of the sun's light faded, the gates opened and Sir Enden and his retinue of two squires and three pages rode out, torches flaming. They trotted to the open plain where the knight prepared to do battle.

A shout rose from the crowd just then and Arista looked up to see a dark shadow sweep across the moonlit sky. It drifted in like a hawk, a silhouette of wings and tail. The crowd murmured and gasped as it circled the castle briefly, moving hesitantly before having its attention caught by torches waved by Sir Enden's entourage on the hillside.

It folded its wings and dove, falling out of the sky like an arrow aimed at the knight of Chadwick. Torches moved frantically and Arista thought she saw Sir Enden level his lance and charge forward. There were screams, cries of anguish and terror, as one by one the torches in the field went out.

"Next!" shouted Luis Guy.

The dwarf led them up the river path to where the moon revealed a large rock protruding out toward the water. To Hadrian it looked vaguely like the dull tip of a broad spear. Magnus thumped the dirt with his boot then pointed toward the river. "We go in here. Swim straight down about twenty feet—there's an opening in the bank. The tunnel runs right under us, curves down and then runs under the river to the tower."

"You can tell all that with your foot?" Royce asked.

Hadrian looked at Esrahaddon. "How are you at swimming?"

"I can't say I've had the opportunity since…," he said lifting his arms. "But I can hold my breath a good long time. Drag me if necessary."

"Let me go first," Royce announced, his eyes on Magnus. He threw his coil of rope on the ground, and tied one end around his waist. "Feed this out to me, but hang on to it. I don't know how swift the current is."

"There is no current here," Magnus told them. "There's an underwater shelf that juts out creating an eddy. It's like a little pond down there."

"You'll forgive me if I don't take your word for it. Once I am down I'll give three tugs indicating that it's safe to follow. Tie off the end and follow the line down. If, on the other hand, I jump in and the rope runs out like you just caught a marlin, haul me back so I can personally kill him."

The dwarf sighed.

Royce slipped off his cloak and with Hadrian holding the rope he descended into the river as if he was rappelling off the side of a wall. He dropped and vanished under the dark water. Hadrian felt the rope slip out gradually from between his fingers. At his side, Magnus showed no signs of concern. The dwarf stood with his head cocked back looking up at the sky. "What do you suppose it's doing tonight?" he asked.

"Eating knights would be my guess," Hadrian replied. "Let's just hope they keep the thing busy."

Deeper and deeper, the rope trolled out then it stopped. Hadrian watched where the line entered the water; it made a little white trail as it cut the current.

Tug. Tug. Tug.

"That's it. He's in," Hadrian announced, "you next, little man."

Magnus glared at him. "I'm a dwarf."

"Get in the river."

Magnus walked to the edge. Holding his nose and pointing his toes, he jumped and disappeared with a plop.

"That leaves you and me," Hadrian said, tying the end of the rope to a birch tree that leaned a bit out toward the river. "You go first—I'll follow—see how well you do. If need be, I'll pull you through."

The wizard nodded and for the first time since Hadrian knew him, he looked unsure of himself. Esrahaddon took three deep breaths rapidly blowing each out; on the fourth inhale, he held it and jumped feet first. Hadrian leapt in right after.

The water was cold, not icy or breathtaking, but colder than expected. The immediate shock caught Hadrian off guard for an instant. He kicked out with his feet, pointed his head down, and began to swim along the rope. Magnus was right about the current. The water was still as a pond. He opened his eyes. Above him, there was a faint blue-gray shimmer but it died at the surface, below it was black. Panic gripped Hadrian when he realized he could not see Esrahaddon. Almost in response, a faint light appeared directly below him. The wizard's robe gave off a blue-green glow as he swam, pedaling his feet and stroking with his arms. Despite the lack of hands, he made good headway.

The light from the robe revealed the riverbank and the rope running down. It disappeared inside a dark hole. He watched the wizard slip through and with his lungs starting to burn, followed him. Once inside he kicked upwards and, almost together their heads emerged from a quiet pool in a small cave.

Royce had the other end of the rope tied to a rock. There was a lantern burning beside him. The single flame easily illuminated the room. The chamber was a natural cave with a tunnel leading out. Magnus stood off to the side, either studying the cavern walls or just keeping his distance from Royce.

When Esrahaddon surfaced, Royce hauled him out. "You might have had an easier time swimming if you'd taken off—" Royce stopped as he saw the wizard's robe. It was dry.

Hadrian climbed out of the pool feeling the river water drizzle down his body. He could hear the drops echoing in the cave like a rainstorm, but Esrahaddon was exactly as he had been before entering the river. With the exception of his hair and beard, he was not even damp.

Hadrian and Royce exchanged a glance, but said nothing.

Royce picked up his lantern. "Coming, short-stuff?"

The dwarf grumbled and, taking hold of his beard with both hands, twisted a bit of water out. "You realize, my friend, dwarves are an older and far more accomplished—"

"Less chatter, more walking," Royce interrupted, pointing at the tunnel. "You lead. And you're not my friend."

Traveling forward they entered into a new world. The walls were smooth and seamless, as if cut by the flow of water. The glossy surface magnified the light from Royce's lantern, making the curved interior surprisingly bright.

"So where are we?" Hadrian asked.

"Under the bank, not far below where we were standing before entering the water," Magnus told him. "The tunnel here corkscrews down."

"Incredible," Hadrian said, his eyes looking about him in amazement at the sparkling walls. "It's as though we're on the inside of a diamond."

Just as the dwarf predicted, the tunnel curved around and around, sloping down. Just as Hadrian lost all sense of direction, it stopped spinning and ran straight. It was not long before they could hear and feel the thunder of the falls. It vibrated through the stone. Here the ceiling and walls seeped water. A thousand years of neglect allowed stalactites of crystal to form on the ceiling and jagged mounds of mineral deposits on the floor.

"This is a bit disturbing," Hadrian remarked noticing a buildup of water on the floor that was getting deeper as they moved forward.

"Bah!" Magnus muttered, but failed to add anything more.

They slogged through the water dodging stone spikes. Examining the walls, Hadrian noticed designs carved into them. Etchings of geometric shapes and patterns lined the corridor. Some of the more delicate lines were faded, missing, perhaps lost to the erosion of a billion water droplets. No words were visible and there were no recognizable symbols. The etching appeared to be nothing more than decorative. Above, almost lost in the growing stone, were brackets for what might have once been banner poles, and on the side walls he spotted mountings for lamps. Hadrian tried to imagine how the tunnel looked before the time of Novron, when multi-colored banners and rows of bright lamps might have illuminated the causeway. It was not long before the tunnel pitched upwards again and they could all see a faint light.

The tunnel ended at a stairway going up. The steps curved and were wide enough for them to take two strides before climbing the next step. When they reached the top, the star-filled sky was above them once more and before long, they stood above ground on the outcropping of rock that made up the base of the citadel. A strong wind met them. The gale was damp, filled with a wet mist. They stood at the end of a short stone bridge spanning a narrow crevasse, beyond which stood the spires of the monolithic tower. It loomed above them so high it was impossible to see the top.

More stairs awaited them on the far side and they moved at a slow but even pace, staying single file, even though the stairs were wide enough for two, or even three, to walk abreast. They climbed five sets of steps, zigzagging in a half-circle around the outside of the tower. As they started their sixth flight, Royce waited until they had moved to the lee of the citadel then called a halt for them to catch their breath. Below, the roar of the falls boomed, but from their perch, protected from the wind, the night seemed still. There were no sounds, no crickets or owls, just the deep voice of the river and the howl of the wind.

"This is ridiculous," Royce shouted over the roar. "Where's the damn door. I don't like being so exposed."

"It's just up ahead, not too much farther," Esrahaddon replied.

"How long do we have?" Hadrian asked, looking at the wizard who shrugged in reply.

The wizard shrugged.

"Does it return here directly after killing, or does it enjoy the night?" Royce inquired. "I should think having been locked up in this tower for nine hundred years, it would want to spend some time flying about."

"It isn't a person, or an animal. It's a conjuration, a mystic embodiment of power. It mimics life and understands threats to its existence certainly, but I doubt it has any concept of pleasure or freedom. Like I said it's not alive."

"Then why does it eat?" Royce asked.

"It doesn't."

"Then why is it killing a person or two a night?"

"I've wondered that myself. It should attempt to fulfill its last instructions and that was clearly to kill the Emperor. It is possible that not finding its target, and not able to travel far from this tower—conjurations are often limited to a specific distance from their creator or point of origin—it might be trying to lure him here. It could have deduced that the Emperor would not tolerate the slaughter of his people and would come to aid the village."

"Regardless, we'd better be quick," Hadrian concluded and led them all in standing up.

The wind resumed as they circled around. It whistled in their ears and buffeted their steps. The damp clothes chilled them despite the hard work of the march. Above, the spires still rose far into the night sky and they all felt a grim sense of drudgery when they reached yet another short bridge, which ended abruptly at a solid wall.

Hadrian watched Royce sigh in disappointment as he looked at the dead end.

"I thought you said there was a door." Royce addressed the wizard.

"There was, and is."

Hadrian did not see a door. There was what appeared to be a faint outline of a door's frame etched in the wall in front of them, but it was solid stone.

Royce grimaced. "Another invisible stone portal?"

"Don't waste your time," Magnus told him. "You'll never open it. Trust me, I'm a dwarf. I spent hours trying to get in and nothing. That stone is enchanted and impenetrable. Crossing the river to get here was nothing compared to opening that door."

Royce turned to the dwarf with a puzzled look in his eyes. "You've been here? You tried to enter the tower. Why?"

"I told you I was on a job for Lord Rufus."

"You said you made him a sword."

"I did, but he didn't want just any sword. He wanted a replica of a sword, an elvish sword. He gave me a bunch of old drawings, which I used to make it. They were pretty good, with dimensions and material listed, but it's not like being able to examine the real thing." The dwarf's stare lingered on Royce suggestively. "I was told others of the same type could be found inside this tower. I came out here and spent all day climbing around, but never found a way in. No doors or windows, just things like this."

"This sword you made," Esrahaddon said. "Did it have writing on the blade?"

"Yep," Magnus replied. "They were real insistent that the inscription on the replica was exactly like that in the books."

"That's it," Esrahaddon muttered. "The church isn't here because of me, and they aren't here to find the heir; they're here to *make* an heir."

"Make an heir? I don't get it." Hadrian said. "I thought you said they wanted the heir dead."

"They do, but they are going to make a puppet. This Rufus has been picked to replace the true heir. There is a legend that only the bloodline of Novron can kill a Gilarabrywn. They will use this creature's death as undisputed proof that their boy is the true heir. Not only will it provide them legitimate means to dictate laws to the kings, but it will also hinder my efforts to reinstate the real heir to power. Who will believe an old outlawed wizard when their boy slew a Gilarabrywn? They will let a few bumpkins try to fight only to die, in order to prove the invincibility of the beast. Then this Rufus will step up and with his sword etched with the name, he'll slay it and become emperor. With Rufus as their figurehead, the church will return to power and reform the Empire. Excellent move, I must say. I'll admit I hadn't expected it."

"A few moderate kings might have something to say about that," Hadrian replied.

"And they know that as much as you do. They have a plan to deal with it, I'm sure."

"So do we still need to get inside?" Hadrian asked.

"Oh yes," the wizard told them, "Now more than ever." He chuckled. "Just imagine if before their boy Rufus slays this beast another contestant slays it first."

The dwarf snorted. "Bah! I told you, you aren't getting through that door. It's solid stone."

The wizard considered the archway once more. "Open it, Royce."

Royce looked skeptical. "Open what? That's a wall. There's no latch, no lock, not even a seam. Anyone have a gem we can try?"

"This isn't a gemlock," The wizard explained.

"I agree and I would know," Magnus told them.

"Try opening it anyway," the wizard insisted staring at Royce. "That's why I brought you here, remember?"

Royce looked at the wall before him and scowled. "How?"

"Use your instincts. You opened the door to my prison and it had no latch either."

"I was lucky."

"You might be lucky again. Try."

Royce shrugged. He stepped forward and placed his hands lightly on the stone letting his fingertips drift across the surface searching by feel for what his eyes might not be able to see.

"This is a waste of time," Magnus said. "This is clearly a very powerful lock and without the key there is no way to open it. I know these things. I've *made* these things. They are designed to prevent thieves like him from entering."

"Ah," Esrahaddon said to the dwarf, "but you underestimate Royce. He is no ordinary lock-picker. I sensed it the moment I first saw him. I know he can open it." The wizard turned to Royce who was quickly showing signs of exasperation. "Stop *trying* to open it and just open it. Don't think about it. Just do it."

"Do what?" he asked, irritated. "If I knew how, don't you think I would have opened it by now?"

"That's just it, don't think. Stop being a thief. Just open the door."

Royce glared at the wizard. "Fine," he said as he pushed his palm against the stone wall and pulled it back with a look of shock on his face.

Esrahaddon's expression was one of sheer delight. "I knew it," the wizard said.

"Knew what? What happened?" Hadrian asked.

"I just pushed," Royce laughed at the absurdity.

"And?"

"What do you mean *and?*" Royce asked pointing at the solid wall.

"And what happened? Why are you smiling?" Hadrian studied the wall for something he missed, a tiny crack, a little latch, a key hole, but he saw nothing. It was the same as it had always been.

"It opened," Royce said.

Hadrian and the dwarf looked at Royce puzzled. "What are you talking about?"

Royce looked back over his shoulder as if that would make everything clear. "Are you both blind? The door is standing wide open. You can see there's a corridor that—"

"They can't see it," the wizard interrupted.

Royce looked from the wizard to Hadrian. "You can't see that the door is standing open now? You can't see this huge, three-story double door?"

Hadrian shook his head. "It looks just like it always has."

Magnus nodded his agreement.

"They can't see it because they can't enter," the wizard explained. Hadrian watched Royce look up, following the wizard's glance and his eyes widened.

"What?" Hadrian asked.

"Elven magic. Designed to prevent enemies from passing through these walls. All they see, and all they will encounter is solid stone. The portal is closed to them."

"You can see it?" Royce asked Esrahaddon.

"Oh yes, quite plainly."

"So why is it we can see it and they can't?"

"I already told you, it is magic to stop enemies from entering. As it happens, I was invited into this tower nine hundred years ago.

It was abandoned immediately after my visit; so I am guessing there was no one to revoke that permission." He looked back at what Hadrian still saw as solid stone. "I don't think I could have opened it though, even if I had hands. That's why I needed you."

"Me?" Royce said, then a sudden shocking realization filled his expression and he glared at the wizard before him. "So you knew?"

"I wouldn't be much of a wizard if I didn't, now would I?"

Royce looked self-consciously at his own feet then slowly turned to look cautiously at Hadrian who only smiled. "You knew too?"

Hadrian frowned "Did you really think I could work with you all these years and not figure it out? It is a little obvious, you know."

"You never said anything."

"I figured you didn't want to talk about it. You guard your past jealously, pal, and you have many doors on which I don't knock. Honestly, there were times I wondered if you knew."

"Knew what? What's going on?" Magnus demanded.

"None of your business," Hadrian told the dwarf, "but it does leave us with a parting of the ways, doesn't it. We can't come in, and I can tell you I am not fond of sitting here on the doorstep waiting for the flying lizard to come home."

"You should go back," Esrahaddon told them. "Royce and I can go on from here alone."

"How long will this take?" Hadrian asked.

"Several hours, a day perhaps," the wizard explained.

"I had hoped to be gone before it returned," Royce said.

"Not possible, besides this shouldn't be a problem for you of all people, I am certain you have stolen from occupied homes before."

"Not ones where the owner can swallow me in a single bite."

"So we'll have to be extra quiet now, won't we?"

Chapter 10

LOST SWORDS

"ITHOUGHT LAST night went well," Bishop Saldur stated, slicing himself a wedge of breakfast cheese. He sat at the banquet table in the great hall of the manor along with Archbishop Galien, Sentinel Luis Guy, and Lord Rufus. The lofty cathedral ceiling of bound logs did little to elevate the dark oppressive atmosphere caused by the lack of natural light. The entire manor had few windows and made Saldur feel as if he were crouching in an animal's den, some woodchuck's burrow, or beaver lodge. The thought that this miserable hovel would see the birth of the new empire was a disappointment, but he was a pragmatic man. The method was irrelevant. All that mattered was the final solution. Either it worked or it did not. This was the only measure of value—aesthetics could be added later.

Right now they needed to establish the Empire. Mankind had drifted too long without a rudder. A firm hand was what the world needed, a solid grip on the wheel with a keen set of eyes that could see into the future and direct the vessel into clear, tranquil waters. Saldur envisioned a world of peace through prosperity, and security through strength. The feudal system so prevalent across the four nations held them back, chaining the kingdoms to a poverty of weakness and divided interests. What they needed was a centralized government with an enlightened ruler and a talented, educated bureaucracy overseeing every aspect of life. With the entire strength of mankind under one yoke, it was impossible to imagine the many goals that could be accomplished. They could revolutionize farming, its fruits distributed evenly at a price that even the poorest could afford, vanquishing hunger. Laws could be standardized, eliminating arbitrary punishment by vindictive tyrants. Knowledge from the corners of the land could be gathered into a single repository where great minds could learn and develop new ideas, new techniques. They could improve transportation with standardized roads and they could clear the stench of cities with standardized sewage systems. If all this had to begin here in this little wood hut on the edge of the world, it was a small price to pay. "How many died?" he asked.

The archbishop shrugged and Rufus did not bother looking up from his plate.

"Five contestants were killed by the beast last night," Luis Guy answered his question as he plucked a muffin off the table with the point of his dagger.

The Knight of Nyphron continued to impress Saldur. He was a sword manifested in the form of a man—sharp, pointed, cutting, and just as elegant in appearance. He always stood straight, shoulders back, chin up, eyes focused directly on his target, his face a hard chiseled mask of contention, daring, almost begging for a confrontation from anyone fool enough to challenge him. Even after days in the wilderness, not a thread lay out of place. He was a paragon of the church, the embodiment of the ideal.

"Only five?"

"After the fifth was ripped in two, few were eager to step forward, and while they hesitated, the beast flew off."

"Do you think five deaths are sufficient to prove the beast is invincible?" Galien asked, looking at all of them.

"No, but we may have no choice. After last night, I'm not certain any more will volunteer," Guy replied. "The previously witnessed enthusiasm for the hunt has waned."

"And will you be ready, Lord Rufus? If no one else steps forward?" the archbishop asked turning to the rough warrior seated at the end of the table.

Lord Rufus looked up. He was taking full advantage of the meal, chewing on a mutton leg that slicked his unruly beard with grease. His eyes stared at them from beneath the heavy hedges of his bushy red eyebrows. He spit a bit of bone out. "That depends," he said. "This sword the dwarf made, can it cut the beastie's hide?"

"We had our scribes check the dwarf's work against the ancient records," Saldur replied. "They match perfectly with the markings recorded on previous weapons that were capable of killing beasts of this kind."

"If it can cut it, I'll kill it," Rufus grinned a greasy smile. "Just be ready to crown me emperor." He bit into the leg again and ripped a large hunk of dark meat off, filling his mouth.

Saldur could hardly believe the patriarch had chosen this oaf to be the Emperor. If Guy was a sword, Rufus was a mallet, a blunt instrument of dull labor. Being a native of Trent, he would ensure the loyalty of the unruly northern kingdoms that most likely could not be gained any other way. That would easily double their strength going in. There was also his popularity, which extended down through Avryn and Calis. This reduced the number of protests against him. The fact that he was a renowned warrior would certainly help him in his first obstacle of killing the Gilarabrywn and crushing any opposition offered by the Nationalists. The problem, as Saldur saw it, was that Rufus, a rough, unreasonable dolt, had not only the heart of a warrior, but the mind as well. His answer to every problem was beating it to death. It would be hard to control him, but it made little sense to worry about the headaches of administrating an empire before one even existed. They needed to create it first and worry about the quality of the Emperor later. If Rufus became a problem they could merely ensure that once he had a son, and once that son was safely in their custody, Rufus could meet an untimely end.

"Well then," Galien said. "It would seem everything is in hand."

"Is that all you called me here for?" Guy asked with a tone of irritation.

"No," Galien replied, "I received some unexpected news this morning and I thought you might like to hear of it, Luis, as I suspect it will interest you very much. Carlton, will you ask the Deacon Tomas to come in?"

Galien's steward, Carlton, who was busy pouring watered-down wine, promptly left the table and opened the door to the hallway. "His grace will see you now."

In walked a plump, pudgy man in a priest's frock. "Luis Guy, Lord Rufus, let me introduce Deacon Tomas of Dahlgren Village. Tomas, this is Lord Rufus, Sentinel Guy, and you already know Bishop Saldur, of course."

Tomas nodded with a nervous smile.

"What's this all about?" Guy asked as if Tomas was not there.

"Go ahead, Tomas, tell the sentinel what you told me."

The deacon shifted his feet and avoided eye contact with anyone in the room. When he spoke, his voice was so soft they strained to hear him. "I was just mentioning to his grace how I had stepped up and handled things here in the absence of the margrave. It has been hard times in this village, hard indeed, but I tried my best to keep the great house in order. It wasn't my idea that they should invade the place, I tried to stop them, but I am only one man, you see. It was impossible—"

"Yes—yes, tell him about the cripple," the archbishop put in.

"Oh certainly. Ah yes, Esra came to live here, I don't know, about a month ago he—"

"Esra?" Guy said and glanced abruptly at the archbishop and Saldur who both smiled knowingly at him.

"Yes," Deacon Tomas replied. "That's his name. He never said too much, but the villagers are a good lot and they took turns feeding him as the poor man was in dire straights missing both hands as he is."

"Esrahaddon!" Guy hissed. "Where is the snake?"

The sudden violent reaction of the sentinel shocked Tomas, who took a step back.

"Ah, well, I don't know, he comes and goes, although I remember he was around the village a lot more before the two strangers arrived."

"Strangers?" Guy asked.

"Friends of the Wood family I think. At least they arrived with Thrace and spend a lot of time with her and her father. Since they got here Esra spends most of his days off with the quiet one, Royce, I think they call him."

"Royce Melborn and Hadrian Blackwater, the two thieves that broke the wizard out of Gutaria, and Esrahaddon are all here in this village?" Saldur and Galien nodded at Luis.

"Very curious, isn't it?" the archbishop commented. "Perhaps we focused on the wrong hound when we approached Arista. It looks as if the old wizard has put his trust in the two thieves instead. The real question is why would they all be here? It can't be coincidence that he turns up in this little backwater village at the precise moment when the Emperor is about to be crowned."

"He couldn't know our plans," Guy told him.

"He *is* a wizard; they are good at discovering things. Regardless, you might want to see if you can determine what he's up to."

"Remember to keep your distance," Saldur added. "We don't want to tree this fox until we know he's led us to his den."

Hadrian folded the blanket twice in length then rolled it tight, buckling the resulting cloth log with two leather straps. He had all the gear left to them on the ground in neat piles. They still had all their camping gear, food, and feed. Royce had his saddle, bridle and bags, but Hadrian had lost his tack along with his weapons when Millie disappeared. It would be impossible to ride double and haul the gear. They would have to load Mouse up with everything and walk the trip home.

"There you are."

Hadrian looked up to see Theron striding from the direction of the Bothwicks, heading for the well with an empty bucket in his hand.

"We didn't see you around last night. Was worried something happened to you."

"Looks like everyone had a lucky night," Hadrian said.

"Everyone in the village—yeah, but I don't think them fellas up at the castle did so well. We heard a lot of shouting and screaming and they ain't celebrating this morning. My guess is their plan to kill the beast didn't go as hoped." The farmer scanned the piles. "Packing, eh? So you're leaving too?"

"I don't see why not. There's nothing keeping us here anymore. How's Thrace?"

"Doing well, rubbing elbows with the nobility she tells me. She's walking around just fine, the headaches are mostly gone. We'll be on our way tomorrow morning, I expect."

"Good to hear it," Hadrian said.

"Who's your friend?" Theron motioned to the dwarf, seated a few feet away in the shade of a poplar tree.

"Oh yeah. Theron meet Magnus. He's not so much a friend as an associate." He thought about that and added, "Actually, he's more like an enemy I'm keeping an eye on."

Theron nodded, but with a puzzled look, and the dwarf grumbled something neither caught.

"What about my lesson?" Theron asked.

"Are you kidding? I don't really see the point in a lesson if you're both leaving tomorrow."

"You have something else to do? Besides the road is a dangerous place and it wouldn't hurt to know a few more tricks, or is this your way of saying you want money now?"

"No," Hadrian waved his hand at the farmer, "grab the sticks."

By noon, the sun was hot and Hadrian had worked up a sweat sparring with Theron who was showing real improvement. Magnus sat on an overturned well bucket watching the two with interest. Hadrian explained proper form, how to obtain penetrating thrusts and grips which was hard using only rake handles.

"If you hold the sword with both hands, you lose versatility and reach, but you gain tremendous power. A good fighter knows when to switch from two hands to one and vice versa. If you are defending against someone with longer reach, you'd better be using one hand, but if you need to drive your sword deep through heavy armor—assuming you aren't holding a shield in your off hand—grip the pommel with both palms and thrust. Remember to yell as you do like I taught you before. Then drive home the blow using all your power. A solid breastplate won't stop a sword thrust. They aren't designed to. Armor prevents a swing or a slice, and can deflect the point of a thrust; that's why professional fighters wear smooth, unadorned armor. You always see these princes and dukes with all their fancy gilded breastplates and light thin metal heavily engraved—it's like walking around in a death trap. Of course, they don't really fight. They have knights do that for them. They just walk around and look pretty. So the idea is when you thrust, you aim for a crease, groove, or seam in the armor, something that will catch and hold the tip. The armpits are excellent targets, or up under the nose guard. Drive a four foot sword up under a nose guard and you don't have to worry much about a counter attack."

"How can you teach that poor fellow anything without swords?"

They both turned to see Mauvin Pickering walking toward them in his simple blue tunic. Gone was the dapper lord of Galilin, instead, he looked much like the boy Hadrian first saw at Drondil Fields. In his hands, he carried two swords and slung over his back two small round shields.

"I saw you from the walls and thought you might like to borrow these," he said, handing a sword and shield to Theron who accepted them awkwardly. "They are mine and Fanen's spares."

Theron eyed the young man suspiciously then looked to Hadrian.

"Go ahead," Hadrian told him, wiping the sweat from his brow with his sleeve. "He's right. You should know the feel of the real thing."

When Theron appeared confused at how to hold the shield, Mauvin began instructing him, showing the farmer where his arm slipped through the leather straps.

"See Hadrian, it helps to actually teach your pupil how to put on a real shield; unless, of course, you expect he'll be spending all of his time warring against maple trees. Where are your weapons anyway?"

Hadrian looked sheepish, "I lost them."

"Don't you carry enough for five people?"

"I've had a bad week."

"And who might you be?" Mauvin asked, looking at the dwarf.

Hadrian started to answer then stopped himself. Alric likely told Mauvin all about the dwarf who had murdered his father. "Him? He's…nobody."

"Okay…" Mauvin laughed, raising his hand and waving. "Pleased to meet you, Mr. Nobody." He then went and sat on the edge of the well where he folded his arms across his chest. "Go on. Show me what he's taught you."

Hadrian and Theron returned to fighting, but slower now as the sharp swords made Theron nervous. He soon became frustrated and turned to Mauvin scowling.

"You any good with these things?"

The young man raised an eyebrow in surprise. "My dear sir, weren't we already introduced? My name is Mauvin Pickering." He grinned.

Theron narrowed his eyes in confusion, glanced at Hadrian who said nothing, then faced the boy once more. "I asked if you knew how to use a sword son, not your name."

"But—I—oh, never mind. Yes, I have been trained in the use of a sword."

"Well, I spent all my life on farms, or in villages not much bigger than this one and I've never had much chance to see fellas beating each other with blades. It might help if 'n I was to see what I'm 'sposed to be doing. You know, all proper like."

"You want a demonstration?"

Theron nodded. "I have no way of knowing if Hadrian here even knows what he's doing."

"Alright," Mauvin said flexing his fingers, and shaking his hands as he walked forward. He had a bright smile on his face as if Theron had just invited him to play his favorite game.

The two paired off. Magnus and Theron took seats in the dirt and watched as Mauvin and Hadrian first walked through the basic moves and then demonstrated each at actual combat speed. Hadrian would explain each maneuver and comment on the action afterward.

"See there? Mauvin thought I was going to slice inward toward his thigh and dropped his guard briefly. He did that because I told him to by suggesting with a dip of my shoulder that this was my intention, so before I even started my stroke I knew what Mauvin was going to do, because I was the one dictating it. In essence I knew what he would do before he did and in a battle that is very handy."

"Enough of the lessons," Mauvin said clearly irritated at being the illustration of a fencing mistake, "let's show him a real demonstration."

"Looking for a rematch?" Hadrian asked.

"Curious if it was luck."

Hadrian smiled and muttered, "Pickerings."

He took off his shirt and, wiping his face and hands, threw it on the grass and raised his sword to ready position. Mauvin lunged and immediately the two began to fight. The swords sang as they cut the air so fast their movements blurred. Hadrian and Mauvin danced around on the balls of their feet, shuffling in the dirt so briskly that a small cloud rose to knee height.

"By Mar!" the old farmer exclaimed.

Then abruptly they stopped, both panting from the exertion.

Mauvin glared at Hadrian with both an amazed and irritated look. "You're playing with me."

"I thought that was the point. You don't really want me to kill you?"

"Well no, but—well, like he said—by Mar! I've never seen anyone fight like you do, you're amazing."

"I thought you both were pretty amazing," Theron remarked. "I've never seen anything like that."

"I have to agree," Magnus chimed in. The dwarf was on his feet nodding his head.

Hadrian walked over to the well and poured half a bucket over himself then shook the water from his hair.

"Seriously, Hadrian," Mauvin asked, "where did you learn it?"

"From a man named Danbury Blackwater."

"Blackwater? Isn't that your name?"

Hadrian nodded and a melancholy look stole over his face. "He was my father."

"Was?"

"He died."

"Was he a warrior? A general?"

"Blacksmith."

"Blacksmith?" Mauvin asked in disbelief.

"In a village not much bigger than this. You know, the guy who makes horseshoes, rakes, pots."

"Are you telling me a village blacksmith knew the secret disciplines of the Teshlor? I recognized the Tek'chin moves, the ones my father taught me. The rest I can only assume were from the other lost disciplines of the Teshlor."

Mauvin drew blank stares from everyone.

"The Teshlor?" he looked around—more stares. He rolled his eyes and sighed. "Heathens, I'm surrounded by ignorant heathens. The Teshlor were the greatest knights ever to have lived. They were the personal bodyguards of the Emperor. It's said they were taught the Five Disciplines of Combat from Novron himself. Only one of which is the Tek'chin, and the knowledge of the Tek'chin alone is what has made a legend out of the Pickering dynasty. Your father clearly knew the Tek'chin, and apparently other Teshlor disciplines which I thought have been lost for nearly a thousand years, and you're telling me he was a blacksmith? He was probably the greatest warrior of his time. And you don't know what your father did before you were born?"

"I assume the same thing he did afterward."

"Then how did he know how to fight?"

Hadrian considered this. "I just assumed he picked it up serving in the local army. Several of the men in the village served his lordship as men-at-arms. I assumed he saw combat. He used to talk like he had."

"Did you ever ask him?"

The thunder of hooves interrupted them as three men on horseback entered the village from the direction of the margrave's castle. The riders were all in black and red with the symbol of a broken crown on their chests. At their head rode a tall thin man with long black hair and a short trimmed beard.

"Excellent swordsmanship," the lead man said. He rode right up to Hadrian and reined in his animal roughly. The black stallion was draped in a scarlet and black caparison complete with braided tassels, a scarlet headpiece with a foot tall black plume spouting from his head. The horse snorted and stomped. "I was wondering why the son of Count Pickering wasn't partaking in the combat today, but I see now you found a worthier partner to spar against. Who would this delightful warrior be and why haven't I seen you at the castle?"

"I'm not here to compete for the crown," Hadrian said simply, slipping on his shirt.

"No? Pity, you certainly appear to be worthy of a chance. What's your name?"

"Hadrian."

"Ah, good to meet you, Sir Hadrian."

"Just Hadrian."

"I see. Do you live here, *just* Hadrian?"

"No."

The horseman seemed less than pleased with the curt answer and nudged his horse closer in a menacing manner. The animal puffed out a hot moist breath into Hadrian's face. "Then what are you doing here?"

"Just passing through," Hadrian replied in his usual amiable manner. He even managed a friendly little smile.

"Really? Just passing through Dahlgren? To where in the world, might I ask, is Dahlgren on the way?"

"Just about everywhere depending on your perspective, don't you think? I mean all roads lead somewhere, don't they?" He was tired of being on the defensive and took a verbal swing. "Is there a reason you're so interested?"

"I'm Sentinel Luis Guy and I'm in charge of managing the contest. I need to know if everyone participating is listed."

"I already told you I wasn't here for the contest."

"So you did," Guy said and slowly looked around at the others, taking particular notice of Magnus. "You are just passing through you said, but perhaps those traveling with you wish to be listed on the roll."

A feint perhaps? Hadrian decided to parry anyway. "No one I'm with will want to be on that list."

"No one you're with?"

Hadrian gritted his teeth. It *was* a feint. Hadrian mentally scolded himself.

"So you're not alone?" the sentinel observed. "Where are the others?"

"I couldn't tell you."

"No?"

Hadrian shook his head—less words less chance of mistakes.

"Really? You mean they could be washing over the falls right now and you couldn't care less?"

"I didn't say that," Hadrian replied irritated.

"But you see no need to know where they are?"

"They're grown men."

The sentinel smiled again. "And who are *these men?* Please tell me so that I might inquire of them later perhaps."

Hadrian's eyes narrowed as he realized too late his mistake. The man before him was clever—too clever.

"Did you forget their names too?" Luis Guy inquired leaning forward in his saddle.

"No," Hadrian tried to hold him off while he struggled to think.

"Then what are they?"

"Well," he began wishing he had his own swords rather than a burrowed one. "Like I said, I don't know where *both* of them are," Hadrian spoke up. "Mauvin is here, of course, but I have no idea where Fanen has gotten to."

"Surely you are mistaken. The Pickerings traveled with me and the rest of the entourage," Guy pointed out.

"Yes they *were*, but they are planning on returning home with me."

Guy's eyes narrowed. "So you are saying that you traveled all the way out here *alone*—passing through, as you put it, and just happened to join up with the Pickerings?"

Hadrian smiled at the sentinel. It was weak, clumsy and the fencing equivalent of dropping his sword and tackling his opponent to the ground, but it was all he could do.

"Is this true, Pickering?"

"Absolutely," Mauvin replied without hesitation.

Guy looked back at Hadrian. "How convenient for you," he said, disappointed. "Well, then don't let me keep you from your practice. Good day gentlemen."

They all watched as the three men rode off toward the river trail.

"That was creepy," Mauvin remarked staring off in their direction. "It can never be good when any sentinel takes an interest in you, much less Luis Guy."

"What's his story?" Hadrian asked.

"I really only know rumors. He's a zealot for the church, but I know many even in the church who are scared of him. He's the kind of person that can make kings disappear. He's also rumored to be obsessed with finding the Heir of Novron."

"Aren't all seret?"

"According to church doctrine, sure. But he really is, which explains why he's here."

"And the two with him?"

"Seret, the Knights of Nyphron, they are the sentinel's personal shadow army. They're answerable to no king or nation, just to sentinels and the patriarch."

Mauvin looked at Hadrian. "You might want to keep that sword. It looks like a bad time to be without your weapons."

Although he had put his lantern out long before the creature's return, Royce could see just fine. Light permeated the walls of Avempartha, seeping through the stone as if it were smoky glass. It was daylight outside, of that he was certain, as the color of light had changed from dim blue to soft white.

As the sun rose, the interior of the citadel became an illuminated world of wondrous color and beauty. Ceilings stretched in tall, airy arches, meeting hundreds of feet above the floor and giving the illusion of not being indoors at all but rather in a place where the horizon was merely lost in mist. The roar of the nearby cataracts, tamed by the walls of the tower, was a soft, muffled, undeniably soothing hum.

Thin gossamer banners hung from the lofty heights. Each shimmered with symbols Royce did not understand. They might have been standards of royalty, rules of law, directions to halls, or meaningless decorations. All Royce knew was that even in the wake of a thousand years, the detailed patterns still appeared fluid and vibrant. It was artistry beyond mortal hands, born of a culture unfathomable. Being the only elven structure Royce had ever entered, it was his only glimpse into that world and it felt oddly peaceful. Still and silent, it was beautiful. Although it looked nothing like anything Royce had ever seen, his reason fought against the growing sensation that somehow all this was familiar. Royce felt calm as he wandered the corridors. The very shapes and shadows touched chords in his mind he never realized were there. It all spoke to him in a language he could not understand. He only caught a word or a phrase in an avalanche of sensations that both mystified and captivated him as he wandered aimlessly like a man blinded by a dazzling light.

He walked from room to room, up stairs and across balconies, following no conscious course, but merely moving, staring and listening. Royce noticed with concern that every movement he made was recorded clearly in centuries of dust that blanketed the interior. Still, he was fascinated to discover that where he disturbed the dust, the floor revealed a glossy surface as clear as still water.

Passing through the various chambers, he felt as if he were in a museum, lost in a moment of frozen time. Plates were still out before empty chairs, some fallen on their sides—overturned in the confusion and alarm of nearly a millennium ago. Books lay open to pages someone had been reading nine hundred years before, yet Royce knew that even to that person who had sat there so long ago, this place, this tower, was ancient. Aside from its dramatic history, by its age alone Avempartha would be a monument—a sacred structure—to the elves, a link to an ancient era. This was not a citadel. He did not know how he knew, but he was certain this was something far more than a mere fortress.

Esrahaddon had left Royce almost immediately after entering the tower after pointing him in the direction he was now following. He told Royce he would find the sword he sought somewhere above the entrance, but that the wizard's path led elsewhere. It had been hours now since they parted and the light outside was already starting to dim. Royce still had not found the sword. Sights and smells sidetracked him, including the musical sound the wind made as it passed through the spires overhead. It was too much to process at once, too much to classify, and soon he found himself lost.

He started to follow his trail in reverse when he discovered his footprints overlapped leaving him a path that moved in circles. He was starting to become concerned when he heard a new sound. Unlike everything he encountered so far, this noise was disturbing. It was the thick rhythmical resonance of heavy breathing.

Every path open to the thief was marred with his own tracks except one. This led to yet another stair where the breathing was louder. How many floors up Royce had wandered he was not certain, but he knew he had not come across any swords. Slowly, and as silently as he could, he began to creep upward.

He had not gone more than five steps when he spotted his first sword. It lay blanketed in dust on a step beside a boney form. What cloth there might have been was gone, but the armor remained. Farther up, he spotted another and yet another. There were two different types of bodies, humans in broad heavy breastplates and greaves, and elves in delicate blue armor. This was the last stand, the last defense to protect the Emperor. Elves and men fallen one upon the other.

Royce reached down and slid his thumb along the flat of the blade at his feet. As the dust wiped clear the amazing shine of the elven steel glimmered as if new, but no etching was on it. Royce looked up the stairs and reluctantly stepped over the bodies as he continued his climb.

The breathing grew louder and deeper like wind blowing through an echoing cavern. A room lay ahead, and with the silence of a cat's shadow, Royce crept inside. The chamber was round with yet another staircase leading up. As he entered, he could feel and smell fresh air. Tall thin windows allowed unfettered shafts of light into the room, but Royce felt that somewhere above him a much larger window lay.

At last, Royce found a rack of elven swords mounted ceremoniously to the wall in ornate cases. Divided from the rest of the room by a delicate chain, the area appeared as a memorial, a remembrance set aside in honor. A plaque on a pedestal stood before the rack and on the walls were numerous lines of elven script carved into the stone. Royce only knew a few words and those before him had been written with such flare and embellishment that he was at a loss to recognize even a single word, although he was certain he recognized several letters.

On the rack were dozens of swords. Each one appeared to be identical and without having to touch them, Royce could see the etchings clearly cut into the blades and the notches hewn into the metal. One spot remained vacant.

With a silent sigh, he steadied himself and began to climb upward once more. With each step, the air grew fresher; currents banished dust to the cracks and corners. Along the stair, more openings and hallways appeared to either side, but Royce had a hunch and continued to climb, moving toward the sound of breathing.

At last, the steps ended and Royce looked up at open sky. Above him was a circular balcony with sculpted walls like petals on a flower. Statues that once lined this open-air pavilion lay in broken heaps on the floor. At their center rested the malevolent sleeping figure of the Gilarabrywn, an enormous black scaled lizard with wings of gray membrane and bone. It lay curled, its head on its tail, its body heaving with deep, long breaths. Muscular claws were armed with four twelve-inch long black nails; encrusted with dried blood, they left deep groves in the surface of the floor where they scraped in the beast's sleep. Long sharp fangs protruded from beneath leathery lips as did a row of frightening teeth that followed no visible scheme but seemed to mesh together like a wild fence of needles. Ears lay back upon its head, its eyes cloaked by broad lids beneath which pupils darted about in a fretful slumber of what dark visages Royce could not begin to imagine. The long tail, barbed at the end with a saber-like bone, twitched.

Royce caught himself staring and cursed at his own stupidity. It was a sight to be certain, but this was no time to be distracted. Focus was all that separated him from certain death.

He always hated places with animals. Hounds bellowed at the slightest sound or smell. He had managed to step past many a sleeping dog, but there had been a few that managed to sense him without warning. He mentally gripped himself and pulled his eyes away from the giant to study the rest of the room. It was a shambles, broken fixtures and rubble. On closer study, however, Royce noticed that the rubble held terrible treasures. He recognized torn bits of Mae Drundel's dress, matted with dark stains and tangled within its folds was a bit of scalp and a long lock of gray hair. Other equally disturbing images lay around him. Arms, feet, fingers, hands, all cast aside like shrimp tails. He spotted Millie, Hadrian's bay mare, or rather one of her rear legs and tail. Not too far away he was stunned to see Millie's saddle and Hadrian's swords. Luckily, they were within easy reach.

As he began to move around the pile, inching his way with the slow discipline of a mantis on the hunt, he saw something. The bodies and torn clothes lay atop the pile of bones and stone. But deep beneath, on the bottom stratum of built-up sediment, Royce caught the singular glint of mirrored steel. It was only a tiny patch, no larger than a small coin, which is what he initially took it for, but its brilliance was unmistakable. It possessed the same gleam as the swords on the stairs and in the rack below.

Barely breathing—each movement keyed to a painfully slow pace that might defy even a direct look—Royce stole closer to the beast and his vile treasure trove. He slipped his hand under the strands of Millie's tail and meticulously began to draw forth the blade.

It came loose with little effort or sound, but even before he had it free Royce knew something was wrong. It was not heavy enough. Even given that elven blades might weigh dramatically less, it was ridiculously light. He soon realized why as he drew forth only part of a broken blade. Seeing the etching on the unnotched metal, Royce realized his hunch was correct. This Gilarabrywn was no animal, no dumb beast trained to kill. This conjured demon was self-aware enough to realize it had only one mortal fear in this world—a blade with its name on it. It took precautions. The monster broke the blade, severing the name and rendering it useless. He could not see the other half of the sword, but it seemed obvious to him where it lay. The remainder of the sword rested in the one place from which Royce could not steal it—beneath the sleeping body of the Gilarabrywn itself.

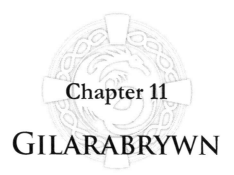

Chapter 11

GILARABRYWN

IT WAS NEARING dusk when Royce, hauling three swords over his shoulder, found Hadrian and Magnus waiting at the well. The village was empty, its inhabitants holed up in their hovels, and the night was quiet except for the faint sounds of distant activity coming from the castle.

"It's about time." Hadrian said, jumping to his feet at Royce's approach.

"Here's your gear," Royce handed Hadrian his weapons. "Be careful next time where you stow it. I do have more important things to do than be your personal valet." Hadrian happily took the swords and belts and began strapping them on. "I was starting to worry the church had grabbed you."

"Church?" Royce asked.

"Luis Guy was harassing me earlier."

"The sentinel?"

"Yeah. He was asking about my partners and rode off toward the river and I haven't seen him come back. I got the impression he might be fishing for Esra. Where is Esra anyway? Did you leave him at the river?"

"He didn't stop back here?" Royce asked. They shook their heads. "Doesn't mean anything; he'd be a fool to come back to the village. He's likely hiding in the trees."

"Assuming he didn't get swept away by the river," Hadrian said. "Why did you leave him?"

"He left me with a very *don't follow me attitude*, which under normal circumstances would ensure that I followed him, but I had other things on my mind. Before I knew it, the sun was going down. I thought he had already left."

"So did you find anything valuable inside? Gems? Gold?"

Royce felt suddenly stupid. "You know, it never even crossed my mind to look."

"What?"

"I completely forgot about it."

"So, what did you do in there all day?"

Royce pulled the bare half-blade from his belt. It gleamed even in the faint light. "All the other swords were in a neat display case, but I found this buried almost directly under the Gilarabrywn's foot."

"Its foot?" Hadrian said stunned. "You saw it?"

Royce nodded with a grimace. "And trust me. It isn't a sight you want to see drunk or sober."

"You think *it* broke the blade?"

"Kinda makes you wonder, doesn't it?"

"So where's the other piece?"

"I'm guessing it's sleeping on it, but I wasn't about to try and roll it over to look."

"I'm surprised you didn't wait until it left."

"With our client leaving in the morning, what's the point? If it was an easy grab—if I could see it and didn't have to spend hours digging through—well, stuff—fine, but I'm not about to risk my neck for Esra's personal war with the church. Besides, remember the hounds in Blythin Castle?"

Hadrian nodded with a sick look on his face.

"If it can smell scents, I didn't want to be around when it wakes up. The way I see it, Thrace has her father, Esra has access to the tower and Rufus will rid the village of the Gilarabrywn. I say our work here is done." Royce looked at the dwarf, then back at Hadrian. "Thanks for keeping an eye on him." He drew his dagger.

"Wha—wait!" the dwarf backpedaled as Royce advanced. "We had a deal!"

Royce grinned at him, "Do I really look trustworthy to you?"

"Royce, you can't," Hadrian said.

The thief looked at him and chuckled. "Are you kidding? Look at him, if I can't slit his throat in ten seconds tops, I'll buy you a beer as soon as we get back to Alburn. Tell me when you're ready to count."

"No, I meant he's right. You made a bargain with him. You can't go back on it."

"Oh please. This little—dwarf—tried to kill me and damn near succeeded, and you want me to let him go because I said I would? Hey, he lived a whole day longer for helping us. That's plenty reward."

"*Royce!*"

"*What?*" the thief rolled his eyes. "You aren't serious? He killed Amrath."

"It was a job, and you aren't a member of the royal guard. He upheld his end just as agreed. And there's no benefit to killing him."

"Enjoyment," Royce said, "enjoyment and satisfaction are benefits."

Hadrian continued to glare.

Royce shook his head and sighed. "All right, okay, he can live. It's stupid, but he can live. Happy?"

Royce looked up at the great motte of the castle where already the torches of tonight's contestants were assembling. "It's nearly dark, we need to get inside. Where's the best seat for this dinner theatre I hear they've been holding at the castle? And when I say best, I mean safest."

"We still have an open invitation to the Bothwicks. Theron is there now and we've been—"

A screeching cry from the direction of the river cut through the night.

"What in the land of Novron's ghost is that?" Magnus asked.

"You think maybe lizard wings found out his rattle was stolen?" Hadrian asked apprehensively.

Royce looked back toward the trees and then at his friend. "I think we'd better find a better place to hide tonight than the Bothwicks."

"Where?" Hadrian asked looking around desperately. "If it comes looking for that blade, it will rip every house apart until it finds it, and we already know the local architecture doesn't pose much of a challenge. It's gonna kill everyone in the village."

"We could run them all to the castle, there might still be time," Royce suggested.

"No good," Hadrian countered. "The guards won't let us in. The forest maybe?"

"The trees only slow it down it won't stop it any more than the houses."

"Damn it." Hadrian cursed. "I should have built the pit out in the village."

"What about the well here?" the dwarf asked, peering into the wooden rimmed hole.

Royce and Hadrian looked at each other.

"I feel so stupid right now," Royce said.

Hadrian ran to the bell, grabbed hold of the dangling rope and began to pull it. The bell, intended for the future church of Dahlgren, raised the alarm.

"Keep ringing it." Hadrian yelled at Magnus as he and Royce raced to the houses sweeping their cloth drapes aside and banging on the frames

"Get out. Everyone out." they yelled. "Your houses won't protect you tonight. Get in the well. Everyone in the well now!"

"What's going on?" Russell Bothwick asked peering out into the darkness.

"No time to explain," Hadrian shouted back. "Get in the well if you want to live."

"But the church? They are suppose to save us," Selen Brockton said, huddling in a blanket in the arch of her doorway.

"Are you willing to bet your life? You're all gonna have to trust me. If I am wrong, you'll spend one miserable night, but if I am right and you don't listen, you'll all die."

"That's good enough for me." Theron said, storming out of the Bothwick house, buttoning his shirt, his massive figure and loud harsh voice commanding everyone's attention. "And it had better be good enough for the lot of you too. Hadrian has done more to save this village from death in the past few days than all of us—and all of them—combined. If he says sleep in the well tonight, then by the beard of Maribor, that is what I'll do. I don't care if the beast was known to be dead. I'd still do it and any of you who refuse, why you deserve to be eaten."

The inhabitants of Dahlgren ran to the well.

Loops were tied into the rope for footholds and while the well was wide enough to lower four or even five people at a time, because they did not trust the strength of the windlass, they only lowered them in groups of twos and threes depending on weight.

Although people moved quickly and orderly, obeying Hadrian's instructions without argument, the process was excruciatingly slow. Magnus volunteered to go in and drive pegs into the walls to form footholds. Young Hal, Arvid and Pearl, being too small to go down first, raced around the village fetching more shafts of wood for the dwarf to drive into the sides. Tad Bothwick went down and worked with Magnus feeding him the wooden spikes as the little dwarf built makeshift platforms.

"Whoa, mister," Tad's voice echoed out of the mouth of the well. "I ain't never seen no one use a hammer like that. It took six weeks to build up these walls, and I swear you look like you coulda done it in six hours."

Outside, Hadrian, Theron, Vince, and Dillon did the work of lowering villagers in. Hadrian lined them up, sending women and children down first into the darkness, where only a single candle that Tad held for Magnus revealed anything below.

"How long?" Hadrian asked as they waited to lower the next set down.

"It would have been here by now if it had flown the moment we heard it," Royce replied. "It must be searching the tower. That gives us some time, but I don't know how much."

"Get up in a tree and yell when you see it."

When everyone was in, Hadrian lowered Theron and Dillon down, leaving only Hadrian, Vince, and Royce above ground where they waited for Magnus to finish the last set of wall pegs. Up in a poplar tree, Royce stood out on a thin branch, scanning the sky while listening to the dwarf hammering the last stakes into place.

"Here it comes!" he shouted, spotting a shadow darting across the stars.

Seconds later the Gilarabrywn screamed from somewhere above the dark canopy of leaves and the three cringed, but nothing happened. They stood still staring into the darkness around them, listening. Another cry ripped through the night. It flew straight for the torches of the manor house.

Royce spotted it in the night sky flying over the hill where the next challenger for the crown prepared to meet the beast. It descended then rose up once more. It issued another screech, then the beast let loose a roar and fire exploded from its mouth. Instantly everything grew brighter as fire engulfed the hillside.

"That's new," Hadrian declared nervously as he watched the ghastly sight. The crowd of challengers lost their lives with hardly the time to scream. "Magnus, hurry!"

"All set. Go! Climb down," the dwarf shouted back.

"Wait!" Tad cried. "Where's Pearl?"

"She's looking for wood," Vince said. "I'll get her."

Hadrian grabbed his arm. "It's too dangerous, get in the well. Royce will go."

"I will?" he asked surprised.

"It's lousy being the only one to see in the dark sometimes, isn't it?"

Royce cursed and ran off, pausing in homes and sheds to call the little girl's name as loudly as he dared. It got easier to see his way as the light from the hill grew larger and brighter. The Gilarabrywn screamed repeatedly and Royce looked over his shoulder to see the castle walls engulfed in flames.

"Royce," Hadrian shouted, "it's coming!"

Royce gave up stealth. "Pearl!" he yelled aloud.

"Here!" she screamed darting out from the trees.

He grabbed the little girl up in his arms and raced for the well.

"Run, damn it!" Hadrian shouted, holding the rope for them.

"Forget the rope. Get down and catch her."

While Royce was still sprinting across the yard, Hadrian slid down the coil.

Thrump. Thrump. Thrump.

Hugging Pearl close to his chest, Royce reached the well and jumped. The little girl screamed as they fell in together. An instant later, there came a loud unearthly scream and a terrible vibration as the world above the well erupted in a brilliant light accompanied by a thunderous roar.

Arista paced the length of the little room, painfully aware of Bernice's head turning side-to-side, following her every move. The old woman was smiling at her; she always smiled at her, and Arista was about ready to gouge her eyes out. She was used to her tower where even Hilfred gave her space, but for more than a week, she had been subjected to constant company—Bernice, her ever-present shadow. She had to get out of the room, to get away. She was tired of being stared at, of being watched after like a child. She walked to the door.

"Where are you going, Highness?" Bernice was quick to ask.

"Out," she said.

"Out where?"

"Just out."

Bernice stood up. "Let me get our cloaks."

"I am going alone."

"Oh no, Your Highness," Bernice said, "that's not possible."

Arista glared at her. Bernice smiled back. "Imagine this Bernice: you sit back down and I walk out. It is possible."

"But I can't do that. You are the princess and this is a dangerous place. You need to be chaperoned for your own safety. We'll need Hilfred to escort us, as well. Hilfred," she called.

The door popped open and the bodyguard stepped in, bowing to Arista. "Did you need something, Your Highness?"

"No—yes," Arista said and pointed at Bernice, "keep her here. Sit on her, tie her up, hold her at sword point if you must, but I am leaving and I don't want her following me."

The old maid looked shocked and put both hands to her cheeks in surprise.

"You're going out, Your Highness?" Hilfred asked.

"Yes, yes, I am going out," she exclaimed, throwing her arms up. "I may roam the halls of this cabin. I may go to watch the contest. Why, I might even leave the stockade altogether and wander into the forest. I could get lost and die of starvation, eaten by a bear, tumble into the Nidwalden and get swept over the falls—but I will do so alone."

Hilfred stood at attention. His eyes stared back at hers. His mouth opened and then closed.

"Is there something you want to say?" she asked, her tone harsh.

Hilfred swallowed, "No, Your Highness."

"At least take your cloak," Bernice insisted, holding it up.

Arista sighed, snatched it from her hands, and walked out.

The moment she left, regret set in. Storming down the corridor, dragging the cloak, she paused. The look on Hilfred's face left her feeling miserable. As a girl she recalled having a crush on him. He was the son of a castle sergeant, and he used to stare at her from across the courtyard. Arista had thought he was cute. Then one morning she had awoken to fire and smoke. He saved her life. Hilfred had been just a boy, but he ran into the flaming castle to drag her out. He spent two months suffering from burns and coughing fits where he spit up blood. For weeks he awoke screaming from nightmares. As a reward, King Amrath appointed Hilfred to the prestigious post of personal bodyguard to the princess. But she never thanked him nor forgave him for not saving her mother. Her anger was always between them. Arista wanted to apologize, but it was too late. Too many years had passed, too many cruelties, followed by too many silences like the one that just hung between them.

"What's going on?" Arista heard Thrace's voice and walked toward it.

"What's wrong, Thrace?" The princess found the farmer's daughter and the deacon in the main hallway. The girl was dressed in her thin chemise nightgown. They both looked concerned.

"Your Highness!" the girl called to her. "Do you know what is happening? Why was the bell ringing?"

"The contest is starting soon if that's what you mean. I was on my way to watch. Are you feeling better? Would you like to come?" Arista found herself asking. She was aware of the irony, but being with Thrace was not the same as being escorted by Bernice and Hilfred.

"No, you don't understand. Something must be wrong. It's dark. No one would ring the bell at night."

"I didn't hear a bell," Arista said, pulling the cloak over her shoulders.

"The village bell," Thrace replied. "I heard it. It has stopped now."

"It's probably just part of the combat announcement."

"No," Thrace shook her head, and the deacon mimicked her. "That bell is only rung in emergencies, dire emergencies. Something is terribly wrong."

"I'm sure it's nothing. You forget. There is practically an army outside just itching for their chance to fight. Anyway, we certainly can't find out standing here." Arista took Thrace's hand and led them out to the courtyard.

Being the second night, the event had moved into full extravagance. Outside, the high grassy yard of the manor's hill was set up like a pavilion at a tournament joust. The raised mound of the manor's motte offered a perfect view of the field below. Colorful awnings hung stretched above rows of chairs with small tables holding steins of mead, ale, and bowls of berries and cheese. The archbishop and Bishop Saldur sat together near the center, while several other clergy and servants stood watching the distant action unfolding on the hillside beyond the castle walls

"Oh, Arista my dear," Saldur called to her, "come to see history being made, have you? Good. Have a seat. That's Lord Rufus out there on the field. It seems he tires of waiting for his crown, but the vile beast is late in showing this evening and I think it is making his lordship a tad irritated. Do you see how he paces his stallion? So like an emperor to be impatient."

"Who is to come after Rufus?" Arista asked, remaining on her feet looking down at the field below.

"After?" Saldur looked puzzled. "Oh, I'm not sure actually. Well, I hardly think it matters. Rufus will likely win tonight."

"Why is that?" Arista asked. "It isn't a matter of skill really, is it? It is a matter of bloodline. Is Lord Rufus suspected of bearing some known ties to the imperial family?"

"Well, yes, as a matter of fact he has claimed such for years now."

"Really?" Arista questioned. "I have never heard of him ever making such a boast."

"Well, the church doesn't like to promote unproven theories or random claims, but Rufus is indeed a favorite here. Tonight will prove his words, of course."

"Excuse me, your grace?" Tomas said with a bow. He and Thrace stood directly behind Arista, both still appearing as nervous as mice. "Do you happen to know why the village bell was rung?"

"Hmm? What's that? The bell? Oh that, I have no idea. Perhaps some quaint method the villagers use to call people to dinner."

"But, your grace—" Tomas was cut off.

"There." Saldur shouted pointing into the sky as the Gilarabrywn appeared and swooped into the torch light.

"Oh, here we go!" The archbishop shouted excitedly, clapping his hands. "Everyone pay attention to what you see here tonight, for surely many people will ask how it came to be."

The beast descended down to the field and Lord Rufus trotted forward on his horse, which he had had the foresight to blind with a cloth bag to prevent it from witnessing the pending horror. With his sword held aloft, he shouted and spurred his mount forward.

"In the name of Novron, I—the true heir—smite thee." Rufus rose in the stirrups and thrust at the beast, which seemed startled by the bold confidence of the knight.

Lord Rufus struck the chest of the creature, but the blow glanced away uselessly. He struck again and again, but it was like striking stone with a stick. Lord Rufus looked shocked and confused. Then the Gilarabrywn slew Rufus and his horse with one casual swipe of a claw.

"Oh dear lord!" the archbishop cried, rising to his feet in shock. A moment later the shock turned to horror as the beast cast out its wings and, rising up, bathed the hillside in a torrent of fire. Those in the yard staggered backward spilling drinks and knocking over chairs. One of the pavilion legs toppled and the awning fell askew as people began to rush about.

With the hillside alight, the beast turned toward the castle and, rising up higher, let forth another blast that exploded the wooden stockade walls into sheets of flame. The fire spread from dry log to dry log until the flames swept fully around ringing the castle. It did not take long for those buildings close to the walls, those roofed with thatch, to catch, and soon the bulk of the lower castle and even the walls surrounding the manor house were burning. With the light of fire surrounding them, it was impossible to see where the Gilarabrywn had gone. Blind as to the whereabouts of the flying nightmare and the intensity of the heat growing all around them, the servants, guards, and clerics alike scattered in terror.

"We need to get to the cellar!" Tomas shouted, but amidst the screams and the roar of the flames devouring the wood, few heard him. Tomas took hold of Thrace and began to pull her back toward the manor. With her free hand Thrace grabbed Arista's arm, and Tomas pulled both back up the slope.

In shock, Arista put up no resistance as they dragged her from the yard. She had never experienced anything like this. She saw a man on fire running down the slope screaming, thrashing about as flames spiraled up his body. A moment later, he collapsed, still burning. There were others, living pyres racing blindly about the yard in ghastly brilliance, one by one collapsing on the grass. Out of instinct, Arista looked for the protection of Hilfred, but somewhere in her soup-like mind, she remembered she ordered him to remain on guard in her room. He would be looking for her now.

Thrace held her arm in a vice grip as the three moved in a human chain. To her left she saw a soldier attempt to breech the wall. He caught on fire and joined the throng of living torches, screaming as his clothes and skin burned away. Somewhere not far off where the fire had spread to the forest, a tree trunk exploded with a tremendous crack! It rattled the building.

"We have to get down in the cellar." Tomas insisted. "Quickly! Our only hope is to get underground. We need—"

Arista felt her hair blowing in a sudden wind.

Thrump. Thrump.

Deacon Tomas began praying aloud, as out of the smoke-clouded night sky, the Gilarabrywn descended upon them.

Chapter 12

SMOKE AND ASH

CRAWLING OUT OF the well into the gray morning light, Hadrian entered into an alien world. Dahlgren was gone. Only patches of ash and some smoldering timber marked the missing homes, but even more startling was the absence of trees. The forest that had hugged the village was gone. In its place was a desolate plain, scorched black. Limbless, leafless poles stood at random, tall dark spikes pointing at the sky. Fed by smoldering piles, smoke hung in the air like a dull gray fog, hiding the sky behind a hazy cloud from which ash fell silently like dirty snow blanketing the land.

Pearl came out of the well. Not surprisingly, she said nothing as she wandered about the scorched world stooping to turn over a charred bit of wood then staring up at the sky as if surprised to find it still there now that the world had been cast upside down.

"How did this happen?" Russell Bothwick asked to no one in particular, and no one answered.

"Thrace!" Theron yelled as he emerged from the well, his eyes focusing on the smoking ruins atop the hill. Soon everyone was running up the slope.

Like the village, the castle was a burned out hull, the walls gone as were the smaller buildings. The great manor house was a charred pile. Bodies lay scattered, blackened by fire, torn and twisted. The corpses still smoked.

"Thrace!" Theron cried in desperation as he dug furiously into the pile of rubble that had been the manor house. All of the village men, including Royce, Hadrian, and even Magnus dug in the debris more out of sympathy than hope.

Magnus directed them to the southeast corner muttering something about the 'earth speaking with a hollow voice.' They cleared away walls and a fallen staircase and heard a faint sound below. They dug down revealing the remains of the old kitchen and the cellar beneath.

As if from the grave itself, they pulled forth Deacon Tomas, who looked battered but otherwise unharmed. Just as the villagers had, Tomas wiped his eyes, squinting in the morning light at the devastation around him.

"Deacon!" Theron shook the cleric. "Where is Thrace?"

Tomas looked at the farmer and tears welled in his eyes. "I couldn't save her, Theron," he said in a choked voice. "I tried, I tried so hard. You have to believe me, you must."

"What happened, you old fool?"

"I tried. I tried. I was leading them to this cellar, but it caught us. I prayed. I prayed so hard, and I swear it listened! Then I heard it laugh. It actually *laughed*." Tomas' eyes filled with tears. "It ignored me and took them."

"Took them?" Theron asked frantically. "What do you mean?"

"It spoke to me," Tomas said. "It spoke with a voice like death, like pain. My legs wouldn't hold me up anymore and I fell before it."

"What did it say?" Royce asked.

The deacon paused to wipe his face leaving dark streaks of soot on his cheeks. "It didn't make sense, perhaps in my fear I lost my mind."

"What do you *think* it said?" Royce pressed.

"It spoke in the ancient speech of the church. I thought it said something about a weapon, a sword, something about trading it for the women. Said it would return tomorrow night for it. Then it flew away with Thrace and the princess. It doesn't make any sense at all, I'm probably mad now."

"The princess?" Hadrian asked.

"Yes, the princess Arista of Melengar. She was with us. I was trying to save them both—I was trying to—but—and now…" Tomas broke down crying again.

Royce exchanged looks with Hadrian and the two quickly moved away from the others to talk. Theron promptly followed.

"You two know something," he accused. "You got in didn't you. You took it. Royce got the sword, after all. That's what it wants."

Royce nodded.

"You have to give it back," the farmer said.

"I don't think giving it back will save your daughter," Royce told him. "This thing, this Gilarabrywn, is a lot more cunning than we knew. It will—"

"Thrace hired you to bring me that sword," Theron growled. "That was your job. Remember? You were supposed to steal it and give it to me, so hand it over."

"Theron, listen—"

"Give it to me now!" the old farmer shouted as he towered menacingly over the thief.

Royce sighed and drew out the broken blade.

Theron took it with a puzzled look, turning the metal over in his hands. "Where's the rest?"

"This is all I could find."

"Then it will have to do," the old man said firmly.

"Theron, I don't think you can trust this creature. I think even if you hand this over it will still kill your daughter, the princess, and you."

"It's a risk I am willing to take!" he shouted at them. "You two don't have to be here. You got the sword—you did your job. You're done. You can leave any time you want. Go on, get out!"

"Theron," Hadrian began, "we are not your enemy. Do you think either of us wants Thrace to die?"

Theron started to speak, then closed his mouth, swallowed, and took a breath. "No," he sighed, "you're right. I know that, it's just…" he looked into Hadrian's eyes with a look of horrible pain. "She's all I've got left, and I won't stand for anything that can get her killed. I'll trade myself to the bloody monster if it will let her live."

"I know that, Theron," Hadrian said.

"I just don't think it will honor the trade," Royce said.

"We found another over here!" Dillon McDern shouted as he hauled the foppish scholar, Tobis Rentinual, out of the remains of the smokehouse. The skinny courtier, covered from head to foot in dirt, collapsed on the grass coughing and sputtering.

"The soil was soft in the cellar…" Tobis managed then sputtered and coughed. "we—dug into it with our—with our hands."

"How many?" Dillon asked.

"Five," Tobis replied, "a woodsman, a castle guard I think, Sir Erlic, and two others. The guard—" Tobis entered into a coughing fit for a minute than sat up, doubled over and spat on the grass.

"Arvid fetch water from the well!" Dillon ordered his son.

"The guard was badly burned," Tobis continued. "Two young men dragged him to the smokehouse, saying it had a cellar. Everything around us was on fire except the smokehouse so the woodsman, Sir Erlic, and I all ran there too. The dirt floor was loose, so we started burrowing. Then something hit the shed and the whole thing came down on us. A beam caught my leg. I think it's broken."

The villagers excavated the collapsed shed. They pulled off a wall and dug into the wreckage, peeling back the fragments. They reached the bottom where they found the others buried alive.

They dragged them out into the light. Sir Erlic and the woodsman looked near dead as they coughed and spit. The burned guard was worse. He was unconscious, but still alive. The last two pulled from the smokehouse ruins were Mauvin and Fanen Pickering, who like Tobis, were unable to speak for a time, but other than numerous cuts and bruises, were all right.

"Is Hilfred alive?" Fanen asked after having a chance to breathe fresh air and drink a cup of water.

"Who's Hilfred?" Lena Bothwick asked holding the cup of water Verna brought. Fanen pointed to the burned guard across from him and Lena nodded. "He's not awake, but he's alive."

Search parties spread out and combed the rest of the area, finding many more bodies, mostly would-be contestants. They also discovered the remains of Archbishop Galien. The old man appeared to have died, not from fire, but by being trampled to death. His servant Carleton lay inside the manor, apparently not content to die by his master's side. Arista's handmaid Bernice was also found inside the manor, crushed when the house collapsed. They found no one else alive.

The villagers created stretchers to carry Tobis and Hilfred out of the smoky ruins to the well where the women tended their wounds. The old common green was a charred patch of black. The great bell, having fallen, lay on its side in the ash.

"What happened?" Hadrian asked, sitting down next to Mauvin. The two brothers huddled where Pearl had once grazed pigs. Both sat hunched, sipping from cups of water, their faces stained with soot.

"We were outside the walls when the attack came," he said, his voice soft, not much louder than a strained whisper. He hooked his thumb at his brother. "I told him we were going home but Fanen, the genius that he is, decided he wanted his shot at the beast, his chance at glory."

Fanen drooped his head lower.

"He tried to sneak out, thought he'd give me the slip. I caught him outside the gate and a little way down the hill. I told him it was suicide—he insisted—we got into a fight. It ended when we saw the hill catch on fire. We ran back. Before we reached the front gate, a couple of carriages and a bunch of horses went by at full gallop. I spotted Saldur's face peeking out from one of the windows. They didn't even slow down.

"We went looking for Arista and found Hilfred on the ground just out front of the burning manor house. His hair was gone, skin coming off in sheets, but he was still breathing so we grabbed him and just ran for the smokehouse. It was the last building still standing that wasn't burning. The dirt floor was soft and loose like it had recently been dug up, so we just started burrowing with our hands like moles, you know. That Tobis guy, Erlic, and Danthen followed us in. We only managed to dig a few feet when the whole thing came down on us."

"Did you find Arista?" Fanen asked. "Is she…"

"We don't know," Hadrian replied. "The deacon says it took her and Theron's daughter. She might still be alive."

The women of the village tended the wounds of those found at the castle, while the men began gathering what supplies, tools, and food stores they could find into a pile at the well. They were a motley bunch, haggard and dirty like a band of shipwrecked travelers left on a desert island. Few of them spoke and when they did, it was always in whispered tones. From time to time, someone would weep softly, kick a scorched board, or merely wander off a ways only to drop to their knees and shake.

When, at last, the men were bandaged and the supplies stacked, Tomas, who had cleaned himself up, stood and said a few words over the dead and they all observed a moment of silence. Then Vince Griffin stood up and addressed them.

"I was the first to settle here," he said with a sad voice. "My house stood right there, the closest to this here well. I remember when most of you were considered newcomers, strangers even. I had great hopes for this place. I donated eight bushels of barley every year to the village church, though all I seen come of it was this here bell. I stayed here through the hard frost five years ago and I stayed here when people started to go missing. Like the rest 'a you, I thought I could live with it. People die tragically everywhere, be it from the pox, the plague, starvation, the cold, or a blade. Sure, Dahlgren seemed cursed, and maybe it is, but it was still the best place I'd ever lived. Maybe the best place I ever will live, mostly because of you all and the fact that the nobles hardly ever bothered us, but all that's over now. There's nothing here no more, not even the trees that was here before we came, and I don't fancy spending another night in the well." He wiped his eyes clear. "I'm leaving Dahlgren, I 'spose many 'a you will be too, and I just wanted to say that when you all came here I saw you as strangers, but as I am leaving, I feel I'm gonna be saying goodbye to family, a family that has gone through a lot together. I…I just wanted you all to know that."

Everyone nodded in agreement and exchanged muttered conversations with the person nearest them. It was decided by all that Dahlgren was dead and that they would leave. There was talk about trying to stay together, but it was only talk. They would travel as a group, including Sir Erlic and the woodsman Danthen south at least as far as Alburn where some would turn west hoping to find relatives while others would continue south hoping to find a new start.

"So much for the church's help," Dillon McDern said to Hadrian. "They were here two nights and look."

Dillon and Russell Bothwick walked over to where Theron sat against a blackened stump.

"'Spect you'll be staying to find Thrace?" Dillon asked.

Theron nodded. The big man had not bothered to wash and he was coated in dirt and soot. He had the broken blade on his lap and stared at it.

"You think it'll be back tonight, do ya?" Russell asked.

"I think so. It wants this. Maybe if I give it back, it will give Thrace to me."

The two men nodded.

"You want us to stay behind and give you hand?" Russell asked.

"A hand with what?" the old farmer asked. "Nothing you can do, either of 'ya. Go on, you both have families of your own. Get out while you can. Enough good people have died here."

The two men nodded again.

"Good luck to you, Theron," Dillon said.

"We'll wait a while in Alburn to see if you show up," Russell told him. "Good luck."

Russell and Tad fashioned a sled from charred saplings and loaded what little they had on it. Lena mashed up a salve, which she applied to Hilfred's burns, and left it and a pile of bandages with Tomas who took it on himself to stay with the soldier. And so it was, that with only a few things to pack up and carry with them, the bulk of the villagers were on their way westward by early afternoon. No one wanted to be anywhere near Dahlgren after sunset.

SMOKE AND ASH

"What are we doing here?" Royce asked Hadrian as the two sat on a partially burned tree trunk. They were just up the old village path from the well near where the Caswell's two little wooden grave markers used to be. Like everything else, they were gone, nothing left to mark their passing. They could see Deacon Tomas sitting with Hilfred who still lay unconscious.

"This job has cost us two horses, over a week's worth of provisions, and for what?" Royce went on, and with a sigh broke off a bit of charred bark and absently tossed it. "We should head out with the rest of them. The girl is likely dead already. I mean why would it keep her alive? The Gilarabrywn holds all the cards. It can kill us at will, but we can't harm it. It has hostages, while all we have is half a sword that it doesn't really need, but apparently would just like to have. If we had both parts of the sword Magnus could put them back together and we could at least bargain from a position of some strength. We could even have the dwarf make us all swords, and maybe even spears with the right name on it. Then we could have a go at the bastard, but right now, we have nothing. We are no threat to it at all. Theron thinks he's going to bargain, but he doesn't have anything to bargain with. The Gilarabrywn set this up only to save itself the tedium of hunting for that sword."

"We don't know that."

"Sure we do. It won't keep those girls alive. It probably had them for lunch already and when night comes, old Theron will be standing out there like a fool with exactly what it wants. He'll die and that will be that. On the other hand, his stupidity will buy time for the rest of us to get away. Considering his whole family is gone and his daughter is most likely already dead, it's probably for the best."

"He won't be standing there alone," Hadrian said.

Royce turned with a sick look on his face. "Tell me you're joking."

Hadrian shook his head.

"Why?"

"Because you're right, because everything you just said will happen if we leave."

"And you think if we stay it will be different?"

"We've never quit a job before, Royce."

"What are you talking about? What job?"

"She paid us to get the sword for her."

"I got the sword. Her old man's got it right now."

"Only part of it and the job won't be finished until he has both parts in his hands. That's what we were hired to do."

"Hadrian." Royce ran a hand over his face and shook his head. "For the love of Maribor, she paid us *ten silver!*"

"You accepted it."

"I hate it when you get like this." Royce stood suddenly, picking up a charred piece of scrap. "Damn it," he threw it into a pile of smoking wood that was once the Bothwick's home. "You're just going to get us killed, you know that, right?"

"You don't have to stay. This is my decision."

"And what are you going to do? Fight it when it comes? Are you going to stand there in the dark swinging at it with swords that can't hurt it?"

"I don't know."

"You're insane," Royce told him. "The rumors are all true; Hadrian Blackwater is a damn loon!"

Hadrian stood to face his friend. "I'm not going to abandon Theron, Thrace, and Arista. And what about Hilfred. Do you think he can travel? You try dragging him through the woods and he'll be dead before nightfall, or do you want to try stuffing him in well all night and think he'll be just fine in the morning? And what about

Tobis? How far do you think he'll get on a broken leg? Or don't you give a damn about them? Has your heart gotten so black you can just walk away and let them all die?"

"They will all die anyway," Royce snapped at him. "That's just my point. We can't stop it from killing them. All we can do is decide whether to die with them or not, and I really don't see the benefit in sympathy suicide."

"We can do something," Hadrian asserted. "We're the ones who stole the treasure from the Crown Tower and put it back the very next night. The same two that broke into the invincible Drumindor, we put a human head in the Earl of Chadwick's lap while he slept in his tower, and busted Esrahaddon out of Gutaria, the most secure prison ever built. I mean we can do *something!*"

"Like what?"

"Well…" Hadrian thought, "we can dig a pit, lure it there and trap it."

"We'd have better luck asking Tomas to pray for Maribor to strike the Gilarabrywn dead. We really don't have the time or the manpower for excavating a pit."

"You have a better idea?"

"I'm sure I could come up with something better than luring it into a pit we can't dig."

"Like what?"

Royce began walking around the still smoldering stick forest, angrily kicking anything in his path. "I don't know, you're the one who thinks we can do something, but I know one thing; we can't do squat unless we can get the other half of that sword. So the first thing I would do is steal it tonight while it's gone."

"It would kill Thrace and Arista for certain if you did that," Hadrian pointed out.

"But then you could kill it. At least there would be the closure of revenge."

Hadrian shook his head. "Not good enough."

Royce smirked, "I could always steal the sword while you and Theron fool it with the blade Rufus was using." Royce allowed himself a morbid chuckle. "There's at least about a single chance in a million that might work."

Hadrian's brow furrowed in thought, and he sat down slowly.

"Oh no, I was joking," Royce backpedaled. "If it could tell the blade was missing last night, it can tell the difference between the real thing and a copy."

"But even if it doesn't work," Hadrian said, "it might give me time to get the girls away from it. Then *we* could dive in a hole—a small hole, that we do have time to dig."

"And hope it doesn't dig you out? I've seen its claws, it won't be hard."

Hadrian ignored him and went on with his train of thought. "Then you could bring the other half of the sword, have Magnus forge it and then I can kill it—see it was a good thing you didn't kill him after all."

"You realize how stupid this is, right? That thing decimated this whole village and the castle last night, and you are going to take it on with an old farmer, two women, and a broken sword?"

Hadrian said nothing.

Royce sighed and sat down beside his friend, shaking his head. He reached into his robe and pulled his dagger out. Still in its sheath, he held it out.

"Here," he said, "take Alverstone."

"Why?" Hadrian looked at him, puzzled.

"Well, I'm not saying Magnus is right, but, well, I've never found *anything* that this dagger can't cut, and if Magnus is right, if the father of the gods did forge this, I would think it could come in handy even against an invincible beast."

"So you're leaving?"

"No." Royce scowled and looked in the direction of the tower of Avempartha. "Apparently I have a job to finish."

Hadrian smiled at his friend, took the dagger, and weighed it in his hand. "I'll give it back to you tomorrow then."

"Right," Royce replied.

"Did your partner leave?" Theron asked as Hadrian approached him walking up the slope of the scorched hill that once was the castle. The old farmer stood on the blackened hillside holding the shattered sword and looking up at the sky.

"No, well sort of, he's headed back inside Avempartha to steal the other half of the sword just in case the Gilarabrywn tries to double cross us. There is even a chance it might leave Thrace and Arista in the tower while it comes here, and if it does Royce, can get them out."

Theron nodded thoughtfully.

"You two have been real good to me and my daughter. I still don't know why, and don't tell me it's the money," Theron sighed. "You know, I never gave her credit for much. I ignored her, pushed her away for so many years. She was only my daughter, not a son— an extra mouth to feed that would cost us money to marry off. How she ever found the two of you and got you to come all this way to help us is…well, I just don't think I will ever understand that."

"Hadrian," Fanen called to him. "Come down here and see what we've got."

Hadrian followed Fanen down the hill to the north edge of the burn line where he found Tobis, Mauvin, and Magnus working on a huge contraption.

"This is my catapult," Tobis declared, standing proudly next to a wagon on which a wooden machine sat. Tobis looked comical in his loud-colored court clothes propped up on a crutch Magnus had fashioned for him, his broken leg strapped down between two stiff pieces of wood. "They dragged it out here when I was bumped from the roster. She's exquisite, isn't she? I named her Persephone after Novron's wife. Only fitting, I thought, since I studied ancient imperial history to devise it. Not easy to do either, I had to learn the ancient languages just to read the books."

"Did you just build this?"

"No, of course not, you silly man. I am a professor at Sheridan. That's in Ghent by the way. You know the same place as the seat of the Nyphron Church? Well, being brilliant, I bribed some church officials who let slip the true nature of the competition. It would not be a ridiculous bashing match between sawdust-filled heads, but a challenge to defeat a legendary creature. This was a puzzle I could solve; one that I knew did not require muscle and a lack of teeth, but rather a staggering intellect such as mine."

Hadrian walked around the device. A massive center beam rose up a good twelve-feet, and the long thick arm was a foot or two longer than that. It had a sack bucket joined to a lower beam with torsion producing chords. On either side of the wagon were two massive hand cranks connected to a series of gears.

"Well, I must say I have seen catapults before and this doesn't look much like them."

"That's because I modified it for fighting the Gilarabrywn."

"Well, he tried," Magnus added. "It wouldn't have worked the way he had it set up, but it will now."

"In fact, we fired a few rocks already," Mauvin reported.

"I've had some experience with siege weapons before," Hadrian said. "And I know they can be useful against something big like a field of soldiers or something that doesn't move like a wall, but they're useless against a solitary moving enemy. They just aren't that fast or accurate."

"Yes, well that is why I devised this one to fire not only projectiles but nets as well," Tobis said proudly. "I'm very clever that way you see. The nets are designed to launch like large balls that open in mid-flight and snare the beast as it is flying, dropping it to the ground where it will lie helpless while I reload and take my time crushing it."

"And this works?" Hadrian asked impressed.

"In theory," Tobis replied.

Hadrian shrugged. "What the heck, it couldn't hurt."

"Just need to get it in position," Mauvin said. "Care to help push?"

They all put their backs to the catapult, except, of course, for Tobis, who limped along spouting orders. They rolled it to the ditch that ringed the bottom of the motte and within range to fire on anything in the area near the old manor house.

"Might want to get something to hide it—rubble or burnt wood maybe, so that it looks like a pile of trash," Hadrian said. "Which shouldn't be hard to do. Magnus, I was wondering if you could do me a favor?"

"What kind?" he asked as Hadrian led him back up the hill toward the ruins of the manor house. The grass was gone, and they walked on a surface of ash and roots that made Hadrian think of warm snow.

"Remember that sword you made for Lord Rufus? I found it, still with him and his horse on the hill. I want you to fix it."

"Fix it?" The dwarf looked offended. "It's not my fault the sword didn't work, I did a perfect replica. The records were likely at fault."

"That's fine because I have the original, or part of it at least. I need you to make an exact copy of what we have. Can you do it?"

"Of course I can, and I will, in return for you're getting Royce to let me look at the Alverstone."

"Are you crazy? He wants you dead. I saved your neck from him once already. Doesn't that count?"

The dwarf stood firm his arms crossed over the braids in his beard. "That's my price."

"I will talk to him, but I can't guarantee it."

The dwarf pursed his lips, which made his beard and moustache bristle. "Very well, where are these swords?"

Theron agreed to the plan as long as he got the piece back and brought the broken blade to the manor's smithy, which now consisted of no more than the brick forge and the anvil. He would hold the blade during the exchange and hand it over immediately should the ruse be discovered.

"Hrumph!" The dwarf looked disgusted.

"What?" Hadrian asked.

"No wonder it didn't work. There are markings on both sides. There's this whole other inscription. See, this is the incantation I bet." The dwarf showed Hadrian the blade where a seemingly incomprehensible spider web of thin sweeping lines formed a long design. Then he flipped it over to reveal a significantly shorter design on the back. "And this side I'm guessing holds the name that Esrahaddon mentioned. It makes sense that all the incantations are the same, only the name is unique."

"Does that mean you can create a weapon that will work?"

"No, it's broken right along the middle of the name, but I can make an awfully good copy of this at least."

The dwarf removed his tool belt hidden beneath his clothes and laid it on the anvil. He had a number of hammers of different sizes and shapes, and chisels all in separate loops. He unrolled a leather apron and tied it on. Then he took Rufus' sword and strapped it to the anvil.

"Carry those everywhere, do you?" Hadrian asked.

"You won't catch me leaving them on a horse's saddle," Magnus replied.

Hadrian and Theron began digging a pit on the side of the courtyard. They dug it on the site of the old smokehouse, making use of the already turned soil to ease their effort. Without a shovel, they used old boards that left their hands black. Within a couple hours, they had a small hole big enough for the two of them to get down fully under the earth. It was not deep enough to avoid being dug up, but it might hide them from a blast of fire so long as it did not come straight down. If it did, they would be like a couple of clay pots fired in sand.

"Won't be long now," Hadrian told Theron as the two men sat covered in dirt and ash looking up at the fading light. Magnus was using his smallest hammer, tapping away with a resounding *tink, tink*. He muttered something, then pulled a heavy cloth from a pouch on his belt and began rubbing the surface of the metal.

Hadrian looked out over the trees, feeling Alverstone inside his tunic. He wondered if Royce made it to the tower. *Is he inside? Has he found Esrahaddon? Can the old wizard do anything to help them?* He thought of the princess and Thrace. *What has it done with them?* He bit his lip. Royce was probably right. *Why would it keep them alive?*

The sound of horses approached from the south. Theron and Hadrian exchanged surprised looks and stood up to see a troop of riders racing out of the trees. Eight horsemen crossed the desolate plain, knights in black armor with a standard of a broken crown flying before them. Leading them was Luis Guy in his red cassock.

"Look who is finally back." Hadrian looked over at Magnus. "You done yet?"

"Just polishing," the dwarf replied. He then noticed the riders for the first time. "This can't be good," he grumbled.

The riders trotted into the remains of the courtyard and pulled up at the sight of them. Guy surveyed the smoldering remains of the old castle for a moment, then dismounted and walked toward the dwarf, pausing to pick up a burnt bit of timber, which he turned over twice in his hands before tossing it away. "It would seem Lord Rufus didn't do as well last night as we hoped. Did you forget to dot an i, Magnus?"

Magnus took a frightened step back. Theron stepped forward quickly, grabbed the original broken blade, and hid it under his shirt.

Guy noticed the act, but ignored the farmer and faced the dwarf. "Care to explain yourself Magnus, or shall I just kill you for lousy workmanship?"

"Wasn't my fault. There were markings on the other side that none of the pictures showed. I did what you asked, your research was to blame."

"And what are you up to now?"

"He's duplicating the blade so we can use it to trade with the Gilarabrywn," Hadrian explained.

"Trade?"

"Yes, the creature took the Princess Arista and a village girl. It said if we return the blade we took from its lair it will free the women."

"It *said?*"

"Yes," Hadrian confirmed. "It spoke to Deacon Tomas last night just before he watched it take the women."

Guy laughed coldly. "So the beast is talking now, is it? And abducting women too? How impressive. I suppose it also rides horses and I should expect it to be representing Dunmore at the next Wintertide joust in Aquesta."

"You can ask your own deacon if you don't believe me."

"Oh I believe you," he said walking up to face Hadrian. "At least the part about stealing a sword from the citadel. That is what you're referring to, isn't it? So, someone actually got into Avempartha and took the real sword? Clever, particularly when I know that only someone with elvish blood can enter that tower. You don't look very elf-like to me, Hadrian. And I know the Pickerings' heritage quite well. I also know Magnus here couldn't get in. That leaves only your partner in crime Royce Melborn. He's rather small, isn't he? Slender, agile? Those qualities would certainly serve him well as a thief. He can see easily in the dark, hear better than any human, has uncanny balance, and is so light on his feet that he can move in almost total silence. Yes, it would be most unfair to all the other poor thieves out there using their normal, human abilities."

Guy looked around carefully. "Where is your partner?" he asked, but Hadrian remained silent. "That's one of the biggest problems we have; some of these cross-bred elves can pass for human. They can be so hard to spot sometimes. They don't have the pointed ears, or the squinty eyes, because they take after their human parent, but the elven parent is always there. That's what makes them so dangerous. They look normal, but deep down they are inhumanly evil. You probably don't even see it. Do you? You are like those fools that try and tame a bear cub or a wolf, thinking that they will come to love you. You probably think that you can banish the wild beast that lurks inside. You can't, you know, the monster is always there, just looking for the chance to leap out at you."

The sentinel glanced at the anvil. "And I suppose one of you was planning on using the sword to kill the beast and claim the crown of emperor?"

"Actually no," Hadrian replied. "Getting the women and running real fast was more the plan."

"And you expect me to believe that? Hadrian Blackwater, the consummate warrior who handles a blade like a Teshlor Knight of the old empire. You really expect me to believe that you're just passing through this remote village? That you just happen to be in possession of the only weapon that can kill the Gilarabrywn at the precise moment in time when the Emperor will be chosen by the one who does so. No, of course not, you are just using what is arguably the most powerful sword in the world to make a trade with an insanely dangerous, but now talking monster, for a peasant girl and the Princess of Melengar, whom you barely know."

"Well—when you put it that way, it does sound bad, but it's the truth."

"The church will be returning to continue the trials here," Luis Guy told them. "Until then, it is my job to make certain no one kills the Gilarabrywn who is, shall we say, unworthy of the crown. That most certainly includes thieving elf-lovers and his band of cut-throats." Guy walked over to Theron. "So I will have that blade you're holding."

"Over my dead body," Theron growled.

"As you wish," Guy drew his sword and all seven seret dismounted and drew their blades as well.

"Now," Guy told Theron, "give me the blade or both of you will die."

"Don't you mean all four?" a voice behind Hadrian said and he looked over to see Mauvin and Fanen coming up the slope spreading out, each with his sword drawn. Mauvin held two, one of which he tossed to Theron, who caught it clumsily.

"Make that five," Magnus said holding two of his larger hammers in his hands. The dwarf looked over at Hadrian and swallowed hard. "He's planning on killing me anyway, so why not?"

"There are still eight of us," Guy pointed out. "Not exactly an even fight."

"I was thinking the same thing," Mauvin said. "Sadly, there's no one else here we can ask to join your side."

Guy looked at Mauvin then Hadrian for a long moment as the men glared across the ash at each other. Then he nodded and lowered his blade. "Well, I can see I will have to report your misconduct to the archbishop."

"Go ahead," Hadrian said. "His body is buried with the rest of them just down the hillside."

Guy gave him a cold look then turned to walk away, but as he did, Hadrian noticed his shoulder dip unnaturally to his right and his foot pivot, toe out as he stepped. It was a motion Hadrian had taught Theron to watch for, the announcement of an attack.

"Theron!" He shouted, but it was unnecessary, the farmer had already moved and raised his sword even before Guy spun. The sentinel thrust for his heart. Theron was there a second faster and knocked the blade away. Then out of reflex, the farmer shifted his weight forward took a step and performed the combination move Hadrian had drilled into him, parry, pivot, and riposte. He thrust forward, extending, going for reach. The sentinel staggered. He twisted and narrowly avoided being run through the chest, taking the sword thrust in his shoulder. Guy cried out in agony.

Theron stood shocked at his own success.

"Pull it out!" Hadrian and Mauvin both yelled at him.

Theron withdrew the blade and Guy staggered back gripping his bleeding shoulder.

"Kill them!" the sentinel hissed.

The seret knights charged.

Four Knights of Nyphron attacked the Pickering brothers. One rushed Hadrian, another launched himself at Theron, and the last took Magnus. Hadrian knew Theron would not last long against a skilled seret. He drew both his short sword and the bastard and slew the first Knight of Nyphron the moment he came within range. Then he stepped in the path of the second. The knight realized too late he was walking into a vice of two attackers as both Hadrian and Theron cut him down.

Magnus held up his hammers as menacingly as he could, but the little dwarf was clearly no match for the knight and he retreated behind his anvil. As the seret got nearer, he threw one hammer at him, which hit the seret in the chest. It rang off his breastplate, causing no real harm, but it staggered him slightly. Realizing that the dwarf was no threat, the seret turned to face Hadrian who raced at him.

The seret swung down in an arc at Hadrian's head. Hadrian caught the blade with the short sword in his left hand, holding the knight's sword arm up as he drove his bastard sword into the man's unprotected armpit.

Mauvin and Fanen fought together against the four attackers. The elegant rapiers of the Pickerings flew—catching, blocking, slicing, slamming. Every attack turned back, every thrust blocked, every swing answered. Yet the two brothers could only defend. They stood their ground against the onslaught of the armored knights who struggled to find a weakness. Mauvin finally managed to find a moment to jump to the offense and slipped in a thrust. The tip of his blade stabbed into the throat of the seret, dropping him with a rapid jab, but no sooner had he done so than Fanen cried out.

Hadrian watched as a seret sliced Fanen across his sword arm, the blade continuing down to his hand. The younger Pickering's sword fell from his fingers. Defenseless, Fanen desperately stepped backward, retreating from his two opponents. He tripped on the wreckage and fell. They rushed him, going for the kill.

Hadrian was too many steps away.

Mauvin ignored his own defense to save his brother. He thrust out. In one move, he blocked both attacks on Fanen—but at a cost. Hadrian saw the seret standing before Mauvin thrust. The blade penetrated Mauvin's side. Instantly the elder Pickering buckled. He fell to his knees with his eyes still on his brother. He could only watch helplessly as the next blow came down. Two swords entered Fanen's body. Blood coated the blades.

Mauvin screamed. Even as his own assailant began his killing blow, a cross slice aimed at Mauvin's neck. Mauvin, on his knees, ignored the stroke much to the delight of the seret. What the knight did not see was Mauvin did not need to defend. Mauvin was done defending. He thrust his sword upwards, slicing through the attacker's ribcage. He twisted the blade as he pulled it out, ripping apart the man's organs.

The two who had killed his brother turned on Mauvin. The elder Pickering raised his sword again but his side was slick with blood, his arm weak, eyes glassy. Tears streamed down his cheeks. He was no longer focusing. His stroke went wide. The closet knight knocked Mauvin's sword away and the two remaining seret stepped forward and raised their swords, but that was as far as they got. Hadrian had crossed the distance and Mauvin's would-be killers' heads came loose, their bodies dropping into the ash.

"Magnus, get Tomas up here fast." Hadrian shouted. "Tell him to bring the bandages."

"He's dead," Theron said as he bent over Fanen.

"I know he is!" Hadrian snapped. "And Mauvin will be too if we don't help him."

He ripped open Mauvin's tunic and pressed his hand to his side as the blood bubbled up between his fingers. Mauvin lay panting, sweating. His eyes rolled up in his head revealing their whites.

"Damn you, Mauvin!" Hadrian shouted at him. "Get me a cloth. Theron get me anything."

Theron grabbed one of the seret who had killed Fanen and tore off his sleeve.

"Get more!" he shouted. He wiped Mauvin's side finding a small hole spewing bright red blood. At least it was not the dark blood, which usually meant death. He took the cloth and pressed it against the wound.

"Help me sit him up," Hadrian said as Theron returned with another strip of cloth. Mauvin was a limp rag now. His head slumped to one side.

Tomas came running up, his arms filled with long strips of cloth that Lena had given him. They lifted Mauvin, and Tomas tightly wrapped the bandages around his torso. The blood soaked through the cloth, but the rate of bleeding had lessened.

"Keep his head up," Hadrian ordered and Tomas cradled him.

Hadrian looked over at where Fanen lay. He was on his back in the dirt, a dark pool of blood still growing around his body. Hadrian gripped his swords with blood soaked hands and stood up.

"Where's Guy?" he shouted through clenched teeth.

"He's gone," Magnus answered. "During the fight he grabbed a horse and ran."

Hadrian stared back down at Fanen and then at Mauvin. He took a breath and it shuddered in his chest.

Tomas bowed his head and said the Prayer of the Departed:

> *"Unto Maribor, I beseech thee*
> *Into the hands of god, I send thee*
> *Grant him peace, I beg thee*
> *Give him rest, I ask thee*
> *May the god of men watch over your journey."*

When he was done, he looked up at the stars and in a soft voice said, "It's dark."

Chapter 13

ARTISTIC VISION

ARISTA DID NOT want to breathe. It caused her stomach to tighten and bile to rise in her throat. Above her stretched the star-filled sky, but below—the pile. Like a nest, the Gilarabrywn built its mound from collected trophies, gruesome souvenirs of attacks and kills. The top of a head with dark matted hair, a broken chair, a foot still in its shoe, a partially chewed torso, a blood soaked dress, an arm reaching up out of the heap as if waving, so pale it was blue.

The pile rested on what looked to be an open balcony on the side of a high stone tower, but there was no way off. Instead of a door leading inside, there was only an archway, an outline of a door. Such false hope teased Arista as she longed for it to be a real door.

She sat with her hands on her lap not wanting to touch anything. There was something underneath her, long and thin like a tree branch. It was uncomfortable, but she did not dare move. She did not want to know what it really was. She tried not to look down. She forced herself to watch the stars and look out at the horizon. To the north, the princess could see the forest divided by the silvery line of the river. To the south laid large expanses of water that faded into darkness. Something out of the corner of her eye would catch her attention and she looked down. She always regretted it.

Arista realized with a shiver that she had slept on the pile, but she had not fallen asleep. It had felt like drowning—terror so absolute that it overwhelmed her. She could not recall the flight she must have taken, or most of the day, but she did remember seeing it. The beast had lain inches away basking in the afternoon sun. She stared at it for hours, not able to look at anything else—her own death sleeping before her had a way of demanding her complete attention. She sat, afraid to move or speak. She was expecting it to wake and kill her—to add her to the pile. Muscles tense, heart racing, her eyes locked on the thick scaly skin that rippled with each breath, sliding over what looked like ribs. She felt as if she were treading water. She could feel the blood pounding in her head. She was exhausted from not moving. Then the drowning came over her once more and everything went mercifully black.

Now her eyes were open again, but the great beast was missing. She looked around. There was no sign of the monster.

"It's gone," Thrace told her. It was the first either of them spoke since the attack. The girl was still dressed in her nightgown, the bruise forming a dark line across her face. She was on her hands and knees moving through the pile, digging like a child in a sandbox.

"Where is it?" Arista asked.

"Flew away."

The princess looked up scanning the stars, no movement at all.

Somewhere nearby, somewhere below she heard a roar. It was not the beast. The sound was constant, a rumbling hum.

"Where are we?" she asked.

"On top of Avempartha," Thrace answered without looking up from her macabre excavation. She dug down beneath a layer of broken stone and turned over an iron kettle revealing a torn tapestry that she began tugging.

"What is Avempartha?"

"It's a tower"

"Oh. What are you doing?"

"I thought there might be a weapon, something to fight with."

Arista blinked. "Did you say to fight with?"

"Yes, maybe a dagger, or a piece of glass."

Arista would not have believed it possible if it had not happened to her, but at that moment as she sat helplessly trapped on a pile of dismembered bodies waiting to be eaten—she laughed.

"A piece of glass? A piece of glass?" Arista howled, her voice becoming shrill. "You're going to use a dagger or a piece of glass to fight—*that thing?*"

Thrace nodded, shoving the antlered head of a buck aside.

Arista continued to stare open mouthed.

"What have we got to lose?" Thrace asked.

That was it. That summed the situation up perfectly. The one thing they had going for them was that it could not get worse. In all her days, even when Percy Braga was building the pyre to burn her alive, even when the dwarf closed the door on her and Royce as they dangled from a rope in a collapsing tower, it was not worse than this. Few fates could compare to the inevitability of being eaten alive.

Arista fully shared Thrace's belief, but something in her did not want to accept it. She wanted to believe there was still a chance.

"You don't think it will keep its promise?" she asked.

"Promise?"

"What it told the deacon."

"You—you could understand it?" the girl asked, pausing for the first time to look at her.

Arista nodded. "It spoke the old imperial language."

"What did it say?"

"Something about trading us for a sword, but I might have gotten it wrong. I learned Old Speech as part of my religious studies at Sheridan and I was never very good at it not to mention I was scared. I'm still scared."

Arista saw Thrace thinking and envied her.

"No," the girl said at last, "it won't let us live. It kills people. That's what it does. It killed my mother and brother, my sister-in-law, and my nephew. It killed my best friend Jessie Caswell. It killed Daniel Hall. I never told anyone this before, but I thought I might marry him one day. I found him near the river trail one beautiful fall morning, mostly chewed, but his face was still fine. That's what bothered me the most. His face was perfect, not a scratch on it. He just looked like he was sleeping under the pines, only most of his body was gone. It will kill us."

Thrace shivered with the passing wind.

Arista slipped off her cloak, "Here," she said. "You need this more than I do."

Thrace looked at her with a puzzled smile.

"Just take it!" she snapped. Her emotions breeched the surface, threatening to spill. "I want to do *something*, damn it!"

She held out the cloak with a wavering arm. Thrace crawled over and took it. She held it up, looking at it as if she were in the comfort of a dressing room. "It's very beautiful, so heavy."

Again Arista laughed, thinking how strange it was to fly from despair to laughter in a single breath. One of them was surely insane—maybe they both were. Arista wrapped it around the young girl as she clasped it on. "And here I was ready to kill Bernice—"

Arista thought of Hilfred and the maid left—no, ordered—to stay in the room. Had she killed them?

"Do you think anyone survived?"

The girl rolled aside a statue's head and what looked like a broken marble tabletop. "My father is alive," Thrace said simply, digging deeper.

Arista did not ask how she knew this, but believed her. At that moment, she would believe anything Thrace told her.

With a nice hole dug into the heart of the debris, Thrace had yet to find a weapon beyond a leg bone, which she set aside with grisly indifference, Arista guessed, to use in case she found nothing better. The princess watched the excavation with a mix of admiration and disbelief.

Thrace uncovered a beautiful mirror that was shattered and struggled to free a jagged piece when Arista saw a glint of gold and pointed saying, "There's something under the mirror."

Thrace pushed the glass aside and reaching down grabbed hold and drew forth the hilt half of a broken sword. Elaborately decorated in silver and gold encrusted in fine sparkling gems, the pommel caught the starlight and sparkled.

Thrace took the sword by the grip and held it up. "It's light," she said.

"It's broken," Arista replied, "but I suppose it's better than a piece of glass."

Thrace stowed the hilt in the lining pocket of the cloak and went on digging. She came across the head of an axe and a fork, both of which she discarded. Then pulling back a bit of cloth, she stopped suddenly.

Arista hated to look, but once more felt compelled.

It was a woman's face—eyes closed, mouth open.

Thrace placed the cloth back over the hole she had made. She retreated to the far edge and sat down, squeezing her knees while resting her head. Arista could see her shaking and Thrace did not dig anymore after that. The two sat in silence.

Thrump. Thrump.

Arista heard the sound and her heart raced. Every muscle in her body tightened and she dared not look. A great gust of air struck from above as she closed her eyes, waiting for death. She heard it

land and waited to die. Arista could hear it breathing and still she
waited.

"*Soon*," she heard it say.

Arista opened her eyes.

The beast rested on the pile, panting from the effort of its flight.
It shook its head, spraying the platform with loose saliva from its
lips that failed to hide the forest of jagged teeth. Its eyes were larger
than Arista's hand, with tall narrow pupils on a marbled orange and
brown lens that reflected her own image.

"*Soon?*" She didn't know where she found the courage to
speak.

The massive eye blinked and the pupil dilated as it focused on
her. It would kill her now, but at least it would be over.

"*You understand mine speech?*" the voice was large and so deep she
felt it vibrating her chest.

She both nodded and said, "*Yes.*"

Across from her, the princess could see Thrace with her head up
off her knees staring.

The beast looked at Arista. "*Thou art regal.*"

"*I am a princess.*"

"*The best bait,*" the Gilarabrywn said but Arista was not sure she
heard that right. It might also have said 'the greatest gift,' the phrase
was difficult to translate.

She asked, "*Wilt thou honor thine trade or kill us?*"

"*The bait stays alive until I catch the thief.*"

"*Thief?*"

"*The taker of the sword. It comes. I crossed the moon to show it the way
twas clear, but hath returned flying low. The thief comes now.*"

"What's it saying?" Thrace asked.

"It said we are bait to catch a thief that stole a sword."

"Royce," Thrace said.

Arista stared at her. "What did you say?"

"I hired two men to steal a sword from this tower."

"You hired Royce Melborn and Hadrian Blackwater?" Arista asked, stunned.

"Yes."

"How did you—" she gave that thought up. "It knows Royce is coming," Arista told her. "It pretended to fly away, letting him see it leave."

The Gilarabrywn's ears perked up suddenly tilting forward toward the false door. Abruptly, but quietly, it stood and with a gentle flap of its wings lifted off. Catching the thermals, the beast soared upward above the tower. Thrace and Arista heard movement somewhere below, footsteps on stone.

A figure appeared in a black cloak. It stepped forward, passing through the solid stone of the false door, like a man surfacing from below a still pond.

"It's a trap, Royce!" Arista and Thrace shouted together.

The figure did not move.

Arista heard the whispered sound of air rushing across leathery wings. Then a brilliant light abruptly burst forth from the figure. Without a sound or movement, it was as if a star appeared in place of the man, the light so bright, it blinded everyone. Arista closed her eyes in pain and heard the Gilarabrywn screech overhead. She felt frantic puffs of air beat down on her as the beast flapped its wings, breaking its dive.

The light was short-lived. It faded abruptly though not entirely and soon they could all see the man in the shimmering robe before them.

"*YOU!*" The beast cursed at him, shaking the tower with its voice. It hovered above them, its great wings flapping.

"*Escaped thy cage beast of Erivan, hunter of Nareion!*" Esrahaddon shouted in Old Speech. "*I shalt cage thee again!*"

The wizard raised his arms, but before he made another move, the Gilarabrywn screeched and fluttered back in horror. It beat its great wings and rose up, but in that last second, it reached down with one talon snatching Thrace off the tower. It dove over the side vanishing from sight. Arista raced to the railing looking down in horror. The beast and Thrace were gone.

"We can do nothing for her," the wizard said sadly.

She turned to see Esrahaddon and Royce Melborn beside her, both looking over the edge into the dark roar of the river below. "Her fate lies with Hadrian and her father now."

Arista's hands squeezed the railing stiffly. She felt the drowning sensation again. Royce grabbed her by the wrist. "Are you alright, Your Highness? It's a long way down, you know."

"Let's get her downstairs," Esrahaddon said. "The door, Royce. The door."

"Oh right," the thief replied. "*Grant entry to Arista Essendon Princess of Melengar.*"

The archway became a real door that stood open. They all entered into a small room. Off the pile, safe behind walls, Arista felt the impact at last and she was forced to sit before she fell.

She buried her face in her hands and wailed, "Oh god, dear Maribor. Poor Thrace!"

"She may yet be all right," the wizard told her. "Hadrian and her father are waiting with the broken sword."

She rocked as she cried but she did not cry only for Thrace. The tears were the bursting of a dam that could resist the flood no longer. In her mind flashed images of Hilfred and that last unspoken word; of Bernice and the cruel way she had treated her; and of Fanen and Mauvin, their happy faces lost. All of this could not be put into words, instead the emotions exploded out of her as she shouted, "The sword, what sword? What is all of this about a sword? I don't understand!"

"You explain," Royce said. "I need to find the other half."

"It's not there," Arista told him.

"What?"

"You said the sword was broken?" Arista asked.

"In two parts. I stole the blade half yesterday, now I need to get the hilt half. I'm pretty certain it is in that pile up there."

"No it isn't," Arista said, shocked that her brain was still working enough to connect the dots. "Not anymore."

The wizard led the way down the long crystalline steps, pausing from time to time to peer down a corridor, or at a staircase. He would think for a moment then shake his head and push on, or mutter, "Ah, yes!" and turn.

"Where are we?" she asked.

"Avempartha," the wizard replied.

"I got that much already. What *is* Avempartha, and don't say it's a tower."

"It is an elven construction, built several millenniums ago. More recently it has been a trap that has held the Gilarabrywn, and more recently still, it has apparently been it's nest. Does that help?"

"Not really."

Although perplexed, Arista did feel better. It surprised her how easy it was to forget. It felt wrong. She should be thinking about the ones lost. She should be grieving, but her mind fought against it. Like a broken limb that refused to support any more weight, her heart and mind were hungry for relief. She needed a rest, something else to think about, something that did not involve death and misery. The tower of Avempartha provided the remedy. It was astounding.

Esrahaddon led them across interior bridges that spanned between spire shafts, up and down stairs and through great rooms. Not a torch or lantern burned, but she could see perfectly, the walls themselves giving off a soft blue light. Vaulted ceilings a hundred feet high spread out like the canopy of a forest with intricately lined designs that suggested branches and leaves. Railings ran along walkways and down steps, appearing as curling tendrils of creeping vines, sculptured from solid stone in vivid detail. Nothing was without adornment, every inch imbued with beauty and care. Arista walked with her mouth open, her eyes shifting from one wonder to the next—a giant statue of a magnificent swan taking flight, a bubbling fountain in the shape of a school of fish. She recalled the crude barbarity of King Roswort's castle and his disdain for the elves—beings he likened to rats in a woodpile. *Some woodpile.*

There was a music to this place. The muted humming of the falls created a low, comforting bass. The wind across the tips of the tower played as woodwinds in an orchestra—soft reassuring tones. The bubbling and trickling of fountains lent light, satisfying rhythms to the symphony. Into this harmony crashed the voice of Esrahaddon as he recounted his first visit to the tower centuries before and how he had trapped the beast inside.

"So since you trapped the Gilarabrywn nine hundred years ago," she said, "you plan to trap it here again?"

"No," Esrahaddon told her. "No hands, remember? I can't cast that powerful of a binding spell without fingers girl; you should know that better than anyone."

"I heard you threaten to cage it again."

"The Gilarabrywn doesn't know Esra doesn't have hands, does it?" Royce put in.

"The beast remembered me," the wizard took over. "It assumed I was just as powerful as before, which means aside from the sword, I am about the only thing the Gilarabrywn fears."

"You just wanted to scare it off?"

"That was the idea, yes."

"We were trying to get the sword and hoped we might also save the both of you in the process," Royce told her. "I obviously didn't expect it to grab Thrace, and there was absolutely no way I could have guessed she would have taken the sword with her. You're certain she took a sword hilt from the pile?"

"Yes, I was the one who spotted it, but I still don't understand. How does the sword help? The Gilarabrywn isn't an enchantment; it's a monster that the heir must kill and…"

"You've been listening to the church. The Gilarabrywn *is* a magical creation. The sword is the counter measure."

"A sword is? That doesn't make sense. A sword is metal, a physical element."

Esrahaddon smiled, looking a bit surprised. "So you paid attention to my lessons. Excellent. You're right, the sword is worthless. It is the word written on the blade that has the power to dispel the conjuration. If it is plunged into the body of the beast it will unlock the elements holding it in existence and break the enchantment."

"If only you had been the one to take it we'd have a way to fight the thing."

"Well, you did save me at least," Arista reminded them. "Thank you."

"Don't thank us too soon. It's still out there," Royce told her.

"Okay, so Thrace hired Royce—I don't know how that transpired, but okay—still I don't understand why *you're* here Esra," she admitted.

"To find the heir."

"There isn't an heir," she told them. "All the contestants failed and the rest are dead I'm sure. That monster destroyed everything."

"I'm not talking about that foolishness. I'm speaking about the real Heir of Novron."

The wizard came to a T-intersection and turned left heading for a staircase that lead down again.

"Wait a minute," Royce stopped them. "We didn't come this way."

"No *we* didn't, but I did."

Royce looked around him. "No, no, this is all wrong. Here I was letting you lead and you clearly don't have a clue where the exit is."

"I'm not leading you to the exit."

"What?" Royce asked.

"We're not leaving," the wizard replied. "I am going to the Valentryne Layartren and the two of you are coming with me."

"You might want to explain why," Royce told him, his voice chilling several degrees. "Otherwise you are jumping to a pretty big conclusion."

"I will explain on the way."

"Explain now," Royce told him. "I have other appointments to consider."

"You can't help Hadrian," the wizard said. "The Gilarabrywn is already at the village by now. Hadrian is either dead or safe. Nothing you can do will change that. You can't help him, but you can help me. I spent the better part of two days trying to access the Valentryne Layartren, but without your hands, Royce, I can't reach it and it would take days, perhaps weeks for me to operate alone, but with Arista here we can do it all tonight. Maribor has seen fit to deliver both of you to me at the precise moment I need you most."

"Valentryne Layartren," Royce muttered, "that's elvish for *artistic vision*, isn't it?"

"You know some elvish, good for you, Royce," Esrahaddon said. "You should pursue your roots more."

"Your roots?" Arista said confused.

They both ignored her.

"You can't help the people back at the village, but you can help me do what I came here to do. What I brought you here to help me with."

"You need us to help you find the true Heir of the Empire?"

"You're normally quicker than this, Royce. I am disappointed."

"I thought you were keeping it a secret?"

"I was, but circumstances have forced me to reconsider. Now quit being so stubborn and come with me. You might look back on this moment one day and reflect on how you changed the course of the world by simply walking down these steps."

Royce sighed and nodded.

"Thank the gods," the wizard said. "Let's get moving."

"Wait a minute." Arista stopped them. "Don't I get a say in this too?"

The wizard looked back at her. "Do you know the way out?"

"No," she replied.

"Then no, you don't get a say," the wizard told her. "Now please, we've wasted enough time, follow me."

"I remember you being nicer," Arista shouted at the wizard.

"And I remember both of you being faster."

They were off again, heading deeper into the center of the tower. As they did, Esrahaddon spoke again. "Most people believe this tower was built by the elves as a defensive fortress for the wars against Novron. As both of you most likely have guessed, that's not true. This tower predates Novron by many millennia. Others think it was built as a fortress against the sea goblins, the infamous Ba Ran Ghazel, only that's also not true since the tower predates their appearance as well. The common mistake here is that this is a fortress at all—that's the result of human thinking. The fact is, the elves lived for eons before man or goblin, and perhaps even before dwarves entered the world. In those days they had no need for fortresses. They didn't even have a word for war as the Horn of Gylindora controlled all of their internal strife. No, this wasn't some defensive bulwark guarding the only crossing point on the Nidwalden River, although that certainly became its use many eons later. Originally, this tower was designed as a center for The Art."

"He means magic," Arista clarified.

"I know what he means."

"Elven masters would travel here from the world over to study and practice advanced Art. Still this wasn't just a school. The building itself is an enormous tool, like a giant furnace for a blacksmith, only in this case, the building works as a focusing element. The falls function as a source of power and the tower's numerous spires are like the antenna on a grasshopper or the whiskers of a cat. They reach out into the world, sensing, feeling, drawing into this place the very essence of existence. It is like a giant lever and fulcrum, allowing a single artist to magnify their power almost beyond reason."

"Artistic vision…" Royce said. "It's a device that will allow you to use magic to find the heir?"

"Sadly, not even Avempartha has that much power. I can't find something I've never seen, or something I don't know exists. What I can do, however, is find something I do know, something that I am very well acquainted with, and something I created for the specific purpose of finding later.

"Nine hundred years ago when Jerish and I decided to split up in order to hide Nevrik, I made amulets for them. These amulets served two purposes, one was to protect them from The Art thus preventing anyone from locating them by divination; the other was to provide me with a means to track them with a signature only I know how to recognize.

"Of course, Jerish and I assumed it would only take a few years to assemble a group of loyalists to restore the Emperor, but as we all now know that didn't happen. I can only hope that Jerish was smart enough to impress upon the descendants of the heir to keep the necklaces safe and to hand them down from one generation to the next. That might be asking too much since—well, who could imagine that I would live so long."

They crossed another narrow bridge that spanned a disturbingly deep gap. Overhead were several colorful banners with iconic images embroidered on them with large single elven letters. Arista noticed Royce staring at them, his mouth working as if trying to read. On the far side of the bridge, they reached a doorstep where a tall ornately decorated archway was drawn into the stone, but no door was present.

"Royce, if you wouldn't mind?"

Royce stepped forward and laying his hands on the polished stone, pressed.

"What's he doing?" Arista asked the wizard.

Esrahaddon turned and looked at Royce.

The thief stood before them uncomfortably for a moment then said, "Avempartha has a magical protection that prevents anyone who doesn't have elvish blood from entering. Every lock in the place works the same way. Originally, we thought no one else but I could enter, oh, and Esra, because he had been invited years ago, but it turns out that if an elf invites you that's all that is needed. Esra found the exact elvish wording for me to memorize for the invite. That's how I got you in."

"Speaking of which…" Esrahaddon motioned toward the stone arch.

"Sorry," Royce said and added in a clear voice. "Melentanaria, en venau rendin Esrahaddon, en Arstia Essendon adona Melengar." Which Arista understood as: *Grant entry to the wizard Esrahaddon and Arista Essendon Princess of Melengar.*

"That's Old Speech," Arista said.

"Yes," Esrahaddon nodded. "There are many similarities between Elvish and the Old Imperial."

"Whoa!" Looking back at the archway Arista suddenly saw an open door. "But I still don't understand. How is it you can grant us—oh." The princess stopped with her mouth still open. "But you don't look at all—"

"I'm a *mir*."

"A what?"

"A mix," Esrahaddon explained, "Some elven, some human blood."

"But you never—"

"It's not the kind of thing you brag about," the thief said. "And I'd appreciate it if you kept this to yourself."

"Oh—of course."

"Come along, Arista still needs to play her part," Esrahaddon said entering.

Inside they found a large chamber carved perfectly round. It was like entering the inside of giant ball. Unlike the rest of the tower and despite its size, the room was unadorned. It was merely a vast smooth chamber with no seam, crack, nor crevice. The only feature was a zigzagging stone staircase that rose from the floor to a platform that extended out from the steps and stood at the exact center of the sphere.

"Do you remember the Plesieantic incantations I taught you, Arista?" the wizard asked as they climbed the stairs, his voice echoing loudly, ricocheting repeatedly off the walls.

"Um…the ah…"

"Do you or don't you?"

"I'm thinking."

"Think faster; this is no time for slow wits."

"Yes, I remember. Lord, but you've gotten testy."

"I'll apologize later. Now, when we get up there you are going to stand in the middle of the platform on the mark laid out on the floor as the apex. You will begin and maintain the Plesieantic Phrase.

Start with the Gathering Incantation, when you do you will likely feel a bit more of a jolt than you would normally because this place will amplify your power to gather resources. Don't be alarmed, don't stop the incantation, and whatever you do, don't scream."

Arista looked fearfully back at Royce.

"Once you feel the power moving through your body, begin the Torsonic Chant. As you do you will need to form the crystal-matrix with your fingers, making certain you fold inward not outward."

"So with my thumbs pointing out and the rest of my fingers pointing at me, right?"

"Yes," Esrahaddon said irritated. "This is all basic formations, Arista."

"I know it, I know it—it's just been a while. I've been busy being Melengar's ambassador, not sitting in my tower practicing conjurations."

"So you've been frivolously wasting your time?"

"No," she said, exasperated.

"Now, when you've completed the matrix," the wizard went on, "just hold it. Remember the concentration techniques I taught you and focus on keeping the matrix even and steady. At that point, I will tap into your power field and conduct my search. When I do, this room is likely to do some extraordinary things. Images and visions will become visible at various places in the room and you might even hear sounds. Again don't be alarmed, they aren't really here, they will merely be echoes of my mind as I search for the amulets."

"Does that mean *all* of us will be able to see who the real heir is?" Royce asked as they reached the top.

Esrahaddon nodded. "I would like to have kept it to myself, but fate has seen fit to force me a different way. When I find the magical pulse of the amulets I will focus on the owners and they will likely appear as the largest image in the room as I will be concentrating to determine not only who wears them, but where they are as well."

The platform was only faintly dust covered and they could easily see the massive converging geometric lines marked on the floor like rays of the sun, all gathering to a single point in the exact center of the dais.

"Them?" Arista asked as she took her position at the central point.

"There were two necklaces, one I gave to Nevrik which will be the heir's amulet and the other to Jerish which will be the bodyguard's. If they still exist, we should see both. I would ask that you not tell anyone what you are about to see, for if you do you could put the heir's life in immense danger and possibly imperil the future of mankind as we know it."

"Wizards and their drama," Royce rolled his eyes. "A simple *please keep your mouth shut* would do."

Esrahaddon raised an eyebrow at the thief, then turned to Arista and said, "Begin."

Arista hesitated. Sauly had to be wrong. All that talk about the heir having the power to enslave mankind was just to frighten her into being their spy. His warnings that Esrahaddon was a demon must be more lies. He was secretive certainly, but not evil. He had saved her life tonight. *What had Sauly done? How many days before Braga's death had Saldur known…and done nothing?* Too many.

"Arista?" Esrahaddon pressed.

She nodded, raised her hands and began the weave.

Chapter 14

AS DARKNESS FALLS

THE NIGHT WIND blew gently across the hilltop. Hadrian and Theron stood alone on the ruins of the manor above what had been a village. A place of countless hopes that lay buried in ash and wreckage.

Theron felt the breeze on his skin and remembered the ill wind he felt the night his family died. The night Thrace ran to him. He could still see her as she raced down the slope of Stony Hill, running to the safety of his arms. He had thought that was the worst day of his life. He had cursed his daughter for coming to him. He blamed her for the death of his family. He put on her all the woe and despair that he had been too weak to carry. She was his little girl, the one who always walked beside him wherever he went, and when he shooed her away, as he always did, he would catch her following at a distance, watching him, mimicking his actions and his words. Thrace was the one who laughed at his faces, cried when he was hurt, the one who sat at his bedside when he lay with fever. He never had a good word for his daughter. Never a pat or praise that he could remember. Not once did he ever say he was proud of her. Most of the time he had not acknowledged her at all. But he would gladly give his own life merely to see his little girl run to him again, just once more.

Theron stood shoulder to shoulder with Hadrian. He held the broken blade hidden beneath his clothes, ready to draw it out in an instant to appease the beast if needed. Hadrian held the false blade the dwarf had fashioned, and he, too, kept it hidden explaining that if the Gilarabrywn knew in advance where its prize was, it might not bother with the trade. Magnus and Tobis waited down the hill out of sight behind a hunting blind of assembled wreckage while Tomas worked at making Hilfred and Mauvin as comfortable as possible at the bottom of the hill.

The moon had risen and climbed above the trees and still the beast had not come. The torches Hadrian had lit in a circle around the hilltop were burning out. Only a few remained, but it did not seem to matter, as the moon was bright and with the canopy of leaves gone, they could see well enough to read a book.

"Maybe it's not coming," Tomas said to them climbing up the hill. "Maybe it wasn't suppose to be tonight or maybe I was just hearing things. I've never been very good with the Old Speech."

"How's Mauvin?" Hadrian asked.

"The bleeding stopped. He's sleeping peacefully now. I covered him in a blanket and created a pillow for him from a spare shirt. He and the soldier Hilfred should—"

There came a cry from the tower that turned their heads. To his amazement, Theron saw a brilliant explosion of white light flare at the pinnacle of the tower. It was there one moment and then faded as suddenly as it had appeared.

"What in the name of Maribor was that?" Theron asked.

Hadrian shook his head. "I don't know, but if I had to guess I'd say Royce had something to do with it."

There was another cry from the Gilarabrywn, this one louder.

"Whatever it was," Hadrian told him, "I think it's headed our way."

Behind them, they could faintly hear Tomas praying.

"Put in a good word for Thrace, Tomas," Theron told him.

"I'm putting a word in for all of us," the cleric replied.

"Hadrian," Theron said, "if by chance I don't survive this and you do, keep an eye on my Thrace for me will you? And if she dies too, see to it we are buried on my farm."

"And if I should die and you live," Hadrian said. "Make sure this dagger I have in my belt gets back to Royce before the dwarf steals it."

"Is that all?" the farmer asked. "Where do you want us to bury you?"

"I don't want to be buried," he said. "If I die I think I would like my body to be sent down the river, over the falls. Who knows, I might make it all the way to the sea."

"Good luck," Theron told him. The sounds of night went suddenly silent, save only for the breath of the wind.

This time with no forest in the way, he could see it coming, its wide dark wings stretched out like the shadow of a soaring bird, its thin body curling, its tail snapping as it flew. It did not dive as it approached. It did not breathe fire or land. Instead, it circled in silent flight, arcing in a wide ellipse.

As it circled, they could see it was not alone. Within its claws, it held a woman. At first, he could not tell who it was. She appeared to be wearing a richly tailored robe but she had Thrace's sandy colored hair. As it circled the second time, he knew it was his daughter. A wave of relief and heightened anxiety gripped him. *What had become of the other?*

After several circles, the beast lowered like a kite and softly touched the ground. It landed directly in front of them not more than fifty feet away on the site of the now collapsed manor house.

Thrace was alive.

A massive claw of scale covered muscle and bone tipped with four, foot-long black nails surrounded her like a cage.

"Daddy!" she cried in tears.

Seeing her, Theron made a lung forward. Instantly the Gilarabrywn's claw tightened and she cried out. Hadrian grabbed Theron and pulled him back.

"Wait!" he shouted. "It'll kill her if you get too close."

The beast glared at them with huge reptilian eyes. Then the Gilarabrywn spoke.

Neither Theron nor Hadrian understood a word.

"Tomas," Hadrian shouted over his shoulder. "What's it saying?"

"I'm not very good at—" Tomas began.

"I don't care how well you did in grammar at seminary just translate."

"I think it said it chose to take the females because it would create the greatest incentive for cooperation."

The creature spoke again and Tomas did not wait for Hadrian to tell him to translate.

"It says: where is the blade that was stolen?"

Hadrian looked back at Tomas, "Ask it: where is the other female?"

Tomas spoke and the beast replied.

"It says the other escaped."

"Ask it: How do I know you will let us all live if I tell you where the blade is hidden?"

Tomas spoke and the beast replied again.

"It says it will offer you a gesture of good faith since it knows it has the upper hand and understands your concern."

It opened its claw and Thrace ran to her father. Theron's heart leapt as his little girl raced across the hill to his waiting arms. He hugged her tight and wiped her tears.

"Theron," Hadrian said, "get her out of here. Both of you get back to the well if you can." Theron and his daughter did not argue and the Gilarabrywn's great eyes watched carefully as Theron and Thrace began to sprint down the hill. Then it spoke again.

"Now, where is the blade?" Tomas translated.

Looking up at the towering beast and feeling the sweat dripping down his face, Hadrian drew the false blade out of his sleeve and held it up. The Gilarabrywn's eyes narrowed.

"Bring it to me," Tomas translated its words.

This was it. Hadrian felt the metal in his hands "Please let this work," he whispered to himself and tossed the blade. It landed in the ash before the beast. The Gilarabrywn looked down at it and Hadrian held his breath. The beast casually placed its foot upon the blade and gathered it into its long talons. Then it looked at Hadrian and spoke.

"The deal is complete," Tomas said. "But…"

"But?" Hadrian repeated nervously, "But what?"

Tomas' voice grew weak. "But it says, I cannot allow those who have seen even half my name to remain alive."

"Oh, you bastard," Hadrian cursed, pulling his great spadone sword from his back. "Run, Tomas!"

The Gilarabrywn rose up, flapping its great wings causing a storm of ash to swirl into a cloud. It snapped forward with its head like a snake. Hadrian dove aside and spinning drove his sword at the beast. Rather than feeling the blade tip penetrate, however,

Hadrian's heart sank as the point of the spadone skipped off as if the Gilarabrywn was made of stone. The sudden shock broke his grip and the sword fell.

Not losing a beat the Gilarabrywn swung its tail around in a sharp snap. The long bone blade on the tip hummed as it sliced the air two feet above the ground. Hadrian leapt over it and the tail glanced off the hillside stabbing into a charred timber. A quick flick and the several hundred-pound log flew into the night. Hadrian reached inside his tunic and drew Alverstone from its sheath. He crouched like a knife-fighter in a ring, up on the balls of his feet, waiting for the next attack.

Once more, the Gilarabrywn's tail came at him. This time it stabbed like a scorpion. Hadrian dove aside, and the long point sunk into the earth.

He ran forward.

The Gilarabrywn snapped at Hadrian with his teeth. He was ready for that, expecting it, counting on it. He jumped aside at the last minute. It was so close one tooth sliced through his tunic and gashed his shoulder. It was worth it. He was inches from the beast's face. With all his strength, Hadrian stabbed Royce's tiny dagger into the monster's great eye.

The Gilarabrywn screeched an awful cry that deafened Hadrian. It reared back, stomping its feet. The tiny blade pierced the pupil and cut a slice. It shook its head perhaps as much in disbelief as in pain and glared at Hadrian with its one remaining eye. Then it spat out words so laced with venom that Tomas did not need to translate.

The beast spread its wings and drew itself up in the air. Hadrian knew what was coming next and cursed his own stupidity having allowed the creature to move him so far from the pit. He could never make it there in time now.

The Gilarabrywn screeched and arched its back.

There was a loud *twack!* A wad of rope netting flew into the air like a ball. With small weights tied to the edges that traveled faster than the center, the net flew open like a giant windsock, enveloping the flapping beast even as it tried to take flight.

Its wings tangled in the net, the Gilarabrywn dropped to the hilltop, crashing down with a heavy thud, the impact throwing up bits of the manor house's stairway banister that flew end-over-end before shattering in a cloud of ash.

"It worked!" Tobis shouted as much in shock as in triumph from the far side of the hill.

Hadrian saw his opportunity and, spinning around, charged the monster. As he did, he noticed Theron following him.

"I told you to take Thrace and run," Hadrian yelled.

"You look like you needed help," Theron shouted back, "And I told Thrace to head for the well."

"What makes you think she will listen to you any more than you listen to me?"

Hadrian reached where the Gilarabrywn lay on its side thrashing about wildly, and dove at its head. He found its open eye and attacked, stabbing repeatedly. With a terrible scream, the beast raked back with its legs, ripping the net open, and rolled to its feet again.

Hadrian, so intent on blinding the beast, had stepped on the netting. When the monster rose up, Hadrian's feet went out from under him. He fell flat on his back, the air knocked from his lungs.

Blind, the beast resorted to lashing out with its tail, sweeping it across the ground. Hadrian got caught while trying to stand up. Too close to be hit by the blade, the force of the blunt tail struck him.

Hadrian rolled and tumbled like a rag doll, sliding across the ash until he stopped in a patch of dirt where he lay, unmoving. Freeing itself fully of the net, the beast sniffed the air and began moving toward the one who had caused it pain.

"No!" Theron shouted and charged. He ran for Hadrian, thinking he could drag him clear of the blind beast before it reached him, only the beast was too fast and reached Hadrian the same time Theron did.

Theron picked up a rock and drew forth the broken blade he still carried. He aimed for the exposed creature's side and, using the rock as a hammer, drove the metal home like a nail.

This stopped the Gilarabrywn from killing Hadrian, but the beast did not cry out as it had when Hadrian stabbed it. Instead, it turned and laughed. Theron struck the blade with the rock again forcing the metal deep, but still the beast did not cry out. It spoke to him, but Theron could not understand the words. Then, having little trouble guessing where the farmer stood, the Gilarabrywn swiped at him with his claw.

Theron did not have the speed or agility that Hadrian had. Strong as he was for his age his old body could not move clear of the blow in time and the great nails of the beast stabbed into him like four swords.

"DADDY!" Thrace screamed, running to him. She scrambled up the slope crying as she came.

From their blind, Tobis and the dwarf fired a rock at the Gilarabrywn, and managed to hit its tail. The beast spun and charged furiously in their direction.

Falling to her hands and knees Thrace crawled to Theron's side and found her father lying broken on the hill. His left arm lay twisted backwards, his foot facing the wrong direction. His chest soaked in dark blood and his breath hitched as his body convulsed.

"Thrace," he managed to say weakly.

"Daddy," she cried as she cradled him in her arms.

"Thrace," he said again, gripping her with his remaining hand and pulled her close. "I'm so—" his eyes closed tightly in pain. "I'm so—pr—proud of you."

"Oh god, Daddy. No. No. No!" she cried shaking her head.

She held him, squeezing as hard as she could, trying by the force of her arms to keep him with her. She would not let him go. She could not, he was all there was. She sobbed and wailed, clutching his shirt, kissing his cheek and forehead, and as she held him, she felt her father pass away into the night.

Theron Wood died on the scorched ground in a pool of blood and dirt. As he did, the last tiny remnant of hope Thrace had held onto—her last foothold she had in the world—died with him.

There is a darkness of night, a darkness of senses, and a darkness of spirit. Thrace felt herself drowning in all three. Her father was dead. Her light, her hope, her last dream, they all died with his last breath. Nothing remained upon the world that *it* had not taken from her.

It had killed her mother.

It had killed her brother, his wife, and her nephew.

It had killed Daniel Hall and Jessie Caswell.

It had burned her village.

It had killed her father.

Thrace raised her head and looked across the hill at *it*.

No one that had been attacked had ever lived. There were never any survivors.

She stood and began to walk forward slowly. She reached into the robe and pulled out the sword that had remained hidden there.

The beast found the catapult and shattered it. It turned and blindly began to search its way back down the hillside sniffing. It did not notice the young girl.

The thick layer of ash that it had created quieted her steps.

"No, Thrace!" Tomas shouted at her. "Run away!"

The Gilarabrywn paused and sniffed at the sound of the shout, sensing danger, but unable to determine its source. It tried to look in the direction of the voice.

"No, Thrace—don't!"

Thrace ignored the cleric. She had passed beyond hearing, beyond seeing, beyond thinking. She was no longer on the hill. She was no longer in Dahlgren, but rather in a tunnel, a narrow tunnel that led inescapably to only one destination...*it.*

It kills people. That's what it does.

The beast sniffed the air. She could tell it was trying to find her; it was searching for the smell of fear it created in its victims.

She had no fear. *It* destroyed that too.

Now she was invisible.

Without hesitation, fear, question, or regret, Thrace quietly walked up to the towering monster. She gripped the elven sword in both hands and raised it above her head. Putting the full weight of her small body into it, she thrust the broken sword into the Gilarabrywn's body. She did not have to put so much effort into it, the blade slipped in easily.

The beast shrieked in mortal fear and confusion.

It turned, recoiling, but it was already too late. The sword penetrated all the way to the hilt. The essence that was the Gilarabrywn and the forces that bound it shattered. With the snapping of the bonds that held it fast, the world reclaimed the energy in a sudden violent outburst. The eruption of force threw Thrace and Tomas to the ground. The shock wave continued down the hill, radiating out in all directions, beyond the burnt desolation to the forest launching flocks of birds into the night.

Dazed, Tomas staggered to his feet and approached the small slender figure of Thrace Wood at the center of a cleared depression where the great Gilarabrywn once was. He walked forward in awe and fell prostrate on his knees before the girl.

"Your Imperial Majesty," was all he said.

Chapter 15

THE HEIR OF NOVRON

THE SUN ROSE brightly over the Nidwalden River. The clouds had moved off and by midmorning the sky was clear and the air cooler than it had been. A light wind skimmed across the surface of the river, raising ripples, while the sun cast a brilliant gold face upon the water. A fish jumped above the surface and fell back with a plop. Overhead, birds sang morning songs and cicadas droned.

Royce and Arista stood on the bank of the river ringing water out of their clothes. Esrahaddon waited.

"Nice robe," the princess said.

The wizard only smiled.

Arista shivered as she looked out across the river. The trees on the far bank looked different than on their side, a different species perhaps. Arista thought they appeared prouder, straighter with fewer lower branches, and longer trunks. While the trees were impressive, there was no evidence of civilization.

"How do we know they are over there?" Arista asked.

"The elves?" Esrahaddon questioned.

"I mean, no one has seen an elf—" she glanced at Royce, "A pure blood elf—in centuries, right?"

"They are there. Thousands of them by now I should think. Tribes of the old names, with bloodlines that can be traced to the dawn of time. The Miralyith, masters of The Art, Asendwayr the hunters, Nilyndd the crafters, Eiliwin the architects, Umalyn the spiritualists, Gwydry the shipwrights, and Instarya the warriors. They are all still there, a congress of nations."

"Do they have cities? Like we do?"

"Perhaps, but probably not like ours. There is a legend of a sacred place called Estramnadon. It is the holiest place in elven culture…at least that we humans know of. Estramnadon is said to be over there, deep in the forests. Some think it is their capital city and seat of their monarch, others speculate it is the sacred grove where the first tree—the tree planted by Muriel herself—still grows and is cared for by the Children of Ferrol. No one knows for certain. No human is likely ever to know, as the elves do not suffer the trespasses of others."

"Really?" the princess looked at the thief with a playful smirk. "Perhaps if I knew that before I might have guessed Royce's heritage sooner."

Royce ignored the comment and turned to the wizard. "Can I assume you will not be returning to the village?"

Esrahaddon shook his head. "I need to leave before Luis Guy and his pack of hounds track me down. Besides, I have an heir to talk to and plans to make."

"Then this is goodbye. I need to get back."

"Remember to keep silent about what you saw in the tower—both of you."

"Funny, I expected the heir and his guardian to be unknown farm boys from some place—well—like this I suppose. Someone I never heard of."

"Life has a way of surprising you, doesn't it?" Esrahaddon said.

Royce nodded and started to head off.

"Royce," Esrahaddon said softly stopping him. "We know that what happened last night wasn't pleasant. You should prepare yourself for what you're going to find."

"You think Hadrian's dead," Royce said flatly.

"I would expect so. If he is, at least know that his death may have been the sacrifice that saved our world from destruction. And while that may not comfort you, I think we both know that it would have pleased Hadrian."

Royce thought a moment, nodded, then entered the trees and disappeared.

"He's definitely elvish," Arista said shaking her head and sitting down opposite Esrahaddon. "I don't know why I didn't see it before. You've grown a beard I see."

"You just noticed?"

"I noticed before, been kinda busy until now."

"I can't really shave, can I? It wasn't a problem while I was in Gutaria, but now—does it look alright?"

"You have some grey coming in."

"I ought to. I am nine hundred years old."

She watched the wizard staring across the river.

"You really should practice your art. You did well in there."

She rolled her eyes. "I can't do it, not the way you taught me. I can do most of the things Arcadius demonstrated, but it's a bit impossible to learn hand magic from a man without hands."

"You boiled water, and you made the prison guard sneeze. Remember?"

"Yes, I'm a veritable sorceress, aren't I?" she said sarcastically.

He sighed. "What about the rain? Have you worked on that incantation any more?"

"No, and I'm not going to. I am the Ambassador of Melengar now. I've put all that behind me. Given time, they may even forget I was tried for witchcraft."

"I see," the wizard said, disappointed.

The princess shivered in the morning chill and tried to run her fingers through her hair but caught them in tangles. Stains and wrinkles dotted her dress. "I'm a mess, aren't I?"

The wizard said nothing. He appeared to be thinking.

"So," she began, "what will you do when you find the heir?"

Esrahaddon only stared at her.

"Is it a secret?"

"Why don't you ask me what you really want to know, Arista?"

She sat trying to look naïve and offered a slight smile, "I don't understand."

"You aren't sitting here shivering in a wet dress making small talk with me for nothing. You have an agenda."

"An agenda?" she asked, not at all convincingly even for her own tastes. "I don't know what you mean."

"You want to know if what the church told you about your father's death is true or not. You think I used you as a pawn. You are wondering if I tricked you into being an unwitting accomplice to your own father's death."

The act was over. She stared stunned at the wizard's bluntness, barely breathing. She did not speak, but slowly nodded her head.

"I suspected they might come after you because they are having trouble following me."

"Did you?" She asked finding her voice. "Did you orchestrate my father's death?"

Esrahaddon let the silence hang between them a moment, then at last replied.

"Yes, Arista. I did."

At first, the princess did not say a word. It did not seem possible that she heard him correctly. Slowly her head began to shake back and forth in disbelief.

"How…" she started to say, "How could you do that?"

"Nothing I, nor anyone else says, can explain that to you—not now at least. Perhaps someday you'll understand."

Tears welled up in her eyes. She brushed them away and glared at the wizard.

"Before you judge me completely, as I know you will, remember one thing. Right now, the Church of Nyphron is trying to persuade you that I am a demon, the very Apostle of Uberlin. You are likely thinking they are right. Before you damn me forever and run into the embrace of the patriarch, ask yourself these questions. Who approved your entrance into the University of Sheridan? Who talked your disapproving father into letting you attend? How did you learn about me? How was it that you found your way to a hidden prison that only a handful of people knew existed? Why were you taught to use a gemstone lock and isn't it interesting that the very gem you used on your door was the same as the signet ring that unlocked the prison entrance? And how was it that a young girl, princess or not, was allowed to enter Gutaria Prison and leave unmolested, not once, not twice, but repeatedly for months without her activities ever being questioned or reported back to her father the king?"

"What are you saying?"

"Arista," the wizard said, "sharks don't eat seafood because they like it, but because chickens don't swim. We all do the best we can with the tools we have, but at some point you have to ask yourself where the tools came from."

She stared at him. "You knew they would kill my father. You counted on it. You even knew they would eventually kill me and Alric, and yet you pretended to be my friend, my teacher." Her face hardened. "School's over." She turned her back on him and walked away.

When Royce reached the edge of the burnt forest, he spotted a series of colorful tents set up around the old village common. The tents displayed pennants of the Nyphron Church, and he could see several priests as well as imperial guards. Other figures moved slowly over the hill near the old castle grounds, but nowhere did he see anyone he knew.

He kept to the cover of the trees when he caught the sound of a snapping twig not too far off. Slipping around, he quickly spotted Magnus crouched in the underbrush.

The dwarf jumped in alarm and fell backward at his approach.

"Relax," Royce whispered sitting down next to where the dwarf now lay, nervously watching the thief.

Glancing down the slope Royce realized that the dwarf had found an excellent position to watch the camp. They were on a rise behind a series of burnt trees where some of the underbrush had survived. Below they had a perfect view of each of the tent openings, the makeshift horse corral and the latrine. Royce guessed there were about thirty of them.

"What are you still doing here?" Royce asked.

"I was breaking a sword for your partner. But I'm leaving now."

"What happened?"

"Huh? Oh, Theron and Fanen were killed."

Royce nodded showing no outward sign of surprise or grief.

"Hadrian? Is he alive?"

The dwarf nodded, and went on to explain the events that transpired that evening.

"After it was dead, or dispelled, or whatever, Tomas and I checked on Hadrian. He was unconscious, but alive. We made him comfortable, covered him in a blanket and put a lean-to over him, the Pickering kid, and that Melengarian soldier. Before dawn, Bishop Saldur and his crew returned, dragging two wagons with them. The way I figure it, either Guy reported what happened and he was coming back with help, or they heard it when the beasty died. They pulled in and fast as rabbits, had these tents up and breakfast cooking. I spotted the sentinel in their ranks, so I hid up here. They moved Hadrian, Hilfred, and Mauvin into that white tent and soon after they put a guard on it."

"Is that all?"

"Well, they sent a detail out to bury the dead. Most they buried on the hill up there near the castle, including Fanen, but Tomas made some big stink and they took Theron down the road to that last farm near the river and they buried him there."

"Perhaps you forgot to mention how you found my dagger?"

"The Alverstone? I thought you had it."

"I do," Royce said.

Magnus reached for his boot and cursed.

"When you investigated my background, you must have stumbled across the fact that I survived my youth by picking pockets."

"I remember something about that," the dwarf growled.

Royce pulled Alverstone from its sheath as he glared at the dwarf.

"Look, I'm sorry about killing that damn king. It was just a job I was hired to do, okay? I wouldn't have taken the job if it hadn't required a uniquely challenging masonry effort. I'm not an assassin. I'm not even good enough to be considered a pathetic fighter. I'm an artisan. Truth be told, I specialize in weapons. That's my first love, but all dwarves can cut stone so I was hired to do the tower work, then the job got changed and after half a year's work I was going to be stiffed if I didn't knife the old man. In hindsight, I can see I should have refused, but I didn't. I didn't know anything about him. Maybe he was a bad king; maybe he deserved to die; Braga certainly thought so and he was the king's brother-in-law. I try not to involve myself in human affairs, but I was caught up in this one. It's not something I wanted; it's not something I looked for; it just happened. And it's not like someone else wouldn't have done it if I hadn't."

"What makes you think I'm upset you killed Amrath? I'm not even mad that you trapped the tower. Closing the door on me was the mistake you made."

Magnus inched away.

"Killing you would be as easy as—no easier than, slaughtering a fatted pig. The challenge would lie in causing the maximum amount of pain before inflicting the death."

Magnus' mouth opened, but no words came out.

"But you are a very lucky dwarf, because there's a man still alive in that tent who wouldn't like it—a man you covered in a blanket and put a lean-to over."

Down below he spotted Arista as she entered the camp. She talked to a guard who pointed toward the white tent. She rushed to it.

Royce looked back at the dwarf and spoke clearly and evenly. "If you ever touch Alverstone again without my permission, I'll kill you."

Magnus looked at him bitterly then his expression changed and he raised an eyebrow. "Without your *permission?* So there's a chance you'll *let* me study it?"

Royce rolled his eyes. "I'm going to get Hadrian out of there. You are going to steal two of the archbishop's horses and walk them over to the white tent without being spotted."

"And then we can talk about the *permission* thing?"

Royce sighed, "Did I mention I hate dwarves?"

"But your grace—" Deacon Tomas protested as he stood in the large striped tent before Bishop Saldur and Luis Guy. The pudgy cleric made a poor showing of himself in his frock caked with dirt and ash, his face smudged, his fingers black.

"Look at you Tomas," Bishop Saldur said. "You're so exhausted you look as if you will fall down any minute. You've had a long two days, and you've been under temendous stress for months now. It is only natural that you might see things in the dark. No one is blaming you. And we don't think you are lying. We know that right now you believe you saw this village girl destroy the Gilarabrywn, but I think if you just take a nap and rest, when you get up you'll find that you were mistaken about a great many things."

"I don't need a nap!" Tomas shouted.

"Calm down, deacon," Saldur snapped, rising abruptly to his feet. "Remember whose presence you are standing in."

The deacon cowed and Saldur sighed. His face softened to his grandfatherly visage and he put an arm around the man's shoulders, patting him gently, "Go to a tent and rest."

Tomas hesitated, turned and left Saldur and Luis Guy alone.

The bishop threw himself down in the little cushioned chair beside a bowl of red berries some industrious servant managed to gather for him. He popped two in his mouth and chewed. They were bitter and he grimaced. Despite the early hour, Saldur was desperate for a glass of brandy, but none had survived the flight from the castle. Only the grace of Maribor could account for the survival of the camping gear and provisions, all of which they had lazily left in the wagons when they first arrived at the manor. In the turmoil of their exodus, they had given little thought to provisions.

That he lived at all was a miracle. He could not recall how he crossed the courtyard, or how he reached the gate. He must have run down the hill, but had no recollection of it. His memory was like a dream, vague and fading. He did remember ordering the coachman to whip the horses. The fool wanted to wait for the archbishop. The old man could barely walk and the moment the flames hit, his servants deserted him. He had as much chance of survival as Rufus.

With Archbishop Galien's death, the command of the church's interest in Dahlgren fell to Saldur and Guy. The two inherited a disaster of mythic proportions. They were alone in the wilderness, faced with crucial decisions. How they handled them would decide the fate of future generations. Who actually held authority remained vague. Saldur was a bishop of the church, an appointed leader, while Guy was only an arm of the security branch. Still, the sentinel actually spoke with the patriarch. Saldur liked Guy, but appreciation for his effectiveness would not prevent him from sacrificing the sentinel if necessary. If Guy still had his knights about him, Saldur was certain the sentinel would take command and he would have no choice but to accept it, but the seret were dead and Guy himself wounded. With Galien also dead, a door had opened, and Saldur planned to be the first one through.

Saldur looked at Guy. "How could you let this happen?"

The sentinel who sat with his arm in a sling and his shoulder wrapped in bandages stiffened, "I lost seven good men, and barely escaped with my life. I wouldn't call that *allowing* it to happen."

"And how exactly did a bunch of farmers defeat the infamous seret?"

"They weren't farmers; two were Pickerings and there was Hadrian Blackwater."

"The Pickerings I can understand, but Blackwater? He's nothing but a rogue."

"No, there's more to him—him and his partner."

"Royce and Hadrian are excellent thieves. They proved that in Melengar and again in Chadwick. Poor Archibald still has fits over it."

"No," Guy said, "I think they're more than that. Blackwater knows Teshlor combat, and his friend, that Royce Melborn is an elf."

Saldur blinked. "An elf? Are you sure?"

"He passes as human, but I'm certain of it."

"And this is the second time we've found them with Esrahaddon," Saldur muttered in concern. "Is this Hadrian still here?"

"He is in the infirmary tent."

"Put a guard on him at once."

"I had him under guard since he was dragged to the tent. What we need to concern ourselves with is the girl. She is going to prove an embarrassment if we don't do something," Guy said and slipped his sword part way out of its sheath. "She is in grief over the loss of her father. It wouldn't be surprising if she threw herself over the falls in a fit of despair."

"And Tomas?" Saldur asked, reaching for another handful of berries. "It is clear he won't be quiet. Will you kill him too? What excuse will you give for that? And what about all the others in this camp that heard him going on all morning about her being the heir? Do we kill everyone? If we did, who would carry our bags back to Ervanon?" he added with a smile.

"I don't see the humor in this," Guy snapped letting his sword slide back down in its sheath.

"Perhaps that's because you are not looking at it the right way," Saldur told him. Guy was a well-trained and vicious guard dog, but the man lacked imagination. "What if we didn't kill her? What if we actually made her the Empress?"

"A peasant girl? Empress?" Guy scoffed. "Are you mad?"

"Despite his political clout, I don't think any of us, including the patriarch, was particularly happy with the choice of Rufus. He was a fool to be sure, but he was also a stubborn, powerful fool. We all suspected that he might have had to be killed within a year, which would have thrown the infant empire into turmoil. How much better it would be to have an empress that would do whatever she was told right from the very start?"

"But how could we possibly sell her to the nobles?"

"We don't," Saldur said, and a smile appeared on his wrinkled face, "we sell her to the people instead."

"How's that?"

"Degan Gaunt's Nationalist movement proved that the people themselves have strength. Earls, barons, even kings are afraid of the power which that commoner can gather. A word from him could launch a peasant uprising. Lords would have to kill their own people, their own source of revenue, just to keep order. This presents them with the undesirable choice of accepting either poverty or death. The landholders will do almost anything to avoid such an event. What if we tapped that? The peasants already revere the church. They follow its teachings as divine truth. How much more inspiring would it be to offer them a leader plucked from their own stock? A ruler who is one of them and able to truly understand the plight of the poor, the unwashed, the destitute. Not only is she a peasant queen, but she is also the Heir of Novron, and all the wonderful expectations that go with that. Indeed, in our greatest hour of need, Maribor has once again delivered unto his people a divine leader to show us the way out of darkness.

"We could send bards across the land repeating the epic tale of the pure, chaste girl who slew the elven demon that even Lord Rufus was powerless against. We'll call it *Rufus' Bane*. Yes, I like it—so much better than the unpronounceable Gilarabrywn."

"But can she be made to play her part?" Guy asked.

"You saw her. She's nearly comatose. Not only does she have no place to go, no friends or relatives, no money or possessions, she is also emotionally shattered. She'd slit her own wrists, I suspect, if she gets a knife. Still, the best part is that once we establish her as empress, once we have the support of the people so fervently on our side, no noble landholder would dare challenge us. We can do what we planned to do with Rufus. Only instead of a messy murder that would certainly invite suspicion and accusations, with the girl we can simply marry her. The new husband will rule as emperor and we can lock her in a dark room somewhere, pulling her out for Wintertide showings."

Guy smiled at that.

"Do you think the patriarch will agree?" Saldur asked him. "Perhaps we should send a rider back today."

"No, this is too important. I will go myself. I'll leave as soon as I can saddle a horse. In the meantime—"

"In the meantime, we will announce that we are considering the possibility that this girl is the heir, but will not accept her unconditionally until a full investigation is conducted. That should buy us a month. If the patriarch agrees, then we can send out rabble-rousers to incite the people with rumors that the church is being forced by the nobles and the monarchs to not reveal the girl as the true heir. The people will be denouncing our enemies and demanding that she take the throne before we even announce her."

"She will make the perfect figurehead," Guy said.

Saldur looked up, picturing the future. "An innocent girl linked with a mythic legend. Her beautiful name will be everywhere and she will be loved." The bishop paused and thought, "What is her name anyway?"

"I think Tomas called her—Thrace."

"Seriously?" Saldur grimaced. "Well, no matter, we'll change it. After all, she's ours now."

Royce looked around. There was not a single sentry left outside. Several still moved about on the hilltop, but they were far enough away to ignore. Satisfied, he ducked through the flap of the white tent. Inside he found Tobis, Hadrian, Mauvin, and Hilfred on cots. Hadrian was naked to his waist, his head and chest wrapped in white bandages, but he was awake and sitting up. Mauvin, though still pale, was alert, his bandages bright white. Hilfred lay wrapped like a mummy and Royce could not be sure if he were awake or sleeping. Arista stood bent over his cot checking on him.

"I was wondering when you would get here," Hadrian said.

Arista turned. "Yes, I thought you would have arrived much sooner."

"Sorry, you know how it is when you're having fun. You lose all track of time, but I did locate your weapons, again. You know how upset you get when you don't have your swords. Can you ride?"

"If I can walk, why not?" he raised an arm and Royce offered his shoulder, helping him to stand.

"What about me?" Mauvin asked, holding his side and sitting up on his cot. "You're not going to leave me, are you?"

"You have to take him," Arista declared. "He killed two of Guy's men."

"Can you ride?" Royce asked.

"If I had a horse under me I could at least hang on."

"What about Thrace?" Hadrian asked.

"I don't think you need worry about her," Royce told him. "I was just by the bishop's tent. Tomas is demanding that they declare her empress."

"Empress?" Hadrian said, stunned.

"She killed the Gilarabrywn right in front of the deacon. I guess it made an impression."

"But what if they don't? We can't leave her."

"Don't worry about Thrace," Arista said. "I'll see she's taken care of. Now you all need to get out of here."

"Theron wanted at least one of his children to be successful," Hadrian muttered, "but empress?"

"You need to hurry," Arista said helping Royce pull Mauvin to his feet. She gave all three of them a kiss and a gentle hug and then pushed them out like a mother sending her children to school.

Outside the tent, Magnus arrived with three saddled horses. The dwarf looked around nervously and whispered. "I could have sworn I saw guards watching this tent earlier."

"You did," Royce replied. "Three horses—you read my mind."

"I figured I needed one for myself," the dwarf replied pointing at the shortened stirrups. He looked at Mauvin with a scowl. "Now it looks like I'll need to get another."

"Forget it," Royce whispered, "Ride with Mauvin. Take it slow and make sure he stays in the saddle."

Royce helped Hadrian up onto a gray mare then started to chuckle to himself.

"What is it?" Hadrian asked.

"Mouse."

"What's that?"

Royce pointed to the horse Hadrian sat on. "Of all the animals he had to choose from, the dwarf stole Mouse."

Royce led them away from the camp, walking the horses across the scorched land where the ash muffled their movement. He kept a close eye on the distant sentries. No outcry, no shouts, no one appeared to notice and soon they slipped into the leafy forest. Once there he turned back toward the river in order to throw off anyone who might look for their tracks. Once he had them safely in a shallow glen near the Nidwalden, Royce ordered them to stay put while he went back.

He crept up to the edge of the burned area. The camp was as it had been before. Satisfied they made a clean escape, he walked back toward the river. He found himself on the trail that led to the Wood's farm and the shell of the old building. Inexplicably, the fire never reached this far and it remained untouched. There was one change, however; in the center of the yard where they first saw the old farmer sharpening his scythe, there was a mound of earth. A stack of stones borrowed from the walls of the farmhouse circled the oblong mound. At its head, driven into the ground, was a broad plank and burned into it the words:

THERON WOOD FARMER

Below that, scratched in into the plank, Royce could just make out the additional words:

Father of the Empress

As Royce stood reading the words, he noticed it—a chill making the hair on his skin stand up. Someone was watching him. On the edge of his sight, a figure stood in the trees. Another stood to his left. He sensed more behind him. He turned his head, focused his eyes to see who they were—nothing. All he saw were trees. He glanced to his left and again nothing. He stood still listening. Not a twig snapped, nor leaf crinkled, but he could still feel it.

He moved away from the clearing into the brush and circled around. He moved as quietly as he could, but when he stopped, he was alone.

Royce stood puzzled. He looked for tracks, where he saw the figures, but none existed, not even a bent blade of grass. At last, he gave up and returned to where he left the others.

"All's well?" Hadrian asked, sitting atop Mouse with the sun on his bare shoulders and chest wrapped in broad strips of white cloth.

"I suppose," he said mounting up.

He led them southwest along the highlands near the falls, following a deer trail that cut through the deep forest. It was the same trail he had found in his hours searching for a tunnel to the tower. Hadrian and Mauvin appeared to be doing better than expected though each of them winced in pain whenever their horse took a misstep.

Royce continued to look back over his shoulder but nothing was ever there.

By midafternoon they had cleared the trees and found the main road heading south to Alburn. Here they paused to check Mauvin's and Hadrian's bandages. Mauvin started to bleed again, but it was not bad and Magnus turned out to be almost as good a nurse as he was a sword smith, fashioning a new pad for his side. Royce searched through the saddlebags and found Hadrian a suitable shirt.

"We should be fine," Royce told them, going through their inventory. "With a little luck we should reach Medford in a week."

"In a hurry are you?" Hadrian asked.

"You might say that."

"Thinking about Gwen?"

"I'm thinking it's time I told her a few things about myself."

Hadrian smiled and nodded.

"You think Thrace will be alright?"

"Tomas seems to be watching out for her pretty well."

"Do you think they'll really make her empress?"

"Not a chance," Royce shook his head and handed the shirt to him.

"Arista told me you two were with Esrahaddon in the tower last night. She said he needed help with something, but wouldn't tell me what it was."

"He was using the tower to look for the Heir of Novron," Royce replied.

"Did he find him?"

"I think so, but you know how he is. It's hard to be sure of anything when dealing with him." Hadrian nodded and winced as he pulled the shirt over his shoulders.

"Having troubles?"

"You try getting dressed with broken ribs sometime. It isn't so easy." Royce continued to look at him.

"What is it? Am I that entertaining?" Hadrian asked.

"It's just that you've worn that silver medallion ever since I've known you, but you never told me where you got it."

"Hmm? This?" Hadrian said. "I've had this forever. My father left it to me."

THE RIYRIA REVELATIONS

If you enjoyed this novel, you will be happy to learn that...

Avempartha is the second in a six book series entitled the Riyria Revelations. This saga is neither a string of sequels nor a lengthy work unnaturally divided. Instead, the Riyria Revelations was conceived as a single epic tale told through six individual episodes. While a book may hint at building mysteries or thickening plots, these threads are not essential to reach a satisfying conclusion to the current episode—which has its own beginning, middle, and end.

Eschewing the recent trends in fantasy toward the lengthy, gritty, and dark, the Riyria Revelations brings the genre back to its roots. Avoiding unnecessarily complicated language and world building for its own sake; this series is a distillation of the best elements of traditional fantasy—great characters, a complex plot, humor, and drama all in appropriate measures.

While written for an adult audience the Riyria Revelations lacks sex, graphic violence, and profanity making it appropriate for readers thirteen and older.

Books in the Riyria Revelations

About the Author

Born in Detroit Michigan, Michael J. Sullivan has raised in Novi. He has also lived in Vermont, North Carolina and Virginia. He worked as a commercial artist and illustrator, founding his own advertising agency in 1996, which he closed in 2005 to pursue writing full-time. His first published novel The Crown Conspiracy was released in October 2008. He currently resides in Fairfax, Virginia with his wife and three children.

Awards for Riyria Books

2009 National Indie Excellence Award Finalist
2008 ReaderViews Literary Award Finalist
2007 Foreword Magazine Book of the Year Finalist

Fantasy Sites Recognition

Named one of the Notable Fantasy Books of 2009
—Fantasy Book Critic
Named one of the top 5 Fantasy Books of 2009
—Dark Wolf's Fantasy Reviews
Named a Notable Indie of 2008—Fantasy Book Critic

Websites

Author's Homepage: www.michaelsullivan-author.com
Author's Blog: www.riyria.blogspot.com

Social Networking Groups

www.goodreads.com/group/show/10550
www.facebook.com/group.php?gid=26847461609
www.shelfari.com/groups/30879/about

Contact

Twitter: twitter.com/author_sullivan
Email: michael.sullivan.dc@gmail.com

5597599R0

Made in the USA
Lexington, KY
26 May 2010